JUST
JANE

Books by

Nancy Moser

FROM BETHANY HOUSE PUBLISHERS

Mozart's Sister

Just Jane

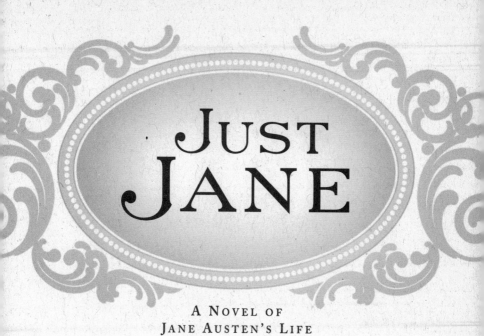

JUST JANE

A NOVEL OF
JANE AUSTEN'S LIFE

NANCY MOSER

BETHANY HOUSE PUBLISHERS
Minneapolis, Minnesota

Just Jane
Copyright © 2007
Nancy Moser

Cover design by Jennifer Parker
Cover photography by Mike Habermann Photography

Published by Bethany House Publishers
11400 Hampshire Avenue South
Bloomington, Minnesota 55438

Bethany House Publishers is a division of
Baker Publishing Group, Grand Rapids, Michigan.

Printed in the United States of America

ISBN   978-0-7642-0356-5

Library of Congress Cataloging-in-Publication Data

Moser, Nancy.
   Just Jane : a novel of Jane Austen's life / Nancy Moser.
      p.   cm.
   ISBN-13:   978-0-7642-0356-5 (pbk.)
   ISBN-10:   0-7642-0356-8 (pbk.)
   1. Austen, Jane, 1775-1817—Fiction. I. Title.

   PS3563.O88417J87   2007
   813'.54—dc22   2007023677

To my two new granddaughters, Lillian and Evelyn.
The world is yours, my darlings.
Find the joy in being just Lillian and just Evelyn.

NANCY MOSER is the bestselling author of sixteen novels, including *Crossroads,* the Christy Award-winning *Time Lottery,* and the SISTER CIRCLE series coauthored with Campus Crusade cofounder Vonette Bright.

Nancy has been married thirty-two years. She and her husband have three twenty-something children and live in the Midwest. She loves history, has traveled extensively in Europe, and has performed in various theaters, symphonies, and choirs.

Cast of Characters

Austen Parents

GEORGE: Born 1731. Pastor of Steventon Parrish in Hampshire.

CASSANDRA: Born 1739. Cassandra Leigh.

The Austen Children

JAMES: Born 1765. Pastor of Steventon Parrish. Married to Anne Matthews. *One child, Anna.* Later married Mary Lloyd. *Two children: James Edward and Caroline.*

GEORGE: Born 1766. Mentally unwell. Sent to live away from home.

EDWARD: Born 1767. Landed gentleman. When he was twelve he was sent to live as the son of a rich, childless couple from Kent, Thomas and Catherine Knight. Upon his adoptive parents' deaths, he took the name of Knight and inherited a vast fortune at Godmersham and Chawton. Married Elizabeth Bridges. *Eleven children: Fanny, Edward, George, Henry, William, Elizabeth, Marianne, Charles, Louisa, Cassandra Jane, Brook John.*

HENRY: Born 1771. Soldier, banker, eventually pastor. Married to Eliza de Feuillide. *No children* (although Eliza had a *son, Hastings,* by her first marriage). Later married Eleanor Jackson. *No children.*

CASSANDRA: Born 1773. Devoted sister to Jane—Jane's muse.

FRANK: Born 1774. Admiral in British Navy. Married Mary Gibson. *Seven children.* Later married Martha Lloyd. *No children.*

JANE: Born 1775. World-renowned novelist.

CHARLES: Born 1779. Admiral in British Navy. Married Frances Palmer. *Four children: Cassandra, Harriet, Frances, Elizabeth.*

Later married Harriet Palmer (sister of first wife, Frances). *Four children: Charles, George, Jane, Henry.*

Other Relatives/Friends

ANNE LEFROY: Aunt of Jane's early love interest, Tom Lefroy. Although twenty-six years older than Jane, the two women were very close.

CATHERINE, ALETHEA, and ELIZABETH BIGG-WITHER: Older sisters of Harris Bigg-Wither of the Manydown estate in Hampshire. Bosom friends.

MARTHA LLOYD: Sister of James's wife, Mary. Martha lived with Jane, Cassandra, and Mother Austen for many years. She married Frank Austen late in life. *No children.*

UNCLE PERROT: James Leigh-Perrot. Brother of Mother Austen. Lived in Bath and in Berkshire. Loyal husband of Jane Cholmeley.

AUNT PERROT: Jane Cholmeley, eccentric, socialite wife of Uncle Perrot. Lived in Bath and in Berkshire. *No children.* James Austen (Jane's brother) was their heir.

INTIMATE CONNECTIONS

ONE

It is a true thing everyone knows that—

I scratch out the words, dip my pen into the well of ink, and try again. It is not the first time I have scribbled and scratched, obliterating one word or phrase while searching for another. I long for the correct word, the indisputable one-and-only connection of words that will capture the essence of my intention. Yet these unfound words tease me by hiding in the shadows of my mind, just out of reach, being naughty and bothersome and—

Aha!

I quickly put pen to paper, eager to capture the phrase before it returns to hiding: *It is a truth universally acknowledged . . .* Yes, yes, that is the phrase that has eluded me. I dip the pen again, finally ready to complete the part of the sentence that has never been in question.

. . . that a single man in possession of a good fortune, must be in want of a wife.

I sit back in my chair of walnut, feeling absurdly prideful I have completed this one line. And yet, it is an important line. The first line of a book. Actually, it is not a book yet. Would it ever by chance be a book?

I peer out the window of the rectory. My mother is bent over her beloved garden, plucking weeds from her asters and lavender hydrangea. *I should go help her.*

But I do not want to venture out. Mine is not a penchant for plantings and pinchings, but for pronouns and prepositions.

Mother stands and arches her back. I suffer her moan without hearing it. She looks in my direction and I offer a wave, which she returns. A lesser—or would it be grander?—mother would observe the gaze of a child who possesses two able hands and immediately summon her outside to assist with the work. But my dear mother (and father too), in spite of having no necessity to do so, condone and even encourage my writing. That it will never amount to anything, that the eyes of family will be the only eyes that will fall upon my carefully chosen "truth universally acknowledged" is also recognized and accepted, yet ignored as unimportant.

"Express yourself, dear child" has always been an invocation in the Austen household, and my sister, Cassandra (two years my elder) and my six brothers (all but one older than I) have always been eager to embrace the unspoken possibilities enmeshed within our parents' entreaty. We do our best to be who we might be—in all our grace, geniality, and glib foolery. That some are more glib and fool than graceful and genial is also not considered a complete disgrace. A person content to be bland will never be anyone's first choice as a companion for an idle afternoon.

Mother goes back to work, releasing me from any hint of guilt. I return to my rich gentleman in want of a wife. If only it were true. We Englishwomen of 1795 have no recourse but to assume it is so. Pray it is so. For how else will we ever prosper? Cassandra and I often huddle together in our shared bed, whispering in the darkness about the inequities of inheritance. How unfair that only the male of the species is permitted to inherit. Alas, the females of our world—if they do *not* find themselves a willing rich man—are bequeathed a life of obligation, forever beholden to the kind heart of some charitable relative to provide a roof that does not leak, a fireplace that does not smoke, and a meal that might occasionally contain meat. Such is our lot if we do not marry well.

I myself can say with some measure of pride that at age twenty, I have prospects. Or at least one prospect. And after all, a woman only needs but one if he be the right one. His name is Tom Lefroy. He is a charming Irishman, the nephew of a neighbour I saw at a ball last Christmas. His eyes are as blue as the Hampshire sky. . . .

We danced every dance. When he took my hand to instigate a cross, rather than merely letting my hand sit gently upon his own, he squeezed it with subtle meaning. And when we slid by, one past the other, shoulder passing shoulder, we did not look straight ahead, as others with less intent would do, but turned our heads inwards, our chins glancing upon our shoulders as our eyes glanced upon each other. With but an instant for conversation, we resorted to single words, words full of teasing. And entreaty.

"Beautiful," he whispered as his shoulder skimmed mine.

"Rascal," was my reply next pass.

"Determined." He offered a wink.

"Ambitious."

The dance proceeded to other movements, silencing our verbal banter. Two dozen couples rose upon their toes, then lowered themselves to just height as they swept up and back, not one step missed, all ably immersed in the elegance of a common sway and parry.

To others it may have been a lark, an amusement on a cold December evening, but for Tom and me it was a sparring, a deliberate caracole, turning, ever turning towards each other and away, despairing of steps that forced time and space between us. I became heady with the sustained implication, as well as the anticipation of more.

But suddenly, as one dance ended and the musicians began the prelude for another, Tom took my hand and said, "Let us hide away."

He pulled me into the foyer, to a bench leaning back against the wall of the mighty staircase but slightly hidden by a tall stand set with a porcelain urn. We fell onto the seat, a jumble of conspiracy, motion, and laughter.

"There," he said, setting himself aright. "Now I have you where I want you."

Before I had time to respond, he leaned forward and kissed me. . . .

Now . . . I put my fingers to my lips, hoping their light pressure will help me remember the one and only. . . .

I do admit that Tom and I behaved in a most shocking manner, dancing with no thought or eyes to another, sitting down together, head to head, knee to knee, discussing *Tom Jones*, and laughing in a way that caused many a matronly stare. That we did not care was shameless. Yet I would not change one moment of our time—which was too fleeting.

Before the third ball, I visited the Lefroy home in Ashe on the auspices of visiting Tom's aunt Anne, a dear friend. Of course, I had hoped to see Tom . . . just to see him would have fed and sustained me, like partaking in one meal, all the while knowing there will be another.

But Tom had fled the house—as if avoiding me? And though I enjoyed my visit with Anne, it did not hold the delicious delicacies I had expected. I now hold on to the hope that Tom was truly called away. Or did he flee because his family teased him about our attraction? Families can be relentless and cruel even as they try to be delightful.

The next day, my feast was complete, as Tom came to call. The presence of his little cousin George was not the ideal—and was a surprise I did not quite understand—but I was so pleased to partake of Tom's company that I told myself I did not mind. And yet . . . I sigh when I allow myself to imagine the meeting I would have desired versus the one that transpired with a thirteen-year-old chaperon who talked about nonsense when I wanted to talk about . . . other things of far more import.

When a fourth ball was planned at Ashe, I held hopes that it was called to honour our upcoming match. In my anticipation I prepared many sets of dialogue that revealed how I would have the evening play out. Tom and I would return to our own special corner behind the urn. As he made his intentions known, he would combine his wit and charm with an eloquence that would impress me to such a degree that I would find myself willing to marry him just in hopes of hearing such eloquence again. And again . . .

Ah, the burdens of imagination . . . when the evening did not play out according to my carefully created dialogue and staging, my disappointment grew to such an extent that others asked of my infirmity. I found a quiet hall and gave myself a good talking to, faulting myself, chiding myself. . . . For in spite of my intense wishes, it is a known fact that people are not characters in a story, bidden by my whim to act and be according to how I wish them to act and be.

A few days after this fourth ball, dear Tom was sent away to London to continue his law studies. He had spoken of them, so I was not surprised. Not completely surprised. He had also spoken of the pressures of being the oldest male of his generation. His father had married for love and lost his inheritance, and as such, had no fortune to pass along. But Tom's great-uncle Benjamin in London . . . ah, there is *the* fortune he needs to cultivate. It is the prudent thing to do for Tom's future—and mine. It is not unusual for the responsibilities and expectations of his gender to take precedent over the needs and desires of a young female with aspiring plans of her own. One's future must be nurtured and finalized to the best of one's ability, in fate's time, not ours.

Yet even with my dashed expectations at the final ball, and my disappointment in Tom's leaving, I take heart in knowing that our initial banter had grown to include some measure of substance. Enough substance that a future together is more than just a girlish inkling or a plot in a story.

And my expectations *are* recognized beyond my own hopeful wishes. My brother Henry's friend, who was here to visit over Christmas, presented me with a portrait of Tom, drawn by his own hand, assuming, of course, that I would delight in it. Which I do. I hold on to that portrait, as it is the only Tom I have seen during these ten long months he has been gone. I expect him to visit our home in Steventon soon, with the proposition to share our future forthcoming. He will go far, my Tom, and I will be a good wife.

I think of him, the oldest boy, the eldest son of twelve children, with five older sisters. . . .

Five older sisters . . . all in want of a husband.

Female names interrupt my thoughts of Tom, listing themselves as though they are real and have but to make my acquaintance: Elizabeth, Jane, Mary, Lydia, and Catherine—no, Kitty. . . . I nod, accepting their introduction, for each seems just right.

Five girls, each in want of a husband. Is this how I can dislodge my story from its hard-fought first line? I will begin with the sisters discussing their lot, chattering over the need for a gentleman who is, of course, in need of them. . . .

It is as good a place as any to begin. At a beginning.

TWO

Mother bursts into my bedroom unannounced. "She is leaving!"

Cassandra and I stop making the bed and exchange a glance. The *she* in question must refer to our cousin Eliza, who has been staying with us.

Mother sits on our bed while Cassandra hurries to close the door. "She cannot leave," says Mother, "not without giving your brother her answer."

It is bad form, leaving my oldest brother, James, waiting. He has wooed Eliza for many weeks, driving over from his rectory in Deane, writing the verses that are his forte, making her laugh. They are a good match, and the family approves. Poor James lost his first wife last spring—dear Anne Matthews felt ill after dinner and died within hours—leaving him alone with two-year-old Anna. Her plaintive cries for Mama led him to send Anna here to the rectory in Steventon to stay with us.

Eliza has also been widowed. Two years ago, her husband of twelve years, Jean Capot de Feuillide, a French landowner, was beheaded by the new French Republic on the same day he was found guilty for attempted bribery while coming to the aid of an imprisoned marquise. Eliza has a child, a ten-year-old son, Hastings, who, alas, suffers from convulsive fits and has trouble speaking well. Yet, a dear boy he is. Once I asked Mother if Hastings reminded her of my older brother George, who suffers similar discomforts and was sent away as a child. She ignored me and told me to go to the garden to dig some turnips for dinner. George is never spoken of. . . . Shakespeare wrote a great truth when pondering the cruel fate to *be* yet not to *be*.

I know letting others care for my brother is for the best, but I do admire Eliza for holding her boy close. Her only boy. Her only child unless . . . She is thirty-five. Four years older than James. It is not an age to dally.

Her Hastings and little Anna play well, which we embrace as a happy sign of a match between their parents. It is quite evident that James and Eliza are two souls in need of companionship, with two children who yearn for the completeness of family in a father and mother united.

With my own mother sitting atop the covers, I abandon the making of the bed. "Perhaps Eliza is just being Eliza. You know how she relishes the game."

Mother shakes a finger. "Love is no game."

Although I hold with my contention, I do not argue with her. For as with games, love is rife with strategies. It demands patience and extends—just out of reach—the lure and promise of a winner. As well as a loser.

"I will not have her disparage our dear James," says Mother. "She has already played our Henry ill."

Yes, she has. A year ago my younger brother, Henry, also wooed our cousin to the point of attachment. Yet she turned him down. Not one to be spurned, Henry quickly became engaged to a sweet girl, Mary Pearson, whose father, Sir Richard Pearson, is in charge of the Naval Hospital at Greenwich. In spite of my prodding, neither Henry nor Eliza will speak of the odd turn of events, though I often wonder if her being ten years his senior was the cause of their parting. Or perhaps they realized that their mutual lighthearted approach to life was not wise. It is preferable if one of a pair is prudent and practical.

James is practical. James will make a good husband for Eliza and little Hastings. He will temper her exuberant nature and she will bring him gaiety. Though, in truth, I do find it hard to fathom Eliza a rector's wife. She, who carries her pug dog like a jewel, who entertains us with her stories of walking in the park in London with the Prince of Wales, or playing cards with the officers at Brighton. Ever since her marriage to Feuillide, she has called herself a countess (though rather more quietly since the trouble in France), and though it is true they did possess five thousand acres and a château, we believe the title an Eliza-ism—one we willingly espouse for her pleasure. Although Eliza and my dear Henry were two fires who threatened to consume each other, in the present case, I see Eliza as the burning fire and James an ember. It is our fervent hope they find a way to warm each other without denying their intrinsic natures.

We hear commotion below and rush to the door and down the stairs. Eliza is one who acts first and explains later.

She is already out the door, her bonnet and cape in place. She gives orders to our servant, John, as well as our father and the coachman she has hired, as to where to put her trunks. Hastings runs a stick over the spokes of the carriage wheel. Again and again. I wish he would stop.

As we approach, Eliza gives us her attention, her face beaming as if all is well and her exit is a planned event, bittersweet in the parting, but acceptable to all.

"Dear Aunt," she says to Mother, kissing both her cheeks in the way of the French. "I am so appreciative of your kind hospitality. Indeed, there is no other place in which I feel so at home than here at Steventon."

"Then why do you leave?" asks Mother.

Eliza blinks as if the question surprises. "I must get back to London."

"But why?"

Eliza pauses a minuscule moment, then turns to her son. "Get in now, Hastings. Yes, you may take the stick with you if you promise not to prod and poke. Up, up, now."

Eliza embraces Cassandra, my father, and then me, cooing sweet nothings that mean nothing. When it is my turn I ask what no one has dared to ask. "Does James know you are leaving? Have you *spoken* with him?" I hope the stress upon the one word invokes the depth of the question.

Our eyes meet, but Eliza quickly looks away. "I will write. You know I always do." She steps into the coach. "I will write to you all.

I promise." She kisses her glove and blows us her farewell. "Ta ta, *ma belle famille*."

Unable to do anything else, we offer our own waves as the coach makes its way down the lane towards London.

And away from James.

As we disperse towards the house, Mother sidles up to Father. "You must send word to James. He must this very day send a post to London, perhaps with a verse of love, cajoling her to answer in the affirmative."

Father shakes his head. "But I have work—"

Mother pulls the sleeve of his waistcoat. "Our work is to make a good match for our children. Eliza's riches . . ."

"Are untenable," says Father, crossing the threshold of our home. "The war between us and France is not over. Any claim Eliza has on her husband's estate is in unsympathetic and greedy hands."

We enter the front room and Cassandra moves a book from a chair so in her distress Mother can sit.

She ignores the offer. "Eliza has her mother's fortune. Your sister did quite well traveling to India to marry Eliza's father."

Father waves away her talk of money. Although it concerns Mother, to the rest of us the match of Eliza and James is a union of family, not fortunes.

Cassandra touches Mother's arm, again offering the chair. With a sigh, she sits and removes a handkerchief from her sleeve, needing it for the comfort of nervous hands, not tears. Mother does not weep easily or often.

"Surely Eliza will not reject two of my sons. Surely not," she says.

As Father pats her on the shoulder, giving her soft words of comfort, Cassandra and I slip away. It is easier than facing the truth that our Eliza—though fresh and vibrant and dear—will not be held captive to our mother's sense of convention.

❦

James will marry today. My new sister-in-law is Mary Lloyd, a family friend from Ibthorpe, just fourteen miles from Steventon. Until today, she lived there with her widowed mother and sister, Martha. It is snowing today—which it is wont to do in January—but I cannot help but feel the snow is a metaphor for the match. Cold. Smothering.

I am being unkind to a friend—though, if truth be told, I have always felt more attachment to Mary's sister Martha than to Mary herself. There is something tight about Mary. Although she seems joyful on this day—greeting friends and family as she accepts their good wishes—when she is off the public stage, when she thinks no one is looking, I see her eyes narrow and her lips draw tight as if to make measure of what pleases her. And what does not.

Being petty, I also notice that her skin—through no fault of her own—does not fit the ideal of smooth ivory, being marked with the residue of the smallpox suffered as a child. I can forgive her that, as I predict I will forgive her other things as she takes hold of the lives of my brother and sweet niece. Hold, and control. For as I have known her as a friend, I have seen how she likes—alas *needs*—to direct the details of a moment. Will James acquiesce? Or will he fight for his right to be master of his own domain?

I hear someone mention Eliza's name within the new couple's hearing and I quickly search for their reaction. They exchange a look. . . . Mary's look pierces and challenges. James's look cowers and makes apologies. I hope Mary's reaction to our cousin will fade with time. I fear otherwise.

James makes quick amends and drapes his arm across the shoulders of his new wife. But Mary shrugs his arm away as if implying she is very capable of standing on her own.

Oh dear. If one does not embrace the thought of touch on one's wedding day . . . even I know what is expected.

Unable to bear James's embarrassment, I seek little Anna. I see her, our little princess who will be four in just months, standing next to Cassandra, as if my sister were her preferred choice of mother.

I shall miss that little girl. For until Cassandra and I are married and have our own children, she has filled a place in our hearts. To have her wrenched away, albeit through a happy event, makes my heart ache from the loss. If only my Tom would come back and save me from my emptiness. If only he would give me reason to hope for a child of my own.

It is time to leave the church and we bundle ourselves against the snow and cold. But when the door is opened we see the snow has stopped. The sun is shining and a bevy of "Ahs" dance between the guests.

"'Tis a good sign," someone says.

It is my hope.

⊱—⊰

Cassandra and I get into our bed and face each other. By winter habit we draw our knees towards our chests and tuck our night-dresses around our cold feet. Once settled, I offer a subject that has been dogging me throughout the day.

"I do not understand men," I say, knowing it is a subject sure to elicit discussion.

"'Tis too broad a statement, Jane," says Cassandra.

I begin again. "Do you think James and Mary love each other?"

"They've known each other their entire lives."

"Knowing is not loving. I know the baker. It does not mean I love him. Nor would I want to marry him."

"I am sure all in all, he is relieved."

As am I. The baker—portly from eating too much of his own goods—would not be a catch.

"But James . . . Eliza rejects him and within days, if not hours, he pursues Mary."

"Mother is pleased."

"I believe Mother is behind it."

In the moonlight I see Cassandra shrug. And she is right. If not for the discretionary interference of concerned relatives and friends, how would any match be made? I heard Mother tell Mary she was exactly the daughter-in-law she would have chosen. I must not take her words as a slap against our Eliza, but as the loving gesture of a mother-in-law welcoming a new member to the family. My own disappointment as to the choice is neither warranted nor welcomed.

Of course, I also heard Mother tell Mary, "I look forward to you as a real comfort to me in my old age, when Cassandra is gone into Shropshire with her Tom Fowle, and Jane—the Lord knows where." I was hurt by that. Does she not believe in my match with Tom Lefroy? Does she not believe that I will marry—at all?

I get back to the subject at hand. "But if James loved Eliza, how could he . . . so quickly . . . ?"

"He needs a mother for Anna. He needs a wife for his household."

Although we Austens are a practical family, and although I know my sister's explanation to be true, it eschews the loftier motivations I long for in my own life.

Cassandra adjusts her pillow beneath her cheek. "I will love but once."

Ah. There. The romance I long for. "In your case it is all that is necessary. Your Tom . . . you are very blessed to be so in love. You with him, and he with you. It is an ideal that is not always grasped, nor made available."

She slides her hand beneath the covers and finds mine. "Both our Toms are far away—in distance but not in heart."

I nod, knowing her formal engagement entitles her to more expansive hope than I can claim. In my heart Tom Lefroy and I are engaged. Does that count?

"We must sleep," she says.

And dream.

THREE

I sit by the window for the light. Embroidering white on white is always difficult, but what other colour befits a bride? I work on a handkerchief for my sister to carry on her wedding day. I will put her new initials—*CF*—on its corner. It will be an honour to aid her as she wipes away her tears of joy upon that happy day.

The day will soon be here. Any day now. It is late spring and we expect Tom Fowle home from the West Indies. He has been gone over a year, and he and Cassandra have been engaged nearly four. What a conscientious man her Tom is, to be so diligent in his quest to earn a comfortable living. Towards that end, it is not every man who would accept a chaplaincy on a ship and go off to distant lands. It is his hope that Lord Craven (his mother's cousin who tendered the invitation for Tom to accompany him) will reward him with a living once he is home. Yes indeed, Tom is a good man. He will be a good provider for Cassandra and their children.

I am sorry to see my sister go. One by one my siblings have left me here in the rectory. Eight children, and all but I on their way towards living their own lives. James, now married to Mary and a rector of his own church in nearby Deane; George, unwell in the mind and sent away. Lucky Edward, adopted at age twelve by a wealthy childless couple in Kent. . . .

Although Father was wary of the arrangement, Mother pushed for it. She was the planner of our futures. That the Knights found Edward amiable, of good character and like temperament, and that they were willing to make him theirs in all ways, appeared to be the hand of Providence. Edward's adoptive father died three years ago, and Edward has inherited great estates at Godmersham and Chawton. Mother's quest on behalf of her son has been amply rewarded, monetarily and otherwise, for Edward and his wife, Elizabeth, have three children with the promise of many more. Children are the true riches of one's life.

Next down the Austen ladder is my dearest Henry. Why does one's heart bond with another, especially when the two temperaments are so vastly left to right? Only God knows. But Henry will always own my heart. He is in the army now, a captain and paymaster, helping to fight the war with France. I am not sure the position suits him, but at least it is a position. Like James, he is a scholar and once talked of becoming a rector. I am proud that he received his master's degree from Oxford.

After Cassandra became the first female sibling, Francis—Frank—was born, just one year before me. Always an adventurous spirit, he joined a frigate at age fourteen and is rising in the naval ranks as a lieutenant in the East Indies. He is a strict man, a wise man. I'm sure he is good to those under him, albeit stern. Charles—the youngest, and two years younger than myself—is also in the navy as a midshipman in Portsmouth.

But the once-bursting rectory was not strictly kept for Austens. For in addition to Father's ministerial duties at the church were the pupils my father taught and boarded here at the rectory. The audible residue of their ever-present clomping towards their garret rooms with ponderous footfalls still rings in my ears.

Yet they too are now gone, a closed chapter in my family's busy life. Perhaps with fewer mouths to feed due to my brothers' departures, Father found a lesser need for the extra income. Boys. So many boys. My whole life has been full of boys with all their bounding, noisy ways.

Life is not busy, nor bounding, nor noisy now. Although Cassandra and I were offered any bedrooms in the near-empty house, we chose to continue our habit of sharing a room. Our one luxury is making the adjoining space a sitting room. It is like having our own home within the home. The two windows afford a commendable view of the garden, the fireplace warms us, and the dark brown patterned carpet conjures the feeling of solid ground beneath our lives. That the walls are only cheaply papered does not matter. My sister and I do not require much. Just enough. And here, we have everything we need to sew, read, draw, and write.

As the only girls amid the cacophony of boys, we are bonded in a way that is most pleasing—and sustaining. We complement each other and see no need for separate lodgings. I have been told our mother once said, "If Cassandra's head was going to be cut off, Jane would have hers cut off too." In our childhood, when Mother was busy with the boys, Cassandra became far more than a sister to me. She was a mother. I continue to love her in both her positions, as well as the many we have added since then: confidante, advisor, sounding board. She is the only one to hear what is truly upon my heart. Somehow, she loves me still.

I do hope her Tom will retain a position close-by. Although I enjoy the entertainment of my sister's letters when we are apart on various family visits, there is nothing more enjoyable than a face-to-face *tête-à-tête* that allows the full breadth of expression and nuance. The other advantage of face-to-face encounters is that once said, our words are gone, evaporated in the air between us, never to be retrieved and held against us. The meanderings of the heart and mind are fickle, and are often wont to be withdrawn or amended.

Cassandra comes in the room, but I continue working, not desperate to hide my work. She knows what I am making for her—yet one more thing I cannot keep secret from her knowledge. I display the handkerchief for her approval. "See, I am nearly—"

My words are abandoned as I see her face. She is as white as my work. Her arms are down, but I see a letter in her hand, held by a mere corner, its fate in danger.

"What is it?" I ask, even as my instincts warn me not to know.

"He is dead," she says.

"Who is dead?"

Through evident effort her arm rises and I retrieve the letter. My eyes skim across the words, then return to the beginning to read them again, hoping to have missed some key word that will change black to white, dark to light.

The dark is unchangeable. Tom Fowle is dead. Three months dead in the West Indies, of fever. To have his anticipated homecoming usurped by this tragic news . . .

I turn to Cassandra to console her, my arms drawing her into a—

She steps away.

I study her for an indication of how I can help. Her eyes are locked into the space between us, never still, surely skirting over her thoughts as mine had skirted over the awful words. Her breathing is pronounced, her chin and lower lip in motion as they fight to find their natural condition. I await the sobs that are her due.

"Please leave me," she finally says.

I want to speak, to offer a thousand words of condolence, to let my own sorrow and pain loose. But I cannot if she does not wish it. Or need it.

She moves towards the window and stands erect, her back to me. I push my own desires aside and leave our room, pulling the door shut behind me.

I hear our mother on the stairs. She sees me in the hall and calls out, "Where is your sister? I must speak to her about the wedding dinner."

Mother does not know. Cassandra came to tell me first. How sinful I am to feel a measure of pride in that.

I hurry down the stairs to protect my sister's pain. "She is resting," I say, touching my mother's shoulder, gently leading her down the stairs.

"There is no time for rest," says Mother. "We have plans to follow and decisions to make."

Decisions, yes. Plans, no.

In an odd thought, I think of the handkerchief I am making for Cassandra, the initials I was about to place in its corner: *CF.*

CA. Alas, *CA.*

My piano instructor, Master Chard, points to the Haydn sonata and says, "You are letting your left hand become too ponderous. The right hand is the butterfly, the bird. The left is its accompaniment. Try it again."

I do my best, trying to will my left hand to tread lightly—with some success.

Master Chard closes his eyes and nods. It is a good sign. As he is the assistant organist at Winchester Cathedral, I know his time is precious. For him to travel fourteen miles to teach *me* . . . I am grateful Father is willing to pay for the lessons. I take solace that of all my siblings, I am the only one with musical ability. Without my efforts the Austen household would remain musically silent. It is the one talent I alone possess, for even my other interest—writing—is shared by both my mother and my brother James. Since I am the lowest of the low, the youngest girl, their talents in that regard take precedence. Mother has always been quite witty in her verse, and James was always talented in writing additions to the family plays we put on as children. He was also the editor of his own publication called *The Loiterer*. It received accolades in London and beyond. My attempts at writing were simply added to theirs until a few years ago when James ceased his publication and Mother found pursuits of more interest than her verse. I have been only too happy to fill the gap and pursue the Austen pen alone. That my father approves is an encouragement. At the front of one of my notebooks he wrote: "Effusions of Fancy by a Very Young Lady Consisting of Tales in a Style Entirely New."

My thoughts make me falter and Master Chard frown. I must concentrate on the music and leave musings of my writing for another time—an impossible notion, all in all. For my mind is never completely free of it. My stories wrap around me like a cozy quilt, and sometimes I long to pull that quilt over my head and pin the blanket shut, allowing me to immerse myself in the world vivid in my mind. At the moment I am quite enamored with a character called Mr. Darcy, the man I chuse as the foil, flirtation, and fancy of Miss Elizabeth Bennet. That neither one realizes they are divinely suited gives apt opportunity for many delightful encounters and sparrings. Mr. Darcy intrigues me and heartens me, for until I find my own Mr. Darcy, I am content to be his creator. Who would not find pleasure in the creation of so perfect a man?

"Miss Jane?"

I blink and bring Master Chard back into focus. I look at my hands. I have stopped playing without volition. It is obvious my thoughts of Darcy and Lizzy have momentarily taken precedence over sharps and flats.

"You digress?" Master Chard says.

"Forgive me. My mind wandered."

"I do not travel all this way for you to—"

I nod. "May I begin again?"

"I think it best."

I turn back to the beginning. I do not remember having turned the page. . . . I take a fresh breath and start again.

I have not played but three measures when I hear the sound of a horse outside. There is a knock and the maid answers. She is given a letter. Although my curiosity begs me to stop the piece, I must not test Master Chard's patience twice in so swift a succession.

Nanny takes the letter back to my father's study, and I resign myself to learning the news later rather than sooner. Yet it must be news of import. A courier does not stop by the rectory every day. Whether it be good news or bad weighs on me, and I hear my left hand turn ponderous once again. With two of my brothers at sea . . . and the war with France still raging . . .

I manage a prayer amid the Bs and Cs, but once again the mental distraction proves too much for my musical ability and I falter.

Master Chard sighs. "Again, Miss Jane, your execution and ability to concentrate leave much to be desired."

I keep glancing towards Father's study, wanting—no, needing—to hear the news. I accept my shortcomings and stand. "I am sorry, Master Chard, but the horseman . . . I have two brothers at sea . . . the war . . ."

He offers a second sigh, more ponderous than the first.

I close the music, then move towards the front door, hoping he will follow. "I promise I will practice with extra diligence before our next lesson."

He gathers his hat. "Only sincere diligence will create art from mere trifles. You do have talent, Miss Jane. But you must—"

I open the door. "And I will, Master Chard. I will."

With a sharp bow, he dons his hat and exits. I feel bad, but not bad enough to delay or dally from the task at hand: I must hear the news.

I make haste to Father's study and find him not alone. Mother and Cassandra are seated before his desk, and when I appear at the doorway, Father beckons me in. "Come, Jane. Come hear the good news."

"'Tis not just good news, 'tis wonderful news," says Mother.

I accept my parents' enthusiasm but look to Cassandra, knowing her assessment is the most important. It is she who has the letter in her lap. But she is neither effusive like Mother nor beaming like Father. Her head is down, her hands crossed atop her heart, her posture suggesting the letter is not something she wishes to touch.

My mind swims as to what news could so delight my parents while bringing such pain to my sister.

Mother snatches the letter from Cassandra's lap and brings it to me. "If Cassandra will not share the news, I will. She has been left a thousand pounds by dear Tom. A thousand pounds!"

It is too great a sum to fathom.

Before I can read the letter for myself, Mother takes it back from me. "Apparently Tom was prudent and made a will before he left on his ill-fated journey to the ends of the earth. He left to earn his fortune, and to secure a position when he returned, yet who could have imagined that he had already accumulated so great a sum?" She put a hand on Cassandra's shoulder. "Marriage or no, it is rightfully yours, Cassandra. Your widow's portion."

I see Cassandra shiver ever so slightly. I know she would give away ten thousand if only to be with her Tom.

Father stands. "It is well and good," he says, "but best discussed another day."

"But when will she gain access?" asks Mother. "She will be much more appealing to future suitors with one thousand—"

Father raises a hand, silencing her words. *Not now, my dear. Not now.*

Cassandra stands. "If you will excuse me, I have work to do."

I step aside to let her pass.

"She should be happy," whispers Mother.

"I am sure she is," Father says.

Mother throws her hands in the air. "Who would know? She neither cries nor pouts, argues nor demands attention. She merely goes on as if nothing has happened."

I do not argue with Mother, for what she says is true, and yet, I know she is not truly disparaging Cassandra's lack of outward emotion. My family is known for its pragmatic, prudent reactions to life's inequities and tragedies. Birth, death, sickness, strife . . . we have been taught by fine example to accept them as life's due. No one is immune, and to rant and carry on is an indulgence reserved for those who have a lesser grasp of actuality and truth.

Lofty pragmatism aside . . . I do worry about my sister. She seems to have withdrawn, taken a step back from life. This is, of course, an understatement. The love of her life is dead. Her plans to marry him dashed. And yet there *is* hope for her to find someone else to love—someone else to love her. My brothers have done so many times. Is my sister any less capable and deserving?

I leave my father's study thinking of my own Tom. I have waited nearly two years. I still hold fast to the hope we will someday marry.

But what if we don't?

I have stopped in the hall, causing Tilly to look at me questioningly as she stokes the fire in the dining room.

I move along to avoid her scrutiny, even as I am unable to avoid my thoughts. What if I were to receive news that Tom Lefroy is dead? Or nearly worse, what if I found myself spurned by him, after all these days spent hoping and planning for a life. . . .

I must find Cassandra.

For my own sake, as well as hers.

Cassandra is in the garden. She pinches wilted blossoms from the heads of the chrysanthemums and places them in a tin bucket. She does not look up as I approach, and I join her chore without preamble.

I do not know how to begin, but it is not a worry. With anyone else in the world I would venture into small chat about the rain we received last evening, or comment on the breadth and depth of the flower beds as they have prospered under the recent near-perfect combination of wet and light. But I know my sister. Where I often offer too many words, she offers only those in need of the moment. I know that when the time is right, she will speak what needs to be—

"I want no money."

I nod.

She offers a bitter laugh. "I want no suitors."

I must interject. "You are still young. You are beautiful. You have much to offer."

She finally offers me a glance. "One thousand pounds."

"Much more than that."

She shakes her head. "I am finished."

I stop her pinching and squeeze her hand. "No, you are not!"

Her smile has lost its bitter edge and is tinged with calm assurance. "You will marry your Tom, and I will live in an attic room and take care of your children so you can write your grand stories."

Her fantasy reignites my fear. "I have not heard from him."

"A wise man must create the foundation of his fortune before he can gain a wife. Your Tom is doing just that. He will come. You are engaged."

"We are not—officially. Though in my heart . . ."

"You are engaged."

I do not argue. How she has turned my attempt to comfort into being the comforted is a talent I have often witnessed, and still find disconcerting.

She goes back to the flowers. "Go now, Jane. As a woman of means I have the right to spend my time as I chuse."

The indication that she will accept Tom's offering allows me to walk away. Although our mother lacks the tact to pronounce it well, it *is* my sister's due.

FOUR

To own silence . . .

How odd that one does not appreciate something, nor even realize its absence, until it is presented as an unexpected gift.

The absence of my brothers and the exit of my father's pupils allowed me to enter a new phase of my life: that of a writer.

I have always written. My first attempts at novel writing—*Catherine, Lesley Castle,* and *Lady Susan*—are evidence of that. But none is quite right. The latter two works are a bit scandalous, with adultery, abandonment of children, and permissiveness beyond the ken of polite society. Years ago, when I read them aloud to the family, Father's eyebrows rose. Yet he did not chastise me, or tell me to stop. I thank him for being patient with me, for what good is a rector who cannot see the joke in sins and sinners?

I have also attempted a series of letters called *Elinor and Marianne.* I enjoy the differences between the two sisters. Perhaps I have shewn that a disparity in character does not indicate a lack of character. . . .

We have always been a family of readers—my father's library has over five hundred volumes, and I have access to them all. And though it is not always considered delicate to admit it, we adore novels. Those of Fanny Burney, Samuel Richardson, Henry Fielding—to name three. And though I hold Fielding's *Tom Jones* dear—for the fact that book inspired the dialogue between my Tom and me—my favourite is Richardson's masterpiece, *Sir Charles Grandison.* It is a massive book, populated by friends. If only I could discuss their failings and follies directly with the characters themselves.

If a book is well written, I always find it too short. The boldness in the craft that these authors possess inspires me to try my hand at it. Not that my busyness will ever amount to much.

I remember sitting in my father's study once, reading while the boys played outside. I heard Henry in the hallway talking with Father, wanting me to come join them in a roll down the green hill behind the rectory. But Father stopped him, saying, "Leave your sister alone, she is enmeshed; she is gone from us." Henry (being Henry) said, "No she is not; she is right there in your study. I saw her through the window." Thankfully, Father held fast, protecting my privacy. His words held more than a kernel of truth. When I read a novel I am not *here*. I am transported to far-off places, my eyes unseeing of the words on the page, busy with a scene being played out in my mind's eye, with my ears engaged, hearing the voices carry from the pen to the present. What a lovely place to be—not *here*.

So, without the boys' chaotic, despotic, and often idiotic presence, the air at the rectory has eased as if a spring breeze has swept away a tumultuous storm, as well as all pressure to constantly *do*. I especially see the change in Mother. Without the need to arrange meals for a bevy of boys, without their beds to make, their clothes to wash, their dirt to sweep . . . her temperament has changed from snappish and sharp to amiable and quite nearly accommodating. 'Tis like a fresh breath is to be had by all.

I enjoy working in the sitting room I share with Cassandra (the blue paper on the walls here is such a balm), and she respects my time here, though, in truth, I do not mind her presence. By her own volition she never intrudes. It is I who occasionally request her participation. I relish her comments when I read to her a line or two out of doubt. She is very wise, and, seeing beyond what I have said, she has an ear for what I mean. I often read aloud to Mother and Father after evening tea, and also accept their comments, though I admit, with less alacrity. 'Tis a distinction I fear implies too much. Mother usually asks for more description of place and costume: "But what colour is her dress, Jane?" And though I have attempted to write more of these details, it is a forced addition that intrudes upon the words that beg to be released. Her request reminds me of a child pulling on a mother's gown, wanting attention. Sometimes attention to the child's needs is required, but at other times it is best ignored.

And so, I ignore Mother's wishes and do what I must do, and write how I must write. If a bubbling stream forces itself to become a torrent, surely disaster will follow. I am what I am, and though I am still learning this measure and meter of words, I must be true to my nature, and yea, even my gift.

For it is a gift—from God, if I may be so bold. I say this not to imply great talent, but to indicate my awareness that I have received something beyond my own choosing. Although in essence I realize I can refuse this offering, I also sense that the prudent act, the one that begs to be tinged with sincere gratitude, requires me to do what I can with this gift and offer it back into the void from whence it came. Whether it will prosper and move along, or disappear like morning fog, I do not know. I should not care. For the gift is not truly mine to hold, but mine to use and return. To *someone's* benefit. I hope.

My musings have delayed my task for the day. I must acknowledge that I have finished that which I started nine months ago. I stack the pages and align the edges. So many hours. So many thoughts—some used and many discarded. But here it sits. *First Impressions,* the story of the Bennet family, which was inspired by my dear Tom's own familial condition. The two oldest Bennet sisters: Jane and Elizabeth, their names taken from my own name and Cassandra's middle name. If someone asks if I used us as the inspiration for our namesakes, I will have to tell them no. If anything, Cassandra gives the most to Jane's character, and I to Lizzy's. But even then, they are not us. Not completely. And never purely. But they are two sisters, dear to each other and different from each other. In that we share a connection.

I am reluctant to be *done,* for I have lived with Lizzy and Lydia, and Mr. Darcy and the duplicitous Wickham. I have invested and divested in them as much as I have in my own Austen family. I am wont to say adieu to them, as I would to those with whom I share blood ties.

I set my hand upon the pages and let a breath go in and out. It is hard to let go, yet it is a necessity in the birth of any child. I tie a string around the pages, adjusting its bow. A pretty package all in all.

There is a knock on the door. "Come in."

Father opens the door, a letter in hand. "'Tis a letter from Henry, addressed to you."

I nod and reach for it.

Father sees the pages. "You have finished?"

"I have."

"Will you read the end to us tonight?"

"If you would like."

He gives me a chastising look. "Of course we would like. It is a good work, Jane. A fine accomplishment."

"I am happy the family is pleased with it."

He strokes his chin, his eyes on the work. "Actually, I know of a man in the publishing business and I was thinking—"

My words do not align with my thoughts. "No, Father. It is not good enough for that."

"Nonsense. Nothing ventured, nothing gained." He turns towards the door. "Tomorrow I will write a proper letter of introduction. Then I will send it to this man, Thomas Cadell."

"He will not publish it."

Father points a finger, then flicks it towards the end of my nose. "We shall see."

Once again I place a hand upon the pages that are mine, all mine.

Until now? Until someone beyond the family reads the words?

I shiver at the thought with dread—

And yes, excitement.

I hold on to hope. And a letter.

The letter Father wrote to the publishers in London—Cadell and Davies—is quite . . . direct. He allowed me to copy it before it was sent:

> *Sirs*
>
> *I have in my possession a Manuscript Novel, comprised in three Vols. About the length of Miss Burney's Evelina. As I am well aware of what consequence it is that a work of this sort should make its' first appearance under a respectable name I apply to you. Shall be much obliged therefore if you will inform me whether you chuse to be concerned in it; what will be the expense of publishing at the Author's risk; & what you will advance for the Property of it, if on perusal it is approved of?*
>
> *Should your answer give me encouragement I will send you the work.*
>
> *I am, Sirs, Yr. obt. hble Servt:*
>
> > *Geo Austen*

In many ways it is an awkward letter, and if I would have had the chance to edit it . . .

I shove away such presumption. He is my father. He deals with businessmen every day. What do I know regarding the form of such correspondence?

I know that I care deeply about its outcome.

Although I am careful not to make anyone else aware, I pore over the letter daily—actually, many times a day. I pull it out of my writing desk and imagine Mr. Cadell reading it and being intrigued, pulling a fresh piece of paper close. He dips quill to ink and writes, *Sir. We would be happy to peruse such a manuscript. Please send posthaste. We have been searching for just such a novel and will surely publish it—at our expense.*

I laugh at the presumption. Yet what good are dreams if they are grounded in logic and probability?

The letter also brings me great pride, for to know that Father thinks well of the story, enough to bother his day by writing a letter and by offering to have it published "at the Author's risk" . . . I am very blessed.

I hear Mother talking to Cook below. I have been alone in my daydreams long enough. There is work to do. Life does go on.

With or without a published book by Jane Austen.

Tilly brings in the post, along with a gust of the November chill. I meet her near the door, eager to retrieve it. There is a letter from Aunt Leigh-Perrot in Bath, a letter from Edward, and . . .

My heart stops.

On top of the pile of three is a letter addressed *to* Cadell and Davies. From my father. Across the front is boldly written: *Declined by Return of Post*.

I turn it over. Father's seal is broken, and resealed.

They read the letter.

They returned it.

They do not want my manuscript.

I have been rejected.

Father comes into the foyer, a book in hand. He sees me. "Ah. Letters." He extends a hand.

I hesitate. For it is not just I who have been rejected. All Father's hard work, writing the letter on my behalf, believing in me . . . oddly, I feel I have failed him.

"Jane?"

I give him the three, keeping the rejection on top. He deserves to see it.

He reads the front, turns it over, then reads the front again. "Declined?"

"They read it but—"

His voice rises. "Declined?"

I take the offending letter away, moving it behind my back. Out of sight. "It was a great risk, Father. *I* am too great a risk. For who will take seriously anything penned by a parson's daughter living in Hampshire? I have no standing, no right, no—"

"But declined?"

I point to Edward's letter, which graces the top of the pile. "Go. Read what your son has to say."

He nods and turns away, then back to me. "I am sorry, Jane. It is a good story."

"You tried, Father. I will always remember that." I kiss his cheek.

He goes back to his study.

And I?

I remove the letter from behind my back and stare at it. My silly imaginings of Cadell writing a far different response evaporate. I need to take the words I have just spoken with such false bravery to Father and hold them as truth: Who am I to expect a publisher to care about my work? I am no one, beyond obscure, never to be known beyond the tight boundaries of tiny Steventon.

Who am I to expect more? Want more? Dream of more?

I retreat to my sitting room and close the door. I open the trunk that holds the evidence of my folly—my follies. Manuscripts written strictly for the amusement of my family. And myself. For I do enjoy the writing process. I do enjoy creating another place and time, populating it with people who could be as outrageous, vainglorious, courageous, or victorious as I will them to be. Through my writing I capture a smidgen of control—if not in my own life, in the lives of my characters. Their happiness, success, justice, or demise depends on me.

If only I had as much control over my own fate. My mind wanders to thoughts of Tom. . . . If only he would come home from his law studies and take me away from all this. Rescue me.

But alas, such happy endings happen only in novels.

Novels that will never be published.

I look down on the stacks of paper, so neatly tied. Hours and hours, days and days of my life . . .

Wasted.

I slip Father's letter under the bow of *First Impressions*. The word *Declined* peeks back at me, teasing me.

Condemning me.

I close the lid of the trunk.

The lid of my dreams.

I dust our room, hating that in winter the smoke from the fireplace makes my work more difficult. Oh, for spring! To open wide the windows and breathe fresh air that smells of the honeysuckle bushes beneath the windows.

Cassandra enters with an armload of fresh laundry. She sets it on the bed and begins folding.

"I can do the dusting," she says, nodding towards my work.

"I am fine."

I see her glance at my writing desk. "I have not seen you writing lately. What are you working on at present?"

I dare not admit that in a week I have written nothing but a letter to Frank. "I have been busy with other things."

"What other things?"

I try to think of how I have spent my time. Oddly, I cannot give her specifics.

"You are *not* writing, are you?"

I plan to hedge, to ease forward an answer that skirts the truth, yet I hear myself say, "No."

"Why?"

I want to repeat my own "Why?" question, genuinely wanting her to give me a reason. For I have none of my own.

"Father told me about the letter to Cadell," she says.

"Declined."

"They must get dozens of such letters every week. It is not a personal affront. They do not know you, Jane. They do not know your work."

I laugh softly. "They will never know. No one will. And why should they be interested? I am nobody. Even if someone were to publish a book, who would purchase it?" I offer a smile. "Besides you and Henry."

Cassandra snaps a pillowcase before folding it. "So you write for fame?"

"Of course. I write only for fame, and without any view to pecuniary emolument."

"Fame and fortune are beyond our influence. Yet our inability to move the pieces about the board does not mean you should not try to be a part of the game."

"Well said, sister. Perhaps it is you who should be the writer."

I pick up a bedsheet to fold it, but she grabs it from my hands. "You must write, Jane. You. As Father must preach, Henry must joke, and Mother must complain. You must write."

Her eyes are intense.

"And what must you do, Cass?"

She hesitates but for a second. "I must encourage." She points to the trunk. "Work on something. Or write something new. I do not care, only that you write."

I nod but reach for the sheet. She slaps my hand away and points to my desk. "Write."

"Now?"

"Now."

She is frozen in place, her finger directing my way.

I move to the desk, but at the last moment detour to the trunk. It is as if I need to see evidence that what she has said is true. I must write. And I *have* written.

I open its lid and see Father's letter mocking me from atop *First Impressions*. I feel no compunction to retrieve that story. Not now. Not yet.

But then I see another I have put away so long . . . it is almost as if I hear Marianne calling to me, "Here, here, Jane! Chuse me! Chuse us! Fix our story. Make it better. Elinor and I have been waiting far too long."

As have I.

I remove the pages of *Elinor and Marianne* and untie the ribbon that binds them together. I begin to read. The book is in letter form and, within pages, annoys me.

"This is not right," I say aloud.

Cassandra smoothes a folded sheet to the pile. "What is not right?"

"These letters. This form. The story does not flow."

"Then change it," my sister says.

I take fresh paper, a deep breath, and begin to do just that.

For I am a writer. And writers write.

Although the act of receiving mail in a small village can test one's patience, the speed with which gossip flies from house to house to house impresses.

I am in the front room when Mother bursts into the house. Her basket—which she had intended to fill with meat from the butcher—is empty, but her face is not. It is brimming with emotions.

"George! Cassandra! Jane, go get your sister. And be quick about it."

I do not have to leave the room, because Father and Cassandra appear in the doorway. Mother removes her cape and I take it from her, draping it over a chair near the fire. I notice the rug is spotted with snow from her feet. I move to stoke the fire to warm her, but she says, "No. None of that now. I have news."

She is in such a flurry, her hand to her chest, her bosom heaving, her bonnet askew, that Father goes to her side. "My dear, calm yourself."

"I cannot calm myself! I have news." But she does sit in the chair he offers.

Cassandra takes a step towards the doorway. "I will get you some tea."

"I do not want tea! I want you to listen."

With a glance between us, Father, Cassandra, and I gather close, set ourselves in place, hopeful she will begin. And yet fearful too. For by her agitated state, the news cannot be good.

Mother tugs at the ribbons of her bonnet but pulls the wrong end, creating a knot. I reach out to help her, but she shoos my hands away and shoves the bonnet behind her head, knot or no knot. In spite of the cold outside, the curls around her face are flattened with perspiration.

It must be very bad news indeed.

"My dear, you must tell us immediately," says Father. "Enough delay."

"But that is what I am trying to do!" She takes a deep breath and rubs her hands together as if to warm them. "I was walking to the butcher's when I came upon Mrs. Newcombe, sweeping the newest snow from her doorway. 'Ah, Mrs. Austen, your ears must have been burning. Is that why you are out on such a cold day?' Of course I asked for details and she said that her husband's cousin, who lives in Greenwich, has a son who is a soldier. He was injured—"

"Was he on a ship with Frank or Charles?" asks Cassandra.

Mother blinks, and I can see the progression of her thoughts dissipate. "No. Yes." She tosses her hands in the air. "Please!"

"Pardon me," says Cassandra.

Mother takes another deep breath and resumes her story. "Actually, the soldier is a friend of our Henry and he was injured and—"

"Henry has been injured?" I gasp.

"No, no. Please let me finish!"

If only she would. . . .

"The soldier was injured and went to the hospital to be treated by Sir Richard Pearson."

"Mary's father?" our father asks.

"The very same."

I try to arrange the facts without interrupting. Mother was talking about the father of our Henry's fiancée, Mary Pearson?

Mother continues. "The soldier heard Mary's father say that his daughter was no longer engaged to our Henry."

"What?"

Mother raises a hand, stopping our questions. "In fact, Henry has married someone else."

This time, she pauses and allows our questions.

"Who, Mother, who?" asks Cassandra.

She shakes her head. "You will never believe it."

"Mother!"

Father takes a step towards her. "Yes, my dear. Enough playing with our emotions."

"Eliza!" she says. "Henry has married our Eliza!"

The next few moments hang in silence, but are soon filled with questions.

"But Eliza spurned Henry years ago, and then she spurned James, and—"

"Yes, yes, but now they are married! At Marylebone Church on December thirty-first."

Cassandra takes a seat on the settee and I join her. "Oh, poor Mary. She must be crushed."

Mother shrugs. "I made the same comment to Mrs. Newcombe, but apparently, Sir Richard implied that it was accomplished with fairly little distress."

"And Eliza does have her own income," says Father. "I used to be trustee of her wealth, but just six months ago she had her assets put directly into her control."

"Was she planning this even then?" I ask.

"I would not doubt it," says Mother. "Although we love Eliza, we are all aware of her penchant for taking control."

I think of my brother, think of his having such a wife. "How will she adjust to having Henry control—"

Mother laughs. "Our Henry does not control his own life well, much less the life of a wife with a son. I believe he may do best with a wife who takes control."

Eliza, our independent, headstrong cousin . . . used to getting her own way. How did she manage this? "But Henry is stationed in Yarmouth, and Eliza lives in London. How did they—?"

"Apparently Eliza took little Hastings to Lowestoft for his health."

I must laugh. "For her purposes."

Another shrug from Mother. And truth tell, perhaps she is right. Does it matter if Eliza set her store on Henry and pursued him? Perhaps she heard about his engagement to Mary and the thought of losing him to another . . . Yes, yes, that would motivate Eliza to action. Plus the fact that Henry has given up all thoughts of joining the church and is now earning a good income as a Captain Paymaster. His income combined with hers . . . and Eliza still holds hope that she will someday receive her proper inheritance from France should that country ever return to normalcy. Yes, indeed, together they can lead the high life which is their preference.

"But why didn't he tell us?" asks Cassandra.

I also admit my hurt, for Henry is my favourite brother, and the bond we have . . . I thought he would have told me.

"They are probably on a wedding trip," says Mother. "He will tell us. I know he will."

"And we will be happy," Father says. It is not a question.

With the slightest hesitation, we all nod. Yes, we will be happy. We are happy. And though surprised, not shocked. Of all the people in our lives, such actions might be expected of Eliza and Henry.

Now . . . if only my Tom would be so bold. . . .

❧⬧

I must thank Eliza and Henry for their help. Although they do not realize they have helped me by simply being themselves, they have.

I am working on *Elinor and Marianne* and have been inspired by the real-life intrigue of Eliza's courtship of Henry, then James, then Henry again. In my story I have a character named Lucy Steele. What if she were engaged to one man—to Edward Ferras— yet ended up marrying his brother?

I dip my quill in the ink. Yes indeed. Thank you, Eliza and Henry.

FIVE

Off to Godmersham to witness my brother's bounty!

'Tis the essence of convenience to have a brother who was made rich through inheritance, though admittedly odd that he has gained his wealth, not from his blood family, but through the family who adopted him. Edward Knight-Austen is his legal name, though I expect the Austen moniker will fall away when he eventually takes on his father's title. No mere "mister" for my brother. Master.

My brother Edward—adopted at twelve by the childless Knights in Kent—also helped his pocketbook by marrying well, for Elizabeth owned her own fortune and property. (That the rich become richer is a perplexing feat, one they have perfected over centuries of practice.) Since their marriage six years ago, Edward and his wife have lived in one of her family's homes, called Rowling, on her parents' Goodnestone estate.

But now all that has changed. Edward's adoptive father died four years ago. Since then, his mother has lived alone in the mansion of Godmersham, but has recently decided having so many rooms to wander in by herself is a bore, and has offered it to Edward, Elizabeth, and their four—soon to be five—children. Five children in six years. Perhaps in their new manor home my brother and his wife should consider separate bedrooms.

I hear the elder Mrs. Knight has just purchased a home in Canterbury. I can only imagine its palatial qualities. I *cannot* imagine she is used to anything humdrum or mundane.

Edward has invited my parents, Cassandra, and me for a summer visit to Kent. 'Twill be a chance for Edward to shew off, though I expect Elizabeth will do the crowing for both of them. To his credit, my brother has never flaunted his wealth, though he readily enjoys it. He realizes how the fates have smiled on him through no merit of his own (but by being a sweet, agreeable boy who captured the Knights' fancy) and acknowledges that he is where he is due to the sacrifice of our parents. To relinquish a son for his own betterment is a true act of love. After seeing Godmersham, perhaps I will wish the Knights had wanted a daughter.

But no. I am suited to Steventon, to the rectory, and to the quiet life we lead. Although I may shew wit to family and close friends, among strangers I have been called standoffish and dull—two traits highly unacceptable in high society. So be it. I see no reason to play a part for others' sake. To pretend to be that which one is not . . . I leave such drama for my characters: Mr. Collins and Lucy Steele aspire to impress. In regard to my own dealings with the upper set, I cannot say I have met any who would make me regret my position, nor any who would inspire me to step up the charm for their benefit—or my own. And if my sister-in-law Elizabeth—now the lady of a great manor—has some of her priggish friends come to call (and if she is appalled by my diffident manner), then I shall declare my mission complete.

I can be quite evil, in a loving sort of way. Yet as everyone knows, Kent is the only place for happiness. Everyone is rich there. Back in Steventon people get so horridly poor and economical that I have no patience with them.

My evil shortcomings are mercifully interrupted by Mother looking out the window of the carriage and exclaiming, "There it is!"

In spite of my stubborn vow to remain unimpressed, I am stunned. How can I be otherwise? The house is set alone on a hill so all can be astonished by its stateliness and offer the proper reaction. It is surrounded by lush parks with groupings of trees planted just so. The entire park is enclosed by a stone wall, a sure way to serve two purposes: shew the world the extent of one's holdings, as well as keep those same people in their proper place—outside.

The carriage stops at the wall and a man unlocks the gate. I admit to feeling a surge of pride that *we* are allowed inside, which proves my ego is not as faultless as I would like to believe.

"Our son has done well," Mother says to Father.

Father answers with an understated "Indeed," although I do notice a slight catch in his voice. Will he ever feel such pride in me?

I dispel the self-pity. Such feelings are not allowed on this day. Perhaps tomorrow.

❦

Despite my best intentions to remain aloof, I stand in awe of the Roman friezes, the intricate carvings at ceiling and fireplace, and the elegance of the Yellow and Chintz rooms. I hear that when Edward travels to his other house at Chawton, the governess and nineteen servants accompany him. He has much responsibility to manage his large estate, and to see to it that the people who live and work here live well and work hard. I would not want such responsibility. Just a small house with Tom, one or two children, and a quiet garden will suffice.

My favourite room at Godmersham is not surprising. It is the library. As I find myself there, alone, I am in awe that I stand in a room that possesses five tables, eight and twenty chairs, and two fires. I sit in a red velvet-upholstered chair with a book and decide that my largest goal during my visit will be to chuse a different chair each day until all are conquered.

I should not be in here alone. Elizabeth invited some of her friends to call and they—along with Mother and Cassandra—are in the parlour having tea. I shall pay for my absence by receiving a tongue-lashing from Mother, a soft chide from Cassandra, and a cold shoulder from Elizabeth. And yet, am I not doing her a favour? She has made it quite clear that I disappoint in such gatherings because I do not fawn and smile and chatter idle nothings for no reason. I know very well that both Elizabeth and her friends see us as the poor relations, and if Mother and Cassandra are willing to accept that role, I would rather be known as the eccentric Jane, off in her own little world. I do not wish to be a part of this elite who come. And sit. Then go. I know I annoy Elizabeth in my refusal to defer. So it is. My world is more desirable than theirs. At least that is my opinion—albeit unsolicited.

This is not the first time I have placed myself in this position. When we visit Mother's brother in Bath, Uncle Perrot, and take the medicinal waters, we come in contact with the upper crust who run in my uncle and aunt's circle. I find that enough of them is too much. Although their ways *have* been useful. I used some of their haughty solicitudes for Darcy's sisters in *First Impressions*. If only people realized that everything they do, everything they say, is fodder for my stories. And for every slight, every double entendre, every bit of keen wit (or lack of it), my pen extends its thanks. I may not *be* one of them, but I *see* all of them. And write them. I dare not use any acquaintance through and through, but I do shop from their actions and character as if at the most extensive store in the land. If I ever do have one of my stories published, and if one of these acquaintances does happen to recognize a certain quality . . . Actually, knowing the unique workings of the human mind, they will probably be more apt to find themselves in places they have not been put. People are odd beings, seeing meaning where there is nothing to be seen, and being blind to the obvious.

My sister-in-law Elizabeth sees herself as lady of the manor. Although admittedly she does hold that title, I find it of interest that those with power and money do not always possess equal portions of intellect and good sense. Elizabeth is a very lovely woman, educated, though not, I imagine, of much natural talent. Her tastes are domestic, her affections strong, though exclusive. But she does not *think* to any great advantage. In the evenings, when grand discussions can be had, Elizabeth allows us to read to her—without comment—and Edward goes to sleep. If it were not for Father, I would die of inane conversation.

And yet, there is also the opposite occurrence . . . to find a person pleasing when one does not expect to do so, when one has resigned oneself to desiring *not* to find a person pleasing . . .

My admission of this sin applies to Mrs. Catherine Knight, the adoptive mother of my brother Edward. Before her husband's death, she was the lady of Godmersham, and though she could have stayed on in that title, she stepped aside to allow Edward and Elizabeth free rein. She remains during our visit now but will take to her house in Canterbury as soon as it is ready.

I admit having apprehension in meeting her, assuming that she, having had more years practice as lady of the manor, would own a loftier air than our own Elizabeth. In that I am proven wrong. If ever there be a woman who deserves every elevation of status and position, it is Mrs. Knight.

I experienced this firsthand this morning when I walked in the rose garden. I did not expect to find company there, but turned a corner to see Mrs. Knight bending over a rosebush, snipping a pink bud.

"Oh," I said, all eloquence eluding me.

"Miss Jane, how nice to see you this morning." She motioned to the flowers. "Do you take to gardening?"

"Only a little. It is my mother who has the gift."

"Ah," she said. "But you have other gifts, I hear."

I felt myself blush, hoping, but dare not assuming, she meant my writing.

"Have you been published as yet?"

I thought of the letter regarding *First Impressions* returned to sender. "Not as yet."

"You must continue to try. It is important for a young person to use their gifts. And it is a parent's responsibility to encourage the transaction." She snipped another bud. "That is why I move."

I did not understand.

At my silence, she gazed at me. "Your brother Edward must assume his rightful place as the head of Godmersham and all that that entails."

"He will do a good job of it," I said.

"He will do a better job of it with me absent. If I remain at Godmersham . . . although I would not mean to interfere, it would be a temptation. Yet a son must rise or fall on his own merits, and does so best when unencumbered by the *status quo*—or by its mistress."

Her smile was delightful. As was her philosophy.

"You are very generous," I said. "And very wise."

She shrugged. "I seek to be both, but assume to be neither. And I *have* arranged to be amply provided for from the estate. So you see my generosity is not without self-service."

Her honesty was disarming. "I stand by my statement."

She offered a little bow. "Thank you, my dear." She scanned the garden. "Now. Which rose should we chuse next?"

Yes indeed, my sister-in-law Elizabeth has much she can learn from this lady.

As do I.

Elizabeth gave birth to a child on the tenth of October. Her fifth child in six years, her fourth son. William. A good name. Full of history.

Two weeks have passed since that happy occasion and it is time to leave. I am ready but for one point—Cassandra is staying behind to help with the new babe. And so I will return to Steventon alone, as my parents' only company.

And they as mine.

Mother is not feeling well at the start of the trip. I suspect her glee at the endless pork, dumplings, and oyster sauce caused her to imbibe too freely—with bad results. I admit to my own temptation. When one is offered all form of succulent things . . . and it was not just at mealtime. Edward made it clear that whenever we wanted to eat or drink, we had only to ask a servant, who brought the item forthwith. One can easily get spoiled.

But with our trip imminent, Mother rises to the occasion. Perhaps the anticipation of arriving home has heartened her indisposition. Although she insists on bitters and asks for bread to settle her stomach, they do their work and she is better.

We stop the first night at the Dartford Inn, and I half expect Mother to take to bed, but she does not. Although she *does* decide that she and I should share a room, leaving Father to have his own. I do not object, as I suppose a man does need his space here and there. As it has been a happy trip so far, I will share the room without protest.

I go up to settle in. Perhaps if it is a quiet night, I can take some time to write. I enter the room and look for my writing box.

It is not there.

And neither are the boxes of my clothes.

I run down the stairs and find the innkeeper. "Sir, my boxes— two leather ones of clothes and papers, and a small writing desk— are not in my room."

He looks over my shoulder at the door leading to the street. "Hmm. They ain't there neither," he says.

"Then, where are they?"

He calls to a boy of about thirteen. "Joseph. Did you bring a wood writing desk and two leather boxes to the room at the top of the stairs?"

It seems a stupid question. I have searched the room. They are not there.

"Uh . . . no," says the boy.

The innkeeper shrugs. "Must still be in the carriage, then."

Good. They are found. "Can Joseph please fetch them and bring them up—"

Mr. Nottley, our driver, overhears. "There are none left in the carriage, Miss Jane."

"Then, where . . . ?"

The innkeeper points to the right. "Another carriage just left.

When they was packing, maybe your boxes got mixed right in."

My heart stops and I stare at him in utter incomprehension. "Left? Where is it going?"

He rubs the stubble on his chin. "Gravesend, I think. The people what got on are sailing for the West Indies."

I feel faint, my head spinning. The man extends a hand, but Mr. Nottley steadies me first. He calls out for Father. "Mr. Austen! Your daughter! Sir!"

Father comes running from up the stairs and helps me to a chair.

"My writing, my desk, my work . . ." It is all I can manage.

"Her things are on a carriage heading to Gravesend," says Mr. Nottley.

"The West Indies," I add. I find it hard to breathe. All my life's work, galloping away, sailing away . . .

"West Indies?" repeats Father. To the men he says, "You must apprehend that carriage at once!"

"I can'na leave," says the innkeeper.

Mr. Nottley takes over. "I will send a man on horseback. We *will* retrieve them."

He leaves to save my worldly possessions. Although the clothing only counts for six or seven pounds, the work . . . 'tis priceless to me.

Mother appears from the parlour, where she had gone to ask after dinner. "What is all the commotion?"

I cannot explain. It is my turn to feel ill.

The innkeeper does it for me. "Her boxes got picked up by another carriage. Your man is going after it."

She sighs. "Well, then. It is taken care of."

My breath leaves me and I offer her a look I know is unkind.

"Well," she says, looking away. "It is."

"Now, now, my dear," says Father. "You must understand how distraught Jane is."

My anger gives me renewed strength and I stand. "If you will excuse me, I will watch for the horseman's return at the window." Mother wisely does not follow.

My thoughts are not generous. That Mother only acknowledges crises if they are her own . . . that she can pass off the tragedy that would ensue—that might still ensue if the man does not catch up with the coach . . .

It makes me wonder. Although she listens when Father and Cassandra implore me to read my stories aloud, I wonder—and this, not for the first time—if she really cares for what I write, or merely endures it, suffering the time as a disagreeable distraction from a more preferred activity.

I hear her talking to the innkeeper. "Some boiled chicken would be nice. And beef. Might you have beef for dinner?"

That she can eat—that she can always eat . . .

I have no words.

❦

Praise God! My prayers are answered.

The coach heading for the West Indies was only three miles away and was intercepted by the horseman. My possessions are returned. After offering profuse thanks to the horseman and Mr. Nottley, after personally seeing my belongings brought to my room, I close the door and assess the tragedy that was thwarted. I kneel on the floor and open the box that holds my manuscripts, old and new. Hours and hours, days and days of work. *First Impressions* is tied with a blue ribbon, *Susan* with green. And *Elinor and Marianne*—the book I work on even now, which I have renamed *Sense and Sensibility*—is in two stacks tied with red. One already edited, and one yet to be.

I slide a page from under the red ribbon and read.

> *Elinor, this eldest daughter whose advice was so effectual, possessed a strength of understanding, and coolness of judgment, which qualified her, though only nineteen, to be the counselor of her mother, and enabled her frequently to counteract, to the advantage of them*

*all, that eagerness of mind in Mrs. Dashwood which must generally
have led to imprudence. She had an excellent heart—her disposition
was affectionate, and her feelings were strong; but she knew how to
govern them: it was a knowledge which her mother had yet to learn,
and which one of her sisters had resolved never to learn.*

I read the last sentence again. It is not quite right. Two *learn*s
too close together . . .

I take the page to a desk by the window, get out my quill and
ink, and change the last few words . . . *had resolved never to be
taught.*

Yes, yes. Much better.

Since I am seated and since my work lies before me, I chuse to
continue my editing. Perhaps Mother will sit with Father by the fire
for hours, allowing me some time to—

There is a knock on the door. "Yes?"

Father peers in, his eyes finding the lost boxes. "You have them."

"I have them."

"A happy ending, then?"

"Indeed."

"Come down to dinner. Your mother has ordered quite a feast
to celebrate your goods being returned safely."

I know my mother's intent has little to do with the longing to
celebrate and everything to do with the desire to appease her appetite.

I glance at the page before me. "I would rather work. . . ."

"All well and good, Jane, but you must eat. Eat first. Then I
promise I will keep your mother occupied so you will have your time
alone. Agreed?"

Father is so dear. What would I do without him?

Mother is ill. Heat in the throat and that particular kind of evacuation which has generally preceded her other illnesses. On the last leg of our journey, we have stopped just miles from home, in Basingstoke. Mother has insisted on seeing Dr. Lyford, and yet, as she sits with him, they discuss the merits of dandelion tea with as much ease as if we were visiting as friends, not patients. In addition, we hear all the news about King George, whom we had apparently just missed as he passed through town on his way back to Windsor. The King is not well either, but we hear it is a problem of the mind more than the body. Although I do not voice it to anyone else, I sometimes wonder about his ability to govern. Especially now with most of Europe under the thumb of the French. We stand alone against the revolutionary Republic. I would not worry even this much if not for Frank and Charles off in the navy, and Henry connected to the army.

I digress. Mother. The focus is on my mother and her sickness. Sicknesses.

As I listen to her laugh and chat I find myself questioning . . . I should not think such thoughts. I am not a doctor. And Dr. Lyford *did* prescribe twelve drops of laudanum at bedtime.

We finish our visit and finally continue home. Home. There is no sweeter word. I could fill a page with but that word and it would still not collect the credit it is due.

Once there, Mother goes right to bed, leaving Father and me to unpack. Yet when James stops by from Deane to greet us, Mother rallies and has a good visit before returning to bed.

I have been put in charge of her laudanum, which somehow pleases me. . . . I administer the twelve drops and she sleeps.

As do I, though I need no medicine to attain that welcome state of peace.

I look at the clock. "But it is three-thirty and she still sleeps," I say to Father. The dinner sits on the table before us—set for three.

Father puts a finger to his lips and with a glance upstairs says, "Do not wake her. She must need the rest. Let's you and I sup, just the two of us." Although I feel a twinge of guilt, I accept his offer and even let him hold out my chair. He moves Mother's dishes to the settee, making the table look right and complete for just us two.

He sits. "There," he says. "Now it is a proper dinner."

Cook has watched all this from the doorway, a platter in her hands. Her face expresses her nervousness, as if she is unsure what to do without the lady of the house in attendance.

"Come, now. Serve Jane and me your offerings. The mutton smells delicious."

So delicious I fear Mother will smell the aroma even in her stupor and come to join us. That I hope against this disturbs but does not stop the sentiment.

Although Father and I have supped together before—when Mother and Cassandra have visited relatives and family—it is a rare treat, especially at this time, having just returned from many weeks of familial togetherness at Godmersham. To eat a meal, just two . . . 'tis a luxury.

"Well, then, Jane. Let us discuss the books we have read lately."

The *highest* luxury.

I am fickle. I admit this as a fault.

I return from Godmersham, put Mother to bed with her laudanum, and congratulate myself in the silence. With Mother abed, and Cassandra gone, I am in control of the household—in control of my own time.

But then Nanny Littlewart, our scrub, takes ill, so we have to hire two charwomen. We also hire a new maid who cooks well and sews well, but knows nothing about helping Father with the dairy. She shall learn her new duties.

As shall I.

The control which I embraced with such glee after returning from Godmersham becomes tedious. Finding time to work on my stories? After writing to Cassandra, Mrs. Birch, my brothers . . . I am tolerably tired of letter writing. I miss the Dashwood women, and dashing Willoughby, and the quite amiable Edward Ferras. Even sharing company with the selfish, greedy Fanny holds an appeal. At this moment they pique my interest and vie for my companionship far more than any being of flesh and blood.

'Tis rude, but 'tis the truth.

I have come to hope (strange but also true) that Mother will have more spurts of healthfulness than time in bed. Yet alas, so far it is an idle wish. Mother has developed amazing symptoms, complaining of asthma, dropsy, water in her chest, liver disorder, and unsettled bowels. Poor Dr. Lyford. I fear he is quite perplexed, as the symptoms do not match any known illness and change with distressing regularity. I make every attempt to be a good daughter, compassionate and kind, and for the largest part, I manage. As Mother comes up with ever more elaborate symptoms, there *is* humor in it, if one takes measure to seek it out.

And so, as the only child at home, the only woman in charge, I indulge in an ample sigh, give orders in the kitchen, make the menu, oversee the cleaning, and make purchases usually left to Mother. The Overton Scotchman was kind enough to rid me of some of my money in exchange for six shifts and four pairs of stockings. The Irish is not so fine as I should like it, but as I gave as much money as I intended, I have no reason to complain. It cost me three shillings and six per yard. It is rather finer, however, than our last, being not so harsh a cloth.

Also with Mother indisposed, I am privy to Father's dealings. Apparently he gave twenty-five shillings apiece for his last lot of sheep and is wanting to get some of Edward's pigs—to which he was enamored on our visit to Godmersham.

Yet it is Father who saves me from total domestic oblivion. He has recently purchased *Fitz-Albini*, actually bought it against my private wishes, for it does not quite feel appropriate that we should purchase the only one of Egerton's works of which his family is ashamed. That these scruples, however, do not at all interfere with my reading can be easily believed. We have neither of us yet finished the first volume. Father is disappointed—*I* am not, for I expected nothing better. Never did any book carry more internal evidence of its author. Every sentiment is completely Egerton's. There is very little story, and what there is is told in a strange, unconnected way. There are many characters introduced, apparently merely to be delineated. We have not been able to recognize any of them hitherto, except Dr. and Mrs. Hey and Mr. Oxenden, who is not very tenderly treated.

We have also bought Boswell's *Tour to the Hebrides* and are to have his *Life of Johnson*; and, as some money will yet remain in the bookseller's hands, it is to be laid out towards the purchase of Cowper's works. I look forward to that.

So, in lieu of being allowed time to work on my own stories, I am privy to the stories of others. Whether they are worthy of my time, and whether I feel my own stories have as much merit as they . . . I cannot say the latter without boast, yet I do make the statement with fullest hope. One day. One day people may read my stories by the fireside after tea. And one day (I must acknowledge this next), they may complain and deprecate my attempts with as much vehemence, glee, and assumed superiority as is exhibited during literary discussion in our humble—but very opinionated—home.

A bell rings from upstairs. It was Father's idea to supply Mother with such a cruel instrument. One evening, when particularly tired, I plan to ask him, "What were you thinking?"

Until then, I head for the stairs. "Coming, Mother."

SIX

I put the breakfast dishes in the cupboard. Nanny usually does this, but she is busy at the back door talking to a peddler. I am glad she is finally well and able to ease my domestic burden. How I wish Mother would follow her example. Although I *can* excel at all things domestic, I am not sure I would chuse to on a regular basis. It makes me wonder if I would make an acceptable mother and wife, taking care of family as well as house *and* keep up my writing. 'Twould be a challenge, no doubt. I take solace in knowing that since Tom has been called to the bar, he will be able to provide the servants needed to make a household run well.

I hear the talking of Nanny and the peddler stop and the door close. I expect to see her come with the rest of the dishes.

She does not.

I call to her. "Nanny? Will you bring the teacups, please?"

I hear the clinking of china. She appears in the doorway, but instead of entering, stops, as if venturing into the dining room would be painful.

I feel my impatience rise. I have much to do. "Come, now. Bring them here."

She blinks, as if remembering the dishes in her hands. She brings them to the cupboard.

"Did you make a purchase?" I ask.

"No. We have no need for tin right now."

I nod. The conversation feels wrong. Nanny's face is active, as if she has much more to say but the words cannot find exit. "Is there something else?"

She draws in a breath, then lets it out.

I set the last bowl in place and face her. "Nanny? Is something wrong?"

Her eyes meet mine but for a second. "I heard news."

"From the peddler?"

She nods. "He travels the county. Extensively."

I know this. Peddlers travel so we do not have to. Better they battle the November chill than us. "And . . . ?"

Her next sigh is one of surrender. "And he was at the Lefroys' last week and your Tom was there at Ashe, visiting, but now he is gone and . . . well . . ."

She did not need to finish.

Tom was home and did not come the scant two miles here? To see me? Nor did he send word so I could go there, to see him?

Nanny offers excuses. "Perhaps he was called away suddenly. Perhaps he had to go back to London to do . . . something."

"Perhaps," I say. I glance at the teacups. "Will you finish?"

"Of course."

I exit the room and find myself at the foot of the stairs. I turn full circle, unsure where to go. Father is in his office, the parlour is too open to whoever might walk by, the garden is cold and can be seen from the house, and my room upstairs passes by Mother's room. . . .

I need escape but have nowhere to go.

My heart pounds in my chest. My throat is tight. Tears threaten.

Needing solitude more than warmth, I grab my coat and bonnet and flee through the front door. To the left lies Steventon. I turn right. I turn away.

I run down the lane.

I do not let my mind grasp the news. And thankfully, it does not fight my will. It thinks of nothing as I button my coat and tie my bonnet, as I dig my gloves from my pocket, as my lungs gasp for air, unused to movement beyond a stroll.

A path leads to the left, off the lane. Fallen leaves try in vain to hide its existence. But I know this path. Since returning from God-mersham, I know many of the paths around Steventon that had previously been unknown to me. Who would suspect (not I) that I would discover the joys of walking alone at the age of twenty-three?

Perhaps those walks were but a preamble to today's excursion, a subtle gift from God, preparing me for my present need for escape by shewing me the way . . . away.

But no. Surely God could not be involved in this awful day.

Suddenly, my mind tosses aside inane busyness and grabs on to the awful news, forcing me to stop my walk and seek the stump of a tree for support.

I sit heavily, as if the news has added weight to my being. Tom was here and did not seek me out. Did not send a message. Did not send an invitation.

Did not want to see me.

"But I have been waiting."

My plaintive words assail the air in awful desperation.

And truth.

For I have been waiting—nearly three years waiting.

I shake my head, finding the ideas unacceptable. As Nanny said, there had to be a reason. A good reason. What Tom and I experienced that Christmas season at the balls . . . it was not nothing. It was special. It was meaningful. We had exchanged much more than simple pleasantries. The way he looked at me—really looked at me—far more intently than any man had ever done. He made me blush, feel beautiful, and feel loved.

Were those feelings misguided? Am I completely ignorant of what is real and what is false?

No. I cannot be so naïve. I write about love every day. I recognize what it is and how it comes about. I cannot be mistaken about this.

I cannot.

There has to be good reason Tom did not come to call.

I stand and head back home. Somehow, I will find out why.

I sit at my desk, paper and quill in hand, ready to write to whoever is capable of ending my pain and offering me the happiness I seek.

Yet I have no idea how to find the truth. I cannot write to my dear friend Anne Lefroy—who is Tom's aunt—and blatantly ask her about Tom. The very fact she has not contacted me . . .

And though I am tempted, I cannot lower my dignity and spill my heart to Nanny and ask her to tap into the servants' grapevine. I will not become a morsel of Hampshire gossip.

Mother is enraptured within her own play, enjoying her part as the invalid. And Father, though dear in his own right, is not one I can go to about issues of love.

I need Cassandra. I need her here. Hasn't Elizabeth had her in Godmersham long enough? William is a month old and by all accounts hale and hearty. Surely, with all their servants, with the help of the governess, with the help of the other children, and Edward, and Mrs. Knight, Elizabeth can relinquish the one person I have to turn to for comfort. Cassandra is my confidante, my life's constant, my sister, my friend, and alas, in many ways, my mother. Only she knows my true heart. Only she is aware of my true love for Tom and how I have waited. She knows every detail of what transpired between us that Christmas and has agreed we are engaged in all ways but public declaration. If she had not believed it so, I trust with my true heart she would have set me right by now. Sisters do such things for each other. Sisters help each other see the truth, no matter how painful.

The fact she has not set me right means I *am* correct in my thinking. Tom and I are to be married.

Aren't we?

Nanny knocks on my door with a letter. "Come by courier, Miss Jane."

I recognize the hand. It is from Anne Lefroy. "Thank you, Nanny."

She does not leave. "The courier says he's to wait for a reply."

I nearly tear the page undoing the seal. The note is short: *I would love to come call, tomorrow at ten? Send word with the courier. I so long to see you, dear Jane.*

"Tell the courier I look forward to Mrs. Lefroy's visit tomorrow at ten."

Nanny's eyebrows rise, she dips a quick curtsy, and leaves the room.

I read the note again. My heart is light. All will be well.

Anne takes my hands and kisses my cheek. "Dearest Jane. How have you been?"

I help her remove her coat and brush off the snow, and lead her to the parlour. "I have been tolerably well—but chilly. Come sit by the fire and warm yourself. I have asked for some hot chocolate, for I know how much you enjoy it."

"I do. How special." She sat in the wing chair by the fire, leaning close, extending her cold hands.

For her to come visit, in spite of the snow . . . she must deem the task most important to risk cold feet and hands. *I* have high hopes for the visit. Since she befriended me when I was only a child, our relationship has been special. To me, Anne embodies the ideal woman: wise, compassionate, witty, courageous, and utterly at ease with herself, and everyone else. Anne, from the well-placed Brydges family, is as much at ease with me, a lowly parson's daughter, as I imagine she is with the King. There is no pretension within her, no tension about her. Beyond Cassandra, she is my dearest friend.

A friend who is here to tell me about Tom?

I am quick to mentally say, *I hope so,* yet I immediately withdraw from the bravado. To know . . . in mere moments I might be drawn to the highest heights.

Or plunged to the lowest depths.

A frightening thing, to *know*.

Suddenly, I want to flee, to leave my guest, run upstairs, slam shut my door, and dive under the covers where nothing ill can reach me. I feel the child again, afraid of the dark, of unseen monsters, and of any truth that dare threaten my happiness.

"Jane?"

I have not been listening. "Yes. Sorry."

"I asked after your mother. Is she doing better?"

Talk of family was a good tack. Talk of family would open the door to talk of her nephew. . . . "She has her good days and bad, often according to the weather, or what I have cooked for dinner."

"Ah," says Anne. "And Cassandra? When will she return?"

"Not soon enough. I miss her terribly."

"For your sake, I also wish she were here. I know she is such a comfort to you."

Her words take me aback. And why will I need comfort?

When I next look at her, she quickly averts her eyes. My stomach clenches.

She is your dearest friend. Just ask what she means.

My heart beats at a higher rhythm as I seek courage. Three words. All I need but say are three words: *How is Tom?* Yet to say them could open a floodgate of other words, other questions: *Where is Tom? Why did he not come to see me? Please tell me a reason why he could be so close, yet not seek me out. Please make the world all right.*

"My husband and I are planning a trip to Italy," Anne says. "I have always wanted to see Rome. Remember that book we looked at when you were small? The one with the drawings of the Coliseum and St. Peter's?"

I nod and realize the conversation has moved on from inquiries after our family's health and activities to things far removed from Steventon and Ashe. Far removed from Jane and Tom. From love. From engagements. From marriage.

I realize I have been distracted again when Anne repeats,

"Remember, Jane? Remember the wonderful visits we have had?"

"I remember them all."

She reaches across the space between us and touches my knee. "You have always been very special to me and I love and cherish you as a daughter—as more than a daughter. As a friend."

Her eyes are intensely blue and full of sincerity. But something else. There is a desperation there, a request, a plea . . . for me to understand something beyond her words? The very fact she is *not* speaking of Tom when he has so recently visited is telling. The normal aside, "And we had the most delightful visit from Tom," is absent, the natural sharing of visits past giving way to future travels.

A diversion. An act of mercy?

I pull from a store deep inside. "When do you leave?"

"Soon, soon," she says, leaning back, looking at the fire again. She is more relaxed. My response has given her indication that the conversation has been successfully turned. "None too soon." She offers me the quickest glance. "I am weary of family right now, of wishing they would . . . or would not . . ."

Ah.

She pulls out a letter. "But here. I have news from a mutual friend, Samuel Blackall."

I cringe. Last January, people tried to pair me with this man— who made it very clear that he was in want of a wife because he was getting his own parish. He much liked the sound of his own voice, and blessedly did not seem in dire need of hearing mine. Yet he made it very clear that I should be greatly honoured at his attention—and intention.

I was not, although I did find our meeting profitable. My Mr. Collins in *First Impressions* benefited much from the flaws and foibles of the forward Mr. Blackall. And though I did not find myself affronted with such a direct proposal as my poor Lizzy, I allowed her to say what I would have said. If Mr. Blackall had been given the chance.

Which he was not.

And now, for Anne to want to read to me any letter containing a single one of his words . . .

Yet as she continues, I recognize the letter for what it is—another distraction. And so I accept it as such.

Anne adjusts the letter to the light. "Here it is. Mr. Blackall says, 'I am very sorry to hear of Mrs. Austen's illness. It would give me particular pleasure to have an opportunity of improving my acquaintance with that family—with a hope of creating to myself a nearer interest. But at present I cannot indulge any expectation of it.'"

I feel my eyebrows rise. This is good news. I had expected to hear Mr. Blackall's entreaty for a deeper bond, the thought of which had the power to send me abed next to Mother. "Ah," I say.

"You are not distressed?" asks Anne.

"I will survive the disappointment. It is most probable that our indifference will soon be mutual, unless his regard, which appeared to spring from knowing nothing of me at first, is best supported by never seeing me."

She smiles, and through her smile I distinguish her true motive. Although I have been spurned by two men today, one was by choice, and that knowledge offers some—however small—satisfaction.

Father chuses this moment to come into the room, carrying a book. "Well, well," he says upon seeing Anne. "What a delight! Jane told me you were coming to visit, but I had forgot. Forgive me, dear Anne, for not welcoming you sooner." They exchange kisses to their cheeks. "And how is the family? I hear your nephew Tom was at Ashe. Is he well? How are his studies progressing?"

I must have gasped because both Anne and Father look at me before returning to their dialogue.

"He is well," says Anne.

She avoids my eyes; I know she does.

She continues. "He has finished his studies, and after his visit, he returned to London. From there he is going back to Ireland to begin his career in law."

"My, my. All grown up."

"In some ways," says Anne.

She looks at me now, and I read the disapproval in her voice. I see the compassion in her eyes.

Father's eyes are diverted to the window. "Oh dear. Look at the snow come down."

Anne stands. "How distressing. I fear I must cut my visit short so I may get back before the roads become impassable."

"How unfortunate," says Father, but he gets her coat just the same. "I will tell your driver."

I hold Anne's bonnet as she buttons her coat. I brush a bit of melted snow from its brim. "I am glad you came," I say.

"I had to see you." She takes my hand and our eyes speak the rest.

Father returns with feathery snow on his shoulders, lacy flakes balancing precariously on his hair. "Your driver is ready."

A quick hug, a promise to write, and she is gone.

I wave from the window.

Father comes up behind me and puts a hand on my shoulder. "How nice she should visit. Visits are so important and mean so much."

As do the absence of visits.

"Well, then," he says, kissing the top of my head, "I must return to work. Are you busy, Jane? Do you have things to do?"

It is an odd question and I face him. "I do."

"Good, good. Keeping busy can be a balm. Yes?"

"Yes, Father."

As he leaves me and goes back to his office, I know that this will be the only gesture of sympathy I will receive from him. Other than Cassandra, my family has never acknowledged my closeness with Tom Lefroy, has never realized the extent of our commitment.

I laugh out loud. Extent of our commitment? Whatever bond was between us has been utterly and unceremoniously broken.

I put my fingers against the cold glass as if touching the snow once removed. *As you have almost touched love, yet remain once removed . . .*

I pull my fingers back and let them find warmth in the folds of my dress.

After my visit with Anne, I head towards my room to sulk, to cry, to fume, to forget, to—

"Jane?"

With a sigh, I swing the door to my parents' room to its full extent. "Yes, Mother?"

She nods to the window. "It is snowing."

"Yes, Mother."

"I do not like snow."

"Yes, Mother."

"It prevents friends from visiting."

I am not sure what to say. Surely she heard me downstairs, talking with Anne.

And then I realize that surely she heard me downstairs, talking with Anne. She heard. She knows what transpired.

"Of course, some people do not possess the manners to visit." She makes a face. "I have little patience with such people. This family knows what is right, even if others do not." She looks right at me. "You know what is right, Jane. I am proud of you for that."

My mind races through her words, wanting her to say them again so I can study them and interpret their true meaning. Does my mother offer me sympathy? Does she know more than she has let on these three years?

Mother snuggles deeper into her pillow and closes her eyes. "I would like to sleep now. My heart is hurting."

This was a new symptom in her parade of feeling. "Should I get the doctor?"

Mother opens one eye. "No. It will pass." She opens both eyes and repeats herself. "It *will* pass, Jane."

I adjust her covers, kiss her forehead, and leave her to sleep.

I hope she is right.

⁂

It will pass, Jane.

I stand once again at a window, watching the snow. But this one is in the sitting room of the bedroom I share with my sister. I should sit. I am weary. But I fear sitting will too easily lead to lying down, which might lead to curling into a ball and clutching my pillow, which will lead to tears and a confinement just as total—and voluntary—as my mother's.

I will not do that. I cannot.

I cannot wallow. I cannot allow myself the total despair of my character Marianne, grieving for Willoughby. To lose one's senses in such a way, to display them for all to see? What did Marianne gain from it but more pain, and deeper sorrow?

I think of Marianne's sister, Elinor. Her suffering after learning that the man she loves is bound to another is just as great as her sister's, yet her response is far different. She binds her grief inside, wrapping it tightly around her heart like yarn around a ball. But in her self-constraint and strength, does she risk having the grief pull too tight, strangling her heart and all other possibilities of love?

Which is the better way? Total release or total constraint? Sense or sensibility?

I think of my own sister. When her Tom died she did not express her grief. She was *not* Marianne. In many ways I have often wished she was—at least to some degree. Cassandra is so controlled and inwards. When I wanted to help I found no way inside her pain, no crack in her regulation to either see her thoughts and feelings nor let my own reach inside. I imagined her pain, but I did not share it. And now, with pain of my own . . . Is there a correct way to grieve? A better way?

Suddenly, Marianne begins to speak in my mind, Marianne from the pages of my story. Marianne who has been so intensely spurned by Willoughby and grieves publicly, with great flourish. She does not realize how her sister Elinor has been suffering in silence, holding on to the secret that Lucy Steele is clandestinely engaged to Elinor's love, Edward—and has sworn Elinor to confidence. To feel such pain without being able to share it . . . as I must hold on to my own pain . . .

I know what I must do. I rush to the manuscript and pull out the right page, ready to make additions. The sisters begin to talk and I hurry to scribe their words to the paper. Elinor speaks first, a bit peeved at Marianne's assumption that she does not also feel deeply.

"You do not suppose that I have ever felt much. For four months, Marianne, I have had all this hanging on my mind, without being at liberty to speak of it to a single creature; knowing that it would make you and my mother most unhappy whenever it were explained to you, yet unable to prepare you for it in the least. . . ."

Elinor's words continue, an outpouring of pent-up frustration and anxiety, finally letting her emotional, indulgent sister realize there are others who suffer too, that indeed, there is another way to suffer.

Marianne was quite subdued. "Oh, Elinor," she cried, "you have made me hate myself for ever. How barbarous have I been to you! You, who have been my own comfort, who have borne with me in all my misery, who have seemed to be only suffering for me! Is this my gratitude! Is this the only return I can make you? Because your merit cries out upon myself, I have been trying to do it away."

The sisters embrace, their sense and sensibility finding common ground. The scene continues in my mind and I let it take hold. The words run across the page of their own volition. I am their servant and keep them supplied with fresh ink and page.

A few paragraphs later the words run faster as the existing plot tightens. What if Elinor's love, Edward, is offered a means to escape his dreadful engagement to Lucy—in fact, is ordered to call it off—yet he declines, for honour's sake, thus losing his inheritance? At a point he could have been freed to wed Elinor, he *chuses* to marry fickle, feckless Lucy because it is the right thing to do.

Ah yes. 'Tis a wonderful twist that will make the story better.

I write faster.

And find my own release.

❦ ❦

I know it is extravagant to think about serving an ox cheek for dinner, but the thought of it, and some little dumplings, will make me fancy myself at Godmersham. In happier days . . .

Although the day is brisk, a day when I would normally take solace inside by the fire, my new penchant for walking in the outdoors has made my desire for ox cheek attainable.

All buttoned and tied with coat and bonnet, I head up the lane from the parsonage to the butcher's. A dusting of snow remains beside the road, and the ground is hard and frozen. Yet the sun shines, teasing me into believing it offers warmth as well as light.

Mrs. Hardy, the butcher's wife, greets me. "Morning, Miss Jane. How was that chicken you bought Monday?"

"Very tasty," I say. "Might you have an ox cheek?"

She smiles. "Ox cheek, you say? It is about time your mother gets past her usual beef and chicken. How is she, by the way?"

"Fine," I say. For I truly believe she is. And I believe her single-mindedness to be otherwise has contributed to her being tetchy and lethargic. With my added burdens I could allow myself to pout, to cry and carry on, or to take to my bed with many an affliction worthy of death and destruction. But I will not. I cannot. And because of that resolve in my own regard, I find it difficult to tolerate such self-indulgence in others. I remember just the other day, Mother making entrée into her dressing room through crowds of admiring spectators. She received the attention she craved, while I had to contain myself from rolling my eyes.

Mrs. Hardy pulls a hunk of meat from a shelf in back. She holds it up for me. "How be this one?"

"Very fine." I can already taste the dumplings. . . . To be polite, I ask after her husband.

"He be fine too, though tired. He was up at Ashe yesterday with a whole passel of meat when he heard the news."

My heart caught in my throat. People knew? Mrs. Hardy knew about Tom and—

"The oldest boy, Tom, is engaged."

My first thought was that he had announced *our* engagement. Could it be I was the last to know? Perhaps he had gone back to Ireland without seeing me because of pressing business. He was an adult now, and perhaps he did not give his aunt Anne the full reason for his actions. Perhaps he *would* have called, had planned to call and—

"Yes indeed," continued Mrs. Hardy. "He's marrying the daughter of Sir Jeffry Paul, who's some bigwig in Dublin. Her name is Mary. The wedding's next year. We're hoping it's here. We would sure like to provide the meat for that celebration."

I want to flee, but know such an act will cause talk. I say something in response, though I have no idea what. Mrs. Hardy wraps the meat; I pay and am on my way.

Usually news feeds me.

But today . . . it destroys.

I walk faster, head down, shoulders drawn forward as if from the cold, when the truth lies in my desire to be away from all people who could inadvertently add to my pain. I need comfort, not anguish.

And yet I know I will receive no comfort. When Cassandra lost her Tom, our friends and family rallied round to offer their condolences.

As was appropriate.

But now, when I have lost my Tom . . . the breaking off of an unofficial and unpublic engagement does not solicit such consolations. I bear my burden alone. I must accept this. I must endure it.

Yet I must also realize that because no one knows the depths of my feelings for Tom (and his for me—truly, truly, I must believe his for me), people are apt to be lax in discretion.

His feelings for me . . .

My pace slows as I realize he has no feelings for me; he marries another.

And yet . . . this is not the first time someone has chosen to marry for reasons other than love. He is an aspiring lawyer, with expectations and responsibilities. Perhaps for his career . . .

"It does not matter."

I speak the truth to the wind—which has become aggressive. I notice for the first time the sun has hidden its face. Dark clouds gather.

How appropriate. A cold shroud for my grief and my shame.

I stop short. Shame? What do I have to be ashamed of?

A horse with its head over the fenced pasture grunts at me and nods its head as if to say, *Yes, Jane, shame.*

Not shame in my actions of three years ago. They were the delighted flirtations of a young girl trying to draw out the delighted flirtations of a young man. They could be forgiven.

But waiting three years . . . letting my imagination create something that was not solid and real . . . there is no excuse for that. I wasted those years; they will never be returned to me. I am twenty-three years old—old enough to know better.

Old enough to learn from my mistakes.

"Never again," I tell the horse.

He nods back at me, sealing the pact.

I hope it is one I can keep.

I love to dance. I come to the ball this evening to do just that. Dance every dance, feel free and young and delighted and delightful. The room is too small and the chairs too few, which in its own way allows for people—since they must stand—to dance.

I feel pretty. Instead of my white satin cap, I wear one of mamalouc. They tell me it is all the fashion now, worn at the opera. Apparently, it is very Egyptian, like a fez with a feather. I know Cassandra will want me to describe it, but I hate doing so. I *can* tell her my gown is made very much like my blue one, but with short sleeves, the wrap fuller, the apron come over it, with a band of the same.

I look across the room and see the two Blackstone daughters— I do not know their individual names, nor care to. I do not like the Miss Blackstones; indeed, I am determined not to like them. I look for the Biggs, who own my friendship to the highest degree. There. Ah. There are Catherine and Alethea.

I am not in much request. People seem apt to not ask me to dance until they cannot help it. One's circumstance varies so much at times without any particular reason.

Or is there reason? Perhaps they know about Tom—I see his brother George here—or even know about Samuel Blackall's having quite enough of my non-interest. Or perhaps they chuse not to appreciate me because I *have* a keen mind and a clever wit. How more fashionable and convenient it would be to be silent, with nodding head and smiling, but ever-locked, lips.

I notice one gentleman, an officer of the Cheshire, a very good-looking young man, who smiles at me, and seems eager to be introduced. Yet I am not sure he wants it quite enough to take much trouble in effecting it. We shall see.

As the Bigg sisters come close, I spot out of the corner of my eye Lord Bolton's eldest son also coming towards me. Considering he dances too ill to be endured, I meet Catherine and Alethea halfway between and take their arms, leading them away from the clumsy Bolton.

"What are you doing, Jane?" asks Alethea.

"Saving my toes."

Since my pride suffers a beating, at least I can save those.

❦

I lie in bed. Alone.

No Cassandra.

No husband.

No Tom.

To the last thought, I sigh. And yet . . . in many ways I am over him. It is not a sigh of despair, but a sigh of acceptance. A *so be it* added to the list of my life's events.

I turn on my side towards the window and see the moonlight cut across the floor and enter our sitting room. It stops at the foot of my desk, as if pointing. . . .

If things had turned out differently, what would I be doing right now? When Tom was home in Ashe last November, if he *had* come to call, if he *had* asked for my hand, what would I be doing right now?

Planning a wedding.

Planning a move to Ireland, where Tom has his work.

Preparing to leave Father, Mother, and Cassandra. And . . . with James's family close, and Edward's just four days away . . . Henry and Eliza in London. Charles and Frank at sea . . . my dear friend Martha Lloyd, the Bigg sisters, Anne Lefroy . . .

How could I ever leave all that I know, all *whom* I know?

To live forever with a man I barely know?

I punch my fist into my pillow, accentuating the truth. For in spite of my romantic notions, in spite of all that seemed evident, Tom and I only spoke a few times. And though I am aware of marriages that are based on fewer meetings than that, our genuine knowledge of each other—of what we feel, who we are, what we desire—is lacking. We spoke of books we had read—our common appreciation of *Tom Jones* fueled many a dialogue—but I never spoke to him about my writing. Would that knowledge have come as a shock to him? Would he approve, or would he think my attempts frivolous or unwomanly?

We flirted shamelessly. We felt the stirrings of desire that come with such attention. And perhaps amid the stirrings, we even felt the seed of love being planted.

But it was not fed, nor watered, nor tended.

And so it died.

Looking back upon it now, I see it could have garnered no other outcome. That I lingered so long in such an undiscerning state embarrasses me and causes me to suffer self-condemnation—albeit in small enough doses to endure. I am wiser now, and perhaps more worldly (even here in tiny Steventon). How much better to realize the value in the rejection. For I am better off here, a single woman amid the soft cocoon of family and friends, than there, married to Tom, living far away, alone from all but him.

'Tis for the best. I know that now. But that does not mean the journey was not painful.

I glance at my desk in the next room. A girl swept off her feet by social circumstance, overcome by the stirrings and temptations of romance, a girl obsessed with novels and happy endings, who loves to discuss those books. A girl who longs to be a heroine, who desires a hero above everything else . . . and yet, perhaps she does not gain him, but is happy just the same.

I throw off my covers, find my slippers and shawl. I go to my desk to begin a new story. I will set it in Bath, that frivolous place of flirtation, fickleness, and frustration. . . .

SEVEN

How ironic. I decide to write *Susan*, set in Bath, and then my brother Edward invites Mother and me to go with him to that very city. Edward has gout and hopes the medicinal waters will give him relief. Elizabeth and the two eldest of their five go too: Fanny and little Edward. My desire to visit that city again—for research—is diluted by my disappointment that Cassandra stays behind in Steventon to take care of Father! She did not come home from Edward's until March, and now, in May, *we* leave *her*?

If I had my way . . .

But I do not.

Our journey proceeds exceedingly well; nothing occurs to alarm or delay us. We find the roads in excellent order, have very good horses all the way, and reach Devizes with ease by four o'clock. At Devizes we have comfortable rooms and a good dinner, to which we sit down about five. Amongst other things we have asparagus and a lobster (which makes me wish for Cassandra to be here), as well as some cheesecakes, on which the children make so delightful a supper as to endear the town of Devizes to them for a long time.

I am plagued regarding my trunk of clothes and manuscripts; it is too heavy to go by the coach from Devizes; there is reason to suppose that it might be too heavy likewise for any other coach. I wonder if we might find a wagon to convey it.

Edward limps into the inn as we are putting on our bonnets. "Good news," he says. "I have found a wagon to convey your trunk on to Bath—but it will not arrive there until tomorrow."

Although I wish to complain because *we* will arrive in Bath this very afternoon, and after nearly losing my life's work once, I am wary of losing it again, I tell him thank-you and get into the carriage. I cannot complain too much when my trip is being supplied gratis by my brother.

Can I?

Although I *can* silently long for our destination to appear with great haste so I can procure a few moments that do not include being knee to knee and arm to arm with another. I can also silently long for a bit of outer silence—and be eternally glad that only Edward's two eldest are on this jaunt. Although I love all my nieces and nephews dearly, I much prefer to enjoy their presence in wide rooms and open fields.

That my mother has taken it upon herself to fill our carriage time with an extensive listing of recent ailments, including each faulty diagnosis from Dr. Lyford, and the strengths and weaknesses of each medicinal remedy or fallacy, only adds to my desire to hurry the horses on towards our destination. *Faster, faster, dear horses, carry me ever faster!*

As Mother continues her discourse, and Elizabeth kindly listens, as Edward finds consolation out the window, I take advantage and close my eyes—for they have bothered me of late—and allow myself withdrawal and respite. Although I dare not hope for sleep in the rocking carriage, I do look forward to letting my mind wander to thoughts of my characters Susan Morland and Henry Tilney. I still am not sure how their story will end. . . .

Mother nudges my knee with a hand. "Wasn't that right, Jane? Wasn't Dr. Lyford utterly wrong about my not having consumption?"

Although I admire Dr. Lyford for his doctoring ability—and commendable bedside manner—I find it easier to say, "Yes, Mother. That is right."

"See?" Mother says to Elizabeth. "It is as I have told it."

May Dr. Lyford forgive us.

Rain accompanies us, adding to our traveler's weariness. We come upon Bath at one o'clock in the afternoon, though 'tis gloomy enough to be one in the morning. I find Bath itself to be on shew as much as all the people who visit there. The buildings are situated in such a way as if to say, "Look at me!" and "Am I not grand?" Both buildings and people have the same motivation, but neither speak of it out loud.

We stop at the Paragon, where my aunt and uncle—my mother's brother—live in No. 1, but it is too wet and dirty for us to get out, and as one does not prevail upon Aunt Leigh-Perrot while looking like a wet pup (a pup who might also dirty her marble), we did not bother them, except to speak to the butler, who told us Uncle Perrot—who suffers from the gout as does Edward—had a better night of it, of last.

As is expected once one arrives in Bath (indeed, why one comes), we are seen and see others. In the Paragon we meet Mrs. Foley and Mrs. Dowdeswell, with her yellow shawl airing out, and at the bottom of Kingsdown Hill meet a gentleman in a buggy, who, on minute examination, turns out to be Dr. Hall—and Dr. Hall in such very deep mourning that either his mother, his wife, or he himself must be dead.

We proceed to the house Edward has let, at No. 13 Queen Square. We are exceedingly pleased with the house; the rooms are quite as large as we expected. The landlady, Mrs. Bromley, is a fat woman (also in mourning), and a little black kitten runs about the staircase. Elizabeth has the apartment within the drawing room; she wants my mother to have it, but for various reasons—not always to my understanding—it is settled for Mother and me to be above, up a double flight where we have two very nice-sized rooms, with dirty quilts but everything comfortable. I have the outward and larger apartment, which is quite as large as our bedroom at home, and my mother's is not materially less. The beds are both as large as any at Steventon, and I have a very nice chest of drawers and a closet full of shelves—so full indeed that there is nothing else in it, and it should therefore be called a cupboard rather than a closet, I suppose.

Mother does not seem at all the worse for her journey, nor are any of us, I hope, though Edward seemed rather fagged last night, and not very brisk this morning; but I trust the bustle of sending for tea, coffee, and sugar and such, and going out to taste a cheese, will do him good.

Mrs. Bromley told us there was a very long list of arrivals in the newspaper yesterday, so that we need not immediately dread absolute solitude; and there is a public breakfast in Sydney Gardens every morning, so that we shall not be wholly starved. I truly have no worries in that regard. Edward is not one to spare the coin in regard to food, and my aunt thinks nothing of setting up card tables for ninety people and feeding them throughout multiple games. I do not particularly like cards. People take it too seriously and gamble. I suppose not having money to lose can also be a facilitating factor in my opinion.

After settling in, I retire down the stairs to the drawing room in order to write to Cassandra. Seizing a quiet minute, I find I like our situation very much; it is far more cheerful than the Paragon, and the prospect from the drawing room window is rather picturesque, as it commands a view of the left side of Brock Street, broken by three Lombardy poplars in the garden of the last house in Queen's Parade. I hope it will be a tolerable afternoon. When first we came, all the umbrellas were up, but now the pavements are getting very white again.

I hear commotion in the hall with the children's effusive jabberings and their parents' attempts to comply. Mother's voice joins them, and I hear talk of proceeding to the Pump Room with haste, so Edward can be made well—by his hopeful expectation if not from the intake and partake of the magic waters.

"Jane?" Mother calls. "Where is that girl?"

I have barely started the letter.

It will have to wait. Bath calls.

Three weeks and counting . . .

I cannot say that I do not enjoy myself here in Bath, yet I can offer the distinction that I enjoy myself best when doing things other than that for which Bath is known. Although both Edward and Uncle take the waters—both by drink and bath—and although Edward has even taken a new electrical treatment that I dare not imagine, I remain a skeptic. Yes, we have been told the benefits of the water are often cumulative, and are often unappreciated until after one has left the city. I do see the convenience in this—for Bath's reputation. One cannot complain well when there is distance. . . .

But in truth, I do not see bountiful benefit in either of the men, and see the greatest benefit coming to the physicians who are as plentiful and as genuine as the sprigs of fruit and flowers in the women's bonnets.

I look at such sprigs now, shopping with Mother, Elizabeth, and my aunt. Before coming to Bath, I was consigned by Cassandra, Martha, and Mary to procure certain items of clothing in the multitude of eager shops that inhabit this city. Among other sundries, Cassandra ordered sprigs for her hat. I peruse the selection before me. Flowers are very much worn, but fruit is the thing. Elizabeth has a bunch of strawberries on her bonnet, and I have seen grapes, cherries, plums, and apricots. A plum or greengage will cost three shillings, cherries and grapes about five. A mite much, I would say. If asked.

Which I am not.

The responsibility is weighty. Although I have been given unlimited power to chuse, it never bodes well to be too at ease with another's budget. But looking here, it appears I can get four or five very pretty sprigs of flowers for the same money which will procure only one Orleans plum.

I put the costly plum down, feeling weary. I realize I cannot decide on the fruit till I write to Cassandra for her preference. I also cannot help thinking that it is more natural to have flowers grow out of the head than fruit (Elizabeth and her strawberries notwithstanding).

Aunt looks over my shoulder at the plum. "Have you found something to suit you?"

"'Tis not for me, but Cassandra."

"Ah." She plucks the plum. "Be that as it may, I hardly think this is quite appropriate for your Steventon."

"Your Steventon" drips with her disdain. Aunt always makes it clear that we Austens are *lesser* to her *more*. And though my mother's own Leigh lineage is hardly impoverished and holds its own honour (their ancestor was the Lord Mayor of London in the 1500s), the Perrot family (which my aunt pronounces Perr-uht, trilling the *r*'s) comes from loftier roots. The entire extent of her right to impale us with her braggadocio escapes me (even though she will insist she has made it perfectly clear), yet I do remember that some King and some river can be claimed as family. We, as mere Austens, are claimed with less enthusiasm.

My aunt puts the plum down with an exaggerated sigh. "I suppose I could take you to a cheap shop. There is one down near Walcot Church that occasionally amuses."

I accept her slight and let my practicality reign. "That might be best."

But with a roll of her eyes, she surprises me by asking the clerk to wrap up two plums.

A gift? I busy myself with silk violets and pretend not to notice. It is best to remain ignorant of a gift until it is properly presented. As I wait for the transaction to be complete, I chastise myself for all the inappropriate thoughts I have entertained regarding my aunt and her haughty ways. She can be a kind woman. Thoughtful in every—

She takes her small bundle and turns towards the door. "Let's move on. I would like to find some lavender ribbon to put around these plums for my hat."

My hat.

As we exit the store, I let the inappropriate thoughts return, finding unkind solace that their bite is nearly as satisfying as any plum on any chapeau.

❦ ❦

Bath causes me to ponder Shakespeare. For indeed, *All the world's a stage, and all the men and women merely players. They have their exits and their entrances; And one man in his time plays many parts.*

The parts people play in Bath are varied, and are actually quite inconsequential. Their desire to be on stage is the driving force here—to be seen, and to see.

And to catch, and be caught by the opposite gender.

Where it is true such negotiations happen in every parlour across England, from the smallest village of Steventon to the great halls of busy London, here in Bath it is more blatant, more persuasive, and utterly endorsed by all.

But not appreciated by all.

It is not that I do not desire a husband. Although a part of my heart will always bear the scar of Tom Lefroy, I have far from given up. That same heart is open and willing to accept the love of another—as long as I am able to return it. No more Mr. Blackalls, if you please. No more men who see a mating with Jane Austen as a pragmatic decision for the sake of a cleaner house, a warm bed, and the propagation of their family name. Get a maid, find a woman of ill repute, and take in an orphan.

Such rude comments are unbecoming, and will certainly not aid in my finding a husband. But is it wrong to want love as an ingredient in a match? Mother and Father love each other. My uncle adores my aunt in a way that perplexes all who know her. Even Tom's parents . . . the entire financial upheaval that currently befalls his shoulders is due to the fact that his father ignored his family's wishes and married for love. It can happen. My brothers have done well in that regard. Although I may not fully appreciate the merits of their wives, I do believe they are happy, and each has chosen well, in his own way.

And what of God? Does He not get involved? Is His will not instrumental towards bringing two people together in a way that is both pleasing to Him *and* suits His plans?

I like to think so, think that someday I will meet a man I am supposed to meet and we will know, just know, that we are meant to be together.

So why must my aunt and mother conspire on my behalf? Do they truly believe I am not capable of making a male head turn, or keeping a chatty dialogue going beyond how-de-dos?

Apparently.

They are conspiring even now. I stand at the door to Aunt's parlour and listen. It is always considered good defense to know the plottings of one's opponent. That I should deem them such is an opinion that would surely earn me a lengthy lecture. Or two.

"If only Jane had my nose," I hear Mother say. "'Tis quite aquiline and is surely a sign of aristocracy, don't you agree?"

"My husband, your brother, has no such nose," Aunt says.

I listen for Mother's reply, but she is silent.

Aunt continues, "Are you insinuating Perrot did not descend from aristocracy because his nose is not large and . . . and hooked? For he is a Leigh too."

I was eager to hear Mother's reply. I have been made aware of the deficiency of my own small nose my entire life.

"'Tis only one sign of aristocracy. There are many others, of course."

"Of course."

"If only Jane was more . . . full. She is so spare."

Mother's words are discreet, but I know their meaning. I cannot help my frame. Unless I eat and eat and eat and become fat and filled out in that fashion, there is no means by which I can ever—

"And her colour is a bit too flushed," Aunt says. "She has the cheeks of a doll."

"At least she does not need to worry about rouge," Mother says.

"And she is nearly too tall."

"Indeed."

Too tall for what? And yet, even as I pretend not to know their intent, I know that my height makes me see eye to eye with most young men.

My aunt sighs. "Does she paint and play the piano well?"

"She is very accomplished at the pianoforte, but has no eye for art. Cassandra owns that talent—but alas, no talent for music."

"Hmm," Aunt says. "It appears your girls must be sold as a pair to get a whole."

I nearly gasp, but am saved from such a reaction by the women's soft laughter. And though my aunt's comment was said in jest, it owns much truth within its edges. In many ways Cassandra and I complement each other. We are better together than apart. We are a truer whole as two, not one.

"There is the concert tonight in Sydney Gardens. Perhaps we can arrange for Jane to sit where it is advantageous," Aunt says.

"I will do all that I can to help."

"As is our duty."

I slip away from the doorway, wishing I could argue with them. But I cannot. Older women framing the romantic pairings of those who are younger?

'Tis been this way since time began, and no amount of *my* disdain or disgust can change it.

The concert entertains and I sit where my aunt and mother have placed me—next to a Mr. Clark, who has high colour such as I, but to an even greater degree. I do not know whether it is caused by his delight at meeting me, his panic for said meeting, embarrassment for being thrust into the matchmaking clutches of my relatives (and surely his), a rash for which he should seek an ointment, or a flush caused by the heat of the evening.

At any rate, it is not attractive. Nor are his teeth, which look as bad as Uncle Perrot's. I try to draw him into conversation, but his yes-and-no answers, offered without adornment, leave me weary. I can never be interested in a man who is not witty with words, and the idea of spending even an evening at his side, with Mother's and Aunt's conspiratorial glances in our direction . . .

I stand and tell Mr. Clark, "If you will excuse me."

By the look on Mother's face, the way she grips my aunt's wrist . . . you would think France had just attacked England.

With great courage I do not surrender and sit down again. I walk between the rows of chairs and away, receiving fewer and fewer looks from concertgoers, as I move past the circle of my acquaintance.

Once through the crowds that linger at the back, I can breathe free, and do so with great alacrity. I take the direction that leads me into the greenery. Lavender hydrangeas tease me on the right with pink nasturtiums bowing to my left. They welcome me, and I know *their* high colour is cause for pleasure, not alarm or discomfort.

As I walk away from the concert area I find myself pleased at the music, once removed. Perhaps I am the recipient of too much fine noise of late. My obvious enjoyment of its lack is telling. I wonder if we can return home soon. I miss Steventon. I miss Cassandra and Father. I miss the solitude of our own garden.

I am looking down at the path and suddenly see two feet—not mine—and feel two strong arms taking mine, holding me back.

"Oh!" I say at the near collision.

"Pardon me, miss," says the young man. "It appears our

thoughts have taken us places our feet have not."

I laugh. "And where were your thoughts taking you?"

He looks to the air, then laughs again. "I cannot remember. And you?"

I do not know this man. I do not wish to reveal too much. But I do like his spectacles. They make him appear thoughtful, an attribute that currently appeals. "I too am devoid of memory," I say. "But I do know that I wished to capture a breeze."

He looks towards the concert. "And less drum."

"Ah," I say. "We also share the vocation of music critic."

His face reddens, but in a nice way. He bows. "Forgive me. My name is Arthur Gould."

I curtsy. "Jane Austen."

"Shall we walk?"

I nod. He is polite enough to head in my previous direction.

"I should not complain about Bath," he says. "My cousins have been very kind to take me in for a visit these past weeks and shew me the sights during my summer holiday."

"Holiday from what?"

"I attend Oxford. I study history. And naval history interests me very much."

I smile. "I enjoy history also. I have two brothers at sea at present. The younger is a lieutenant on a frigate, and the elder is a commander in the Mediterranean. And one brother, Henry, has just left the militia and is currently seeking opportunities in Dublin."

"Really? What do they think of the problem of the French, the Revolution, and Bonaparte?"

I spot a bench. "Shall we sit?"

And though I do not care much for politics and war, what ensues is a wonderful discussion about my brothers and their views—of them I can talk for hours.

That Mr. Gould does not mind is definitely in his favour.

I am surrounded.

Midmorning, on the day after the gala evening at Sydney Gardens, I am called from my room to the parlour. Aunt Leigh-Perrot has come to visit and sits stiffly in a chair, her hands in her lap. Mother sits nearby as I enter. "Come, Jane. We must speak to you."

My mind skitters across any indiscretions I might have visited since they saw me last, and can think of nothing. Yet it is evident I have done something to offend.

I stand before them, my hands clasped in front. I make no preamble, more than willing to let them speak first.

My aunt does the honours. "I have heard that you went walking alone, with a stranger."

"While you should have been at the concert with us," Mother adds.

"I went walking alone, and met a stranger by happenstance."

"You spoke?"

They make the word sound scandalous. "We did."

"Did you walk with him?"

"As we spoke."

"Did you sit with him?"

"On a public bench, for all to see." My words, said to clarify and amend their concern, sound slightly wrong and nearly confrontational. I rush to remedy anything misconstrued. "We rested a moment. He spoke of his studies at Oxford. He is studying history and has an interest in all things naval. We spoke of Charles and Frank." Surely the presence of my brothers—albeit in subject if not in true presence—would appease them.

My mother and aunt exchange a glance as if conceding this point. And yet they are not through.

"We hear he is not well . . . not well appointed," Mother says.

"He is poor," Aunt says. "He is here strictly on the grace of some odd cousins." She nods her head at this and adds, "Odd in many ways, I have heard."

I realize it is not the best of times to bring up my aunt's opinion of us lesser, odd Austens.

"Are his cousins female?" Aunt asks.

Her question confuses, but I answer. "I do not know."

"Is he the eldest son?"

Again, "I do not know."

She shrugs. "At least in that way he might have the chance of inheriting the uncle's estate. As will your James."

Aunt and Uncle are childless, so my oldest brother, James, is due to inherit, when the time comes, a fact that surely makes his mercenary wife, Mary, quite gleeful.

Mother's eyes perk up. "Is he the eldest male in his generation? Because then . . . my objection might be lessened if he was due to inherit and be able to give you—"

I raise my hands in in protest. "Mother, I am not engaged to this man. I simply spoke with him in friendly conversation for a short time, during which I did not procure either family or financial information."

She looks shocked. "But was he not amiable?"

"He was very amiable, but—"

"I could make inquiries," Aunt says. "Mrs. Fellowes might know, or the Mapletons."

"The latter, I would think," Mother says. "You like the Miss Mapletons, don't you, Jane?"

I spent Friday evening with the Mapleton women and am obliged to submit to being pleased in spite of my inclination. Together we took a very charming walk up Beacon Hill and across some fields to the village of Charlecombe, which is sweetly situated in a little green valley, as a village with such a name ought to be.

My mother awaits my answer.

"I find Marianne sensible and intelligent, and even Jane, considering how fair she is, is not unpleasant. I do not see them very often, but just as often as I like. I have heard that their father, Dr. Mapleton, is quite a success here. No other physician writes so many prescriptions as he does. Whether that be good or bad, I dare not fathom."

My aunt cocks her head. "A rather biting assessment from such an acquaintance as yourself."

I feel myself redden. I realize my comments are too honest and reveal far too much for the ears of my aunt and mother. Such bits of sarcasm are best kept for Cassandra's ears alone.

"I do not mean to offend, Aunt, but merely mean that I do not think you should bother them with questions about—"

Aunt waves away my concern. "'Twill be no bother. Your uncle and I know everyone in Bath, and all are glad to tell me what I need to know."

I do not mention that Aunt did *not* know Mr. Gould. . . .

"How old are you now, Jane?"

"Twenty-three."

Aunt Leigh-Perrot shudders. "Too old, too old. If not Mr. Gould . . . I am disappointed no other young man has caught your fancy during your time here."

"And Edward speaks of leaving soon," Mother adds.

Aunt drops her hands to her lap. "Well, then. I must expedite my inquiries regarding your young man."

"He is not my young man!"

Mother and Aunt are visibly aghast at my declaration. I admit my words were too forceful. I take a breath to calm myself. "Forgive me. It is just that I have no real interest in Mr. Gould, and were we not seen together, I would not have mentioned him—so short and without meaning was our acquaintance."

The brows of both women furrow, making them look their age. "You cannot be so choosy, Niece," Aunt says. "You and Cassandra—older than yourself by two—must make efforts to find a mate, and a proper situation."

Mother leans towards Aunt confidentially. "Since Tom Fowle

died, Cassandra shews no interest in finding another. We all have tried to get her to dance at balls and to make it known that she *is* available, haven't we, Jane?"

She has spoken the truth. "Yes, we have, but . . ." I cannot say more without breaking a confidence. Only I know that my sister has no intention of ever marrying.

"At least she had a fiancé," Aunt says. "But you, Jane . . . you have not done your duty in eliciting male interest."

Her words cut deeply. First, by bringing to mind my sorrow in regard to Tom and a marriage that is not to be, and second, by reminding me that my sorrow has to be borne alone. Aunt speaks from an ignorance that cannot be remedied.

She stands, ready to leave. "In spite of your objections, I will make inquiries. It is my duty."

I cannot argue. My aunt's domination is not something I can battle alone. Mother rises to see her out.

I pity poor Mr. Gould.

❦

"He is gone," Mother tells me.

It takes me a moment to realize the "he" is Mr. Gould.

My face must reveal my true feelings, because Mother asks, "Does that make you happy?"

Relief is a closer feeling, yet I *can* speak a truth. "I am sorry to hear that." In spite of my aunt's and mother's matchmaking schemes, in spite of the fact that Mr. Gould *was* a nice enough fellow, I do not wish to procure a mate through coercion or manipulations. Although I know such means are often used (and often necessary) in the pairings of young people, I still embrace the hope that I can find a husband through my own means, my own charm, and my own destiny.

It is the stuff of novels.

How appropriate.

❦⟶❧

I pack my trunk. It is time to go. Although I have enjoyed our visit to Bath, it is a place for visits, not residence. And six weeks is enough of gaieties, gallivants, and gambits.

Edward is the one who instigates our retreat—for two reasons. He has not been well these last two days; his appetite has failed him, and he has complained of sick and uncomfortable feelings, which, with other symptoms, make us think of the gout. Perhaps another fit of it might cure him (*and* another round of treatments), but I cannot wish it to begin at Bath.

But the most pressing reason for our departure is that rent day at Godmersham approaches. Twice a year—in January and July—the workers on Edward's estate come to the house and dine with him amidst music and merriment. But just the men. The women of the estate are not invited. Actually, I see no great affliction in this segregation, for I can imagine both genders benefit from an occasional evening free of the other. Such a statement is not meant to be disparaging of either side, though I can imagine some might take it as such.

Mother comes in the door, her bonnet in hand. "Are you ready? The carriage awaits."

I close the trunk and latch it. "I am ready to get home," I say.

Mother gives me a quizzical look. "Home? We are not going home. I wish to visit my other Leigh cousins at Adlestrop and Harpsden and Great Bookham."

My breath leaves me in a sigh. Yes, Mother had mentioned such visits, but I had not realized she was set upon them. "But Father and Cassandra . . . they are eager for our return."

"Oh, fiddle-dee. They are fine. I did not travel all this way to slip by my other relations. They are expecting us."

"You contacted them?"

"I certainly do not wish to appear on their doorstep un-announced." She set her bonnet. "So come, Jane. It is time for our next adventure."

My enthusiasm will impress no one, nor fool the same. Apparently there are still more relatives to tax and annoy.

❦

I enjoy family as much as the next person, but cousins, all those cousins at Adlestrop, and then seeing another cousin, Edward Cooper, who lives in my mother's childhood home in Harpsden near Reading . . . Mother thrives in the extra travels, and I . . . survive.

These cousins are affable enough, and their hospitality genuine and appreciated, but as Mother wants to pass by my beloved Hampshire and continue into Surrey, south of London—which is hardly on the way—I feel like asking to be let out. I will make my own way home.

The distance from Steventon was only one reason I do not relish our trip to Great Bookham. Aunt Cooke, yet another of Mother's cousins, has just published a novel of her own: *Battleridge, an Historical Tale Founded on Facts.* I admit that envy is present in my desire *not* to visit her. I should own pride in her accomplishment and have hopes for some interesting discussions regarding the creation of a novel. But from what Mother has said of Aunt Cooke, I regard our visit with trepidation.

Which is fulfilled during our first evening together.

We have barely settled in the parlour when Aunt presents herself before us, holding a book. And I know then, I know. . . .

"Have you seen my book?" she asks, holding its tan leather in front of her chest.

"No," Mother says, reaching for it. "Let us see." She examines the cover with due respect and leafs through the pages.

She hands it to me. "See, Jane? Perhaps someday one of your stories will be published."

Aunt Cooke raises her eyebrows. "You are making attempts to write?"

I glance at Mother, wishing she would be the one to state my progress, but Mother looks back at me, forcing me to list my accomplishments. Or not. "I have written a few stories."

"They are quite good," Mother says.

Her praise surprises me. Not that she hasn't said as much among the family during one of my readings, but she is not one to praise me elsewhere.

Aunt looks a bit distressed and turns towards a cupboard from which she produces two more copies of her book. "I have a copy for each of you. I will be eager to hear what you think." She hands one to Mother and keeps one for herself. I, of course, already have one in my hands.

I am being expected to read it—during our visit. Although I am a lover of novels, my aunt's presumption offends. I vow never to do such a thing to others—*if* I ever get published. If they wish to read my work, I will be pleased, but I will not force it upon anyone. Ever.

"Perhaps you would like me to read aloud to get you started. You may follow along in your own copies."

Joy.

I laugh aloud, then clamp a hand over my mouth, not wanting anyone in the house to awaken.

It is two in the morning. I am reading my aunt's novel in bed, by candlelight. The late hour does not indicate an inability to close its pages, but a fascination with its style, its . . . mediocrity.

I feel the guilt that is appropriate in such a judgment, and yet . . . I have read dozens of novels and, as such, have learned to recognize what is good and what is not, what is new and enlightening, and what is typical and so very *done*.

Every plot twist, every locale, every deep sigh and bated breath in Aunt's novel has been done oft before. A grotto, an imprisoned heroine in a dark tower, a lost document in a false-bottomed chest . . .

Yet even as I roll my eyes, I find satisfaction. For unwittingly Aunt has given me an element to use in my current story, *Susan*. My entire manuscript revolves around a young girl who puts too much stock in such elements, living their fantasy rather than real life. It makes fun of these novel components that my aunt has embraced with such fervor. I wonder . . . if I add a lost document in a false-bottomed chest in *Susan*, *if* my story is ever published, and *if* Aunt Cooke ever deems it worthy of her time, will she recognize that her book was the seed of that improbable (but very convenient) ingredient?

I laugh again at the thought; the idea of a future date when Aunt Cooke sits in her bed, reading *my* book. She will come upon the paragraph about the hiding place, draw in a shocked breath, put a hand to her chest, and exclaim, "But that is my idea!"

Yours and many before you, Auntie.

"I finished your book, Aunt Cooke," I say at breakfast.

The shocked face and hand to the chest I imagined are reenacted over eggs and biscuits. "Oh, my dear. You do me great honour."

Not particularly . . .

Mother butters a biscuit. "You must have been up all hours, Jane. You will be wrecked for the day."

"Perhaps," I say—and I *am* tired. "But it was worth it."

I enjoy my double entendre, as I do the glee it produces in my aunt. "Oh, Jane. I knew you would like it."

Mother looks skeptical but hides the extent of her feelings behind the biscuit.

"The covering is very lovely," I say, for I have vowed to tell the truth—as far as the truth will go without offending.

"I agree," Aunt says. "I was very pleased. It was not the colour I had imagined, for I thought a pale aubergine would have been more appropriate than conservative oatmeal colour, but the gold lettering makes up for any disappointment."

Personally, I think the publisher knew what he was doing. A calm oatmeal was needed to offset my aunt's exuberant and lofty word choice and plot.

"Which part did you like best?" Aunt asks.

The end? Indeed, she puts me on the spot. How can I remain true to my convictions yet not offend—for what good would offense do? I can tell from her actions she does not want real opinion.

I hit upon a solution. "I found the false-bottomed chest interesting."

"I knew you would like that! I read a similar story once myself and thought it so delightful that I decided to incorporate it into my own story. Feel free to use it, Jane, if it suits your needs."

It is difficult to hold in a smile. "Thank you," I tell my aunt. "Perhaps I will."

EIGHT

Father paces. Mother sits by the fire, tugging at her handkerchief. Cassandra's head is down and shakes no-no-no in disbelief. I am too aghast to do much other than watch them.

Aunt Leigh-Perrot arrested for theft?

In between bouts of pacing, Father pauses and reads us more of the letter from Uncle Perrot. "He says the shopkeeper who accuses her is Miss Elizabeth Gregory. She has a millinery shop over on Bath and Stall Street and—"

"We were there!" Mother says, turning to me. "Remember the ivory lace I purchased for my blue hat?"

Before I can respond, Father says, "Lace. That is exactly the item in question. Apparently your aunt ordered and paid for some black lace but, after leaving the shop with your uncle, was accosted by the shopkeeper, who accused her of taking some white lace—without paying."

"That is absurd," Cassandra says.

"Did she have the white lace with her?" I ask.

"Unfortunately, yes," Father says. "And since it was deemed worth more than twelve pence, it is a capital crime."

"Which means?" I ask.

Father looks up from the letter. "Which could elicit her death by hanging, or exile to Botany Bay in Australia for fourteen years."

"For a little bit of lace?"

"'Tis the law," Father says.

"'Tis a ridiculous law," I say.

"The law is not the concern," Cassandra says. "She did not do it. She could not."

"She would not," Mother says. "She and Perrot have plenty of money. She buys what she wishes when she wishes."

"I agree," Father says, perusing the letter again. "Something is not right here."

Mother stands. "What is not right is that my brother's wife is in gaol."

Father clarifies. "She'll be staying in the gaoler's house in Ilchester until the trial."

"When will that be?" I ask.

"Months. They fear months."

Mother looks at Cassandra and me. "You girls. You must go, be with her. Comfort her in this difficult time."

"Perrot has moved in with her," Father states.

"'Tis not enough. She must feel the arms of our family embracing her. Girls! Go ready your trunks at once."

Cassandra and I look at each other, and my sister's unnerved look certainly mirrors my own. Mother wants us to go to gaol with our aunt? We both look to Father, who blessedly takes Mother's arm, stopping her traverse from the parlour up the stairs to make ready for our trip.

"Now, now, dear. We cannot send the girls. Perrot says the conditions are crude, the gaoler's children loud and unruly . . . and perhaps the comfort we imagine from such an arrangement would be more an imposition—"

"Ridiculous," Mother says. "The girls have always been a relief to any in the family who need comfort. Besides, we have both heard stories regarding women of status committing suicide after being accused of shoplifting."

Cassandra draws a breath. "Surely not!"

Mother considers this but a moment. "I would hope not. And I do suppose Aunt's fortitude and courage will prevent her from even thinking of such a thing."

I could add the traits gumption, self-importance, and pride to the list, but remain silent.

She moves towards the stairs. "Cassandra, is your blue dress mended?"

"Not yet, but—"

Father interrupts. "My dear, you must not rush into such a thing. You must give us time to carefully consider and—"

Mother throws up her hands. "Fine. To satisfy you, I will write first and make the offer. Both girls. Or at least one."

She departs the room to do just that, leaving the three of us recovering in her wake.

I am the first to speak. "Father, although I wish to help . . ."

He raises a hand, stopping further explanation. "I will not send you unwisely, daughters. I promise you that."

I am relieved. Father always keeps his promises.

I ask for God's blessings on crude gaolers' houses, and gratitude for the wisdom of Aunt Leigh-Perrot. For in spite of Mother's offer that Cassandra and I join our aunt's misfortune as she resides at the gaoler's house, and possibly attend the very trial in which she is accused, Aunt mercifully declines. "I will not allow these elegant young women to suffer at my side." Our wave of relief is drenching.

And our aunt's defense counsel is traitorously inept. His name is Joseph Jekyll, and he himself spreads gossip that she is guilty of the crime to which she is charged and is, in fact, a kleptomaniac. He also very vocally shares his opinion that Uncle Perrot is far too submissive to his demanding wife.

The latter holds a modicum of truth, but the former is completely false.

Or so I believe.

That I even consider the possibility that Aunt would steal disturbs me. I couch these traitorous thoughts in the possibility that Aunt put the white lace amidst her purchase of black lace without thinking. A mistake by a woman who by these very eyes has been seen to pick up numerous items for her perusal as she shops while keeping up a lively banter with whomever her companion might be, as well as the clerks who flock to her service. If she is guilty, it is surely an inadvertent gaffe.

I keep all these doubts and dealings to myself. I will allow justice to be done—if there is such a thing. The punishment of death or banishment for so small a theft? I know God's commandments. I hold close "Thou shalt not steal," but imposing the same harsh penalty for theft as for murder? This is truly absurd. I pray that someday men in power will remove this offense to common sense. Perhaps as the century turns over . . .

1800. I still find it difficult to write the number, and too many letters suffer a smudge as I err on the date. This change of year from one century to the next is sobering, as if something more is expected from each of us, as if the chasm between December thirty-first and January first is deep and wide, and in order to pass over it one must take stock with self-probing questions:

What have I done with my life?

What shall I do with the rest of it?

Unfortunately, at age four and twenty I find my life distressingly devoid of measurable accomplishment.

I am not married.

I have no home of my own.

I have no children.

I write novel after novel . . .

But to what avail? Beyond family—who patronize me, albeit with love—who cares? Will anyone ever care? Will anyone ever hold a book by Jane Austen in their hands?

Yet during such times of doubt I remember the failings of Aunt Cooke's *Battleridge* and deduce that if that book can be published, then surely . . .

It is an arrogant thought, full of traits I am most apt to shift upon others than accept as my own, traits unconscionable and unflattering as we begin a new century.

And yet I own them, and own the dream that someday my

writing will matter to someone beyond myself. If that reveals a pride unbecoming. . . ?

I accept the fault, even as I dream the dream.

※ ※

For unto whomsoever much is given, of him shall be much required: and to whom men have committed much, of him they will ask the more.

I grew up with that verse ringing in my ears. Father still uses it in many a sermon, and more importantly lives the words, inspiring us to do the same.

As I do today.

I bundle against the cold, grateful it is not snowing. We have done our own suffering in the rectory this winter, with cold drafts and too much snow. And James broke his leg and now cannot get out at all—even though he told Aunt Leigh-Perrot that he and Mary (as the heirs) would attend the trial. That is not to be.

There are so many not-to-be's during a hard winter. Not-to-be's, not-to-do's, and being-too-much—together, that is. It is a strain upon the most loving family to be with one another too much. The knowledge that one cannot escape, cannot venture out for a walk, an errand, a visit, or a dig in the garden accentuates the condition and makes the walls tilt inward, the ceiling loom low. Air! I need air!

That is one reason why I venture out today. E'en though the air be bitter, the sky is blue, and the sun shines (I wish to ask the Almighty about this dichotomy when the chance arises). I carry a basket of bread, some baby clothes Mother has made, and a small blanket I have bound. The items will surely not revoke troubles, but may ease a few.

The poor are dissatisfied with reason. Wheat will not be cheap this year: and every other necessary of life enormously dear. The poor man cannot purchase those comforts he ought to have: beer, bacon, cheese. A lack of firewood has even caused the death of a few elderly. Can one wonder that discontent lurks in their bosoms? I cannot think their wages sufficient, and the pride of anyone is hurt when they are obliged to ask for relief. That they can receive what is offered . . . I am sensible to the task in their acceptance. I wish I could do more.

I know all the families in Steventon—over thirty there are—and am aware of many sufferings. But today I go to the Wilson family, where Agnes Wilson bore her sixth child just three months ago. No mother leaves her house—or even her room—before a month has passed, but with the cold, Agnes's confinement has surely been forced.

The leafless trees that edge the house are mournful, and I hear a baby cry inside. I knock on the door.

Mr. Wilson answers, barely cracking the door against the cold. His face is flushed and it takes him a moment to realize who has come. "Ah. Miss Austen."

I lift my basket for him to see. "I come with a welcoming parcel for the new child—and for its family."

A little girl squeezes in front of her father, eying me, then the basket.

"Come in," Mr. Wilson says.

The front room is dark—which strikes me as odd, considering the sunny day, but then I see that a quilt has been tacked against the window, against the cold.

Four other children rally round the basket, and I realize I could be invisible for all they care. 'Tis the food they want.

'Tis the food they will get—though I set it on the table near their mother, who holds baby number six at her breast. I am ashamed I do not know its name. I remove the basket's outer covering. Upon sight of the bread, the children go, "Ahh!"

I pull out the baby clothes and blanket. "I hope these can be of some use," I say.

Agnes smiles and pulls the baby from her breast, buttoning her dress. "You are so kind. Sit, Miss Austen. Please, sit. Would you like a warm drink?"

I do sit but decline the drink. I do not wish to *take* anything from what must be meager stores. "May I hold the baby?" I ask. It has the look of a boy. "What is his name?"

"John," she says and hands the baby over. Just fed, he fits nicely into the crook of my arm and looks up at me with brown eyes. I run a finger along his cheek, marveling once again at a baby's intrinsic softness.

"Shoo, children," Mr. Wilson says.

"We want bread!" the eldest says.

"Later."

I know I am the cause of the delay, and I vow to leave as quickly as is polite. But then Mr. Wilson sits down too. "Wife here has been longing for news of the town—gossip I calls it but—"

"Jack!"

"Gossip I calls it and gossip it is, but if it will make you happy, I am not too proud to ask Miss Austen for a bit of it. After all, we all know we are surrounded by a neighbourhood of voluntary spies. Might as well get some fun from it."

I try to think of something that will ease Agnes's boredom and curiosity. "My brother Henry was in Ireland for seven months and met Lord Cornwallis and—"

"Ain't he the Governor-General of India?" Mr. Wilson asks.

"He is."

"Then, what's he doing in Ireland?"

I have to think. "Quelling the rebellion, I believe." I realize a political discussion will serve no one well, so I move back to talk of Henry. "My brother arrived back in London this January. Unfortunately, his wife's young son is not doing well."

"I is sorry to hear about the boy," Agnes says. "What's wrong with 'im?"

I regret mentioning Hastings's problems, yet have no recourse but to reply. "He has fits." It is as concise as I can put it.

Agnes nods. "We've known one like that. The fits made the child less than whole." She taps her head. "It often seems like mental and bodily sufferings are closely sewn."

She speaks the truth. I try to think of news less melancholy. "My brothers Frank and Charles are at sea, and Frank is near Egypt and is a commander and—"

"Have you heard about Lord Lymington?" Mr. Wilson asks.

"No, I have not." I have not thought about the Portsmouth family in many years. The eldest boy, Lord Lymington, was a pupil of Father's before my birth. I heard about his stuttering and how he was taken out of school and sent to London to be cured. I knew not the results, but found it telling that only his two younger brothers went to Eton for their education.

Mr. Wilson leans closer. "Apparently the family married him off to a woman aged forty-seven—and him only thirty-two."

"Why would they do that?"

Mr. Wilson and his wife exchange a glance. "Sounds to us like they want to make sure he don't get any children out of the match. Not that Lord Lymington knows the what-all about that." He checks to make sure no children are listening. "It's said he thinks it takes fifteen month to born a baby."

"He's obsessed with funerals too," Agnes whispers. "Likes the servants to make a play of it. And then he beats them." She shudders.

Mr. Wilson continues. "He don't keep track of his own finances neither. Some bigwig does that for 'im." He sits back. "Seems to me the family is fixing things so the second son can inherit."

I have no notion what to say. Such gossip is far from edifying, yet rings true with what I have heard. I manage to say, "I am sorry to hear that."

Mr. Wilson flips a hand. "No sorriness here, not for the likes a 'im. No man like that should inherit Hurstbourne Park."

Blessedly, the baby in my lap cries, allowing me the chance to leave. I stand and offer little John to his mother. "I will be going now. I would like to get home before it snows again." Too late I remember the sunny day.

I am let out with the Wilsons' thanks for the contents of my basket. I notice that while visiting, the sun has disappeared and it *does* look like snow.

By whatever excuse, I am more than ready to return home to the rectory, which has the blessing of owning a place in neither the high nor the low of society.

The middle ground is far good enough for me.

Father bursts in the front door as Cassandra and I set the table.

Mother helps him off with his coat. "Gracious, George, what is wrong? You are flushed."

Coat removed, he faces us. "She is innocent!"

We do not need explanation of who "she" is.

"Aunt's trial is over?" Cassandra asks.

"James and Mary are back from the trial. I passed them coming home from the church."

"Why did they not stop?" Mother asks.

"James is exhausted. For him to travel with a broken leg to support Aunt Leigh-Perrot . . . he said he will come call tomorrow."

Mother pouts. "I would have liked to hear from him directly."

Father cocks his head. "Would you rather wait, then?"

We all exclaim, "No!" Father is appeased and continues. "The jury was only out ten minutes."

Mother leads him to a chair. "Details. We need more details."

We all sit as Father's audience.

"Even though Aunt Leigh-Perrot had counsel—"

"Mr. Jekyll, who speaks against her," I add.

Father sends me a look to be silent. "Mr. Jekyll was not allowed to argue in her defense."

"Then, what role did he—?" Mother asks.

Father raises a hand. "At first. He was not allowed at first. It started with Miss Gregory of the store, who had brought the charges. She gave her account, stating how Aunt stole the lace, how she trembled from fright when she was confronted, how her face turned red."

"I would be frightened too if accosted in such a way," Mother says. "Falsely accused by some crazed woman on the street?"

Father sighs, and it is obvious he desires our silence but has resigned himself to our commentary.

"Then it was brought to the court's attention that the shop's clerk, Charles Filby, had been bankrupted three times, and there is evidence that seven other customers have found extra items in their purchase bundle—luckily all returned before they were stopped and accused. That is when the tide changed." He nods once with satisfaction. "Aunt Leigh-Perrot was allowed to speak in her own defense."

Having witnessed many speeches by my aunt, I guess the implication of this statement. "She was eloquent, no doubt?"

"Indeed she was. According to James, before her discourse was complete, there were many tears in the room—from men as well as women."

Mother puts a hand to her bosom. "Whatever did she say?"

"She spoke of her lifelong reputation and how she would neither risk it nor bring pain to her devoted, loving husband—who apparently sobbed during her monologue. He had to cover his face with a handkerchief so she could continue."

The thought of Uncle Leigh-Perrot with a cloth over his face nearly brought a smile. Nearly.

"Then she brought many witnesses to defend her honour." Father shrugs. "And that was that."

Mother takes a deep breath. "That is quite enough, I would say."

Father stands. "I am sorely hungry."

We get back to our tasks. And as I place the plates, my thoughts apply themselves to the fact that the deplorable situation just visited by my aunt and uncle has done nothing to dispel my opinion regarding the littleness of Bath.

To live here, in sane and reasonable Hampshire, is a blessing beyond measure.

⋘—⋙

Summer goes on, as summers do, and I am happy with visits from family—until Edward takes Cassandra home with him. Elizabeth has born herself a namesake and needs help. To the rescue, Cassandra! But the Elizabeths' gain is my loss, and at the end of October, I pretend to be happy that the weather is fine for my sister's journey, but only for her sake, not mine. The sun may be shining, but my heart is overcast.

I wander the rectory with the need to once again gauge and measure this home, as it holds one fewer Austen. Where the walls should feel expanded with extra room, they lean close. I know it will take days to push them back again, yet I have done it before. It seems Cassandra is perpetually needed somewhere not here; her ability to be calm in the face of chaos, to partake of the what-needs-to-be-done items of any household, makes her presence worth more than gold or fine silver. I, owning no such attributes, am left behind. To fend. To make do. To suffer at her absence.

After my inventory of leaning walls, I find Father in his study, his elbows on his desk, his hands covering his face. Is he also mourning Cassandra's departure?

"Father?"

He removes his hands, pulls in a breath, and sits upright. "Oh. Yes. Jane."

I have pulled him from another place. "Are you unwell?"

I watch his eyes and see he is making a choice of answer.

Although I never rush to bad news, I do not want him to scuttle around the truth.

"Tell me true, Father. What troubles you?"

He lets out the breath he has been saving and sweeps an open hand across the papers on his desk. "'Twas a bad year. Money is tight."

"How tight?"

He puts a hand on a paper and hesitates. I realize I am not a son, but he *can* tell me. I try again. "Father? How tight?"

"Half."

I do not understand. "Half what?"

"Our best year was six hundred pounds, but this year . . . we have only cleared three hundred."

I realized the yield of the crops was less, but not by this amount.

He sighs and adds, "And the war taxes have trebled, and horse taxes too . . . we must sell the carriage."

I move to stand behind him and lean low to wrap my arms about him, my head next to his. "I am so sorry, Father. I—" My eye is caught by the sight outside of Mr. Harker speaking with Mother regarding planting new trees on the right-hand side of the elm walk. Mother has been fretting about whether it would be better to make a little orchard of it by planting apples, pears, and cherries, or whether it should be larch, mountain ash, and acacia. She frets so much and with such alacrity that I have said nothing and am ready to agree with anybody.

But now, seeing them proceed, I question the wisdom. "Should we be going to the expense of planting new trees when—?"

He takes my hand. "A few trees cost little and offer hope for the future."

I shrug, only supposing it is so for his benefit. I am not one to worry much about money. To have enough is enough. But now, the thought that there is not enough is disconcerting.

Father offers a smile. "Do not worry, dear Jane. I have traversed many a trouble in my sixty-nine years, and will no doubt traverse many more."

I kiss his cheek and leave him, closing the door quietly behind me.

My last glimpse shews him staring down at the papers with furrowed brow.

❧ ❦

During a horrendous storm, we lost two great elms in the garden and four trees in the grove. And we were not the only ones who suffered damage. The Lefroys at Ashe lost their dining room chimney, making quite a mess within that room. I give thanks that our storm raged without, not within. The rectory remained safely intact.

Although the storm is all that has been talked about for weeks, we recover and do not dwell on the loss. Father will not allow it. In fact, he has insisted that we go about to neighbourhood gatherings and balls.

I happily comply. Monday last, the three of us and James had a very pleasant day at Ashe. We sat down fourteen to dinner in the study, the dining room with its crumbled chimney being uninhabitable. Mrs. Bramston talked a good deal of nonsense, which Mr. Bramston and Mr. Clerk seemed almost equally to enjoy. There was whist and a casino table, and six outsiders. Rice and Lucy made love with their avid flirtation, Matthew Robinson fell asleep, James and Mrs. Augusta alternately read Dr. Finnis's pamphlet on the cowpox, and I bestowed my company by turns to all.

And tonight there is a ball. Just yesterday it was settled that Mrs. Harwood, Mary, and I should go together, but shortly afterwards a very civil note of invitation for me came from Mrs. Bramston. I might likewise have gone with my dear friend Anne Lefroy. How delightful to be given three methods of going. I will be more *at* the ball than anyone else.

I dine and sleep at James's home in Deane, where I have help with my hair, which I fancy looks very indifferent. I hope nobody abuses it so I can retire delighted with my success. Hair has never been my crowning glory, and I would just as soon cut it off than be consistently mundane. It would surely be a way to put myself into every conversation—something I am *not* wont to do.

We arrive to the ball on time, as James is ever punctual. As I enter I count nearly sixty people. Though some will not dance—by choice or lack of partner—I still imagine a good brace of couples. Fifteen or sixteen perhaps. A jolly lot, to be sure.

I begin to take stock of those present, making mental notes I will share with Cassandra in my letters. I see the Portsmouths, Dorchesters, Boltons, Portals, and Clerks, though there is a scarcity of men in general, and a still greater scarcity of any that are good for much. There are very few beauties, and such as there are, are not very handsome. Miss Iremonger does not look well, and Mrs. Blount appears to be the only one much admired. She has a broad face, diamond bandeau, white shoes, pink husband, and fat neck. The two Miss Coxes are here: I trace in one the remains of the vulgar, broad-featured girl who danced at Enham eight years ago; the other is refined into a nice, composed-looking girl, like Catherine Bigg.

I cross the room and see Sir Thomas Champneys. I spot his daughter and think her a queer animal with a white neck. Mrs. Warren, I am constrained to think, is a very fine young woman, which I much regret. I hear she is with child, but as the music starts, she dances away with great activity, looking by no means very large. Her husband is ugly enough, uglier even than his cousin John; but he does not look so *very* old.

I nod to the Miss Maitlands, who are both prettyish, with brown skin, large dark eyes, and a good deal of nose. The general has got the gout, and Mrs. Maitland the jaundice. Miss Debarie, Susan, and Sally are all in black, but do not carry off such severity well. I am as civil to them as their bad breath allows.

As I get a cup of punch I chastise myself for being so biting in my assessment, but diminish my mental punishment by the fact that I must find something of interest to share with Cassandra. As she consoles and advises me, I amuse and entertain her. 'Tis our lot and obligation to each other.

James Digweed approaches and I apply a smile.

"Miss Jane." He bows.

I curtsy. "Mr. Digweed."

"How nice to see you tonight," he says, his eyes scanning the room. "But where is your lovely sister?"

"In Kent, at my brother's."

His face is genuinely sad—something else I can relate to Cassandra. "I am sorry to hear that. Please send her my best."

"I will."

He puts his hands behind his back, shewing his fine blue waist-coat and brocade vest to full advantage. "I am sorry to hear of your loss of trees. Those two great elms . . ." He shakes his head, then blinks as if the recipient of a fresh thought. "Surely they fell from utter grief at your sister's absence."

He is so serious and gallant that with difficulty I retain my smile. "Surely 'tis true."

At the lack of my sister, he asks me to dance. I comply. It is the least I can do for his sorrow.

By the end of the evening, I have partnered with Stephen Terry, Tom Chute, and James Digweed, as well as Catherine. There were commonly a couple of ladies standing up together, but not often any so amiable as ourselves.

I return to Deane exhausted, yet refreshed. Dancing will do that. As will enjoying good company.

I am well content.

❦ ❧

To add to my state of contentment, I go to Ibthorpe to visit Martha Lloyd. Her mother is not well, and as I have experience in that regard—knowing how it strains the nurse e'en more than the nursed—I come to offer diversion. And help, if asked.

Three of the endless Debaries come to call within hours of my arrival. As they had recently visited us at Steventon, I endure a recount of their great uncle's passing in London (*great* in their assessment of him, not in regard to a familial title). They persist in being afflicted. I find these stories of their love and attention to such uncle, who was unknown thitherto by us, to be directly linked to his death. He was obviously a man who owned enough riches to cause the entire Debarie clan to proclaim sudden interest. I do wish the whole thing settled soon so we can be spared further mention of his laudable traits. And I do hope for the Debaries' sake, generosity was one of them.

Upon leaving, the Debarie sisters urge a visit from Martha and me to their nearby parsonage. We say we will try, and close the door.

I quickly bar it with my body.

"What are you doing, Jane?" Martha asks.

"Barring further entry against all persons in order that I might have you to myself for at least an hour."

She giggles and gives me a curtsy. "But what about our return visit to the Debaries'?"

I shake my head with vigor. "We cannot go."

"Whyever not?"

I approach her confidentially. "Don't you know that it is not an uncommon circumstance in this parish to have the road from Ibthorpe to the parsonage much dirtier and more impracticable for walking than the road from the parsonage to Ibthorpe?"

As my bosom friend she takes no time in agreeing with me. "Yes, yes, I do believe you are right."

"To further our cause, shall we pray for rain?"

"Absolutely," Martha says. She raises praying hands at her chin and bows her head.

I do the same and pronounce, "Amen!"

What Martha does not know is that e'en though my prayer appeared short, it had another purpose unconnected to the Debaries. For its content contained no mention of roads but was filled with gratitude for having such a friend as she.

⁂

I will admit Mrs. Lloyd sincerely ill. I have been so long in the presence of my mother's phantom complaints, and also in Bath (where illness is embraced and thought about at every minute) that I find myself suspect of all *her* symptoms. I silently offer apologies and help Martha's duties of care the best I can. Although I find the best cure is to be busy and ignore all illness, in Mrs. Lloyd's case such action—no matter how determined—is not available.

But that does not mean Martha and I cannot enjoy our visit. I find her so unlike her sister Mary. Although through her marriage to James, Mary is my relation, I find my true sister's heart connected to Martha.

Our best times are had after Mrs. Lloyd is set to sleep for the night. We retire to Martha's cozy room and feel the freedom of a closed door. We speak freely and at great length. That our hours of sleep are adversely affected does not matter. I would not trade such times for all Uncle Debarie's riches.

We dress for bed but wrap ourselves in quilts as we sit in two ratted but comfortable chairs by the fire. I bring my feet up to the chair's cushion and tuck the quilt beneath them. "I finished another story," I proclaim. Martha is the only one outside the family who is privy to my attempts.

Her eyes light up, a true sign of friendship. "Does this book contain a Mr. Darcy in it?"

"Of course not."

"Another *like* Mr. Darcy?"

I shake my head. "Are you smitten?"

"You know I am. 'My good opinion once lost is lost for ever.'"

I laugh. "You know his words better than I!"

"If you would let me read *First Impressions* one more time, *I* will have it published. By memory."

"Is that a threat?"

"A promise," Martha says. Her eyes flash with a combination of firelight and sincerity. "It is a good book, Jane. Very good."

"'Tis not a book yet."

"But it will be. It must be."

Her words are a balm. And yet . . . . "I have no avenue to get it published. Mr. Cadell and Davies sent back a letter regarding—"

"Unopened. I know. They sent back a *letter.*"

"They did not deem the story readable."

"They did not *read* the story. They read a letter about the story. *That* is what they returned."

I offer a shrug, though it is a true point I have oft wanted to embrace.

She reaches across the space that separates our chairs and waits until I let myself loose from the guilt and take it. She squeezes. Hard. "You must try, Jane. You must not let your work remain hidden. Its light must shine for all the world to see."

"It is not worthy of the world's eyes."

She lets my hand go with emphasis. "*That* is a lie." She sits back. "You have spent countless hours creating stories for your own amusement?"

"They do amuse me."

Martha pulls her own blanket close. "If this is true, then you, Jane Austen, are the most selfish of all beings."

I am shocked by her words. And hurt. "I am not selfish. You have read them. My family—"

"Four, five people have been so honoured?" She shook her head. "'Tis deplorable, Jane. Hundreds, yea even thousands, must enjoy your work."

The idea ignites me with excitement. And fear. "But . . . how?"

"You try. If you do not ask the question, the answer is no."

Her words hang in the air between us as if they own substance beyond their sound.

Martha wisely allows a bit of silence. Finally she asks, "You will do this, Jane?"

I find my answer honest. "Yes. I will."

"You offer a promise?"

With a deep breath, I say, "I do."

❦—❧

My joy continues. I have much to be joyful about. My time with Martha has invigorated me, as has the occurrence of my birthday. I am now five and twenty, and though some would suffer fear and frustration at that fact (considering my unmarried state), I refuse to allow myself such an ungrateful opinion. I have prospects—though neither they nor I know it. After all, 'tis I who danced nearly every dance at the balls this season. I am not a wallflower, but a flower yet to fully bloom.

And professionally . . . though 'tis true I have not been published, I have three satisfactory manuscripts complete and in my proud possession. I am poised with promise. I will not falter in my determination to continue my writing *and* pursue publication. I have no thought as to how this latter will come about, but I trust some divine plan will aid its completion—or no.

But that is all the future, a shaded place that offers few glimpses and allows no regret.

The regret will come later.

I do not dwell in that place of maybes or possibilities. I am happy now, and now is what sustains me. After nearly two weeks at Ibthorpe, I have the continuation of pleasure in Martha's company, for she accompanies me the fourteen miles to home, and I find that any distance has little meaning when in good company. We tease that our initial plan was to have a nice black frost for walking to Whitchurch, and there throw ourselves into a post chaise, one upon the other, our heads hanging out at one door, and our feet at the opposite. What a stir we would have made!

As I near home, I make note that my parents have been alone during my absence. Have they missed me as they have missed Cassandra? I cannot imagine what they do alone in only each other's presence. In their thirty-six years of marriage, through eight children and a bevy of Father's pupils in residence, they have not oft suffered a silent house.

Like it or not, they are soon to have that silence quelled. We pull up front.

I see by a carriage that James is here. I mention it to Martha.

Her face lights. "My sister! What a delighted happenstance if Mary is also here."

I hold less delight at the possibility but do not dispute my friend's happiness.

We make our entrance, letting the driver bring in our bags. Martha spies Mary sitting in the parlour and the sisters embrace. I remove my hat and see Mother and Father standing to greet me. They exchange an odd glance, but then Mother comes forward with an embrace.

"How are you feeling, Mother?" I ask. I feel a bit guilty for not wondering more after her health during my visit at Ibthorpe.

She takes a small step back, then says, "Well, girls, it is all settled. We have decided to leave Steventon and go to Bath."

I am in no mood to visit my aunt and uncle. I look forward to some time at home with Martha. "Can we not wait for a visit?" I ask.

Mother looks at Father, who steps forward. "'Tis not a visit we speak of, Jane. We will move to Bath. We will reside there."

One word screams through my mind. *No!*

I remember nothing else.

"She awakens." It is Martha's voice.

I open my eyes and find myself on the settee in the parlour. Martha holds my hand and looks upon me with worried countenance.

So it was not a dream.

"Water," Father says. "Give her some water."

A glass is held to my lips, but I push it away. I sit and gaze upon those gathered.

Mother sits in a chair nearby. "See? She is better. I was not mistaken in telling her."

"You spoke too plain, my dear," Father says. "Too plain too quickly. Jane was barely in the door when you accosted her with the news."

"I thought it best to let her know posthaste. There is much to be done."

My muddled mind attempts to grasp the subject behind their bickering. "I do not understand," I say. "I must have heard you incorrectly. Surely, I heard—"

"You heard correctly," Mother says. "While you girls were gone, your father and I decided we have had enough of Steventon and wish to—"

Father suppresses her words with a hand to her arm. "Not so harsh, my dear. We cannot expect Jane to comprehend our reasoning when we ourselves took many days to meld the factors into a decision."

I set my feet upon the floor, needing its solidity. I rub my hands over my face, accepting the pain as a measure of this moment's reality in time.

"Fine. You have questions?" Mother asks.

I remove my hands and stare at her. A bitter laugh escapes. "We are to move? To Bath?"

"Yes, yes," Mother says. "It will be ever so grand. We have always enjoyed Bath."

They have enjoyed Bath.

Mother continues. "With Uncle and Aunt there and so many acquaintances coming and going at all times of year, why, we shall have a merry parade of friends come to see us."

"We have friends here. A lifetime of friends."

"Well, yes . . . but . . ." Mother has no answer.

Father takes over. He sits beside me on the settee and takes my hand in his. "I am seventy years old, Jane. My health is less than it once was, and I . . . I am weary. The farm did not gross well and . . . I wish to retire."

Silent until now, Mary raises a hand. "James will take over the parish. We will move here and—"

"Yes, yes," Father says. "Let us get Jane acclimated to the idea before we express the details."

But it was too late. By the satisfaction on Mary's face, and with full knowledge of her eternal desire for *more*, I wonder about her influence.

"Four decades," Mother says. "Four decades your father and I have slaved for this parish, giving our all to bring life and light to our neighbours and—"

"Pleasant years that have brought us much joy," Father says.

Mother acquiesces with a shrug. "Of course. But now—"

"Now, your mother and I are entering a new season of our lives."

"It can be a new season for you and Cassandra too," Mother says. "There are many eligible men in Bath and—"

I spring from the settee. "I do not care for eligible men!"

"Enough of that, young lady!" Mother says. "You must care. Your father's provision for us is barely enough to take care of myself, much less *two* unmarried—"

She stops short and reddens. She looks at Father and says, "I am sorry, George. You have been a fine provider. I do not mean to degrade or offend or—"

"I am too old to be offended by facts," he says. "And what your mother says is the truth." The fresh breath he takes is ragged. "I know this is hard, Jane, but think of this: from Bath we can more easily take holiday in Devon and Wales. You would like that, would you not?"

"Of course, but—"

"Never mind that," Mother says. "Once I get settled in Bath I shall be very content to remain forever. I see no need to travel farther."

I wait for Father to contradict her, to hold fast to his travel plans that *would* please me and be of some consolation.

But he offers only a shrug, and with that one act relegates holidays in Devon and Wales to oblivion. Then he reaches once again for my hand. I have no choice but to give it to him. "What we do, we do for all. You do understand that, don't you, Jane?"

I look down at his eyes, pleading with me to ease his guilt.

I will not.

I cannot.

I do not—and go to my room.

I sit at my desk and write a letter to Cassandra. I do not know if my parents have sent word to Godmersham of this crisis, this tragedy, and I am not about to reenter their presence to ask. *I* must tell Cassandra the awful news, whether first-heard, second, or tenth.

Martha has kindly left me alone to do this deed. I do not wish for her to behold the scrape of my angry pen against the paper, nor witness the heat in my cheeks and the stone of my chin. I do not want her to hear the words I press to the page being spoken aloud. I do not usually speak as I write, but find no other venue for the appalling discourse that threads through my being. I believe that the true art of letter writing is to express on paper exactly what one would say to the same person by word of mouth, and I know I will now talk to Cassandra almost as fast as I could if she graced the room before me.

They cannot do this to us! Their selfishness knows no bounds. Do they not think of our friendships here? Steventon is the connective tissue that holds us firmly to this life. It is borne in deep roots that rise through our bones and vessels and burst through the air unto the stars. This tissue cannot be severed lest our very hearts stop beating and we fall to the ground, our lives unused.

I find I am without breath and allow myself a moment to catch some air. I dip my pen and continue my tirade.

How dare they make such a decision without our contribution! Like two naughty children, scheming when left alone, they throw common sense aside and do what they desire, with no thought or inclination to the consequences, nor to the wishes or needs of others. Such actions are unconscionable, despicable, and with no evidence of the love that supposedly is present between parent and child. As the youngest daughter, I realize I am the lowest of the low, but since it is my life that is affected as much as theirs, should I not be consulted? Should my very existence not be recognized as viable and worthy of opinion? Must I be ignored?

Apparently yes.
My hand shakes as I make a closing.

I await your words, which surely will match mine in their intensity and utter despair. In them, I hope to read of a solution to our awful predicament. Save us, dear sister! Find a way to save us.

I sign my name, blot the ink, and fold the letter, sealing it with blue wax. I take it downstairs and only relinquish it long enough to put on my coat.

Mother looks up from her embroidery. "Surely you are not going out, Jane. Not in this cold."

What does she care? "Surely I am."

Martha stands. "Would you like me to go with you?"

"No," I say, though I appreciate the kindness of her offer. "I will return shortly."

I go outside. Although I usually let one of the servants take the outgoing letters, I cannot risk delay in posting this particular brief. Nor can I risk the chance that I will calm myself and have second thoughts.

This letter must reach Cassandra in all its fervid glory. Although she may chuse to consign its burning words to the fire, I will not regret writing them. For I had to write them.

Write them or die.

NINE

I pass by my bedroom and am taken aback, as I find my brother's wife, Mary, inside. She stands before two French agricultural prints above our dresser, perusing them with hand to face, as if they hang at a museum.

I can *see* the possessive look in her eye as she assesses how these will look above her own dresser, in this very room, when she and James move in.

"Mary." I allow my voice to hold a hint of sternness. She has tested me once too often these past months.

She starts like a child stealing a candy. "Jane."

Yes, yes, we know our names. . . .

"May I be of assistance?" I ask.

It is her turn to be taken aback. Her face fumbles for control, but then she waves a hand towards the pictures. "These are lovely."

"Yes," I say. "They are." I wait. I will not make this easy for her *if* she has the gumption to—

"I was wondering if they are staying?"

Her audacity astounds. "They are not. Edward gave them to Cassandra and me. As a gift. They belong to *us*."

She blinks. "There is no need to be peeved, Jane. Your parents have told James and me to peruse the contents of the house for items we may desire."

Desire? Has anyone inquired of my desire? In this? In anything?

I move to the door and point downstairs. "You have already put your mark on other pictures: the battle piece, the Mr. Nibbs and Sir William East, not to mention all the assorted manuscripts and writing instruments dispersed over the house."

"I have not put a mark on anything, Jane. Nor 'tis there much value in the things we *have* chosen."

As expected, Mary's sense of value relates to pence and pounds, and her ability to look to herself first. Does she not realize that these pictures possess great value to me? For in their brushstrokes and shade, outline and perspective, they enfold the lot of my memories as distinctly as the Pembroke table conjures images of Mother locking away her valuables in its drawer, and Father's desk elicits the memory of his smile in the moment he looks up from his work when I enter the room. Does she not realize the intrinsic and sentimental value in familiar things that are as much a part of a life as skin and sinew?

Already Father's churchly flock is deserting him to pay court to his son. E'en the brown mare, which, as well as the black mare, is to devolve on James at our removal, has not had patience to wait for that and has settled herself even now at Deane. I suppose that everything else will be seized by degrees in the same manner.

"I know your parents wish to keep the moving expenses to a minimum, so—"

I will not be distracted. "Your eagerness at the expense of others is not admirable, Mary."

She offers a not-too-convincing rendition of "appalled" before saying, "I am not taking what has not been freely given."

I wish to add that nothing is free, but know I have gone too far already. There will be repercussions for my angry torrent.

I move deeper into the room. "If you will excuse me, I have a letter to write."

She is as eager to be relieved of my company as I am of hers.

I look at my writing desk, where I *will* write a letter. Poor Cassandra. She will soon be privy to yet another outpouring of my ungracious heart.

There are times when one must create a victory—even if it is as unacknowledged as it is unaccommodating and unacceptable. To others.

To me, the victory is embraced as a necessity, a bit of salve to ease my distended nerves.

Our family has been invited to an anniversary fete for Mary and James. Martha, as Mary's sister, is, of course, going. As are Mother and Father.

I, however, have declined. The image of well wishes and hearing the outpouring of "May you have many more happy years" would be vinegar on open sores.

Distressingly, as the rest leave for the celebration, no one asks my reason for staying behind. Do they fear the answer? Or do they truly not care? My utmost hope is that they *know* e'en though they do not acknowledge.

Yet why should they know of *that* distress when they seem oblivious to all other? The tears I cry over our move are worthy of the most tragic actress, in the most tragic and sorrowful scene. That my parents are unmoved, that they have yet to ask my true opinion . . .

I am nothing to them. And in Bath, I will be less than that.

Steventon holds my life. Every moment, every life-breath, every emotion, laudable and not, has a root here. I am who I am because of this place, this house, this garden, this town, these neighbours. . . .

Who will I be in Bath? In that place that prides itself on providing roots to few, that thrives on commotion, noise, and the flighty visits of strangers hoping to take more than they give?

I look out the window as the carriage moves towards the party. Mother waves. I stand erect. And still. Another attempt at rebellion that will be unappeased.

It is all I have.

And *that* frightens me more than anything else.

I pull a volume from the shelves in Father's office. It is a collection of William Cowper's poems. I hold it to my chest. Just two years ago we purchased his complete works.

Martha looks at me from across the room. "Another 'dear friend' you cannot part with?"

I close my eyes and recite from my favourite, *The Task*: "'God made the country, and man made the town. What wonder then that health and virtue, gifts that can alone make sweet the bitter draught that life holds out to all, should most abound and least be threaten'd in the fields and groves?'"

"It will be all right, Jane. There is health and virtue to be found in Bath too."

"Health, perhaps, but virtue?" I harrumph, knowing I am unfair, but not caring. Of late, each task is a step closer to the precipice.

Martha finishes straightening a stack of books on the floor. "This stack to sell is small—compared to the rest." She nods at the commodious shelves that hold over five hundred volumes. "Your father wants to move as few as possible."

In a fit of drama I go to the shelves and spread my arms wide across them, barring them from the possession of all others. "These are as few as possible. Surely these are a part of me that cannot be sold."

"But there are so many, Jane. The expense of moving—"

I whisk myself round to face her. "Father and Mother should have thought of that and included it as key to their decision."

"Jane . . ."

I run a hand along the titles. These are not all great books, but they are my books, and I have read every one. "In part I write because of these."

"What did you say?"

I realize I have whispered the words. "Nothing. Let us continue our inventory. Perhaps James will buy a few so at least they remain on family shelves. Yet I suppose Mary will want them gratis."

"Jane . . ."

I accept her admonition but do not embrace it.

&—&

"Father, no!"

He puts his hands behind his back. "I am sorry, Jane. But we cannot bring the pianoforte to Bath. We cannot bring our new tables either. Only the beds will go, for those are of personal comfort. I do not think it will be worthwhile to remove any of our chests of drawers either. We shall be able to get some of a much more commodious form, made of deal and painted to look very neat. Your mother and I have thought at times of removing the sideboard, or the Pembroke table, or some other piece of furniture, but upon the whole we have ended in thinking that the trouble and frisk of the removal would be more than the advantage of having them at a place where everything may be purchased, so—"

"But my piano?"

He blinks as though his last recitation was for his own benefit, not mine. "It must be sold with the rest."

I resist throwing myself across its keys as I had done last week against the bookshelves. I resist but still am tempted.

I stand tall, knowing Father responds best to strength and logic. "It is *my* piano, Father. I am the only one who uses it."

"Which is a point in favor of selling it."

Oh dear. I had not meant it that way.

I step towards him. "So much of what is mine is being discarded and—"

"Discarded, Jane?"

"Appropriated, then," I say. "Can I not keep something that provides me with so much joy?" I quickly add, "And also provides the family with joy as they listen to my musical attempts?" I dare him to say otherwise.

"Of course, Jane. We always appreciate your music."

"Then, let the music continue in Bath," I say. "There, Aunt and Uncle will be able to appreciate it too."

"Your aunt has her own pianoforte, and I am sure she will allow you to use it whenever you wish."

Now I know what Charles and Frank feel in the final moments of a battle. It is time to take a final stand. "I wish to take the piano, Father. I will pay for its removal, if needed."

"You have no money, Jane."

"I have a bit. Enough." I do not know if this is true.

Father walks towards me, and I know by the sallow look in his eyes that I am defeated. He puts a hand on my shoulder. "I am sorry, Jane. But it cannot be. I must say no."

I manage to look him clear in the eyes. "To me, Father. You must say no to me. Again." I step back, causing his arm to fall. "But fear not, for I am well used to it."

I leave him before I say even more.

A letter has come from Cassandra. I remove myself to my room—our room. Of late it is the sole place where I partake of my sister's correspondence. No more reading the pages in the parlour, where others can intrude. They take everything else away from me; they will not take my sturdy boat on a rough sea. Cassandra is the one person who will *not* tell me how I must do what is asked without complaint, implementing my duty as a good daughter.

She has been three months absent, and my tolerance of others having her in *their* presence is tested to breaking. I can be a very loving relation and a very excellent correspondent, but when pushed I degenerate into negligence and indifference. I have done all but beg *Come home to me, Cassandra. You are my only relief.*

I sit and open the letter. My habit is to peruse it once quickly, then go back and savor every word.

But at the second paragraph my perusal is halted:

> *Perhaps you could consider giving your small cabinet to Anna.*
> *Mary has written me saying she would enjoy it very much. Mother*
> *has also written, saying she approves. Apparently, they want to*
> *move very little.*

The rest of the letter can wait. How can my sister betray me? I know her suggestion is made with good intent—as well as with Mother's and Mary's prodding—but have I not had enough stripped from my possession?

I pull out fresh paper.

> *Dearest Cassandra,*
> *You are very kind in planning presents for me to make, even*
> *though my mother has shewn me exactly the same attention, but as*
> *I do not chuse to have generosity dictated to me, I shall not resolve*
> *on giving my cabinet to Anna till the first thought of it has been my*
> *own.*

I sit back in my chair, my heart pounding. I do not oft speak to my sister in this manner. Yet I do not oft find myself in this deplorable position of losing the foundation of my very life.

I look upon the harsh words. Should I toss the paper to the fire? Or should I allow myself the fire of the words?

I decide on the latter. Cassandra will understand I do not blame her. I will make it known by the tone of the rest of my missive. But she must also be made aware of the injustices being done in her absence. Done to her as well as to me.

I look across the sitting room, where the cabinet in question sits unawares. It has always been mine. As a child I used the bottom drawer as a bed for my doll. My niece will not have it. No one will.

Mother appears at the door. "Jane, I have decided to have two maids in Bath. A steady cook and a housemaid."

"Is not Nanny coming with us?"

"Nanny's husband is decidedly against her quitting service in such times as these, and I believe would be very glad to have her continue with us. But you know, Jane, in some respects she would be a great comfort, and in some we should wish for a different sort of servant. Nothing is settled at present with her, but I should think it would be as well for all parties if she could suit herself somewhere nearer her husband and child than Bath. Mrs. Rice's place would be very likely to do for her. Yet, as she is herself aware, it is not many that she is qualified for."

So we have dispensed of dear Nanny too—though it does appear Mother has at least given more thought to her disposal than that of my cabinet.

"Does Father know of your idea of servants?" I ask.

"Not as yet."

"I assume there will be a manservant also, of middle age," I say. "Someone who can undertake the double office of husband to the former and sweetheart to the latter. No children to be allowed on either side."

Mother rolls her eyes. "This is not one of your novels, Jane."

It could be.

Thankfully—for her sake—Mother is called away before I can mention my cabinet *not* being assigned to Anna.

The battle is not over. But it will be won.

Hopefully, in my favor.

I hug Martha close, her bonnet to my ear. "Do not go."

"I must. Mother is not well."

I know this to be a truth, but it does not lighten my sorrow. "You leave me alone."

She is wise enough not to say, "But your parents are here." As a bosom friend she discerns my meaning.

Martha approaches the carriage. "Cassandra will be home soon."

"Not soon enough. And Mother wants me to travel with *her* to Bath to look at rental properties."

"But surely Cassandra will come too?"

"If I am consulted."

Sadly, we both know the probability of that.

Cassandra is home!

We meet her at the door with strong embrace. "Welcome!" Father says.

"I am ever so glad to be home," she says.

"You leave our grandchildren well at Godmersham?" Mother asks.

I take Cassandra's coat and bonnet. "All six of them."

"And baby Elizabeth?"

"Quite healthy with rosy, fat cheeks, and four brothers and a sister to croon and coo over her."

"I do wish to see her," Mother says. She turns to Father and bats his arm. "We should go to Kent for a visit."

"And when would we have time for that?" he says. "You and Jane are to leave for Bath at the end of the week."

"Cassandra too," I say.

Mother holds the door so Cassandra's luggage can be brought inside. "No, Jane. Cassandra must stay here."

My worst fear is realized. "But why?"

"She has items to sift through for the move. Being at home, you have had the advantage, Jane."

I see no advantage.

Cassandra and I exchange a plaintive look.

There is nothing we can do.

❦—❧

"They do not think straight nor long enough to discern the truth. That they could make such a decision in the few days I was at Martha's speaks strongly of their impulsiveness."

Cassandra leans over the washbasin and rinses her face. When she is finished I hand her a towel. "They *must* have been months contemplating it."

"I do not think so," I say, getting under the covers for a sleep that may not come easily. "There is all indication that a lightning bolt from heaven has been responsible for sending us towards this hell."

Cassandra gets in bed. "I hate how you have suffered. If only I could have been here with you."

"So you could witness how gleefully Mary, and even our James, descended upon our meager riches?"

"Apply a bit of mercy, Jane. They did not instigate this change in our lives—nor in theirs. That they find joy and excitement in the prospect is to be expected."

As always, she is the voice of reason. I sit up in bed, adjusting the pillow behind me. "The very least they can do is not express their glee in my presence."

She offers me the look I deserve. Yet I am unappeased. "Please, Cassandra, do you not find our fate despicable for the fact that we have had no say in it, *and* for its unfortunate fruition? We are held captive from a life of our own."

"Do you have another life to go to, Jane? Do I?"

I dislike the truth. "There is no choice, then. We must marry the first man who asks. Whether Digweed, Blackhorn, Holder, or . . ." Amid my sarcasm, I smile. "Or?"

Cassandra adjusts the covers before answering. "I know you

wish me to mention dancing four dances with Mr. Kemble at the last ball, but I will not."

"Because I teased you about him being so stupid a man? Because I said that I would have rather you danced two of them with some elegant brother-officer who was struck with your appearance as soon as you entered the room?"

She ignores my query. "The men do not swarm about me, Jane, no matter how *you* testify to my merits."

"At least you are dancing, sister. It is the best way to meet and—"

"I have no wish to meet and . . . anything."

She has made this blanket statement before. "But Tom has been gone two years."

"Three."

I trust she knows. "I realize you loved him, but I also believe he would wish you to marry and be happy."

"I am happy," she says, pulling the cover over her shoulder. "Happy enough to have truly loved. Once."

I think of Tom Lefroy and know that I have not truly loved. Not as yet.

Cassandra continues. "As much as we believe we will dislike Bath, Jane, there may be advantage there."

I roll my eyes but am curious. "Oh, do tell me what it is. I am waiting, all pins and needles in expectation."

Cassandra takes a long, hard breath, as if what she is about to tell me is of the utmost difficulty. "'Fire is the test of gold; adversity, of strong men.'"

"So saith Cassandra Austen?"

"So saith Seneca, a Roman philosopher. Father had a book—"

"I have no wish to hear the wisdom of dead Romans."

"Then listen to me."

"I am."

"Are you?"

I hesitate but for a moment. "I will."

"Good, because in many ways, you and I are of one cloth. We are perfectly content to embrace home and garden. Big cities like Bath . . ." She shakes her head. "It is not for us, Jane."

I am surprised by her words. "I agree. I truly dislike—"

She stops what would have been a rant by raising a hand between us. "I know what you dislike because I dislike it too. But because we are being forced into a situation and locale we would never have chosen otherwise, we are forced to adapt. And grow." She touches a finger to her own forehead and points towards mine. "We will learn things we would not have learned if left to our own devices, dear sister. And because of this knowledge, we will be better for it, even if it comes buttoned too tightly, and in rough fabric. Use it, Jane. Use it in your books. Nothing will be a waste if we declare it so."

And right then, as I have many times in the past—and no doubt will feel many times in the future—I know my dear sister is right.

She returns to the origin of our discussion. "Besides, we have no place to go but to live with our parents. So . . . 'Whither thou goest . . .'"

I complete the verse from the book of Ruth. "'I will go; and where thou lodgest, I will lodge: thy people shall be my people, and thy God my God.'"

Cassandra turns her back to me, ready to sleep. "Amen."

DEEPEST
AFFLICTION

TEN

Cassandra arrives home to Steventon.

And I leave.

With Mother.

Alone.

The person in whom I take solace is now taken from me. With whom should I seek solace now?

We leave on the fourth of May. A favourite month forever bound to this horrible occasion. The sun mocks me by shining. How dare it do such a thing!

I walk through the house that has been my home. I have lived here twenty-five years, four months, and nineteen days. There is not another house that has ever been home. Every moment of my life, remembered or not, has been embraced by these walls, this floor, this ceiling. Every emotion I have felt was felt here. All the family I have ever had shared this space, their laughter and tears still present as I walk from room to room. Other than my parents, I have lived here more than any of my siblings. My brothers all gone. And Cassandra often at Edward's for months at a time helping with their never-ending creation of progeny. Yes, I too have traveled and visited elsewhere. But if days were added on to days, I am the one who has spent the most time amid these rooms. This is my house more than any other's. And yet I was not asked to give it up. I was not consulted. The decision was forced upon me. As others move towards the future with anticipation, I do not.

I am not ready, nor do I wish to be.

I hear Mother coming from the back and slip up the stairs, needing more time alone. As I enter that which soon will be my room no more, I hear her stop at the front door and commence talking with Father regarding our carriage.

I close the door on my sitting room and lean against it. Although the ownership of this space is fairly new—having only come into Cassandra's and my possession after the departures of our brothers, it is a place that is fixed in my memories. The joy it has brought has made it a place beyond worth. That we are to leave it behind, that my parents have already done so in mind and emotion if not yet in act, disturbs me nearly beyond bearing.

How can they let it go? Does it not elicit cherished times in their hearts? Are they so cold that our departure means nothing to them?

I hear as well as feel a soft knock on the door against my back. "Jane?"

As it is Cassandra, I let her in. She does not ask what I am doing, standing near the door alone. Instead, she takes me in her arms and offers commiseration.

It is my only solace.

❦

Our journey away from one life and on to another is free from accident or event. I find this disconcerting. Should we not suffer tragedy and turmoil? At least some small drama to mark this journey? If I would write such a scene, I would make it so.

As it is, we change horses at the end of every stage, and pay at every turnpike. We have charming weather, hardly any dust, and are exceedingly agreeable to one another—as we do not speak more than once in the first three miles.

Between Luggershall and Everley we take a grand meal. We cannot with the utmost exertion consume more than a twentieth of the beef. That we neither one have the appetite hints that Mother feels at least a part of the discomfiture of leaving as I. Or maybe the jostling of the carriage is the cause. . . . The main value of the meal is the procurement of a cucumber that will, I believe, be a very acceptable present, as my uncle talks of having inquired as to the price of one lately, when he was told a shilling.

We have a very neat chaise from Devizes; it looks almost as well as a gentleman's, at least a very shabby gentleman's. Unfortunately, when I get into the chaise I discover that Cassandra's drawing ruler is broke in two at the top where the crosspiece is fastened on. I hope she will beg my pardon. Yet it seems appropriate that something go awry on this day.

In spite of the advantage of the chaise, we are three hours coming from thence to the Paragon. The first view of Bath in fine weather does not answer my expectations. I think I see more distinctly through rain. . . . The sun is behind everything, and the appearance of the place from the top of Kingsdown is all vapour, shadow, smoke, and confusion.

It is half after seven before we enter the house. The manservant William, whose black head is in waiting in the hall window, receives us very kindly, and his master and mistress do not shew less cordiality. They both look very well, though my aunt has a violent cough. We drink tea as soon as we arrive, and I give the present of soap, basket, and cucumber. Each is kindly received.

I have not been two minutes in the dining room before Uncle questions me with all his customary eager interest about my brothers Frank and Charles, their views and intentions. I do my best to give information.

As we settle in, I find I have the pleasure of my own room up two pair of stairs, with everything very comfortable about me. Again, I nearly wish it were not so. I should not hold comfort. Not on such a day. Not after such a journey.

I go to bed, assuming I will not sleep.

I should not sleep.

As an act of rebellion.

But alas, I grow tired and soon know that my weak body cannot contend with my rebellious heart.

My heart surrenders.

I sleep.

I have been awake ever since five and sooner. I would like to claim it as a partial victory towards my rebellion but know the truth lies in having too many clothes over me. I thought I should have them by the feel of them before I went to bed, but in the night I had not the courage to alter them. I am warmer here without any fire than I have been lately with an excellent one—a fact I am wary to admit.

In spite of our journey, Mother's health is commendable and I secretly wonder whether her ailments at home were brought about by boredom. With all her sons moved away, and no more pupils . . . she moved from chaos to calm. And where I prefer calm, I do believe she prefers otherwise.

Our purpose here is to find a house so when Father and Cassandra join us (soon, Cassandra, come soon!) we shall have a place for them to stay. I do not use the word *home* because the distinction is too vivid in my heart to offer the word indiscriminately.

Our work began back in Steventon. Before arriving we made inquiries. There are three parts of Bath we think likely to have suitable houses: Westgate Buildings, Charles Street, and some of the short streets leading from Laura Place or Pulteney Street. Westgate Buildings, though quite in the lower part of the town, are not badly situated themselves; the street is broad and has rather a good appearance. However, Charles Street is preferable; the buildings are new, and its nearness to Kingsmead Fields would be a pleasant circumstance, as it leads from the Queen Square Chapel to the two Green Park streets.

The houses in the streets near Laura Place are above our price. Gay Street is too high, except only the lower house on the left-hand side as you ascend. Towards that, Mother has no disinclination. It used to be lower rented than any other house in the row, from some inferiority in the apartments.

But above all others, her wishes are fixed on the corner house in

Chapel Row, which opens into Prince's Street. Her knowledge of it is confined only to the outside, and therefore she is equally uncertain of its being desirable as of its being available. In the meantime she says she will do everything in her power to avoid Trim Street, expecting Cassandra to express a fearful presentiment of it, due to its lowly nature.

Today, when my uncle goes to take his second glass of water from the baths, I walk with him—he limping with his walking stick—and in our morning's circuit we look at two houses in Green Park Buildings, one of which pleases me very well. We walk all over it except into the garret. The dining room is of a comfortable size, the second room about fourteen feet square. The apartment over the drawing room pleases me particularly because it is divided into two, the smaller one a very nice-sized dressing room, which upon occasion might admit a bed. The aspect is southeast. The only doubt is about the dampness of the offices, of which there are symptoms. If I am to live in Bath, I wish to live in an amiable space. And I wish to find it soon. . . . The pace as we peruse the market is unbearably slow.

Soon after, a friend, Mr. Evelyn, speaks to the proprietor of No. 12 Green Park Building and finds that he is very willing to raise the kitchen floor. But all this I fear is fruitless. Tho' the water may be kept out of sight, it cannot be sent away, nor the ill effects of its nearness excluded.

Beyond our search of property, I think of other ways to make our move here more amenable. My hope is that we can tempt Martha's mother to settle in Bath—for her health. I send word that meat is only eight pence per pound, butter twelve, and cheese nine and one half. I carefully conceal, however, the exorbitant price of fish: a salmon has been sold at two shillings, and nine per pound for the whole fish. The Duchess of York's removal is expected to make that article more reasonable, but till it appears so, I say nothing about salmon.

As diversion, I meet with a Mrs. Mussell for a gown. We discuss it at length, and she tells me her intentions. It is to be a round gown, with a jacket and a frock front, open at the side. The jacket is all in one with the body and comes as far as the pocket holes, about half a quarter of a yard deep all the way round, cut off straight at the corners with a broad hem. No fullness appears either in the body or the flap; the back is quite plain in this form, and the sides equally so. The front is sloped round to the bosom and drawn in, and there is to be a frill of the same to put on occasionally when all my handkerchiefs are dirty. She is to put two breadths and a half in the tail, and no gores—gores not being so much worn as they once were. There is nothing new in the sleeves: they are to be plain, with a fullness of the same falling down and gathered up underneath, just like some of Martha's, or perhaps a little longer. Low in the back behind, and a belt of the same.

My mother orders a new bonnet, and so do I—both white stripes, trimmed with white ribbon. I find my straw bonnet looking very much like other people's, and quite as smart. Bonnets of cambric muslin are a good deal worn, and some of them are very pretty, but I shall defer one of that sort till Cassandra's arrival. Black gauze cloaks are worn as much as anything.

All in all, this attention to fashion detail by the seamstress overwhelms me. I have never taken so much interest in costume—until now. Of course, Steventon is not so devoted to fashion as Bath. Whether I learn to appreciate such concentration remains to be determined.

Once home, Aunt beckons me. In spite of her cough and being deafer than ever (and Mother's sudden cold), we are to have a tiny party here tonight. I hate tiny parties, as they force one into constant exertion. Miss Edwards and her father, Mrs. Busby, and her nephew Mr. Maitland, and Mrs. Lillingstone are to be the whole of it. I am prevented from setting my black cap at Mr. Maitland by his having a wife and ten children.

Such is my lot.

After having tea last week with Mrs. Busby, I realize I scandalized her nephew cruelly; he has but three children instead of ten—though one would obviously be too many for my purposes.

Purpose. I find I have little here. Yet in this place I am not afraid of doing too little. It is my inclination, as my vigor is lacking.

To expedite the matter, today I plan a walk with a new acquaintance, Mrs. Chamberlayne. As we are not that well acquainted, I would opt for another day in fuller company, but she presses the duet of just us two.

I am not completely comfortable with those I do not know well. Small talk and chitchat can only take one so far until it becomes tedious. True friendship and confidentiality take time—and true effort. Neither of which has been procured by Mrs. Chamberlayne and myself. Nor—though I risk being unfair—am I entirely sure I wish the opportunity. First impressions are strong and hard to break, and my initial determination of Mrs. Chamberlayne's potentiality as a bosom friend has been, so far, weak.

I pride myself on being a good walker. And Mrs. Chamberlayne . . . well, surely the stance of those we passed must have been agitated by our wake. Cassandra will surely be impressed when I tell her of our progress. We go up by Sion Hill and return across the fields. In climbing a hill Mrs. Chamberlayne is very capital; I could with difficulty keep pace with her, yet would not flinch for the world.

On plain ground I am quite her equal. We post away under a fine hot sun, she without any parasol or any shade to her hat, stopping for nothing, and crossing the churchyard at Weston with as much expedition as if we are afraid of being buried alive.

That she can maintain conversation while traversing with such vigor is a feat to which I give her due credit.

Her choice of conversation is less laudable. . . .

"So. Miss Jane. You are not married. Why?"

I nearly trip. "I have not found the right gentleman."

"Hmm."

She has my interest. "Why do you say it so? 'Hmm.'"

Her pace slows but a little. "You are not so young. So naïve."

"I assure you, I am neither."

"Then pray tell, what constitutes the 'right one'?"

The answer seems obvious, but I offer it anyway. "The right one is the one you love. The one who loves you."

She laughs, puts a hand to her mouth, then quells her amusement. "Surely you jest?"

"I do no such thing. Although I am aware of marriages made for other reasons—"

"Many other reasons."

"I continue to hope for a marriage of love."

"You will continue into spinsterhood."

"So be it." My words are more forceful than truthful.

"I hear your sister is older, and also unmarried."

Before I can answer, she adds, "I remember you in Gloucestershire when you were very charming young women."

The comment appears a compliment yet owns a bite.

I move to answer her original query. She can belittle me but not Cassandra. "My sister loved fully and truly, but her fiancé died helping others while in the West Indies."

She offers a slight bow of her head in acquiescence. "I grieve for her sorrow."

"As do I." I decide to take the offensive. "And you? How is your dear husband?"

We walk three paces in silence. Then she says, "Mr. Chamberlayne seems to think it strange that I should absent myself from him for four and twenty hours when he is home, tho' it appears in the natural order of things that he should quit me for business or pleasure. Such is the difference between husbands and wives. The latter are tame animals whom the men always expect to find at home ready to receive them; the former are lords of the creation, free to go where they please."

I know not what to say. For I have known such women, and e'en placed such a situation in *First Impressions,* when Charlotte marries

Mr. Collins and admits to Lizzy that she much prefers solitude to his company.

"So you see, Miss Jane, I—"

"I am sorry for you." The words are presumptuous, and I wish I could take them back. "Forgive me, I should not have—"

"No, no," Mrs. Chamberlayne says. "Sympathy and compassion soothe the inequity just a little." She stops and takes a new breath. "Well, then. Shall we walk back through this park? It is a shorter way."

We walk in silence, each in our own thoughts and contemplations of the strange society of love and marriage.

After seeing what she is equal to, I cannot help feeling a regard for her.

As to agreeableness? She is much like other people.

And I—be it good or bad—am not.

Mother is in heaven, her boredom summarily dismissed.

Between house hunting, Aunt's entertaining, and going out, Mother lives in a state of anticipation. That it is May and therefore *not* the true season frightens me, for my memories of more-to-do daunt me. Such excitement entices when one is on holiday but overwhelms when such frivolities happen with great occurrence near one's residence. Plenty much is often too much.

This morning I go with Mother to help look at some houses in New King Street, but they are smaller than I expected to find them. One in particular out of the two is quite monstrously little. The best of the sitting rooms not so large as the little parlour at Steventon, and the second room in every floor capacious enough to admit a very small single bed.

Our views on the Green Park Buildings seem at an end as we observe dampness still remaining in a house which has been only vacated a week, with reports of discontented families and putrid fevers being the *coup de grace*. We now have nothing in view. When Cassandra and Father arrive, we will at least have the pleasure of examining some of these putrefying houses again. They are so very desirable in size and situation that there is some satisfaction in spending ten minutes within them.

We correspond with Father, reporting our findings, but Father in particular—who was very well inclined towards the Row before—has now ceased to think of it entirely. At present the environs of Laura Place seem to be his choice. His views on the subject are much advanced; he grows quite ambitious and actually requires now a comfortable and a creditable-looking house.

Then let him come find one.

It is discouraging. In such a large place, one would think acceptable housing could be found. Yet . . . perhaps we will find none and go home to Steventon!

I cannot allow such thoughts. The door is closed. I have no recourse but to walk away. . . .

To add to our distress, news from home does not inspire confidence in our pilgrimage here. Father is not pleased with the money that has been raised through the selling of our possessions. Mr. Bent seems bent upon being very detestable, for he values the books at only seventy pounds. Sixty-one guineas and a half for the three cows gives one some support under the blow of only eleven guineas for the dining tables—which are nearly new. Eight for my pianoforte is, alas, about what I expected to get. But ten shillings for Dodsley's poems pleases me to the quick, and I do not care how often I sell them for as much. When Mrs. Bramston has read them through, I will sell them again! Mary is more minute in her account of their own gains than in ours. I sigh to consider that the whole world is in a conspiracy to enrich one part of our family at the expense of another.

There is no quarrel as to which part is which.

ELEVEN

I walk.

A great deal.

It is my only sanctuary and escape while I wait for Father and Cassandra to join us here. In this place. This awful place.

As I walk the streets I walked previously as a visitor, I am struck by the metamorphosis of my outlook. How could I have viewed this regal place with pleasure on one hand, only to view it with utter disdain on the other?

'Tis not a hard question. As a visitor I'd had Steventon to return to. I'd had a home. Here, I have only Aunt and Uncle's house as an abode, with viewings of all others a poor comparison to the comfort and familial ambiance of Steventon. How can any home replace it?

I fear it cannot.

How can any town replace the village of my youth? The country roads, the gardens, the people I knew—and who knew me. People from poor to wealthy, servant to gentry. I was known by them. I spoke with them. I knew of their lives. Our lives intertwined. The strands were neither perfectly made nor always tightly woven, but the bond was attempted and accepted in its attempt.

There seems to be no attempt to interweave here. I walk among grand new buildings, quickly built to fill the need of incoming residents and visitors. As we have seen in old *and* new, the quality is often poor. Slipshod. Many have a veneer of all things fine. Yet upon closer inspection . . . there are cracks in the veneer. Shaky foundations.

So it is with the people.

There is no Wilson family with six babes I can help with bread and blankets. Actually, this is not true. I know the poor must be here, but they are handily shoved in some dark corner where we do not have to be bothered with them and where they do not disturb the pristine ambiance of our fantasy world.

There is no mingling of classes as in Steventon. There is no glue of daily contact to bind us together as one entity. Yet e'en as the classes go to great lengths to keep separate, I feel a fragility surrounding me, as if the town holds its breath. As if it is built as a house of cards, susceptible to a careless expulsion of one breath.

I pass a baker opening the door of his shop for business. He smiles and we exchange a "Good morning." His amiable greeting reminds me that I am being harsh. There are good people in Bath. Good aspects. And to many—like my aunt and uncle and my parents—appealing aspects. Perhaps it is only I who do not appreciate what is here. Perhaps I am ungrateful. Perhaps I see wrongly. Feel wrongly. Judge wrongly.

I hesitate in my walk and consider returning to the Paragon.

But before my mind can make such a distinction, my feet take up their pace once again and continue away.

I accept their dictate. It is as good as any other.

"You should not go out alone, Jane," Aunt tells me as I untie my bonnet.

"Whyever not?"

She adjusts a footstool for my uncle's aching legs. "Tell her, Perrot."

He gives her a look, as if trying to discern what *she* would like him to say. I hear her whisper, "Big city . . ."

"Ah yes," he says. "This is not Steventon, Jane. This is a big city with people from all over Europe."

"Good people," Aunt adds.

He gives her a quizzical look because I sense he was going to warn me about bad people—which her comment has sorely quashed. "There are certainly good people," he says. "Bath has been quite victorious in quelling the petty crimes for which other cities of thirty-four thousand must endure. But the fact remains it is a cosmopolitan city, Jane. And you, who are used to tiny Steventon . . ."

I am still unsure what they are trying to warn me about: the stray criminal or the cosmopolitan dandy who lies in wait for a wandering Hampshire maiden.

"You should have friends, Jane," Aunt says. "It is odd you go out on your own with such frequency."

Ah. Here is the genuine reason for their disapproval. I am not social enough; I have found neither husband nor bosom friend within the city boundaries.

"Make some inquiries, Jane," Aunt says. "And accept kind invitations."

Is there such a thing as an unkind invitation?

Aunt tucks a blanket around Uncle's legs and stands erect. "If you have trouble in such respects, I can do it for you."

It seems I am doomed to trouble on all accounts.

My morning begins as best it can, for I find a letter from my little brother on the table. I do so love hearing from Charles, as well as Frank—my sailor brothers.

I devour its content. Charles has received thirty pounds for his share of a privateer's spoils and expects ten more. He says he is buying gold chains and topaz crosses for Cassandra and me. But of what avail is it to take prizes if he spends his profit in presents for his sisters? He must be well scolded.

His current ship, the *Endymion*, has received orders to take troops to Egypt—which I should not like at all if I did not have hope of Charles's being removed from her, somehow or other, before she sails. He is uncertain of his own destination but desires me to write directly, as the *Endymion* will probably sail in three or four days. I shall write today to thank him, reproach him, and extend my continued prayers for his safety.

As I take out paper on which to make my reply, the servant Albert brings in a note. "For you, Miss Jane."

It is from Mrs. Chamberlayne. She wishes to walk this afternoon. I do not wish to go, but then I hear Aunt and Uncle in the next room. . . .

"Have Jane take you up to the waters," Aunt says. "She does not mind and she has nothing better to do."

Nothing better to do than sit in a house of my elders.

I call Albert back and write a quick note to be brought to Mrs. Chamberlayne, accepting her offer.

At least I will be *out*.

❦

On our walk, I am prepared to wind myself in order to stay abreast of Mrs. Chamberlayne's hearty pace but find that today her rate is not quite so magnificent. It is nothing more than I can keep up with, without effort, and for many, many yards together on a raised narrow footpath I lead the way.

Our discussion today is less insightful, and of little interest—though plenty agreeable, as every time I say, "Is not that tree beautiful?" or "What a lovely day it is," she agrees. I attempt more enlightening conversation, even offering some gossip about Charles's ship.

"Would you like to hear a bit of royal intrigue?" I ask.

"If it is interesting."

Would I be sharing it if it were not? I continue. "This February, my brother Charles, who is on the frigate *Endymion*, had the King's son, Prince Augustus Frederick, come aboard."

"The Duke of Sussex?"

"The very one." We turn past a row of yellow houses. "The ship was visiting Lisbon as apparently the climate there is a balm to His Majesty's asthma. His presence was special enough, but interest was added in regard to the Prince's companion." I wait for her to ask.

She does not.

I consider halting my discourse but continue on, hoping she will spark to life at some point in its telling. "His companion was his wife, Lady Augusta Murray."

"That is nice."

I shake my head. She does not understand the ramifications. "She is the woman he married without asking the approval of the King or the Privy Council. The marriage was annulled soon after—even though they had a baby son."

"My son is two next week."

My pace slows from the shock of her transition. It is my turn to give the dull answer. "That is nice."

We walk on in silence. Apparently she has no interest in the true love shewn by the Prince in living on with his "amiable Goosey" in spite of government decree. I find such dedication romantic.

"We are leaving Bath in two days."

I say what I am expected to say. "I am sorry to hear that." Yet, in truth, I am content to end our friendship, which ends as most friendships in Bath must end—with a departure. As such, these friendships, and all others I attempt here in Bath, pale with my true friendships with Martha, or Anne Lefroy, or Catherine Bigg.

It is not that I expect a discussion of world events or life-and-death matters, but there must be a connection that delves into the open—open not closed—recesses of one's thoughts and heart. I have seen my dearest friends at their best—and worst, and they have seen me, and love me still.

And yet, I do not fault Mrs. Chamberlayne for our lack of connection merely because of a dearth of meaningful conversation. Martha and I also banter about nothing quite successfully. The difference lies in our ability, and yea, even our shared anticipation of deeper dialogue. To have no chance of such give and take is as of little worth as a drop of rain fallen on the sea.

Our walk nears its end, and as we part and say our adieus, there is no regret or desire for another meeting.

There is no feeling at all.

❦

I am in a mood. A mood that the arrival of my sister will correct. *Soon, Cass. Come soon and keep me from my wickedness.*

I find it harder and harder to play nice with visitors, or to even wish for their presence. I am content to escape to my high room and bar the door from all who would call and interrupt my . . .

What do I do up here?

Pout.

I pout.

And conspire regarding how to bring justice to my plight. Perhaps if I run away, back to Steventon, and put a herb in the tea of the new tenant to the farm, Mr. Holder . . . with Martha's knowledge of medicinal preparations, she could offer advice for something that would make him ill. Not deathly, just ill enough to find that taking on the trials and tribulations of a new farm is beyond his bearing.

To relieve him of his plight, he would beg my father to return.

Oh, the satisfaction I will have moving Mary's possessions from the rectory and onto the road. Once they are cleared, I will march inside, give her the smallest curtsy as my farewell, and shut the door.

Actually, Father and Mother do not need to come back with me. I will live there alone. Or with Cassandra. The two of us could make do. Somehow.

I know it is folly, and doubly, a waste of time and energy. I should be writing.

I peer at my trunk of manuscripts but cannot bring myself to open its lid and take them out. I am not sure why I am so restrained. Is it because my thoughts are disjointed, flitting from this to that without lighting for more than a moment? Is it because my emotions are raw and as variable as my mother's taste in real estate? Is it because I feel inept at creating a satisfactory story for my characters when I cannot even create a satisfactory story for myself? Is it because I have no confidence in my own desires? After all, my desire to stay at Steventon meant nothing to the world. Why should I believe my desire to be published carries any more weight or is any more valid?

I know the answer lies in all those reasons, and their overhanging presence is a cloud that threatens to push me lower and lower into a place . . .

From which I dearly hope I can recover.

❦ ❧

I am bad. Very bad.

Mother has just told me the news that Marianne Mapleton has died. When we last visited Bath, I privately disparaged the girl, saying she was not one I wished to nourish as a dear friend.

And now she is gone.

"How?" I ask.

"She had a bilious fever. She was believed out of danger on Sunday, but a sudden relapse carried her off the next day." Mother shakes her head. "Such a kind girl. The most beautiful. Intelligent. And charitable too, I hear."

"It seems you have all manner of attribute covered."

"You wish to dispute me?"

"No, no, Mother. It is just that . . . I find it interesting that on early death, many a girl has been praised into an angel. Many on slighter pretensions to beauty, sense, and merit than Marianne."

At first, she does not respond. Then she says, "Bitterness does not suit you, Jane."

I pull within an extended breath, knowing she is right, and wondering why this new, bitter Jane has emerged.

But I know the answer to that.

❦ ❦

They have arrived! My loneliness is over!

I hug Father and smell the musk of his travel that is accentuated by the warm days of June. But it is Cassandra I *need* to embrace, and I go to her and cling to her as a drowning woman clings to a buoy in the water.

"I am so glad you are here," I whisper in her ear.

"As am I," she whispers back.

Mother waves a handkerchief at the door. "Yes, yes, my turn now."

She embraces the travelers and leads them inside her brother's home—which will certainly be filled to capacity with the number of guests suddenly doubled. Secretly I hope Mother *and* Aunt feel the tightness of the air. Perhaps it will be instrumental in nudging our removal from this place to a place of our own. I do so desperately wish for such a place in hopes that somehow, once settled, I will regain a notion of my former contentment.

I fear I will not.

But hope I will.

❦ ❦

We have found lodging!

It is more expensive than what Father originally wanted to spend, but at least it is not too cramped. Nor too damp. But I worry.

He embraces optimism again, yet our finances seem to state he should be holding on to what he can, buttoned tight within an inside pocket.

No. 4 Sydney Place is only nine years old and faces Sydney Gardens. Our rental stands in a row of terraced houses that are four stories tall. The city, with its Pump Room and commerce, stands close across Mr. Pulteney's bridge along the wide Great Pulteney Street.

Out the back is land that is (so far) undeveloped, offering us at least a glimpse of green country vistas. Like those we left behind in Steventon? Far from it. Perhaps if I squint my eyes when taking perusal of the green, I can imagine and remember. . . .

"There!" Father signs the papers in Uncle's study with the solicitor. "Three years accounted for."

"Accounted for?" I ask as he comes into the hallway.

"Leased. We are leased for three years."

My legs are weak. I lean against the wall, making a painting of St. Paul's Cathedral go askew.

"Jane? Are you unwell?"

Completely. Absolutely.

Cassandra takes my arm. "Come. Let us get some air."

She leads me outside, and after a few breaths I do feel better. Physically.

But emotionally?

"Are you all right now?" asks Cassandra.

I ignore her question for one of my own. "Three years? We are to be in this detestable place three years?"

Her look is quizzical. "Father is retiring here. You knew that, Jane. The lease should not be unexpected."

And it isn't. If only I will admit as much.

I take her arm and walk. "I, more than anyone, know of their commitment here. But hearing the words: three years . . . I am but stifled already."

"You feel stifled from being cooped up in Uncle's house."

"With old people."

She nods once. "I am here now. And we are to have our own home. We will manage, Jane."

We have no choice.

Which, in itself, is the real problem.

❦—❦

We are moved. As I meander between sitting room and bedroom, up stairs that creak (from some hidden damp, no doubt), I admit that our new residence on Sydney Place is elegant. And very fashionable.

The details of cleaning and unpacking distract me.

Momentarily.

❦—❦

As we are now settled, I have no excuse.

I open my trunk of stories and take out *Susan*. Since the story is set in Bath and I am *in* Bath . . .

I untie the bundle and look down at the thousands of words lying in wait in my lap.

In wait for what?

For me to diddle and piddle with them?

Towards what end?

Although I was isolated from any sort of publishing in Steventon, it seems a place closer to my aspirations than here, where real contacts might be made.

Odd.

I am diverted by a noise outside and look out the window as a young child screams. Yet I am relieved to see he is not hurt, just willful. He wants a candy, and his mother has said no.

A cart goes by, loaded with wooden boxes. As the little boy bolts from his mother in front of the horse, it blessedly halts its forward movement but rises up with a fierce neighing, causing the cart to roll backwards and two boxes to fall from its back.

Beautifully suited gentry give the accident a passing glance and do not offer the poor driver help. He jumps from the cart and tries to calm the horse. His eyes are on the fallen boxes. Does he fear some hooligan will snatch one?

Such commotion. Did those boxes contain something of value?

He manages to move the horse and cart to a post, where it is tied. With great effort he gets the boxes back on board. He is on his way. The crisis is over.

Like the driver returned to his mission, I return my attention to the pages before me. I pick up the first page and begin to read. Yet after but a few lines, I realize I have not retained a single word. My eyes skim across the alphabet but do not allow the scribbling to be formed into cognizant thought.

Cassandra comes into the room, and upon seeing the trunk open, and seeing the pages in my lap, says, "I am sorry to disturb you. Carry on."

She begins to leave but I call her back. "There is no need to go," I say. I retrieve the string and retie it around the stack of pages.

"What are you doing?"

"Putting it away."

"But why? I think it is a fine idea that you begin your work again."

"A fine idea, to be sure, but a useless one."

"Why do you say that?"

I gaze out the window at the people strolling by. They should be an inspiration to me. I should take the accident I have just witnessed and place it among the folds of my story. I *could* do that. I *have* done such a thing.

But I do not want to.

"Jane? Tell me what you mean."

It is frightening to put the truth into words, but I will do it. For my sister's sake.

"They do not speak to me, Cass."

She intuits who "they" are. "Not at all?" she asks.

I shake my head. "As my will has been silenced, so have theirs. They do not wish to speak."

"But can you not wake them? For surely they will give you comfort and companionship. They are family to you."

At this moment, I am not too keen on family.

"Perhaps one day, when it is an extremely good day, when I feel energy instead of this dreadful lethargy . . ."

"You must awaken them, Jane. You must."

I am not so sure.

TWELVE

We suffer the commotion of leaving Steventon and moving to Bath, yet near as soon as Father and Cassandra arrive, he wishes to be off again. "To the sea!" he proclaims as often as we let him.

I do not argue with him. I love the seaside towns of Devon and Dorset. I love taking long walks, smelling the salt air, and watching the sea gulls dive and dip. And the ships . . . If a man, I would have been a sailor like my brothers. I know it.

Mother *does* argue. "But we cannot leave Bath! We have only just arrived!"

She is right, of course, and I see her view with more logic than Father's, but I do not wish to stay *here*, and so I urge Father on, using my enthusiasm to aid him in achieving his way.

Which he does. Repeatedly, and as often as he can.

In these towns, many that we visited on holiday when we lived in Steventon, I can momentarily lift reality aside and pretend that the home we will return to is the rectory. It is a silly game I play with myself, but if it aids me getting from one day to the next . . . I see no harm in it.

Today, as we do during as many days as possible, Cassandra and I go sea bathing. We stand on the edge of the ocean, the breeze making the curls around our caps dance.

A man signals us forward. "Come now, ladies. It is your turn."

Cassandra and I ascend the steps into the wood box of the bathing machine, our swimming clothes in hand. Two other women follow. The doors close and we begin to undress. It is awkward to keep our balance, especially when the horse draws us into the sea until the surface of the water is on a level with the floor of the dressing room.

I feel the movement of the water against the cart and hear the attendant unhitching the horse and moving him to the other end to be ready when it is time to be pulled to land again.

"I cannot see!" says one of the other women. "Why don't they put a window in these things?"

"For privacy, silly," says her companion.

Although the lack of a window makes perfect sense, I cannot help thinking a window in the top of the bathing box would be a logical solution. Until men can fly, there would be no threat of a voyeur.

But no one has inquired as to my opinion on the matter.

"There is no air! It is unbearably hot," complains the first woman again.

"Then hurry your change so we can go out!" says the second.

I agree. This transitional phase from street to sea is never pleasant. It is no time to dally. Or complain, as there is no remedy but speed.

I feel a hand on my arm and assume it is Cassandra. "Give me your dress. I will put it on the high shelf with mine."

I do as I am told and quickly put the bathing dress over my head. It is made of linen. Other years we rented one, but since Father has informed us that he plans on much travel to coastal places, we have been allowed to purchase our own, ready-made. I much prefer this, as wearing what someone else has worn is in many ways disagreeable. The least of reasons being the deplorable fit. One size for everyone is not fashionable. Although, fashion has not a thing to do with sea bathing. After all, look at the great pains made to keep us from ever seeing anyone else but those in our cart. Vanity, thou art frivolous.

"Ouch!" says the first voice. "You stepped on my toes."

"If you will only be ready we can open the door."

"I am, I am. You other two?" she says, implying us. "Are you ready?"

"We are," I say.

The door is opened and I squint at the sudden sunlight. The

other two women perch at the end of the box as if having second thoughts. Their discussion proves my impression.

"It will be cold. I know it will."

"Of course it will. But it will be good for us. Three dips is the normal prescription."

A robust woman comes into view, standing in the water by the back steps. She is the Dipper. I have seen her before. She is very strong.

She holds out her hand to the woman. "Come on now, dearie. Don' hold up the lot by being timid."

The swimmer-to-be shivers, yet the air is warm. "But I cannot swim," says the woman.

"No need," says the Dipper. "I'll 'ave 'old a ya. One, two, three dunks, an' you're done."

"I will go," says the other woman.

"Thata girl."

She descends the step with her companion watching after her, hand to mouth. Her fear is ridiculous. We are in but three feet of water, and though the waves come at a steady but unpredictable pace, they are not such to elicit fear. Neither Cassandra nor I know how to swim, but that does not stop us from traversing each afternoon to the shore, where we put our names on the list, hoping to get our turn. We do not do so for medicinal reasons. We go for the sheer joy of it. There is something freeing in feeling the power of the waves crashing around my legs, and the tide pushing, swirling, pulling. It is a battle of sorts. I come so often because I am not allowed to stay long enough on any one dipping to truly satisfy. And perhaps, just perhaps, it is the fact that my two brothers have taken the sea as their lives that I enjoy it so. Somehow, so far away, we can share this common element.

After much dialogue, the companion is shamed into going and makes quite a squealing spectacle as she is dipped—only twice, because she begs for it to stop.

Finally, it is our turn. I let Cassandra go first. She goes without a single squeal and with a dignified composure I cannot hope to match. For I find it difficult to come up from the dip and not sputter and rub my eyes. Although seawater may be medicinal, neither my sight nor my taste appreciate its saltiness.

Her dunking complete, Cassandra sits in the water as I take my turn.

"Take a deep 'un, dearie. Here we go."

The Dipper does her thricely duty amid the waves. I am released. I do not know where the prescribed three dips originates, but cannot help but find a parallel between its restorative power and the early Christian baptisms where people were immersed in water and dipped under, thrice. Restored in body. Restored in soul. Restored in mind? Father, Son, and Holy Ghost?

As I come up I hear the second woman call to the first, "See, Abigail? I am swimming."

The swimming woman stands with one foot on the ground and does the arm stroke, getting quite a respectable distance by a series of little hops, yet deceiving no one.

"You pretend," Abigail says.

The swimmer drops her arm, stands still, and says, "I challenge you to do better."

The Dipper chimes in, "You'll do no such thing. Come o'er 'ere where I can see ya. I don' need no drownings today."

I agree completely.

"Hello."

Cassandra and I, rejuvenated from our sea bathing and back in our street clothes, turn towards the masculine voice. A handsome face greets us. And a lovely smile.

He tips his hat. "I saw that you walked in from the seaside?"

I put a hand to the curls that peek out from my bonnet. The

damp curls. "We have returned from sea bathing."

He looks in that direction. "I have never indulged."

"You should," I say. "It is very invigorating."

"Does it heal one's constitution, as they say?"

Cassandra answers. "I would think the results are variable. According to the degree of one's illness—"

"And expectations," I say, then risk adding one more word. "And gullibility."

He laughs. "And how high are your levels of those . . . attributes?"

I feign a frown and shake my head. "Oh, low, very, very low."

"So you are neither expectant nor gullible?"

"Nor ill," Cassandra adds.

"Although we are quite healthy," I say. "I will admit that we desire to *be* expectant, and conspire to hold gullibility at bay."

"A good plan to aspire to."

"If we do not *ex*pire first."

We all laugh. How rare to find a gentleman who knows how to parlay language in such a witty fashion. How delightful.

He removes his hat and offers a bow. "William Jones, at your service, ladies."

We curtsy, and Cassandra, being the eldest, offers introductions. "We are the Austen sisters: I am Cassandra, and this is Jane."

"A pleasure." He turns to his right. "Shall we walk?"

I could think of nothing better.

❦

The appeal of Sidmouth increases a hundredfold after meeting Mr. Jones. He is a clergyman, in town to visit his brother, who is a doctor here. We have met twice since that first happy happenstance—with Cassandra as our chaperone, of course. I am glad to have her along, not because being in a gentleman's presence makes me nervous, but because by her very presence I am relieved of having to remember what I said, what he said, and what I said again. This allows for our sisterly time alone to be utilized for discussions of his intentions, and what he *really* might have meant by what he said after hearing what I said.

The whole affair makes me giggle. Cassandra too—which makes me very pleased. For I do not wish to have feelings for anyone whom Cassandra dislikes.

She assures me William Jones is very amiable.

I stand before the mirror and attempt to tame my curls, for he is to call today. Call here, at our residence in Sidmouth.

"You look lovely," Cassandra says, watching my flutterings.

"I can never claim that trait, but I am grateful for your encouragement."

"*He* needs no encouragement, you know."

I turn away from the mirror to see her face. "Do you think . . . ?"

"I believe he is quite in love with you."

"Has he said something?"

She points to her eyes. "With these. I can see by the way he looks at you."

"Perhaps he partook of bad oysters."

She puts her hands on her hips. "Perhaps he feels the pangs of love."

I put a hand to my midsection. "Is this what it feels like?"

"Only you can say."

"But how do I know?"

Cassandra shrugs, which is not an answer I can fathom. "I have only loved one man and the love grew so gradually, from childhood to grown, that I am not sure I can speak of love's measure, or absolute knowledge." She twists a curl by my forehead, then steps back, obviously pleased. "Is this feeling the same as that which you had towards Tom Lefroy?"

I am torn by her question. "I do not know. That seems a lifetime ago. I was not the same Jane then as I am now. Should I feel the same?"

"You were very young then."

"I was very ignorant of . . . life."

Cassandra nods. She understands. For in the three years since Tom, I have felt a myriad of emotions hitherto unknown to me. I had been a happy young woman, nearly a child, who flirted and laughed at balls, and whose largest dilemma was whom to dance with first. Now I am older and have been introduced to disappointment, frustration, sorrow, anger. . . .

"Does a person love the same way twice?" I ask.

"I would not know." She takes my hand and draws me to standing. "It is time. He will be here soon."

"So . . . what do I do?"

"You follow your heart."

I remember a quote from Blaise Pascal that Father taught me: *The heart has its reasons which reason knows nothing of.*

I hope to prove the quotation wrong.

Father and Mr. Jones engage in a rousing discussion regarding the simple fact that though men *appear* to be good, it does not mean they truly follow God's decrees. William points out that we often judge people by their manners, when such manners can cover a multitude of flaws of what should be true, godly character. Father heartily agrees.

I am content to observe—and delight in their connection. Although I have little history of bringing suitors to meet my parents, what plays out between them fulfills my imagination.

Their discussion complete, William looks in my direction and smiles. Father smiles. Mother smiles. Cassandra smiles.

The world is good and right.

"I was wondering, Mr. Austen," William says, "if I might be allowed to meet up with you again in the near future. Jane says you are traveling on to another coastal town?"

"We are," Father says.

"Are *you* leaving Sidmouth soon, Mr. Jones?" I ask—with far too much panic in my voice.

"I must." He looks at Father. "But with your permission, once my business is complete, I would like to come visit with you again. You name the city, and I will be there."

Oh my.

My panic subsides and my heart follows Pascal's quotation. I am a stranger to reason.

"I think that would be delightful," Father says, shaking William's hand. "Come, let me shew you our itinerary."

The men leave the room and Mother is immediately at my side, taking my hands in hers. "Oh, Jane, he is all I hoped for you! I am so pleased."

She hugs me tightly, more tightly than she has ever embraced me.

I am glad to have finally pleased her.

I have pleasure on so many accounts.

God is good.

"You daydream again," Cassandra says as the carriage jostles us towards our next coastal destination.

"Mmm."

"He will be there," she whispers.

As soon as we arrive at the inn, even before I remove my bonnet, I check with the owner. I have sent word through William's brother as to our final schedule. He, in turn, is to leave word at the inn as to where he is staying. To see him! Soon, I will see him!

I must admit my affection has grown in his absence. I am not naïve enough to call it true love. But with my imagination added to my memories, I have all hopes that love will evolve. And is that not the best kind of love? One that once born grows larger?

"Excuse me, sir?" I ask the owner. "Is there a message left for Miss Jane Austen?"

He nods and pulls a letter from a box. "Came two days ago."

He has been here two days? My heart races. I must not keep William waiting a moment longer!

I rush to my room, where Cassandra unpacks. Immediately she sees it in my hand. "What does he say?"

"I have not opened it yet." I toss off my bonnet and sit by the window to read. I break the seal and gaze for the first time upon William's writing. He owns a lovely cursive. Very readable and neat.

Dear Miss Austen . . .

I had hoped for *Dear Jane.*

But as I read the words, the importance of the salutation evaporates.

I regret to inform you that William has had an accident and has been killed. Please know that his thoughts were upon you. He was so excited about seeing you again. . . .

"Jane?"

My head shakes back and forth of its own volition. The letter falls from my hand, its words too heavy to hold.

Cassandra picks it up and reads. Her shaking head joins rhythm with mine. "No! No! It cannot be!"

I press my hands against my face, covering my eyes. Surely they did not just see the words, read the words, accept the words.

Surely, they did.

I feel Cassandra slip into my bed, beside me. My back is to her, and we do not speak, but I move over as best I can. She puts a hand on my shoulder. "I am so sorry, Jane. I know what you suffer."

And for the first time since hearing of William's death, I realize she does. I turn towards her and adjust our two frames in the space meant for one. Even in the moonlight I can see her face. "You *know*."

She nods.

"What am I to do?"

"You hurt."

I begin to cry and she touches her forehead to mine. There is comfort there, but I move on to another emotion and pull back. "But why, Cass? Why would God take him? We had just found each other. Why, when I finally found a man I might truly love?"

"Why did God take my Tom?"

"It is like we are doomed to be two old spinster women."

"I am accepting of that," she says.

I sit up, throwing the cover against her. "But I am not! I know you want no one but Tom, but I have not made such a choice. I am willing—if I find the right one. I am open to the idea of love and marriage and family and—"

"Then it will happen."

"When?"

"I do not know."

"But why would God bring this man into my life, tease me with his charm and amiability, please Father and Mother with hopes of our future, and then take him from me?"

"I do not know."

I dislike her answers. "Who *does* know?"

She opens her mouth to speak, and I know the same three words perch on its edge. She wisely does not let them loose.

I lean against the wall at the side of the bed and draw my knees to my chest, pulling my gown around them. "Do you ever wonder if we are a disappointment to our parents?"

"Because we are not married?"

I shrug, for that is a part of it. But there is more. "All their sons have done well and prospered. But we . . . we . . ."

"What would you have us do? The avenues of accomplishment open to women are narrow."

"We *could* marry. Have children. Stop being a burden. Give them some true time alone."

"They know my view of it."

"But Mother made it clear that moving to Bath would open marital possibilities."

"For you, Jane. Not for me. There will be none but Tom for me."

She frustrates me, for of the two of us it is Cassandra who has more to offer a man than I. She is adept at all things domestic, she is intelligent, calm in the face of calamity, constant, versed in child rearing, and loves far beyond herself. I am a gray, dusty moth to her lovely butterfly.

We allow silence to fill the space between us. It is not awkward, as it might be in the presence of others. We accept each other's silence as a part of our dialogue. Words are not the only thing that speak.

"If I do ever marry, you will live with me," I say. I did not plan to say it, but the words move unbidden from thought to fruition.

"Your husband may not approve."

"Then he will not be my husband." I hold out my hand. "Shake on it, Cass. Make a pact of it."

She hesitates, but only for a moment. We shake hands.

Though others may come and go, live and die, satisfy and disappoint, the two Austen sisters will remain united.

Forever.

THIRTEEN

We have returned to Bath. I am as pleased as I would expect.

And yet . . . I *have* decided there are little rubs and disappointments everywhere. We are all apt to expect too much. If one scheme of happiness fails, human nature turns to another; if the first calculation is wrong, we make a second better. We find comfort somewhere.

We must. It is our never-ending quest.

I try to hold on to, but not dwell on, the lovely months in the west country at the shore, nor dwell on what could have been with my William. (Was he ever *my* William? I ponder this.) Yet I know what good such dwelling achieves.

Our lives attempt to find a rhythm here, but I find the rhythm of my left hand does not match that of my right. I work against myself, yet cannot seem to come to a complete stop so that I may get a better start at things, in good time, in even time.

I have many excuses, some worn by overuse. But just to keep things interesting I add new complaints to my list: the house at Sydney Place has an odd smell that one gets used to once inside but that assails the senses anew each time one returns. And the new furniture we have procured here is right enough but will always be wrong because it is not our old furniture. Plus, I grieve over the lack of a piano. Yes, I can visit Aunt Leigh-Perrot and play hers, but that is not the same as spending time each day in a private communion with music before others are about. There is a place I visit while playing—a place that I miss.

Privacy is an issue here, as Mother and Father, with no cares or responsibilities, have taken it upon themselves to be social flutterbees, going out, coming in, having others in, going out—none soon enough. That they insist Cassandra and I meet and greet annoys me. We are not wallflowers, nor hermits, but the obvious intent behind the meetings embarrasses. "We are like flowers in a stall, ready for picking," I tell Cassandra. She responds with, "They fear we will wilt."

Their fear is unfounded. On my part, I have no plans to wilt. But to be presented with such desperation, as though we are a bargain because of some flaw . . . *Come see, come buy. They are not so terribly out of season!*

Not yet.

Age is our flaw. Time, that endless taskmaster, ever moving, unrelenting . . .

Were it not for the marriage issue, I would find my age quite pleasant. At twenty-six I am old enough to know something of the world and young enough to hope for something better. Wise, yet naïve? If there can be such a state, it is mine.

I sit near the window and work on my needlework. I do more of it now, as it gives me something to occupy me when unamusing people come to call. Too often have I been caught thinking: *I wish I had a piece of work handy so my time would not be a total loss.* So now, ever wiser, when we have visitors, I take up my work with an eagerness which it does not often command. Although I have socks to darn, I have been informed *that* is not proper. And so I make a pretty case for a pillow, ivory with yellow and pink flowers. Father reads the paper, and Cassandra sits nearby putting embroidery on a moss green reticule to match her newest dress.

She displays it for my perusal. "Do you think this is enough? Or should I put another row along the open—?"

Mother rushes into the room, causing me to prick my finger. She waves a letter. "Young Hastings is dead!"

Eliza's son, by her first husband, the French count. Poor little Hastings!

Cassandra takes the letter from her. "It was the fits. They had come more frequently of late."

"He has not been well," Father adds. "Never been well."

It was a truth we none could argue. Ever since the chubby little boy had come into our lives to be our special pet to pamper and play with, we recognized he was unlike other children. His speech never developed correctly, and he took to repeating very formal phrases such as calling someone "My very valuable friend." Yet as lofty as the words sounded, they seemed said from memory, as if he had learned the sounds but knew not the meaning.

Mother pulls a handkerchief from her sleeve and sits by the fireplace. "He has been in much pain. For years," Mother says. "Fifteen long years of agonizing existence."

Whenever I think of Hastings, I am reminded of my older brother, George, who is also not *right*. Second born, and nine years older than I, he was sent away as a child. It has been years since I have seen him, but I *have* heard he is well. Well enough. Unlike dear Hastings, George can function.

Cassandra finishes reading the letter and tells us the rest of its contents. "The boy has been buried in Hampstead beside his maternal grandmother. Eliza is going to Godmersham for a few weeks."

I nod. "She and Henry will find solace at Edward's. Henry so enjoys it there."

With a glance to Mother, Cassandra says, "Henry is not going. He is staying in London to attend to business with his new banking position."

Mother shakes her head. "They are apart far too often."

I have noticed this quirk in their relationship, but have accepted it as an agreed upon situation for two very independent spirits. Although Henry is my favourite brother, I do acknowledge—at least in private—his many faults.

"He had better behave himself," Father says.

"Meaning?" I ask.

Mother receives another glance, this time from Father. "He had just better, that is all. Life is hard work, not all pleasure."

"They should be having their own children," Mother says. "Especially now . . ."

"But Eliza is ten years older," I say. "There is no need to offer details. Eliza is forty years old. The fact that she and Henry have not already had a child warrants speculation that she is unable. For surely, they *do* share affection to its fullest extent.

"It is none of our business," Cassandra says. "We must each write, offering our condolences, and let them handle the grieving as they will."

She is right. As always.

Death is part of life. And accepting that fact as quickly as possible is the Austen way.

❦ ❧

Yes, indeed. The Austen way has its merits.

The next year Henry and Eliza come to visit. I wonder if being in Bath will be bittersweet for Eliza, bringing back memories of her son, who sought help here. But if that is so, she does not mention it.

The two of them are as vibrant as ever. The air moves when they enter a room, the light brightens and colours enrich. And once they have entered, the four corners, the ceiling, and the floor, all come to attention.

Henry falls into a chair in the parlor. Eliza gracefully takes command of a settee next to Father. Oddly, he reddens at the very nearness of her. I am not surprised. Eliza has that effect on men of all ages. She seems to make them more aware that they are men.

And she, a woman.

Mother, Cassandra, and I sit on various chairs, drawing them close to hear the news. Henry has intimated that there is an adventure to tell, which, considering the players, does not surprise.

"So," Father begins, looking at lovely Eliza. "Henry says your trip to France was eventful?"

Henry leans forward and lowers his voice. "We barely made it out with our lives!"

Eliza rolls her eyes. "Your son exaggerates—although we did

have to resort to subterfuge to escape."

Mother pulls in a breath. "Escape? So you did have to escape?"

Eliza quells her concern with her hands. "No story should be told from back to front." She flashes Henry a look.

He tips an imaginary hat and sits back, giving her free reign. "I ask extreme forgiveness and defer," he says.

"As you should." Eliza sets her hands in her lap and begins. "Since the peace with Napoleon was declared last year, Henry and I thought it would be the proper time to return to the home I held with my late husband and claim the lands, and the Feuillide assets. It is only fitting that such properties be released now that our countries are not at war."

"You would think," Henry adds.

"It did not go well?" Mother asks.

Eliza glares at her husband. "See? They guess the ending because of your intrusion. Now, hush!"

I offer encouragement. "Please tell. Tell all of it, in any order."

Eliza begins again. "Once in France, we discovered that since my dear husband died as a confessed murderer—though he was completely innocent, I assure you—"

"He was beheaded for those crimes," Mother says.

"Mother!" Cassandra says.

"But he was."

Eliza raises a finger to make a point. "Many innocent people were executed during the horrors of the Revolution. It was not always guilt that led to death, but proximity, breeding, and bad luck."

"We know that, my dear," Father says, patting her knee. "Please continue."

"So . . . as my husband was treated with injustice, so was I. My claims as his wife were null. Our house, our land, our accounts, are all gone, eaten up by the greed of those who took what was not theirs."

"I am so sorry," Cassandra says.

Eliza shrugs. *"C'est la vie."*

"We could have used the money, my dear," Henry says.

"That is a universal statement, dear one, and as such, not worth stating."

I have heard that Henry's banking venture in London is not going as well as he had hoped. . . . For his sake, I try to get the story backed away from finances. "You mentioned escape?"

"Oh yes, indeed," Eliza says. "For once the French disappointed us with the news, they took no time in informing us that, as we were British subjects, they had a right to intern us in Verdun. As prisoners!"

"No!" Mother says.

"Yes," Eliza says.

"And so we made our escape," Henry says.

"Henry, be quiet," Father says. "Let Eliza tell it."

Henry harrumphs and pretends offense, but I see the glimmer of humor in his eye. I imagine they have perfected the bantering in many tellings of this story.

"Although Henry's use of the term *escape* is overly dramatic, there was the essence of danger in our returning home. I took charge. We agreed that Henry should be relegated to an invalid role under the cover of our traveling carriage. No one at the posting stations could detect my nationality, as I have a perfect command of French. I speak as those at Napoleon's court and disarmed all suspicion."

"Bravo!" Father says, clapping.

"Soldiers stopped you?"

"Of course. The country is still in upheaval," Eliza says. "And let me tell you how pained I am to see the tricolour flags waving in place of the beloved fleur-de-lis."

"Talk like that could get *you* beheaded, my love," Henry says.

"I will say what I wish."

"In England," I say. "Say what you wish in England."

She does not argue.

"At least you are home!" Mother says.

Eliza looks at me. "You have my permission to use this, Jane. If you ever need such a scene in one of your books."

"Actually, you have much in your life that is worthy of a novel's plot," I say.

Henry laughs. "That belies the believability of a novel's plot."

Eliza pretends to be offended. "*You* married me."

He blows her a kiss. "And you married me."

They are a pair. That is *not* fiction.

I sit at my writing desk. It has been far too long. I credit—or blame—Eliza's words for my position: *You have my permission to use this, Jane. If you ever need such a scene in one of your books.*

Intrigue in France after a war, a masquerade for one's life, deception, lost fortunes . . .

I place my pen on the page and will my mind to engage.

It does not.

Certainly I can build a story on this scenario. Two impulsive lovers risking all to raise their station in life?

I think of Eliza's true background.

A woman ten years her husband's senior.

With a disabled child—who in spite of her best efforts, dies.

A woman whose father was not the man her mother married but most likely Warren Hastings, a ranking official in the far-off land of India.

A woman who married a Frenchman she did not love—for money.

A husband who cared little for his imperfect son.

A revolution.

Flight to a safe land.

The husband returns to regain his property.

He is caught, tried for murder, and beheaded.

In a far-off land, the wife woos one brother, yet marries another. . . .

I cannot write this. No one would believe it.

In truth, I cannot write anything.

I put the blank page away.

I am exhilarated as the carriage leaves Godmersham and heads to Steventon. Cassandra and I have just spent time at Edward's. With seven children and an eighth on the way, we helped Elizabeth rather than let her play weary hostess. On our part I will complain and say the pleasure and fun usually present in our visits was set aside for more practical occupations.

In Elizabeth's defense . . . the poor woman. Her time between pregnancies shortens. I wish I could talk to my brother about such things, but I cannot. Anyone can see she is being worn out. A woman's place may include birthing babies, but receiving a deep breath between them seems the least of fair.

Cassandra sits across from me and taps her toe against mine. "You glow."

"I am happy with the prospect of seeing Hampshire again."

"And James and Mary?"

I smile. "Hampshire has much to anticipate."

"Ah. You think ahead to our visit to the Biggs in Manydown, do you not?"

I raise a hand. "I confess."

"I have missed Catherine and Alethea."

"I have missed *everything*."

But not for long. Soon, soon, I will be home, among true friends.

Manydown is an estate that breathes history. The Bigg-Wither family and their ancestors are listed in the legendary Domesday Book, that book commissioned by William the Conqueror in 1086 to appraise the depth and breadth of England's land and resources. Since 1679 Manydown has only had three owners, including the present lord of the manor, Lovelace Bigg-Wither.

He himself greets us at the door, his portly body capped by an abundance of white hair. His life is so useful, his character so respectable and worthy, that I have never met a more generous country squire. "Welcome, girls. Welcome! My own daughters have been waiting for you with bated breath."

"And impatient hearts!" Alethea comes down the elegant staircase to embrace us. Dear Catherine comes right after. The foyer chitters with greetings.

There are six daughters in the Bigg family (there had been seven, and two sons, until a son and daughter died years ago). But we count the three oldest as our dear friends. The eldest of the three is Elizabeth Heathcote, who—like her father—is widowed, though her grief is quite new. Just last spring her husband died at age thirty. She lives at Manydown now with her son. They are not here to greet us, but I know we will often have the pleasure of their society.

Without anyone's bidding our luggage is taken upstairs to our rooms—we each get our own, one next to the other. Our coats and bonnets vanish as if by a magician's trick, and we are whisked away up the grand stairs to the elegant drawing room that affords a grand view of the estate's fifteen hundred acres. The leaves of the trees have fallen, allowing us to see farther, between the branches.

As we continue our chatter, suddenly the brother Harris lifts up from the settee where he has been lying. He trips as he tries to stand and I can see that he has grown even taller. Although twenty-one, he moves like an adolescent, uncomfortable with his gawky frame.

"Harris!" I say. "You frightened me."

Instead of verbally responding, he runs a hand through his blond hair and asks forgiveness through a bow. He is a man of few words by habit and necessity. In his youth he suffered horribly with a stutter and was sent to a special teacher to overcome it. Which he has. To some extent. I am of the opinion that with such consuming attention being given to his speech, he has never felt at ease, and so either says the wrong thing rightly, or the right thing wrongly. And yet there is a charm about him . . . in many ways he is a stumbling, fumbling puppy you wish to cuddle and comfort.

Catherine once intimated a story about him. On one occasion Harris had instructed a wine punch to be created—with awful results. When his guests made faces at the concoction, he reportedly said, "Gentlemen, my punch is like you. In your individual capacity you are all very good fellows, but in your corporate capacity you are very disagreeable."

Although often too blunt, I do admire his wit as well as the content of his observation. For I too have witnessed such a phenomenon. People, by their very nature, offer diversity regarding whether their strength is shewn in solitude or company. Eliza and Henry are the sort that prosper in a crowd. Cassandra and I prefer our own society—or the combined asset of simply being with each other. Neither penchant can be called all good or all bad. Full benefit can be accomplished by learning to find contentment in both situations. Father has often quoted St. Paul in the hopes of aspiring us to achieve such a goal: *I have learned, in whatsoever state I am, therewith to be content.* I have heard the words often enough but find the application a challenge.

The Bigg-Wither family fills the room, and we feel completely welcomed.

Old friends are the best friends.

Five women. In one bedroom. On one bed. We sit in our nightclothes with pillows in laps, shawls about shoulders, blankets askew to warm cold feet, and candles flickering with our movement and chatter. In the company of these women, I am content. They are family to me. Sisters. Confidantes. I often wonder if men bond in this way. I will never know.

There is a knock at the door, and Catherine climbs off the bed to answer it. It *is* her room. . . . As we are not properly attired, she merely cracks the door.

Harris pushes the door wide with his foot. He carries a massive silver tray with teapot, cups, and cake upon it. "Food for the frivolous!"

"Harris! You cannot come in here," Elizabeth says.

"It appears I can."

He sets the tray on a chest, and I notice he wears a butler's jacket—as well as he can, considering it is many sizes too small.

He displays the cake plate. "Miss Jane asked for this. Pumpkin cake."

"I did no such thing!" I say.

"Well, then . . ." He takes the cake towards the door.

"No! Do not take it away!" I say.

He turns towards me. "So you *did* ask for the cake?"

"No, I did not. You know very well I did not, but . . ." I look at my friends. They are all smiling. This is not the first time in the past week that Harris has singled me out. "But I *will* eat it. We must not let it go to waste."

He bows and brings the cake to me as I sit on the bed. Cassandra, Alethea, and I scramble to get ourselves more covered, but he seems not to notice. He simply places the whole of the cake in front of me upon the covers, then bows and leaves, closing the door behind him.

Catherine goes to the door, opens it, and yells into the hall, "You forgot the lemons for the tea!" She quickly closes the door and puts a chair in front of it. "There," she says. "We are now safe from my brother."

"I do not believe one of us is safe from him," Elizabeth says. She pours the tea and hands cups and saucers all around.

I pretend I do not know what she is talking about. I get off the bed, go to the tray, and cut the cake to serve. "Does everyone want a piece?" I ask.

"You are evading the question," Alethea says.

I serve the first piece and lick a crumb from my finger. "I heard no question."

"We all have noticed his attention this week," Catherine says as she takes the first piece.

I determine to feign ignorance and do not respond.

"Jane . . ." Elizabeth says.

"I still hear no question."

They all moan at my evasion. "Fine," Elizabeth says. "You force us to speak plainly."

"It is what I prefer," I say. Actually, it is what I desire. For I know of what they speak. I have seen Harris pay *me* particular attention. I have enjoyed it. But I wish for others to tell me what *they* have seen and what *their* interpretation might be.

Catherine takes the cake knife away. She holds me by the shoulders, her blue eyes intent on mine. "Harris shews great interest in you, Jane."

"I would hope so. I have known him my entire life."

She sighs with exasperation. "He prefers you above all others."

"All other what?" I ask. Their faces reveal their frustration. I have taken the ruse far enough. I take Catherine's hands in my own. "Forgive me. Yes, yes, I have noticed his attentions."

"You've encouraged them," Cassandra says. There is a hint of censure in her voice.

"I have merely been kind."

"More than kind," Elizabeth says, finishing the cake service. "I know my little brother. He has spoken more in the past week than he has spoken in mixed company in years."

"Ever," Alethea says.

Catherine leans forward, our foreheads close. "I would love to have you as a real sister," she whispers.

The others hear and concur. "Oh yes!" Alethea says. "It would be the ultimate perfection."

I look to Cassandra. She does not frown. She does not shake her head against the notion.

"He has not asked," I say.

"He will—if we encourage him," Elizabeth says. She sets her cake aside and heads towards the door.

I run after her, holding her back. "You will do no such thing."

"Little brothers need sisterly encouragement. It is a fact."

"But not about this," I say.

"'Twould be *so* perfect," Catherine says. "Since our older brother died, and the rest of us are girls, Harris is due to inherit Manydown and all that it entails. As his wife, it would all be yours."

Alethea raises a hand. "Would you let us stay until we find our own mates, O Jane, lofty mistress of the manor?"

"No, no," Elizabeth says. "That will never do. Harris and Jane will need all the bedrooms for their many children."

I feel myself blush, but the idea is not unpleasant—although but a few children would suffice. I never wish to be like Edward's Elizabeth, having child after child to her own disintegration.

"You cannot make such plans for her, Elizabeth," Catherine says. She turns to me. "How many children have you wanted, Jane?"

"Two or three would be fine, but—"

"That will not do!" Elizabeth says. "You come from a family of eight children, and we had nine. You must keep up, Jane!"

I look to Cassandra and find her smiling. "I would be happy to help care for them."

I am surrounded.

In a loving embrace.

Catherine moves to the library doors and surprises me by shutting them as she leaves. "I must go see Father about something. If you will excuse me."

It is the poorest of excuses and so thinly veiled that both Harris and I can see through it.

For she has left us alone. All have left us alone.

Although no one has spoken of our nocturnal marriage discussion all day—at least not in my presence—I have heard whisperings and have witnessed Catherine and Elizabeth halting all talk when I came in the room. I suspect a conspiracy has been set in place. And now, alone with Harris, with all family safely tucked elsewhere (or with their ear to the door), I suspect what is coming.

And find that I accept the idea, if not embrace it.

I sit on the blue-and-gold brocaded settee and retrieve a book from a nearby table. I open it, but do not look at its pages. Harris stands by the fireplace, fingering a gold candlestick, making the lit candle jump and jerk. Although I have never felt awkward with him before, knowing what might transpire has changed my ease to disease.

I wish for him to speak first. But by his nervous actions it appears he wishes the same of me.

I, who can write dialogue for characters with a lucidity and speed of water going over a falls, cannot think of a word to say. But finally, as the silence threatens to consume the very air in the room, I burst out, "I so enjoy being here at Manydown. Your family is—"

"Would you marry me?"

I steal a fresh breath, then let it out. And then I say, "Yes, I believe I will."

To his merit, he removes his hand from the candlestick—thereby preventing any further topples—and comes to me. He sits beside me and takes my small hand in his large one. "Will you, r-r-really?"

His stammer makes him seem e'en younger than his twenty-one years, but also endears. "I will. Really."

He leans close, kisses my cheek, then stands. "We must tell the family!"

Hand in hand we leave the library, and the close proximity of my friends tells me they already know our news. "We are betrothed!" he says.

Hugs, kisses, and hearty congratulations abound.

So this is what it feels like.

❦

I snuggle into my bed, bringing the covers to my chin. "I am going to be married!" I tell the candlelight.

I spread my hands and feet to the four corners of the ample bed—which is far larger than my bed back in Bath—and wonder about the extent and decoration of our marriage room. Surely it will be even grander than this. And if it is not to my liking? As the mistress of the house, the bride of the inheritor of the great estate of Manydown, surely I will be free to change it.

I throw off the covers and climb out of bed. A friendly fire warms the room. No more cold toes and rush to the covers as Cassandra and I have always been forced to suffer. When I am mistress of Manydown, I will make sure every room is as amiable and warm as this one, made cozy with the dance of firelight.

I walk to the windows and feel the weight of the heavy green-and-gold jacquard. It is a fine fabric but lacking in warmth because of its regal appearance. "I would prefer velvet," I tell the room. A good compromise that will maintain the abundance of the room yet enhance its warmth.

I notice that in the recent moments "warmth" has shewn itself to be of import to me, and I wonder (and quite correctly too, if the strength of my feelings can be trusted) that it is not just physical warmth that makes itself essential to my preferences, but a warmth of spirit, as if God presides and approves. A warmth of atmosphere and setting. For as with people, a room, and nigh e'en an entire place, possesses character and spirit. A place can be inviting or repellant, engaging or abrasive. Freeing or confining.

I think of Bath, and a pall enshrouds me.

But . . . just as quickly, I am able to throw it off, for that place will no longer be my home! All that I have endured may be pushed away, as a bad dream is shunned the next morning. For here I have awakened! Here, in the Hampshire I love, I can find release from my captivity. Here, I will find delight. Delight in a home, new sisters, future children, and a new . . .

Oddly, the word sticks in my throat and I let go of the drapery. I force myself to say it. "A new husband."

Harris.

Gangly Harris, with his awkward presence of body, and his even more awkward presence of words. Or lack thereof.

I do not hold his verbal impediment against him. He is improved, and still young enough to improve more—though I do wish he would have found discretion of word choice during his treatment, as well as word pronunciation.

Unwittingly, my mind thinks of Mr. Darcy and Willoughby in my novels. Although Mr. Darcy does not speak often, when he does I have made him eloquent and wise. And though Willoughby is effusive, he is charming.

Harris is none of these.

The thought comes as a wee small voice and weakens my knees. I retire to the bench at the dressing table. I take up the comb and pull it through my hair. A tangle stops me, allowing blessed distraction.

But the thought returns: *Harris is none of these. He is neither eloquent, wise, effusive, nor charming.*

"But his family is."

You do not marry his family.

In the mirror I see my head shake no. "But I am marrying them. I will be a Bigg-Wither. I will be embraced as a daughter and sister."

And a wife.

I watch myself shudder.

I gasp at the observation. Why should I shudder? A woman fresh from a proposal does not shudder. A woman with the congratulations, embraces, and kisses of her new family still palpable in her memory does not shudder.

And yet I did.

I did.

I whisper aloud, "God, help me understand! Let me know what to do."

I shudder again—and realize perhaps the Almighty has already answered.

I cover my face with my hands, my head shaking of its own accord.

What have I done?

I knock softly on the door to Cassandra's room. Surely she is in bed, perhaps asleep.

It cannot be helped. My need cannot wait.

I hear soft rustling. She cracks the door, then seeing me, opens it wide. "Jane?"

I brush past her, closing the door behind me. "I must talk."

She moves to the chairs by the fire. "There is much to talk about. I am not surprised you cannot sleep."

I wait until she is seated to tell her the substance of my insomnia. She points to the tea tray nearby. "It is cold, but—"

"No," I say. "I do not wish for tea."

The discord in my voice makes her look at me closely. "There is something wrong."

"Completely."

"Are you afraid of being a wife?"

I hesitate a moment, then understand her concern. "Not that. I understand *that*." My married friends have spoken of such things. On occasion.

She continues. "I know being the mistress of such a large estate will be daunting. It is a large leap from rectory to mansion."

"I—"

"But you will have help here. Beyond the servants are Elizabeth and Alethea and Catherine, and though I expect they will also marry, they will always be ready to help you—"

"No!" She blinks at my interruption. I breathe deeply and reach across the space between us to touch her knee. "What you fear . . . that is not the problem."

She searches my eyes, and I see hers grow wide. She touches my hand. "Oh, Jane . . ."

I withdraw to the safety of my chair, now requiring the space between us. If only it were larger, if only I could retreat to the dark corners and tell her my awful thoughts from there. But I cannot. I must stay here and tell her the truth—she, above all others, will allow its say.

"Jane, tell me."

I must. I must say it plain. "I have second thoughts."

"But why?"

I rise from the chair, unable to be still as the words tumble from my lips. "I am not sure. There are a dozen reasons to indicate this is a blessing from heaven itself. For my fortune will be my family's fortune. Father will not need to worry about our fates after his passing— nor Mother's. I will be able to take care of us all here at Manydown."

"If Harris would agree."

"He would agree. I would make him agree. I am the one to gain. That he even shews interest in me . . ."

"Do not belittle your attributes, sister."

"You know I will not, I do not, but the world can attest to my age. In two short weeks I will be seven and twenty. Harris is over five years younger."

She shrugs. "Such a small disparity across a lifetime . . ."

Silence settles and I take refuge behind my chair. "I would be free from Bath. I would be home in Hampshire."

"A definitive joy."

"He is a nice enough man. And his family is dear. A closer association would be pleasing to all."

Cassandra shakes her head. "Jane . . . I only hear points that validate your previous agreement, and yet you say you have—"

"Second thoughts." I return to my chair, leaning my elbows on my knees. "I cannot do it. I cannot marry him."

I wait for her reply, I wait for the words *But you must! You gave your consent.*

The words do not come. Instead, Cassandra says, "You do not love him."

It is a statement, nay a question. "He is a nice man."

"You do not love him."

"Love need not be a prerequisite. Love may grow and—"

"You are a romantic, Jane."

I do not understand how this pertains.

She explains. "I too was swept up in the moment of last evening, and I too felt true joy for your betrothal, but as I sit with you now . . . I know you could never marry without love. Nor could I."

"This past week I have tried to think of him all the time, think about him more than myself."

"I do not ever imagine you lovesick, pining away, wishing to know a man's every move and mood."

"But surely that is the way it is, the way love is. Did you not think of your Tom in such a way?"

She hesitates, then nods. "I did. Many times a day I wondered what he was doing so many, many miles across the ocean. At such times I often wondered if he was thinking of me, two minds with but a single purpose."

"That is the stuff of love! Two becoming one in every way."

"I fear it is a rarity among marriages."

"Mother and Father feel that way. I know they do. And our

brothers . . . I believe they truly love. They have found the mates of their souls."

"And Harris is not yours?"

It is time to say it. "He is not. And I fear he can never be."

"Then . . ."

She waits for me to offer action. "Then . . . I must refuse." I lean back in the chair with a weighty sigh. "How do I do such a thing? I have no wish to hurt Harris, or his dear family." I think of something else. "Will they remain our friends after such an offense?"

"I am sure they will."

I bolt upright as a new thought surfaces. "And Mother and Father . . . am I being selfish by retracting our arrangement? My marriage to Harris would give them great security and peace of mind. The benefits are immense, and my cost small in comparison. Perhaps I should let it stand. Marry and bring benefit to our parents. And to you, Cassandra. To you too!"

She rushes to my chair, kneeling beside me. "Stop that! I will not have you raise material gain as a reason for marriage. Yes, it is done— far too often, as you and I have oft discussed. Our parents are content where they are. They are not wealthy, but they eat and drink and find happiness in each and every day. They do not need more, especially the *more* that would come at the expense of their daughter's happiness. You say your sacrifice is small. That is a lie. To relinquish your hope to marry for love as a means of putting a fancier roof over our heads, or eating better cuts of meat . . . such an exchange is neither desirable nor commendable. In fact, it is loathsome and despicable."

I smile and applaud her monologue. "Bravo, dear sister. With an eloquent fervor such as yours, Parliament would stand and take notice."

She blushes and returns to her chair. "By arresting me for lunacy."

"The truth is never lunacy," I say. And I mean it. For though the list of reasons in favour of marrying Harris are lengthy and convincing, my sister's reasons for breaking the engagement have their own authority.

"I should not marry Harris," I say.

"You should not marry Harris."

My breath leaves me. "Whatever I do tomorrow is wrong."

"But must be done."

"But how . . . ?"

"We wait until morning and then you just . . . do it."

God help me. God help us all.

⟨⟨⟩⟩

The seating does not suit his frame.

It is an odd thought to entertain at such a life-changing moment. I should be concerned with the colour of his eyes, the wave of his hair, even the cut of his waistcoat. Not the fact that Harris looks ridiculous poised on a blue silk settee with delicately turned legs.

The existence of such petty trivialities does not speak well for my character. I hope they are merely an indication of my extreme discord and sadness over what has transpired, and yea, e'en fear over what I must do. Never, in all my years, have I ever imagined myself in such a position.

Although I would rather stand across the room, or sit in a chair at some distance, I know I cannot. I sit beside him on the settee, my body angled to create the greatest separation.

It is obvious he holds no suspicion as to the reason I called him here alone, for he bridges the gap I created and kisses my cheek. I do not draw back, and immediately wonder if I should have. Shunning his kiss would have been one way to broach the subject before us.

'Tis too late now.

He takes my hand and smiles. "We have many plans to make, Jane. I wish my dear mother . . . but my sisters . . ." He lets me fill in the words, and I recognize this habit as one I would have had to live with.

I withdraw my hand. "Harris . . . the wedding . . ." I chastise myself for giving him incomplete sentences and hasten to state the truth. "I cannot marry you."

His head pulls back. "Pardon me?"

I must say it again. "I cannot marry you."

He blinks. "Why not?"

"It is not you. You are the best and kindest of men. And your family is as dear to me as my own."

"Then why?"

Presented with such a direct question, I am mute. My reasons slip into hiding and will not venture out.

"I can give you much," he says.

I touch his hand. "But I can give you little." An answer to his *why?* question surfaces. "You deserve a wife who will adore you. I am not that woman."

"I can do with less," he says.

"I . . . cannot."

I rise. There is nothing else I can say.

To him.

But there are others . . .

Cassandra and I are in the Manydown carriage on our way to Steventon. My sister sits across from me, studying me in that way she does.

"Do not stare," I say, for after telling the Bigg sisters of my disgrace, I am in no mood for scrutiny.

"I am proud of you."

I allow my jaw to drop. "Proud for hurting a family I love?"

She nods once. "I am proud of you for letting your heart rule your mind."

I am confused. "Most would be chastised for such a thing."

"And in most events the chastisement would be deserved."

"But not in this case?"

"Your heart does not love him, Jane. And though every material element pointed towards your union, you did not let such practical matters sway your instincts."

I laugh. "Practical matters help pay the bills. Instincts own no practical worth."

"That is not true. Instincts are given to us by God to guide us. It takes a strong woman to listen to those instincts and ignore what the world says to do."

"Because of my instinctive decision I have doomed us all to a life of penury."

My sister shrugs. "God provides. He always has and always will."

"Your faith is much stronger than mine, sister."

"It is not a contest, Jane."

"Good. Because I would lose."

❧ ❧

The carriage approaches the Steventon rectory, and my stomach adds new knots to the old. "Do not say a thing to Mary. Not a word."

Cassandra adjusts a glove. "I have already agreed, Jane. You know you can trust me."

I can trust Cassandra. With my life. But I cannot trust my sister-in-law Mary. Material matters rule James's wife, and I cannot bear the tongue-lashing I will receive if she finds out why we are returning from Manydown early. *You stupid, stupid girl! To give up Manydown and all that it entails? What were you thinking?*

The carriage pulls up front and as we exit, James appears at the rectory door, his face replete with questions. He accepts our luggage, but as he begins to take it inside, I intervene with the next portion of our plan.

"Will you please take us to Bath, James?"

"Now?"

Cassandra straightens our luggage into two neat lines. "Now, please."

"But why?"

I see Mary hovering in the hall. James sees the direction of my gaze and steps outside into the cold December air, closing the door behind him.

"But why?" he asks again.

"I cannot say—now," I explain. "But if you will get your carriage . . ."

"Trust us, brother," Cassandra says. "We need you to do this."

He looks at each of us in turn, his dark eyes searching ours. His perusal complete, he says, "Then I will do it."

We each kiss his cheek.

"Come inside while I get the carriage ready."

I hesitate. I do not want to enter the house and deal with Mary's questions, and yet I can think of no way to avoid it. With a shared look of despair between Cassandra and me, we enter the rectory.

Mary is there to meet us, hands clasped in front.

"So. You come and force my husband to get the carriage—when he has a sermon to write?"

"We are sorry, Mary," Cassandra says. "It cannot be helped."

"And why not?"

My mind swims with lies about Father or Mother being ill and needing us in Bath. Or Uncle Perrot . . . he is often not well. But I cannot share the lies lest I cause James more worry than I already have. "There has been a disagreement," I say. I hope, but know it will not be enough of an explanation.

"About what? And with whom?" Mary asks.

"I prefer not to say—at this time." Perhaps the hope of someday hearing the details will defer further questioning.

My hope is dashed as Mary asks, "Whom did you offend? Mr. Bigg-Wither? Catherine? Elizabeth? Alethea?"

She does not mention Harris, probably because he has been

away at school. Yet even though, I can honestly answer that I have offended them all.

"We have simply had a change of plans," Cassandra says.

"Because you caused problems at Manydown," Mary says.

"I—"

James saves me by coming inside. "The carriage is ready."

Cassandra and I say quick good-byes to Mary and withdraw. James kisses her cheek and follows.

Mary stands at the door and her questions attempt to reach us as we pull away.

Miles. We need many, many miles between us and all that has happened.

Once the horses find their rhythm, James asks, "Now. I deserve an explanation."

He does. And I have to be the one to tell him. "Harris proposed last night."

"Young Harris? Proposed to you?"

I take offense. "I am not that much older than he."

James shrugs. "I had heard he is in search of a wife."

"As are all young men due to inherit," Cassandra says.

"But more than that. He and his father have had words, though in Harris's case they are few and often rude. I have heard tales of one evening when Harris had some wines poorly mixed and was quite offensive to—"

"We heard of that too," Cassandra says.

"He could not tolerate his father's chastisement, so he moved to Wymering, where he could do as he pleased."

"But he is still due to inherit Manydown," Cassandra says.

"He is. But father and son often clash."

As my visits at Manydown have always been spent with the Bigg girls, I am surprised at the news, yet not at the fact I am unaware.

James clicks at the horses, then continues. "I do not say this to disparage your new husband, Jane. I am very happy for—"

"I accepted. Then changed my mind."

"This morning she told him," Cassandra says. "Told the family."

James turns to see my face. "You broke your engagement?"

I try to think of a way to couch my answer, but end up saying a simple, "Yes."

"An engagement is a contract between two families. The Biggs have a famous lawyer and judge in their family, Sir William Blackstone. He could make trouble if they pursue it."

I had not thought of that. "Surely, they will not. They cannot. They would not want that."

"No," James says. "I do not believe they will. But they could."

Cassandra defends me. "She feels guilty enough, James. Do not add to her pain."

I want to make him understand that I *do* grieve my behaviour. "My motives were wrong and I find them heavy in their awful burden. I am the first to admit I was tempted by the idea of wealth and position, as well as the love I have for the Bigg girls. I was caught in the moment and said yes. Although I was immediately swept into a celebration of our union, I think even before I left the room I knew it was wrong. And I deeply regret hurting so many because of my one moment of weakness."

Cassandra slips her hand through my arm as her seal of approval.

James nods but once. But it is enough. "We are all imperfect beings, Jane. We all make mistakes. I commend you on amending yours so quickly. A bit of pain now is better than a bushel of pain in the future."

"You are too good to me, brother."

"And wise," Cassandra adds.

In spite of the cold, I see James blush. "Do you think Harris truly cares for you?"

I am shocked by the question, because I have not asked it

myself. "No, I do not believe he does."

"Well, then," James says. "Although love does grow after the vows, it is best to have some deep affection at the onset."

Yes, indeed. My brother is wise.

And forgiving.

I pray the rest of the world is as generous.

❧—❦

I am a coward.

I return to Bath with my tail between my legs. No, that is not correct. I do not come cowed, but embarrassed. There is a difference.

Mother and Father wait in the sitting room for us to explain why we have returned so early. With James driving us, unscheduled, and him with a sermon to write.

We defer the answer until we freshen ourselves, but finally it comes time for them to hear of my folly. I have informed Cassandra she does not have to subject herself to this discourse, but she, being the dearest sister, will not have me face it alone. If only I could make time retreat two days. Three or four would be better, for I call myself guilty of leading Harris towards the proposal. Women *do* have that power. I had that power and wielded it with glee at Manydown, flirting and cajoling Harris into a submission to the will of our female conspiracy. If bitter, I could blame the Bigg sisters, but I do not. In the end, right or wrong, I hold my own counsel.

Although I do not believe women can move a man who has no intention to propose, if there is a little affection, a little interest, and a little openness to marriage, I know a woman *can* make the *little* seem *enough*. My largest hope is that Harris joins me in feeling relief at the dissolution of our engagement. Oddly, in such matters it is the woman who has the upper hand. It makes me think of one of my stories, sitting in my trunk upstairs. It is nearly impossible for a gentleman to break an engagement without bringing shame to the lady. Edward Ferras was willing to marry the simpering Lucy Steele rather than cause her shame. Of course, I took care of that situation by making Lucy fall for his equally simpering brother. (Stupid, stupid girl! Did she not know what she had left behind?) Elinor can thank *me* for her happiness with Edward.

As I can thank myself?

Time will tell.

Actually, that I am the one who mended the mistake of our own betrothal is a blessing for all. I spared Harris the pain of discovering our incompatibility too late, or if caught in time, the choice of whether to break the engagement himself and cause me pain. It is discouraging that the right thing is not often the easy thing.

Lost in my own musings, I find myself at the door to the sitting room. Cassandra takes my hand and we enter. Will I be as eloquent in front of my parents? I fear both Cassandra and I are a disappointment to them.

But again, time will tell.

"So," Mother says, taking charge. "You are home early and obviously swore James to secrecy. It was most unpropitious for him to have to rush off home again with nary a word."

Father stands behind and touches her shoulders. "Now, now, dear. Give the girls time to explain before you expect the worst." He looks at me—not Cassandra—as if knowing I am the culprit. "I am sure it is nothing. I am sure our worried imaginings far outweigh the circumstances." He looks hopeful.

I must dash that hope.

As Mother has procured the settee for her own use, Cassandra and I have no choice but to sit apart, our united front physically challenged.

"Jane?" Mother asks. "We have been kept waiting long enough."

The telling will be no easier one minute from now. . . . . "I broke an engagement."

"Engagement?" Mother asks. "Since when were you engaged?"

"Since last night." Was it only last night? Surely it was months ago.

Mother stares at me. She has no words. Or too many.

Father takes over. "More, Jane. We obviously need more."

With a look to Cassandra, drawing on the constancy of her support, I tell the story in its entirety.

Mother releases her posture and falls back against the cushion of the settee. "You had him and you threw him away?"

Although she makes it sound like a fish story, I nod. "I could not do it. I am sorry to disappoint you, and I know it may be hard for you to understand but—"

Father circumvents Mother's chair and comes towards me. I search his face for his intent. Will he scold or . . .

He stops in front of me and holds out his hands. I take them and he urges me to standing. Beneath his grayed eyebrows, his eyes are kind. "It takes courage to chuse integrity over circumstance."

"Integrity!" Mother says. "Stupidity is more like it!"

Father ignores her and continues. "Although my practical nature grieves the easement in our position that the marriage would ensure, my paternal nature accepts your decision as wise, at least in your own eyes. And in the end, we all must live with our own decisions. Allowing others to decide for us does not guarantee a better decision but almost always guarantees a fuller regret, and regret is a poison I wish on no one."

I fall against his chest, needing his arms around me. He complies, and I thank God for such a man.

Such a father.

FOURTEEN

Know thyself.

To thine own self be true.

I thank my father for urging me to read through his library as a child. For where else would I have harvested these wise words? Whether it be the wisdom of Thales or Shakespeare, I embrace their assurance that my existence is not without merit, and my choices are not without some level of worthy insight. For who would I be if I tried to be someone besides Jane? The posers of the world try so hard to be what they are not, and yet . . . how fatigued they must be. Perhaps I am not smart enough to be one of them. Nor strong enough in constitution.

Thank God.

And so, after returning to the prison of Bath, after rejecting a chance to break free via Manydown and marriage, I hold on to the meager strength of being . . . just Jane.

I will admit that "just Jane" seems to gain insight from hard times. I wish to ask the Almighty about this, for why do we learn more from struggles than victories?

I am certain He has His reasons.

I do not think of reasons. I merely try to live rightly. Yet I have never chosen struggles for the sake of gaining wisdom. I am not so bold.

So. I am . . . home. After nearly two years in residence I must bestow to Bath its lawful title (if not its emotional one). The rest of December slogged by—in all ways. I managed Christmas, managed the new year, and can admit to allowing myself some pleasure in them both. Life went on. One can either go with it, or let it leave you behind.

I do not cry about the could-be's anymore. For what good are tears but for making my already full cheeks more pronounced with blush and swelling. That my family (yea, e'en Mother) allowed me this decision is enough to send me forward, not back. Plus, the letters I have received from Catherine, Elizabeth, and Alethea, assuring me that our friendship is indelibly signed by all involved, mercifully relieve that burden and imply that, all in all, my choice was the right one. Can it be that sisterhood carries more lasting fortitude than marriage?

I do not know. Yet. But I am willing to believe it, if need be.

One member of the family is still intent on marrying me off—to most anyone who holds a half inch of breeding. Although Aunt Leigh-Perrot knows nothing of Harris—I thank God that Mother has been able to keep the secret; surely shame is a factor—Aunt continues her matchmaking assault with all canons blazing. She continues to find fault with me, but I am learning to accept her discontent and disapproval of all things *Jane* as a matter of perma-nent residency.

Considering I am so lacking in any attribute she deems worthy and marketable, it astonishes that she finds any suitors willing to take me.

Yet, somehow, she does.

Today she has asked to tea a young man she and Uncle met at cards last weekend. According to my aunt, my past absences from card playing are socially suicidal.

She means to rectify my error this very afternoon.

In his defense, Reginald Clemmons is handsome enough, nice enough, and even on occasion witty enough to meet any woman's standards of courting. And perhaps at another time, with a few more months between Manydown and the present, I could have found a way to be charming to him—though I will never be charm-ing enough, according to my aunt.

As I stand in the doorway of the sitting room at the Paragon, watching Aunt shew Mr. Clemmons the door, Cassandra comes up behind me. She has been witness to this afternoon's foray, a second fiddle if Mr. Clemmons was not impressed with my first violin.

"Brace yourself," she says.

I am a little surprised by her warning. "I did well. I smiled. I was polite."

"But you did not elicit a proposal, on the spot, in Aunt's presence." She giggles softly. "That would have been preferred."

I know she is more right than wrong.

Aunt closes the door and turns on me. "Jane, I can count the words you said to Mr. Clemmons."

I stifle a shrug that would surely send her into an even longer lecture. "I am sorry, Aunt Perrot. I attempted to speak well to him."

"Well to him? Well is not enough, young lady! You need to speak brilliantly in new company. To capture a man, a woman must sparkle. You, my dear, are too often a dull stone."

Unsuspected fury overtakes me. I do not deserve such a comment. And why does she not speak of Cassandra's reticence? Not that I would wish my sister to endure such a complaint, but . . .

Words well to the surface and I let them out, even as I know I should not. "Perhaps I do not wish to sparkle, Aunt. Sparkle falsely. I say what comes to mind. I will not waste energy creating idle chatter meant only to impress."

Cassandra comes to my defense. "Your characters sparkle, Jane."

I grab on to the diversion. "Which is even more reason why I personally cannot. For I only have so much sparkle within me, and I chuse to save it for them."

Aunt Perrot stands in the foyer, her head wagging in utter disgust. "What are we to do with you two?"

Leave us alone is not an acceptable answer.

Instead I think of one better, one I can blame on others wiser than I, men who have gone before us all.

"Know thyself, Aunt Perrot. To thine own self be true."

She appears confused and thankfully has no more words—at least none that bear stronger wisdom than that which I offered.

I allow her condition and make advantage of it by quickly taking my leave.

My brother Henry falls into a chair in my bedroom and slings a leg over its arm. He has always sat thus, as though having two feet on the floor at the same time constitutes some measure of surrender.

Surrender to what?

Convention, society, and the ever-present risk that life might dare turn boring.

So far, he has done a good job defeating all three. Between Henry and Eliza . . . I admire their gusto, their *zeste pendant la vie.* Although they do not shun the boundaries of society, they bend them and refuse to be broken by them.

If only I possessed such strength.

"So, sister. How have you been? What are you doing with your life?"

He does not know of Harris. Although I can easily call Henry my favourite brother, I know his limitations in regard to discretion and secrecy. According to his knowledge, I have suffered no intrigue, and no humiliation.

I point to my writing desk. "I have copied out *Susan.* I am not sure why, but—"

"Is Father going to pursue its sale?"

I do not want to complain but . . . "Father has not pursued any publication of my work since the letter regarding *First Impressions* was rejected."

He allows both feet to hit the floor. "Whyever not?"

"It *is* a poor prospect."

He stands, ready to fight. "It is no such thing!"

"I am no one, dear brother. I have no recognition, no—"

"You have no recognition because you have not let yourself be recognized. Your writing is good, Jane. Excellent. Engaging. Fresh."

I laugh at his exuberance. "You have always been a good brother, but—"

"But nothing! I know I often do not act as though I have a brain in my head, but I do. A good one. One good enough to recognize talent and know when it is wasted."

My spirit, recently tested, tried, and tired, ignites with his words of confidence. But I am wary. To try and to fail seems impossible, even though I know what should be done, even though I know that failure, though painful, is not fatal.

He goes to my writing desk and finds the stack of pages, all neatly transcribed. He reads aloud the first line: "'No one who had ever seen Susan Morland in her infancy would have supposed her born to be a heroine. Her situation in life, the character of her father and mother, her own person and disposition, were all equally against her.'" He looks up at me. "No one ever supposed you to be a heroine either, Jane. But you are, or rather you *can* be."

His exuberance fills me up. "I do not wish to be a heroine, but . . . I would like others to know the ones I have created."

"Exactly!" Suddenly, he gathers the pages. "Is this complete? All copied?"

"Yes, but—"

"Then I will take it with me. I am now your agent."

"But, Father—"

"Has not done his job. Besides, he is retired, yes? And another *besides*, you need a young, virile, delectably charming man to be your champion." He tucks the manuscript under his arm and gives me a sharp bow. "Henry Thomas Austen, at your service."

I surprise myself by rushing towards him, wrapping my arms round his neck, nearly causing the pages to topple. "Thank you, Henry! You will never know—"

"Exactly." He pulls back to look at my eyes. "*You* will never know what you can be until you try. Even the Bible speaks of the shame in keeping a light hidden under a basket. We must let the world see you shine, Jane. And I will do my best to make that happen."

Cassandra and I return from a walk. The day, though still cold, is sunny enough to have lured us outside. Too much indoor air constrains me. I must breathe free—even if the day is brisk and my toes grow cold.

As we approach our lodging, Mother pops out the door, looking left, then right, directly at us. "There you are! I paid no attention to which direction you had gone."

We hurry to the entrance, not wanting Mother to catch her death. "What is wrong?" Cassandra asks.

As soon as the door is closed, Mother answers, breathless. "Not a thing is wrong, not a single thing."

Father comes into the foyer as we remove our coats and bonnets. "Indeed, girls. Come in by the fire, and let us tell you what has transpired since you have been gone."

Gone? The clock on the mantel indicates only forty minutes have passed. What could have charged our parents with such effusions?

We are seated by the fire, in our parents' chairs (yes, indeed, something is about!). Father takes a letter from the table behind the settee. It is obvious this is the source of the happiness.

"We have received good news?" Cassandra asks.

Father smiles—at me. "We shall let Jane read it. It is a message from your brother."

"Sent by special messenger," Mother adds.

With difficulty I breathe. My heartbeat takes exception and vies for a place of equal importance. I take the letter in hand and recognize Henry's messy cursive.

"I hope you do not mind we opened it ahead of you," Father says. "Though it was addressed to you alone, with the special courier. . . ."

I shake my head at his disclaimer. I read aloud:

"Dearest Sister,

I have the best of news. I assigned one of my business partners, William Seymour, to offer your book Susan to an acquaintance, a publisher in London, Richard Crosby. Mr. Crosby has agreed to publish it and will pay ten pounds."

"Ten pounds, Jane," Mother says. "A fair amount, to be sure."

I am not counting my purchases, but I am pleased. Any income of my own represents freedom for myself, as well as freedom for my parents. I will be ten pounds less a burden to them now.

"Is there more?" Cassandra asks. "Read more."

There is more, and I return to the letter. "'He'—I believe Henry means Mr. Crosby—'promises early publication and intends on advertising the book as "in the Press" in a brochure called *Flowers of Literature.*'"

"Advertisement, Jane," Father says. "Actual advertisement. It appears Mr. Crosby is genuine."

"Of course he is," Mother says. "Our Henry would not elicit the help of a charlatan."

"Let her finish," Cassandra says.

"That is about all," I say, scanning the short rest. "Henry will get me the payment as soon as possible and will keep me informed." I read the last line, then look up from the letter. "He says he loves me and is proud of me."

"Of course he is," Father says. "As are we all." He comes to me and lifts me into an embrace. Mother follows, and then Cassandra.

I feel as if the very world has embraced me.

It is a beginning.

Cassandra sits on her bed, brushing her hair.

I do the same from the window seat. "Ten pounds, Cass. What I can do with ten pounds!" I tap my chin, then pretend to get an idea. "I know! With such great wealth, I will buy a cake. You know how interesting the purchase of a spongecake is to me."

She gains a mischievous look, gets off the bed, and opens a drawer of her dresser. "This proves what you really think of money."

She holds something behind her back. "What do you have there?" I ask.

"You may remember a certain letter you sent me that mentions your true heart in regard to payment for your work?"

"I remember no such letter."

She laughs, pulls a letter from behind her back, and shoves it under my nose. "Here. True evidence of your greed."

I glance at the letter's date. "This is dated January 16, 1796."

"I was visiting Tom and his family in Kintbury. You were at home."

"You kept this?"

"I keep all your letters."

At first hearing, I am impressed, and then fearful. "All my letters? E'en the ones where . . ."

"You are completely honest?"

"Where I am distressingly honest."

"I have them, Jane. But fear not. I will not ever let others read those of a more intimate and . . . emotional nature. I will not let you suffer shame or embarrassment. Ever. I promise."

I believe her but still feel a bit nervous that my letters still exist. Then I have a thought. "I have not kept yours."

She shrugs. "There would be no reason. I am not the writer. I am not witty. My letters do not entertain."

"Of course they do. They entertain me greatly."

"Then their mission is complete." She waves away this discussion and points at the letter from seven years previous. "Read at the bottom of the first page."

I scan to the place and immediately know what has caused her interest—and teasing.

"Read it aloud, Jane. Let the whole world hear your views on publishing fame and fortune."

I clear my throat and begin. "'I write only for fame, and without any view to pecuniary emolument.'" I lower the letter to my lap. "I will not refuse the ten pounds, if that is what you are trying to get me to do."

"You may have your ten quid if you admit your change of heart."

"I have a proposal for you."

"Haven't we had enough of proposals?"

To think that my sister believes she is *not* witty? "I will sacrifice fame for a bit of pecuniary emolument."

She puts a hand to her chest dramatically. "You mean you chuse coin over commendation?"

"Absolutely. I am quite happy being unknown—as long as my work is most well known."

"This may be a problem when 'a novel by Jane Austen' appears on the cover."

Although I have never seriously entertained this predicament, I find it is something to think about. "Truly, sister, I do not want fame."

She snatches the letter away from me. "Then, alas, you shall just have to live with fortune."

It would be nice to try.

I intercept Cassandra in the hall as she carries fresh sheets to our rooms. "Cassandra, would you go with Mother to the milliner for me?" I ask. "I have something else I . . ." I defer. I do not wish to say more.

Astute as ever, she takes a step towards me. "You have some plans? A secret rendezvous perhaps?"

"You know very well there is no one who currently holds my interest."

"Bath society is very disappointed."

"As intended." I hear Mother downstairs. "Will you go in my stead?"

"If you will tell me what you intend to do with your time."

I pull her into our room. "I wish to start another novel."

Her face lightens and she hugs me with the sheets between us. "What about?"

"I am not completely sure, but since Mr. Crosby is publishing *Susan,* and since I have two other novels awaiting his interest once *Susan* is publicly accepted . . ."

"You are a novelist now. A real novelist."

I both revel and am petrified by the title. "If that is so true, then I must do what novelists do. I must become what I am. I must write."

"Bravo!" She kisses me on both cheeks. "I am eager to read the scratches of your mighty pen!"

"Jane?" It is Mother. "I am waiting."

Cassandra presses the sheets into my arms and takes on one duty so that I may take on another.

I sit at my desk, pen poised over paper, spirit willing, mind ready.

To begin a new venture, a new story, is a supreme act of faith. It is obvious by the pile of manuscripts in my trunk that I have owned much faith in all my years. Faith that my work has some merit and meaning to others beyond myself. Yet intertwined in each and every word is something beyond faith. Need.

I need to write.

Although I may not sparkle to my aunt's liking, although I am not completely comfortable being among people I do not know, I do know that I have a voice living within my pen, one that speaks in full volume once it touches a page.

I make no claims of art or eloquence or even intelligence. My work will not live through the ages like Shakespeare or Burney or Cowper. I have no such aspirations. I merely desire to write stories about what I know, what I see, and what I feel. Through these stories I reveal more of myself than ever is revealed through direct knowing—barring Cassandra's knowledge of me. And yet even my dear sister does not—cannot—know all the thoughts and emotions that flit through this awkward mind and heart. Does one mortal ever completely know another?

I think not. And good it is too. For those increments of our being that are kept to ourselves are seldom worth sharing, whether it be due to their darker side or their inane mediocrity. I admit I possess both varieties.

And yet . . . through my characters these nether regions of my constitution find a voice which the reader can embrace or disdain with little consequence to myself. It is not Jane Austen who is man-hungry and frivolous like Lydia Bennet, not Jane Austen who wears her heart on her sleeve like Marianne Dashwood. And though I easily decry my characters with their faults—stating they are most certainly not mine—I also must admit that Jane Austen is not strong and wise like Lizzy Bennet, nor constant and loyal like Elinor Dashwood. I cannot claim to share the high attributes nor the low faults of these characters. Yet through them, I do release a part of myself. What I wish to be. What I am glad I am not.

And so, I sit at my desk, determined to begin again.

Yet I admit, this time it is different.

I am afraid.

For two reasons.

One, because I have a publisher who believes in me. I am no longer writing merely for myself, my family, and an indistinct audience of my own imagination. What if Mr. Crosby does not like what I write? I do not wish failure when I am on the verge of success.

My second reason to fear is that I have never written here, in Bath. I have copied over what I wrote elsewhere. I have edited the words and phrases that were born in another time and place. But I have not written anew anywhere other than Steventon. I have never written in a place that still does not feel like home, in a town that seems overridden with frivolous strangers and far too few sincere friends.

In addition, I have only written as an ignorant young woman, at ease with her life, content in most ways, and hopeful of the future. I have never written with the scars of lost loves, broken engagements, and betrayal as stubborn lodgers in my mind. Logically, I know such experiences should add to the depth and breadth of my writing. But I fear otherwise.

I remember a French proverb Eliza taught me: *Qui onques rien n'enprist riens n'achieva.* I repeat its translation aloud for my own benefit. "He who never undertakes anything never achieves anything."

And so, shoving fear aside, I begin.

It is my birthday. December the sixteenth. The sun does not awaken me by shining in my window. It is the moon that makes me arise. I move to the window and see that it is full. A full moon on my twenty-ninth birthday.

Is it an omen of a larger event? For as others before me, I am aware that the fullness of the moon often brings about extreme behaviour. Or does the extreme behaviour merely become notable because the orb of the moon is noticed?

As he often does, Shakespeare interrupts such thoughts, and I take up Juliet's words. "'O, swear not by the moon, th'inconstant moon, That monthly changes in her circled orb, Lest that thy love prove likewise variable.'"

I am happy to leave the inconstant moon to itself. Its power is not something I wish to ponder on my birthday. I accept its existence with simpler thanks, for it *is* beautiful, and its glow makes the darkness less dark.

I look to the clock on the mantel and notice the time. Three o'clock. It is too soon to arise.

And yet . . .

I turn away from the moon and see that its light has cut a swath across the pages of my work on the desk, accentuating its presence.

But not because it is good work. For it is not. There is something wrong about the book that I cannot wholly determine. The characters are interesting enough. The story revolves around the Watson family, which consists of a sickly father who is a parson on the verge of death, and his six children: two sons and four daughters. The eldest son has married a dislikable woman for her money, the other son is a novice doctor, and the four daughters are in search of husbands. They all realize that once their father dies they will be left at the mercy (and charity) of their brothers. The youngest daughter, Emma, who until now has been brought up by a rich uncle and aunt, has returned to the small village of her family, but finds no solace there. Because she has been so distanced from her family she disdains their ways. Greatly.

Being careful not to awaken Cassandra, I move to the desk, wishing to reread a line I wrote last night regarding Emma's disparaging view of her sisters' quest for suitable mates: *To be so bent on marriage, to pursue a man merely for the sake of situation, is a sort of thing that shocks me; I cannot understand it. Poverty is a great evil; but to a woman of education and feeling it ought not, it cannot be the greatest. I would rather be a schoolteacher (and I can think of nothing worse) than marry a man I did not like.*

I read it again and find nothing distinctly wrong with it, yet nothing distinctly right either. Surely after writing so many novels (albeit unpublished ones, for I am still awaiting Mr. Crosby's fulfillment of his promise to publish *Susan*) I should know what is good and what is not. This not knowing is disconcerting.

Despite the early hour, I hear rumblings in my parents' bedroom next door. Father has not been well this autumn, suffering fevers that come and go. He is currently in the midst of one, and I expect Mother is up, attending to his nocturnal needs.

Since this is my birthday, I expect that, with the morning, I will be greeted with good tidings as well as the question, "And how would you like to spend your day, Jane?" It is Sunday, and after attending church I believe my best choice for amusement is to stay at home and work on these perplexing pages. 'Twould be better for Father too, to not feel the guilt of being unable to accompany me to some soiree, or to venture out when it would best benefit his health to stay abed.

With a nod, sealing the decision, I cast a shawl about my shoulders, sit at my desk, take up my pen, and angle my pages so the moonlight lightens them.

Hopefully I will be able to *en*lighten them beyond their insufficiencies.

It is my birthday wish.

❦

I retrieve the post and find a letter from my dear friend Anne Lefroy. I break the seal eagerly, for Anne's letters can always be relied upon to be packed with interesting tidbits about my Hampshire acquaintances and friends. Without her reliable and steadfast accounting, I would truly feel lost here.

Dearest Jane,

I do not wish to cause you pain, but I must inform you that there is news from Manydown. Young Harris has married. Her name is Anne Howe Frith. Her father is a lieutenant-colonel in the

North Hants Militia. Harris and his wife are at Quidhampton and
seem very happy. I am to meet them at the Prices' tomorrow. Every-
one in the neighbourhood seems pleased with the bride.

I know she says this last not because I worry over Harris's happiness—alas, to my disgrace, I do not—but to let me know that it
is done and there is no drama or strife involved. And also to assure
me that because Harris *has* found a suitable match, my Manydown
disgrace can be completely set aside without malice. I have already
been the recipient of kind friendship from Harris's sisters, but his
marriage successfully closes the door on the flaws and foibles of the
past.

For which I am grateful. It is true I am alone, but with Tom,
with Harris . . . it has all been for the best.

I read the rest of Mrs. Lefroy's letter:

I have just had my solitary breakfast and tho' I try to keep up
my spirits I cannot always succeed when I look back to the happy
days when in my husband's absence I was surrounded by my chil-
dren. The contrast is too much for my feelings and I feel forlorn and
wretched beyond description.

I am saddened by her sadness. I feel guilty too, for as with her
children, I have also abandoned her company. And though I know
she keeps busy helping the poor, I also know there is little contentment at home. Her marriage is without glee. Reverend Lefroy is
kind enough but lacks the zest for life that Anne deserves in her
mate. If only I could go to her now. Surprise her. We would rush
into each other's arms, both benefiting from the renewal of our special bond.

But I am without means of seeing her. Unless someone takes
me, or comes to fetch me, I am confined here.

Finished with Anne, I am surprised to find a letter from James.
This, in itself, is not odd because he writes to us often. The oddness
falls on the fact this letter is addressed to me. Just to me.

I set the other items from the post on the foyer table and open it.

> Dear Jane,
>   *I am grieved to inform you that your dearest friend, Mrs. Anne Lefroy, has been killed in a riding accident.*

I discover I have held my breath. Only my body's need for another causes me to break the moment with even the slightest movement or sound.

Anne gone? Impossible! For her words still ring in my mind!

I look to the table. Yes, indeed. There is her letter! Written in her own hand.

She cannot be dead. Cannot.

But she is. James's words are indisputable: . . . *your dearest friend, Mrs. Anne Lefroy, has been killed in a riding accident.*

With difficulty I read the rest of the letter.

> *It was last Friday. She and a servant rode to Overton to shop. I saw her there and she commented on the stupidity and laziness of her horse. On the way home, it bolted. The servant says he tried to contain the beast, but as Mrs. Lefroy was trying to dismount, she fell. Her head was injured in such a way that was beyond Dr. Lyford's skill, and she died at three o'clock in the morning on December the sixteenth. I am so sorry, Jane. I know what a kind and wise mentor she was to you all of your years.*

That delightful woman who took me under her loving wing and led me into adulthood? I had long ago forgiven her for being the one to send her nephew Tom away lest our attraction go too far. She was correct in her action and thought only of the Lefroy family, and even me. If I had been married to Tom all these years . . .

I may have been happy, but probably not. Not in Ireland, moved so far.

As I had moved so far from Anne here in Bath.

In many ways I had abandoned my friend. Not that I could have prevented her horrible accident, but to have been close enough to be able to spend more time with her before this tragic end . . .

I look to the letter again, hoping the words magically changed.

. . . *she died at three o'clock in the morning on December the six-teenth.*

I gasp. December the sixteenth was my birthday. I remember the clock in my room. Three o'clock . . . it was the time when I awakened!

My legs are weak. I seek the strength of a chair.

It is meager comfort compared to the strength Anne gave to me. No more.

I can take no more.

Father wants us to move. And so we do. To Green Park. It is damp here, and not as amiable as Sydney Place. Although Father has not said so—indeed has said we moved because our lease on Sydney Place has run out—I do believe our move is an attempt to save money. Bath is not a place where one can live on frugal means.

We do not have the view of the fields behind us as we did on Sydney Place. Am I being punished for complaining about that natural aspect in comparison to Steventon? Is that why I have lost any view of nature? It does me no good to think in such a way. Father did not move to vex me, nor is my heavenly Father punishing me.

I vex myself. I am in a mood of late. Anne's death still weighs upon me, and Father's health is variable and worrisome. The war is going again (will Napoleon ever be completely defeated?) and I fear for Charles and Frank. And my writing is *not* going—going well, at least. In addition, neither Henry nor I have heard a word from Mr. Crosby regarding the publication of *Susan*. It has been a year. . . .

As I say, I am in a mood. Justified or not, I find no pleasure here.

Father joins us at breakfast. Cassandra and I both jump from our seats to greet him and help him get settled, for his presence has been rare of late.

"There, there," he says, setting his walking stick against his chair. "Do not fuss over me. I am not an invalid, you know."

It is his pride that makes the statement, for in the first weeks of the new year he has been visited by a variety of doctors. William Bowen has visited to offer him medicinal comfort for his condition, and just yesterday morning, Father was stricken in exactly the same way as heretofore: an oppression in the head, with fever, violent tremulousness, and the greatest degree of feebleness. The same remedy of cupping, which had been so successful, was immediately applied—but without such happy effects. Apparently, the warm cups did not extract the bad blood to enough extent. The attack was more violent, and at first he seemed scarcely at all relieved by the operation. However, towards the evening he got better, had a tolerable night, and here appears this morning as if nothing transpired.

I pour him some tea and he takes the cup with trembling hand. He sets it down again, the threat of spills imminent.

"Here. I have filled it too full."

He allows me to adjust the cup's measure and drinks. Cassandra brings him the plate of scones and ham and he takes a serving of each, though one far smaller than he used to chuse. We return to our seats.

"You are feeling better today, Father?" Cassandra asks.

"I am. I feel no fever." He points to the ham. "Would you pass me the ham, please? I think I would like a piece."

We are silent. We do not wish to be rude but . . .

He sees his own error. "Oh. I see I have a piece already. My forgetfulness is because I have not had course to read lately, not as I usually do. I have always said: a mind disengaged with vital thought gets used to blankness."

I laugh softly, wishing to make light of yet another example of his recent loss of memory. It worries me. I do not like seeing my father *less*.

Suddenly, he pushes back his chair and rises, and taking up his stick, walks to the window. The day is bleak. The sun casts no shadows.

But he sees otherwise. "A fine day. Fine indeed."

Mr. Bowen descends the stairs to join our trio of women who await news on Father's condition. "I do not know how he does it, ladies," Bowen says. "It appears that the Austen constitution is admirable. Every symptom is so favourable that I am sure of his doing perfectly well."

Mother's sigh is more extravagant than Cassandra's or my own. She shews Mr. Bowen the door. "There," she says upon closing it. "It will be all right."

I say a silent prayer of thanks—and hope—and go about my day.

But as the day advances, all these comfortable appearances change. The fever grows stronger than ever, and our sighs of relief change to sighs born in fear.

As the evening progresses, I send for Mr. Bowen. He comes at ten.

Cassandra and I wait outside the closed bedroom. I am tempted to put my ear to the door to hear their words more plainly but do not, for in truth, I do not want to hear. If I could leave completely and not have to see Mr. Bowen or Mother when they exit the room, I would be most pleased. To hear will be to know and be asked to accept, and I wish to do neither.

"Let things be as they were this morning," I pray.

Cassandra slips her hand through my arm. "He was not well e'en then, Jane. Not completely."

"At this moment I will accept 'not completely' as far better than . . ." I cannot say it.

The voices in the room go silent, but footsteps come close. My heart races as the door opens. Mother is crying and falls into our arms.

Mr. Bowen softly closes the door and faces us. His countenance shews his reluctance to speak. But he does. He does.

"I am sorry, ladies. But I must pronounce his situation to be most alarming."

Mother sobs. I shake my head no.

It is Cassandra who finds words. "Is there no hope?"

"There is always hope, but . . ."

He shrugs and I find it a disconcerting action. How dare he shrug my father's life away!

"There must be something we can do!" I say. The anger feels a far better alternative than defeat.

"I will come back tomorrow morning. I plan to bring a physician with me. Dr. Gibbs."

"Bring as many as you can," I say. "Certainly Bath has more than its share of those adept at healing. I want them all here. All."

Cassandra gently nudges Mother towards me, where I take up her comfort. "I will shew you out," she tells Bowen.

I do not regret my outburst. Certainly the reputation of this place must be good for something. It is time it proves its healing claims.

Cassandra returns to us. "One of us must be with him at all times," she says.

"All of us," I say.

Mother nods and dabs at her eyes. "Yes, yes. We must all be there with him. And we must pray. Pray without ceasing."

That we can do.

This morning Mr. Bowen has brought with him Dr. Gibbs. They have asked that we leave the room.

Cassandra and I stand in the hallway, supporting our mother. She has a handkerchief clutched in her hand, much used during the difficult night, where sleep was fitful and worries large.

"What will we do?" Mother asks. It is a question we all ask, if not aloud, within ourselves.

"He has come round before," Cassandra says. "Perhaps—"

"No," Mother says. "Not this time. I feel it."

Even as I am about to say, *Do not say such a thing,* the door opens and Bowen and Dr. Gibbs come out. They close the door behind them. Bowen only glances at us, his eyes finding the floor as quickly as possible.

And I know.

"How is he?" Mother asks, but surely she also knows.

Dr. Gibbs takes her hands in his. "Only a miracle, Mrs. Austen."

She looks to Mr. Bowen, who has seen Father the most often. "William?"

He is forced to look up, to meet her eyes. His are full of frustration and apology. "I am so sorry. It is a lost cause."

Although I expect Mother to wail, screaming "No!" into the rafters, she does not. She only nods once, her eyes ahead, unseeing, as if, for this one moment she is alone, accepting the fate that is being played out before her.

She turns towards the door. "I must go to him."

Cassandra and I begin to follow, but Bowen gently holds us back with a touch to our arms. "Give them a moment."

"But only a moment," Dr. Gibbs says.

"We will be downstairs," Bowen says, and the men retire.

My head begins to shake no, no, no, no, no.

"Jane, are you all right?"

No, no, no, no, no.

"We have been prepared. He has not been well for months."

My head continues of its own accord. "There is no real preparation."

She slips her hand through mine and we wait for our turn to say good-bye.

"I am not sure I can do it," I say.

"You must," Cassandra tells me. "If not for his sake, to prevent regret."

I know she is right, yet I have never been at a deathbed. Although James lost a wife, Eliza a son, and my dear Anne was lost to me, I have never been *there*, to see, to witness the transition from this life to the next.

Heaven. Father will soon be in heaven with God, the Christ, angels, and all those who have gone before him. I will see him there one day. Yet such comfort is fleeting. I want him here, now, for many, many more days and years.

The door opens. "Come in, girls," Mother says. Her face is red, her cheeks damp, but there is a strength of her chin that reveals her determination to get through this whole.

Hearing the commotion, Bowen and Dr. Gibbs hurry up the stairs and follow us inside. We go to our father's bed, one on either side. He is not awake and breathes heavily.

I take his hand. It has no strength. "Can he hear?"

"Only God knows," Mother says, "though it is well if you speak to him as if he can."

Cassandra leans near him, speaking close to his ear. I cannot hear what she says, and have no need to hear. I will have my own chance to say what must be said.

And yet, as she kisses his cheek and rises, giving me my turn, I find words elusive. Me, who holds words as my dearest friends. Yet what does one say to the rock of my life, the one stable constant no matter where we have lived? Father is my encourager, my champion, my guardian. He epitomizes all things Austen. Without him, who am I? Who are any of us?

"Jane . . ."

I know. I must do it now or relinquish the chance. I sit on the edge of the bed and pull his hand to my breast. "I love you, Father." I feel the slightest movement in his fingers, as if he has heard. I squeeze his hand, acknowledging. I search his face for a smile, an opening of the eyes, e'en an attempt to open his eyes. . . .

But it is not to be.

Father takes a sudden intake of breath, lets it out, but does not return it with another.

Breathe, Father! Breathe!

Mother rushes close. "George? George?" She jostles him as if he is in deep sleep. "George! Wake up!"

Dr. Gibbs slides beside me, takes Father's hand, and feels his wrist. He puts his ear to Father's chest. Then he stands and says the words we despise: "He is gone."

Inadvertently, we take a step back, as though giving him room. Giving his soul room to rise to heaven?

I look above Father's head, wondering if something transpires that I cannot see.

Mother speaks first, directing her question to Dr. Gibbs. "He did not suffer, did he?"

"He did not. Being quite insensible of his own state, he was spared all the pain of separation. I would say he went off almost in his sleep."

"It is twenty past ten," Cassandra says.

"Midmorning," Mother says. "He always liked midmorning."

I am not sure how valid this observation is but realize the moment of death is probably not a time where thoughts observed contain sense. One must say something and so . . . so it is.

But if one must say something, why have I said nothing?

After having such a revelation, I say, "I must write to the brothers."

I kiss Father's forehead, take a final look, then leave to attend to my task. Run to attend to my task. For I do not wish to be in attendance when . . . whatever happens next, happens. Death is already present in this house. I do not need to see it linger.

Am I a coward?

Absolutely.

❦ ❧

Henry is here. And James. And the other brothers have been notified of our loss—their loss. The service at Walcott Church is simple and to the point. Father would have found it quite acceptable. Even as a rector he was not one to go on and on as others I have heard. More words do not necessarily mean the best words.

He is gone from us, but it is not the end of life. He is without strife. He is happy. *And God shall wipe away all tears from their eyes; and there shall be no more death, neither sorrow, nor crying, neither shall there be any more pain: for the former things are passed away.*

I shall try to be happy also. Not happy that he is dead, but happy for . . .

It will take time.

❦ ❧

"So how much do I have to live upon?" Mother asks.

We, Mother, we. For there are also Cassandra and I who must survive.

James sits back from the table scattered with papers containing financial facts and figures. "With Father gone, his clerical stipend ends and you are left with but two hundred ten pounds."

"But your father said we have investments," Mother says.

James ruffles through the papers and pulls out one. "Which in a good year could bring another one hundred twenty per annum."

"I say we need a few more zeroes at the end of those numbers!" Henry says.

"Care to make that happen?" James asks.

Henry reddens, but says, "Presently my income from the bank is a bit tenuous, but I could offer fifty a year."

"As will I," James says.

I wonder if James has cleared his offering with his wife, Mary. If not, surely she will have plenty to say about it, none of it charitable.

"And Frank has offered one hundred," Henry says. He covers his mouth with a hand. "He wished for it to be a secret."

Mother shakes her head. "Secret or not, I will not accept it. It is far too much considering he is now engaged to a Ramsgate girl with no means of her own."

The "Ramsgate girl" has a name: Mary Gibson. Although we have not met her, we find her haltingly acceptable. She is only nineteen to Frank's thirty, and comes from no wealth whatsoever.

"Let him give what he has promised, Mother," Henry says. "For he is now appointed Flag Captain of the *Canopus*. It is a captured French ship that Frank is going to use to chase other French ships. He *has* the money, Mother. Or will have."

She shook her head. "He needs the income for his own family—such as it is. I will only accept fifty from him. I will not be the source of hardship for any son."

What about daughters?

Although I am more than willing to take Frank's hundred for the sake of our cause, I know the look on Mother's face. She is intractable. At least in this.

"Edward is good for a hundred," Henry says. He lifts his glass. "*Vive* Edward!"

"Do you really think we can speak for him?" Cassandra says.

"I was just there. I am sure of it," Henry says. "Godmersham brings in that amount with nary a labor done."

We have not heard from the youngest, Charles, off at sea watching the Atlantic for American ships wanting to trade with France.

He is just starting out in his career and cannot be expected to donate any excess.

"But I can help," Cassandra says.

"How so?" James asks.

"I have the interest from what my Tom left to me," she offers.

Henry claps. "Excellent! How much is that?"

"Fifty per annum. Give or take."

James does the figures. "That equals around . . . four hundred fifty pounds a year."

"Bravo!" Henry says. "Certainly enough for three women to keep a house."

"Not well," Cassandra says.

"Well enough," Mother says. She looks round the table, skimming over me. "Thank you, dear children, for coming to my aid at such a difficult time."

The meeting disperses, save for me.

No one comes back to the room to say, "Jane? Are you coming?" No one notices that I did not say a word during the discussion of a future that includes me. Just as no one asked, "Jane, what do you think of this?" Or even, "Jane, what can you give to the pot?"

Of course my answer would have been "Not much" and "Nothing." For I have nothing to give. Our family is crippled without Father. And I am the offending appendage, hanging limp and without use. A burden. Something to be cut off and tossed away.

I am nothing but air and matter.

And matter, I do not.

Although our income is workable, it is not enough to stay on in the Green Buildings. We must move to furnished lodgings at No. 25 Gay Street. It being wartime, and this being Bath, prices are high. Ever a frugal family, we now face a different layer of frugality.

Mother has let the servants go.

Now it truly is just us three.

Three women, left to fend for ourselves. Living on the charity of others.

Mother has large plans to spend the summer months visiting relatives, sponging off their kindness, and I accept that plan as essential and preferable to staying here, in these rooms that offer no inspiration beyond my aspiring to be away from them. The stone façade and stately pediment above the door belie the less than stately rooms inside.

No inspiration to write, that is a certainty. But I determine to try again, for it is the one thing that has any chance of earning an income.

I pull out the manuscript about the Watson family, intent on continuing the story. I sit at my desk and try to take my thoughts to that place rather than this.

I had left off with my heroine, Emma, who is visiting her family's meager home after growing up in riches elsewhere, deciding that sitting at the bedside of her dear father is preferable to other company. For all he requires is gentleness and silence.

I close my eyes a moment, attempting to find the image of Emma and her father that I had last left in my mind. Ah . . . there it is. I begin to write:

In his chamber Emma was at peace from the dreadful mortifi-cations of unequal society and family discord; from the immediate endurance of hard-hearted prosperity, low-minded conceit, and wrong-headed folly, engrafted on an untowards disposition. She still suffered from them in the contemplation of their existence, in mem-ory and in prospect; but for the moment, she ceased to be tortured by their effects. She was at leisure; she could read and think, though her situation was hardly such as to make reflection very soothing. The evils arising from the loss of her uncle were neither trifling nor likely to lessen; and when thought had been freely indulged, in contrasting the past and the present, the employment of mind and dissipation of

unpleasant ideas which only reading could produce made her thank-
fully turn to a book.

The change in her home, society, and style of life, in consequence
of the death of one friend and the imprudence of another, had indeed
been striking. From being the first object of hope and solicitude to an
uncle who had formed her mind with the care of a parent, and of
tenderness to an aunt whose amiable temper had delighted to give
her every indulgence; from being the life and spirit of a house where
all had been comfort and elegance, and the expected heiress of an easy
independence, she was become of importance to no one—a burden on
those whose affections she could not expect, an addition in a house
already overstocked, surrounded by inferior minds, with little chance
of domestic comfort, and as little hope of future support. It was well
for her that she was naturally cheerful, for the change had been such
as might have plunged weak spirits in despondence.

I lift my pen, finding myself troubled by these words, yet not quite knowing why. I continue with a few lines more, then stop suddenly.

It is not right. The words I write today, the words I have written on previous days, are full of dark foreboding and bitterness. Emma is always right and is quick to find fault in all others. But where it could be presented otherwise, there is no light or comedy in her world. She despairs of her situation as a visitor in her family's home, being welcomed but ungrateful. She is destined to become a victim. Her fear of what will happen when her father dies, her fear of being penniless, is . . . is . . .

My fear. And too closely, my reality.

I, Jane Austen, who grew up living with enough, have now dipped below that measure.

I am living what Emma fears! I am . . . I read the last lines again: . . . *important to no one—a burden on those whose affections she could not expect, an addition in a house already overstocked, surrounded by inferior minds, with little chance of domestic comfort, and as little*

*hope of future support. It was well for her that she was naturally cheer-
ful, for the change had been such as might have plunged weak spirits in
despondence.*

At this moment I acknowledge a new truth. I cannot continue
with this book. To do so would be to indulge in a darkness I dare
not contemplate or even acknowledge. The emotions are too
unpleasant to visit.

I put my pen down. I slip the page which I have just written to
the bottom of the stack. I stare at the multitude of pages, contemplating what I must do.

I must . . .

I must let it go. I cannot write this book, this book about a
father's death and the dire consequences to his daughters. I cannot
write the scene where he takes his last breath. I cannot write about
the grief of their present and fear for their future.

I take up the pages and put them in the trunk with my old
manuscripts. Yet I know this one will not be removed to be revised
and pampered into a better result. This one will remain here forever.
Unfinished. A thing to be escaped *from.* For I cannot visit it again.
I cannot go to its place and speak for its characters or feel what they
feel.

I close the trunk and lock it. I stand back, my heart pounding.

Start something else, my mind tells me.

But I sense such a thing is not possible. I can do but one thing
here, in this place, in this time of my life. I can either live or write.

I cannot do both.

FIFTEEN

Cassandra has not been well since Father's death. Although we discuss it privately, neither one of us knows if it is due to a physical ailment or grief, for we *do* know it is possible to make oneself sick.

Whichever the cause, she has gone off to Ibthorpe to visit Martha and her mother, hoping the change of scene will help. I write gay and witty letters, trying to cheer them and feel a part of their camaraderie. And yet, last night I received word that Mrs. Lloyd is gravely ill. Moving from one bastion of grief to another was not Cassandra's intention. Sometimes I do not like growing old, for age brings with it the irrefutable and unstoppable fact of others growing even older. And becoming ill. And passing on. Although we all know death does *not* discriminate by age. . . .

I continue the letter I write to my sister:

> *I received your letter last night, and wish it may be soon followed by another to say that all is over; but I cannot help thinking that nature will struggle again and produce a revival. Poor woman! May her end be peaceful and easy, as the exit we have witnessed! And I daresay it will. If there is no revival, suffering must be all over; even the consciousness of existence I suppose was gone when you wrote. The nonsense I have been writing in this and in my last letter seems out of place at such a time; but I will not mind it, it will do you no harm, and nobody else will be attacked by it. I am heartily glad that you can speak so comfortably of your own health and looks, tho' I can scarcely comprehend the latter being really approved. Could traveling fifty miles produce such an immediate change? You were looking so very poorly here; everybody seem'd sensible of it. Is there a charm in a hack post chaise? I assure you, you were looking very ill indeed, and I do not believe much of your being well already. People think you in a very bad way, I suppose, and*

pay you compliments to keep up your spirits. At any rate, as a com-
panion you will be all that Martha can be supposed to want. And
in that light, under those circumstances, your visit will indeed have
been well-timed, and your presence and support have the utmost
value.

I look up from the page, finding it exhausting to act merry and
sarcastic when one feels frightfully neutral. I try to think of some
question I can ask that has nothing to do with death and sickness.
I am only partially successful:

You told me some time ago that Tom Chute had had a fall from his
horse, but I am waiting to know how it happened before I begin
pitying him, as I cannot help suspecting it was in consequence of his
taking orders as he was going to do duty or was returning from it.

I have little compassion for men who avoid their duty. It is
nearly a year since that lout Napoleon declared France an empire,
and three months since he declared himself Emperor. The audacity
of that little man, making up for his lack of stature with grand aspirations. He needs to be dealt with. Completely. I am ever so proud
of Frank and Charles and the supremacy of our Royal Navy in protecting us from Napoleon's acts of bravado and greed.

Which reminds me, I must write them next, to encourage them
in their work for our empire.

God save the King!

And my brothers.

And dearest sister.

※

On April 16, 1805, Martha's mother passed on. It was not unexpected, yet somehow death still elicits a blow. I am glad Cassandra
is there to comfort and assist.

The good coming from the bad (for I do look for such things) is that Martha is now free to move to Bath. She is a dear sister, in my heart if not in blood, and I look forward to having her here. It has long been my wish. That the benefit comes later than I had originally hoped is accepted with open arms. Although it will take Martha a few months to address the move, our attention is diverted towards this happy occasion.

It is now June, Cassandra has returned to us, and we are all on our way to Godmersham for a visit with Edward and family. We stop at Steventon and gather our niece Anna, since Mary has just given birth to her second child, Caroline. Unlike our own parents, who sent us out as babies to be weaned and attended, Mary is a different sort of mother and nurses her own children with great fervor. To see her cuddle and coo the baby against her breast . . .

I have been told that after I was christened at the age of fourteen weeks, I was sent away until I was nearly two and more manageable. All of my siblings were done so as well. Of course, I do not remember this, and yet . . . I have often wondered if I would have become a different sort if I had owned a mother who doted and coddled me. Cuddled me. Cooed to me. Would Mother and I be closer now? Or would I have become too dependent on love instead of feeling the need to guard myself from its very existence? It is not that I do not need love. I do. But I am wary of it. Once given, will it be accepted? Or will it be removed? Of course, I have always had Cassandra to love me. As a sister *and* a mother.

Perhaps such a different upbringing would have been for the better, perhaps for the worse. Our dear Eliza and *her* mother were as close as bosom friends. So who fared best? Who became the better adult? It is an unanswerable question owning too many unequal variables. Life is what it is.

I sound like Father.

This Austen pragmatism *was* learned through being brought up the way I was brought up.

So . . . it is not all bad.

With my own brothers dispersed, and our household down to just the three of us, the chaos and merriment we find at Godmersham is an elixir to frazzled nerves and frayed emotions. My sister-in-law Elizabeth comes from a large clan of ten brothers and sisters, many of whom live nearby in Goodnestone with their widowed mother, Mrs. Bridges. Edward and Elizabeth already have nine children of their own.

Although I am of the sort who embraces silence and solitude, on this visit I embrace every trampling footfall and every joyous peal of laughter. In the evenings we often take a quiet walk round the estate, with little George and Henry to animate us with their races and merriment. We are also putting on a play called *The Spoiled Child*, which is a monstrous hit in London. Whether it be a hit in Godmersham will be determined by our greater—and lesser—talents.

Although I enjoy these happy moments with the children, I am more than willing to let Elizabeth, Cassandra, and the governess, Anne Sharp, take care of their cries, both plaintive and pouty.

Speaking of Anne Sharp ... I can say that a highlight to my stay is our new acquaintance. I find her bright, well-read, and able to converse rather than chatter. I seek her out whenever I can—as I do now.

I climb the back stairs to the children's nursery with a book for Anne. Fanny, age twelve, grabs my free hand, pulling me into the room.

"Auntie's come to play!" Fanny says.

Ten-year-old George (always my favourite, my "itty Dordie") runs forward to touch me. "Tag!" he says. "You're it!"

I make after him, dodging Henry and William, aged eight and seven, sidestep little Lizzy, five, and Marianne, four, and end up being assaulted by two-year-old Charles, who runs into my legs with arms wide.

"Oomph!" I say, picking him up.

Louisa, just one, crawls across the carpet at record speed. I extend hugs and kisses all round and receive many more in return. Only little Edward, age eleven, is absent, as he does not feel well. His papa and mama have determined to consult Dr. Wilmot. Unless he recovers his strength beyond what is now probable, his brothers will return to boarding school without him.

Although my sister, Cassandra, is the true nurturer between us two, I am the one my nieces and nephews seek to play games, or rough and tumble. Yesterday (though starting out a very quiet day with my noisiest efforts being writing a letter to Frank), William changed all that as he and I played at Battledore and Shuttlecock. We have practiced together two mornings in total and have improved a little; we frequently keep it up three times, and once or twice, six.

"Welcome, Jane," Anne says (for we are on a first-name basis, at least in private).

"I do not mean to interrupt," I say, making Fanny twirl beneath my arm again and again.

Fanny lets go and bobbles in her walk. "I am dizzy!"

"Me! Me!" William says.

Marianne jumps up and down. "Me! Me!"

Louisa cries because Marianne has jumped on her hand. Anne goes to the rescue, kissing tiny fingers, making them well. "There, there," she says. "Let us go find your blocks."

Suitably distracted from the crisis, Louisa is set down and begins to play. And, as it is a rule that what one sibling has, the others want, Henry and William join her to shew the proper way to build a tower.

Three down . . .

Fanny takes my hand again, wanting more twirls, but Anne saves me by sending her off to ask a servant to bring us some tea.

We sit in the window seat that overlooks the grounds. Unwittingly, we both sigh at the same time—and laugh at the happenstance.

"Well," Anne says.

"Well," I say. I bring the book front and center. "I found a book in the library I thought you would enjoy. *Gisborne*. Cassandra recommended it, and having begun, I am pleased with it—and I had quite determined not to read it."

Anne accepts the book but does not open it. "I would rather read your stories, Jane."

"I wish Cassandra would stop telling you about them."

"As do I," Anne says. "I would rather you do the telling. And let me read—"

I shake my head vehemently. "No one reads my stories."

"But Cassandra said you used to read them aloud at Steventon."

"Godmersham is not Steventon. Here the audience is . . . more discerning. Besides, Steventon was a lifetime ago."

"But I, who discern much . . . do you not have them with you?"

"I always have them with me. I could no more leave them behind than a mother could leave her children."

Anne cocks her head and smiles. "So . . . ?"

Although I know Anne will be forthright and honest, I cannot let her read my work—perhaps because she is so forthright and honest. "I make you this promise," I say. "Perhaps someday. *If* one of my stories gets published—"

"When."

Her support touches me. "When. I shall send you a copy of your very own."

"Signed by the author, I hope?"

"Of course," I say. " 'Twill make it worth a penny more."

As we laugh, Elizabeth enters the room. Anne stands. I do not. Elizabeth's eyebrows rise. "Jane."

"Good afternoon, Elizabeth."

I can tell that the next question she begs to ask is, *What are you doing here?* but to her credit, she does not voice the words.

Instead, she says, "Mrs. Austen would like to see the children after tea. Would you make them ready?"

"Of course," Anne says. "Right away."

Elizabeth turns to leave but hesitates in the doorway. "Jane? Are you coming for tea?"

"We have sent Fanny to bring us some here," I say.

She blinks, nods, then leaves us.

Anne slowly returns to the window seat. "Jane . . . please do not feel you need to stay when you have been summoned—"

I put a hand on her arm. "I do not stay because I need to, but because I want to."

"But Mistress Elizabeth . . . I know she does not approve of your befriending me, a mere servant."

"You are not a mere anything, Anne. And I will befriend whom I please—to be pleased." I look towards the door and, in spite of my bravado, feel a stitch in my stomach, but I offer a smile. "By her reaction you would think I was nurturing our friendship on purpose."

"I do not wish for there to be friction on my account."

"Not on your account. If any friction is to be had, it will be on mine." I look out the window at my brother's vast estate and long for the more intimate garden at Steventon. The more intimate house. "You are the only friend I have entirely to myself, Anne. I will not discard such a blessing to earn points with anyone."

Fanny defers any argument by coming in the nursery, followed by a servant with a tea tray.

"Ah," I say. "Tea is served."

❦

Elizabeth comes into the library (where I have found a slice of solitude) and says, "My mother would like you and Cassandra to come visit her at Goodnestone, by turns."

There is an essence of peeved in her voice, or surprise at the invitation. "That sounds lovely," I say. "And very kind of her."

Elizabeth shrugs, then turns to leave. "She asks that Cassandra go first. Richard will take her tomorrow morning, when she is ready."

"She will be very happy to go, as will I when my turn arises." I realize this has a second meaning that is not kind. Truly, I do not mean it to be so. But before I can think of a way to offset the implication, Elizabeth continues.

"Fanny and Anne are off to read romance stories in the garden. They are bringing with them a gypsy basket of bread and cheese and wonder if you would join them."

I stand and set my book aside. "That sounds delightful."

Upon her exit, I again feel the essence of Elizabeth's feelings for me—or against me. I do not know why I do not get along well with two of my sisters-in-law, Mary and Elizabeth, yet am quick to make excuses for them: they are set in their ways and do not appreciate my independent nature. And I am set in my independence and find their choices to accept the inevitable limitations of society—the pressure to marry for money and produce a constant stream of children—an act of surrender. Not that I am always strong within myself. But I strive to *be*. Do they?

Elizabeth is also determined to make sure I know my standing as compared to hers. For instance, a Mr. Hall walked off this morning with no inconsiderable booty. He charges Elizabeth five shillings for every time he dresses her hair, and five shillings for every lesson to her lady's maid, Mrs. Sace. In my eyes it is far too much, for he allows nothing for the pleasures of his visit here, for meat, drink, and lodging, the benefit of country air, and the charms of the housekeeper, Mrs. Salkeld. And Mrs. Sace's society. Yet towards me he was considerate, charging only two and six for cutting my hair. He either respects my youth or my poverty. Yet how did he know what I could afford? I am but certain Elizabeth informed him of my lower, lowly status.

How kind of her. If only I could return a like favour.

It is my turn to accept Mrs. Bridges's hospitality. Acquaintances warned that I would find Goodnestone dull. I wish when I had heard them say as much, they could have heard the son's—Mr. Edward Bridges's—solicitude and could have known all the amusements that were planned to prevent any hint of dullness.

On the first night of my visit, Edward, who was not expected to be at home, dined with us. He had been, strange to tell, too late for that day's cricket match, too late at least to play himself, and, not being asked to dine with the players, had come home. It is impossible to do justice to the hospitality of his attentions towards me; he made a point of ordering toasted cheese for supper entirely on my account.

The Bridges sisters—Harriot, Sophie, and Marianne—are quite delightful. Actually, the first two own that trait, while Marianne lies sick. During my visit, there is some drama about a ball in Deal, and how the girls will get there, and who was asked first, and by whom, and on and on. . . . I feel in the way—for I have not been invited. They are all very kind and assure me I am most welcome, but I have sent word for my brother to fetch me early next week. My clothes will run out by then, so it is as good a time as any to make my exit.

Edward Bridges comes and goes. He dined at home yesterday; the day before he was at St. Albans; today he goes to Broome, and tomorrow to Mr. Hallett's. He is a delightful young man who continues to be very kind—and handsome.

I see him now, coming down the front stairs, ready for Broome. He, in turn, sees me and smiles.

"Miss Jane, how nice—but surprising—to see you up so early this morning. It is not e'en breakfast yet."

"I arose on account of the sun streaming in the windows of my fine room. It was not my choice to rise between six and seven. Yet I used the time well. I have written to my sister."

He raises a finger and goes to a drawer in one of the entry tables. "Knowing you are such an avid writer, I bought you a gift." He pulls out some fine writing paper tied with a blue ribbon.

"You are too kind, Edward. My visit here has been filled with your kind attentiveness. You make a girl want to seek you out just to see what other kindness you have in store."

Suddenly, Edward takes hold of my free hand. "I enjoy providing for your every need, Miss Jane. And I believe I would enjoy doing so on a permanent basis."

I can only blink at him.

"Would you consider marrying me?"

I pull my hand away and laugh, then cover the offending sound with a hand. "I am sorry, I did not mean—"

He nods. "I know my proposal is surprising. I did not expect it myself when I came downstairs this morning. But to see you here . . ."

"My vision of loveliness caused all rational thought to be abandoned?"

He reddens. "Perhaps it was a bit hasty."

"Perhaps." I touch his hand, but only for a moment. "But very flattering nonetheless."

He finds his own laugh. "What *would* Mother have said if we had gone to awaken her with the news?"

"She would have just as soon gone back to sleep, assuming it was merely a dream."

He takes my hand once more, his face sincere. "She would not object, you know."

"So she is hoping you will marry a penniless girl?"

"Your character is priceless."

I offer him a curtsy. "Now, Edward. Off with you to Broome. I will see you when you return and perhaps we will play some Sackree. Although I cannot afford to lose more than ten shillings on the game, I would just as soon lose to you as anyone else."

He bows, takes his hat and riding crop, and is gone.

I stand in the foyer alone, quite glad there is no one else yet awake to witness this latest happenstance. I should have said yes to Edward, quite before he could find his reason, and become a legal part of this fine family.

But once again marriage and I have narrowly slid past each other, like two dancers, barely touching in the pass, ending on opposite sides of the line.

Why does it seem inevitable?

I stand before the armoire in my room, about to chuse a dress for the day. My green flowered perhaps? But with hand poised to pull it from its peg, I remember the news of yesterday: Prince William Henry, the Duke of Gloucester, has died. As the brother of King George III, and far from the line of succession, his passing is not cause for elaborate nationwide mourning. Yet respect must be shewn. Must we buy black lace, or will ribbon do?

My next thoughts are cold, and yet . . . his death does not move me, though it *will* cause the hearts of dozens to ache. The Bridges girls are not among that number, however, as they are very well pleased to be spared the trouble of preparation this ball has caused. For with a national mourning there can be no large balls, at least not for a time, so their previous perplexity as to the logistics is now moot. And I too can relax, knowing that I am not in the way of their plans.

I heard that the Duke's third child has taken over his title. Two older sisters, passed over. The only boy gets the lot of it.

And the girls get nothing.

But by marriage.

Such it is, and there is not a thing any of us can do to change it. Royalty or peasant or somewhere in between.

And yet . . . knowing that doing well for myself is invariably attached to finding a husband . . .

I think of Edward Bridges. I think of Harris. Two proposals refused. That some women long for one proposal, while I have declined two—to fine men with much to commend them. Declined for different reasons. It is as though two different Janes experienced the same event. But is that not appropriate? I am not the same now with Edward as I was then, with Harris. The past years are enough to change every pore of my skin, and every feeling of my mind. Which makes me wonder: What Jane will I be years from now?

And will I be married or still a spinster?

Yet here exists the larger question: Do I have a right to continue to refuse offers of marriage that would pull me (and my mother and sister) from the poverty of our current situation and place us within a condition of financial ease? Society would be appeased if I allowed myself this decision, for *it* has made the rules which hang above every opportunity. *It* imposes the penalty for not adhering to its wishes.

Guilt. How odd to suffer more guilt for this man-made wrongdoing against society than any guilt I suffer for wrongdoing against the Almighty. Guilt for wrongs against the Lord stem from an inner knowing of right and wrong added to the biblical guidance of a lifetime. The rules of our faith are wise and when followed allow all to benefit. When I break these rules, I feel guilt because I *know* I have done wrong. I acknowledge it and am forgiven. Then I try to do better.

But guilt for wrongdoing against society does not stem from any inner knowing. These rules that are forced upon us make little sense. So why should we feel guilty for ignoring them?

Perhaps it is not guilt at all, but something darker. Perhaps what we feel is fear. God offers grace and forgiveness for a contrite heart. But society offers cruel consequences and never forgives.

Or forgets. Once crossed, there is no second chance to do better. Society remembers each sin and gleefully catalogues it, holding the new offense against us. If it could pin a sign upon us, to eternally declare our sin to the world, I believe it would. The depth and breadth of this injustice is appalling, unwavering, and unavoidable.

Does society have the right to impose this marital path which may bring unhappiness, e'en as it carries with it freedom from financial worries? Must a woman chuse her own counsel and poverty, or society's counsel and means? Must stability and peace of mind be attained only by surrender to self?

I hope not, but fear it is so.

Until such time as I find true answers . . . unable to change society I will attempt to change myself.

Right now I seek a dress. I pull the green one from its peg. Black or no black, mourning or no mourning, in these things I will let others tell me what is proper.

As for the rest?

God help me. God help us all.

HUMBLE HOPE

SIXTEEN

I sit in Manydown, happy.

Hmm. I need to adjust my words.

Happily, I sit in Manydown?

I laugh at my private attempts to edit, as well as my concern. For it does not matter how it is said; it matters only that there be truth within the words.

"You laugh."

Cassandra gets dressed behind me. I simplify the cause for my laughter by saying, "I am happy." I turn from the chair by the window to face her. "We have had a delightful visit here at Manydown."

"We have."

"I am so grateful the Biggs have forgiven the humiliation of my engagement to Harris."

"Long ago, Jane. It has been nearly four years. And Harris is married elsewhere."

"I do wish him happiness."

"A commendable wish." She comes to me and shews me her back. I button her buttons. With no forethought, I whisper in her ear, "I do not want to go back."

Her dress secured, she faces me. "We cannot be gone from Bath forever, Jane. Ibthorpe, Godmersham, Goodnestone, a holiday with Edward in Worthing, then Steventon with James, and now Manydown ... we have imposed on the hospitality of others long enough."

I know she is right. It is March. We have been gone since the previous June! Though nothing is ever directly stated between Mother, Cassandra, and me, none of us has spoken of our return home. Do we withhold all mention of it, for fear of breaking the spell of our jolly visits?

As Cassandra adjusts the sleeve of my dress, I state aloud what might not be pleasant to hear. "I had hoped one of our brothers would offer . . ."

She drops her hand and levels me with a look. "So you want more? Is the hospitality and generosity of our family and friends not enough?"

I am ashamed. "I appreciate all that has been done. It's just that . . . I know our time here is drawing to an end."

"As must all things."

I realize my happiness has dissipated, abandoning me to this other emotion. How dare happiness leave me so discourteously!

If I could catch it and hold it captive, I would.

Cassandra is at the door of our bedroom. "Are you coming? Are you ready to enjoy *this* day?"

I will try.

❦

We are home in Bath.

We must move.

Again.

What little we have at Gay Street must be trimmed e'en more to move to Trim Street. What an apt name. Years ago, when we first moved to this city, we had distinctly and determinedly avoided this neighbourhood, assuming Cassandra would express a fearful presentiment about moving here. We successfully avoided it then, but now . . .

Our situation is untenable, our choices few.

I sit in our Gay Street residence, at the table we eat upon, and wrap the few dishes Mother will let us move. *"It is not as though we are going to have any grand dinners, Jane."*

Not as though we could, for we do not rent a house now, but only a few rooms within someone else's abode. When James found out, he had the audacity to say, "But what space do three women really need?"

I suppose a closet would suffice, though from what I have seen of our lodging at Trim Street, the exaggeration is not great.

To myself I complain aloud, making the walls aware of my displeasure. "The move to Bath was for nothing. We are nothing. We have nothing. These narrow circumstances are—"

Suddenly, Mother appears in the doorway. Her chin is set and her voice quivers as she says, "It has not been for nothing, Jane. Your father and I had three years here in Bath, three years to enjoy each other and have time for ourselves. That was worth everything to me. That was worth even these narrow circumstances."

I put down the dish I am wrapping and go to her. "I am so sorry, Mother. I am selfish."

She does not argue with me.

I walk the rooms of Trim Street, wrapping a shawl tighter against the chill of this new residence. The tour does not take long. Four rooms. A parlour with a small table to dine upon in the corner, a kitchen, and two bedrooms. I would venture outside to escape these inner spaces, yet the neighbourhood has little to commend. There is no garden. No open space to allow my thoughts room. I am trapped. The notion to curl into a ball and draw my shawl o'er my head offers itself for my consideration.

It is an option.

Mother comes from the kitchen after making herself a cup of tea. "What are you doing, Jane? You appear lost."

It is an apt term, yet a condition that will not benefit further exposure. Mother cannot improve our situation. She is doing her best. She and Cassandra also suffer. The diminishment of our station is a shared falling from society's grace. Although Uncle Perrot and Aunt have been kind and most solicitous, they can only do so much. And truth be told, we are not their responsibility. Society has a secret: the fate of widows and spinsters falls behind its screen; there, but unseen. And as we huddle in this frightening place, society's largest hope is that we will remain hidden so they need not deal with us. We are a pesky fly that spoils the tranquil air of their existence. They would just as soon swat us as open a door and set us free.

Mother sits in her favorite chair, which *did* accomplish the move from Gay Street. "You do not answer me, Jane."

I must say something. "Perhaps I am a bit lost. I do not adapt to change easily."

"So I have seen. You must learn to adapt, Jane. Especially now, when change has become our roommate." She sips her tea. "I do my best to use our income wisely. Yet even with your brothers' help, we must be careful with each farthing."

"I know." I know.

"Speaking of farthings . . . perhaps you should take up the pen, Jane. You sold one story. . . ."

"It has not been published, and it has been nearly three years."

Mother purses her lips and sighs. "At least you received pay for it."

At least. But the least is not enough. My pride wishes for a book in my hand. For certainly with that book, other publishers would take note of my work. I would have a publishing history. As of now, I have nothing.

Although not privy to my thoughts, Mother disputes them. "You *do* have a trunk full of manuscripts that you insist on taking with us anywhere we go. They have become an additional traveler."

"I dare not leave them behind." I remember the time when they had been left in the coach and nearly ended up in the West Indies. Since that time, my work has never left my presence.

"Why *don't* you write now, Jane?" Mother asks. "It might make you feel better."

I shrug and say, "We shall see," but I know I cannot write here, cannot write feeling as I do now.

For it is not possible to enter the lives of my characters and fix their problems and crises when I cannot even fix my own.

❦ ❦

Summer has come, and Frank will wed Mary Gibson. Although tentative in our approval because of her youth and family standing, we now accept her. If Frank is happy . . .

He deserves happiness. And pride. Just last October, the naval superiority of the British navy was established at the Battle of Trafalgar. Frank carried Lord Nelson's second-in-command aboard his ship, the *Canopus*, but alas, was at Gibraltar getting provisions when the battle occurred. Frank mourns he was not present when our fleet of twenty-seven ships encountered thirty-three Spanish and French ships. Our enemies lost twenty-two vessels. We lost none.

But we did lose Lord Nelson. He died late in the battle, assuring his hero status. He has become a demigod. And though I take nothing away from his character, I am not alone in growing weary of the mania which has swept the nation these past months. Everything is "Trafalgar." It seems no polite gathering can avoid a replaying of the battle, with even women knowing details usually kept from their more delicate sensibilities. There is even a "Trafalgar stitch." And according to this public aggrandizement, Lord Nelson saved us from Napoleon's invasion, while in truth, Napoleon had backed away from such an idea months before. I find it interesting that human nature is so well disposed towards those who are in interesting situations that e'en a person who either marries or dies is sure of being spoken of kindly. The entire thing is quite the phenomenon and, though enjoyed at first, becomes tedious.

Victories notwithstanding, the war is not over, and I fear it will never be. Seventeen years and counting, it alters direction upon

Napoleon's whim. We have won the sea, but now he bothers Europe inland. How can one man impose so much turmoil upon so many nations? Once we are rid of him, I pray history never repeats itself.

In this lull before what will surely be another Napoleonic storm, Frank marries. Huzzah! Huzzah! And one more huzzah!

Indeed, my dear brother is the most courageous man I know— e'en beyond his naval career. For in the wake of his marriage he has brought forth the most splendid prospect. He has asked Mother, Cassandra, me, and even Martha Lloyd to come join him and his new bride in renting a house in Southampton! Situated there, he will await new orders and will be close to the port of Portsmouth. If any man claim bravery, I dare it to be lifted beside my brother's bravery at volunteering to share a house with five women.

The fact that Mother has agreed so easily to take leave of Bath surprises me, but when I inquire after her reasons, she only says, "It is time."

Beyond time.

On October 10, 1806, we move into lodgings with Frank and his young bride, Mary Gibson—temporarily, while we search for a house to lease. Mary, married but three months, is already pregnant. Alas, my brothers are certainly doing their part in bringing new Austen children into the world. November brings Edward and Elizabeth's tenth child. Her name is to be Cassandra Jane. In this—as in all things—I am quite willing to let my own dear sister take first billing. Soon after our move, Cassandra leaves us to visit Godmersham for Christmas, to offer aid as only she can. As she leaves I wish to call her back. *You cannot go! Not when we have just found a good place to be.*

For Southampton is a good place, and I am happy. Happiness is such a flighty occasion that one cannot always discern its requirements, nor its measure. For here we are in a cramped lodging that is no better than what we had left on Trim Street, and yet, here I am happy. Here I feel release and hope, like an escaped prisoner breathing deeply of fresh air after a long confinement.

I am content and merely wish for everyone to stay in place so we can enjoy it. But alas, it is not to be. Cassandra's defection to Edward's is followed by Martha's visit to the Fowles' through the holidays and into February. I am left with Mother and her string of illnesses, perceived and real, and my new sister-in-law, little Mary Gibson. Mary suffers fainting fits that I notice usually occur after eating too much.

Hmm.

I say if one plus one equals a dislikeable two, then stop the addition. But it is awkward for me to offer such advice, for she does not know us. Yet I vow to eventually bestow *all* my vast wisdom upon her. Fortunate girl.

In the absence of the two most able domestic mavens, and in the presence of two other women—one old and one young—who suffer various ailments and complaints, I am left to handle the household.

I do my best, which cannot be measured well by any lofty standard.

Unfortunately, we receive a visit from two who have no qualms about telling me my shortcomings.

We have a New Year's visit from James, his Mary, and their newest child, Caroline. Where is my breath of free air? Where is my moment to bask in the sun of sanity and serenity?

Some place very far from here.

I love my brother. I love my niece, in her cuddly newness. And I . . . I . . .

I will not put words to my feelings about my other sister-in-law Mary. Two sisters-in-law named Mary . . . I wonder what I should call them in private. "Little Mary" for Mary Gibson, and "big Mary" . . . no. That is unkind. Perhaps "little Mary" would suffice for Frank's bride and "the other Mary" for James's. "The other Mary" is a well-suited name, saying more, and yet less, than I might imagine.

At any rate, they come and I do my best (though certainly not good enough) to entertain and offer every creature comfort.

Surprisingly, in the case of the other Mary, I do better supplying creature comforts than entertaining. During our evening readings, we suffer a misstep as *Alphonsine* proves unreadable. We are disgusted within twenty pages, as, independent of a bad translation, it has indelicacies which disgrace a pen hitherto so pure. So we change it for *The Female Quixote*, which now makes our evening amusement to me a very high one, as I find the work quite equal to what I remembered it. Little Mary, to whom it is new, enjoys it as one could wish. The other Mary, I believe, has little pleasure from that or any other book.

What subject does intrigue the other Mary?

Money.

"It is too bad you are forced to live like this," she says one evening, scanning a disgusted eye over our lodging—our temporary lodging, which is not meant to hold three extra visitors.

"We are very happy here," Frank says. "It is a good arrange—"

"I am so blessed to have a husband like James, whose provisions exceed any wife's expectations."

I do not believe her. For though she has no trouble heralding her husband's income, I cannot fathom it will ever exceed Mary's expectations. I fear her expectations flow towards the Godmersham way of life more than the finest life available in the Steventon parsonage.

I soon find myself wishing that only James had come to visit, and yet . . . too soon I find that he is not as amiable a guest as I had imagined. The company of so good and so clever a man ought to be gratifying in itself; but his chat seems forced, his opinions on many points too much copied from his wife's, and his time is spent walking about the house and banging the doors, or ringing the bell for a glass of water.

Who is this man? Where is *my* James, who could entertain me with his great thoughts and humour? Where is this fine eldest son who emulated our father? Father would not have been so weak and ineffectual, nor as demanding, as this strange visitor I do not know.

Or particularly like.

I blame the other Mary for his new deficits, though if I admit a larger fact, I know there is plenty of blame for James to share. A man does not grow browbeaten and tetchy without assent.

I wish I could say their parting comes too soon. But I am greatly comforted that it will not come later, especially after having witnessed the full extent of their house-guest shortcomings. As it is, I hope my memories will fail by the next time they develop an inclination to come call.

Upon our good-byes, I lean against the door. Relief tops the exhaustion of my bones—and soul. I take solace in knowing I have been left to the comfortable disposal of my own time. There will be no more torments of rice puddings and apple dumplings. And perhaps—upon a length of time—I will even come to regret that I did not take more pains to please them.

"'Tis none too soon," Mother says. "James did not seem to mind the expense their visit produced—and me, on a short income."

"James did not mind it, and his Mary encouraged it."

She shrugs, which, all in all, is the limit of what one can do at such times.

"I do manage—with the finances," she says. "Would you like to see?"

"Of course." That Mother has been forced to deal with numbers when they were never within her vocabulary is a sad fact of widowhood. She leads me to a small table, which she has confiscated as a desk, and pulls out a booklet of paper.

"See here? I began 1806 with 681 pounds and begin 1807 with 991. All this after spending 321 to purchase stock. Frank has also been settling his accounts and making calculations, and we both feel quite equal to our present expenses; but much increase of house rent would not do for either of us. Frank limits himself, I believe, to four hundred a year."

I nod, having little knowledge about such things, yet wise enough to know Mother's increase in income (in spite of having to entertain James and company) is a fine hope for our future.

If only I had something to offer.

We find a house to let in Castle Square. The landlord is the Marquis of Lansdowne. His own home has been newly built alongside. It looks to be a mock-Gothic castle. I leave him to his home and gladly take his leftovers. Our space includes a pretty walled garden where we can grow fruit and vegetables. And we are near the sea. Second to the rolling green of Hampshire, I do love the sea.

I miss Cassandra and want her home again. I try to cajole her return by telling her that Frank and Mary wish her home in time to help them with their choices for the house, and that they desire me to say that if she is not home straightaway they shall be as spiteful as possible and chuse everything in the style most likely to vex her: knives that will not cut, glasses that will not hold, a sofa without a seat, and a bookcase without shelves. All teasing aside, we do want her here to help chuse the final details of our home.

Beyond the house, we are very much pleased at the prospect of having a garden. To be privy to our own green just out the door will be a salve to all our constitutions. The garden is being put in order by a man who bears a remarkably good character, has a very fine complexion, and asks something less than the first man we asked. He informs us that the shrubs which border the gravel walk are sweetbriar and roses, but the latter of an indifferent sort. We mean to get a few of a better kind, and at my own particular desire, he procures us some syringas. I could not do without a syringa. We talk also of a laburnum . . . to have the mix of the lilac and yellow sprays . . . I can think of nothing lovelier. The border under the terrace wall is being cleared away to receive currants and gooseberry bushes, and a spot has been found that should prove very proper for raspberries. Fine prospects and fine berries. With such I shall surely find contentment.

The alterations and improvements within doors also advance very properly. The garret beds are made, and Cassandra's and mine will be finished today. I should like all the five beds completed by the end of this week. There will then be the window curtains, sofa cover, and a carpet to be altered. Martha's rug is just finished and looks well, tho' not quite so well as I had hoped. I see no fault in the border, but the middle is dingy. Mother plans to knit one for Cassandra as soon as she returns to chuse the colours and pattern—another incentive for her to find no more delay in leaving Godmersham.

Finally, our dressing table is being constructed on the spot out of a large kitchen table belonging to the house. We do so with the permission of Mr. Husket, Lord Lansdowne's painter—domestic painter, I should call him, for he lives in the castle. Domestic chaplains have given way to this more necessary office, and I suppose whenever the walls want no touching up, he is employed painting the face of m'Lady. 'Tis common knowledge that she was the Marquis' mistress before she became his wife, and all know the extent such women embrace to showcase their wares.

I am being petty. I have no cause to disparage the Lady of the castle, for she is nice enough and regularly drives by in a phaeton drawn by eight very small ponies, which greatly delights the children of the neighbourhood. Surely the ability to delight children makes up for past, less seemly, habits of delight.

There are many acquaintances to be made here. In fact, such acquaintances increase too fast. Although we previously lived in the world of rectories and rectors, socialites and hopeful wannabes, in Southampton we find yet another environ, for we are in Frank's world. The world of the navy.

They are, all in all, an enjoyable and gracious lot, and by our relation with Frank our lowly status is elevated. In most eyes at least . . .

I enjoy being around people who are my opposite. People who replace my reserve with exuberance. People who have the ability to make everyone feel at ease, to make everyone feel as if their place in society, as well as their temperament, is something to be accepted. It is a gift not many people (young or old) possess. Such people are genuine in who they are and allow others like me to be the same. There is no playacting. Only gracious acceptance.

To such people I sing high praises. To the few who make me feel as though their friendship is but charity, I am mute.

Regarding my muteness? It is to their benefit.

We sit together in the evening. We always sit together. For there is no recourse. When he is home Frank sits with us, one stallion amongst five mares. Little Mary embroiders some nit-nat for the baby, Mother dozes, and the rest of us read *Clarentine*, by some relative of Fanny Burney.

The relative does not succeed, and I suffer quite enough. I stop my reading and hold the opened book as evidence. "I must say I am surprised by how foolish this book turns out to be. I liked it much less on the second day of reading than at the first, and it does not bear a third day at all. It is full of unnatural conduct and forced difficulties, without striking merit of any kind."

I wait for someone to argue with me, to fight for the merits of *Clarentine*, but Mother barely opens one eye, Mary rethreads her needle, Cassandra picks another book from the table nearby, and Martha yawns.

Another rousing evening in Southampton.

I close the book with a snap. If truth be known, I think we are all of us too full of merit, which if pressed can be found to be the most unnatural conduct of all. We are too polite, too full of sisterly accommodation. There is never a raised voice or, heaven forbid it, full-out hysterics. Although I have often witnessed as much from Mother, or me, or even occasionally Cassandra (when sorely vexed), in the presence of these two new sisters, we contain ourselves.

Contain ourselves too tightly. If cordiality could maim. Or kill . . .

I know Martha would forgive me if I were to push decorum aside and reveal my true self—for she has seen glimpses of that horrid creature in past visits, but little Mary . . . we are still too new in our acquaintance, and her condition too delicate, and her breadth of experience too shallow, to accost her with any full display of feeling—sincere or not.

And then there is Frank. My dear, dear brother who is so

different from the stodgy James, the vivacious Henry, the business-
man Edward, and the adventurous Charles. Frank is . . . constant.
Looking across the room at him now, I can nearly see the cogs of
his mind working as he sits with one leg crossed, one foot bobbing
slightly to its own rhythm. His gaze is towards the window, which
is dark in the winter night. It is as though he sees beyond it. To the
sea. The constant sea, that comes and goes without bidding or
direction.

Yet Frank is completely unlike the sea in that he does not storm.
I have heard the tale of Frank at sea, where another seaman was
swimming in the ocean and my brother calmly said, "Mr. Paken-
ham, you are in danger of a shark—a shark of the blue species." His
words were so calmly stated that the man thought Frank made a
joke. He did not.

I watch him change the direction of his gaze from the window
to the fire grate. Ah! I see a bit of kindling has escaped to the carpet.

I gasp and stand, ready to act, but Frank acts first—I cannot use
the term *swifter*, because he simply strides across the room and
shoves it back to the grate with the toe of his boot, not e'en missing
a footfall as he continues his gait to the bookshelf, where he peruses
the shelves.

To the surprise of all, Frank—of the frigates, blue sharks, and
navy—is also in the process of making a very nice fringe for the
drawing room curtains. He is too perfect.

We are all too perfect. Every company needs one person to hate,
one who appalls others by their selfish ways, their candid remarks,
or their bad taste in bonnet or boot. To have no one who offends
vexes my nerves. I am not one to demand adventurous agitation,
but I could sorely use a dose of domestic animation.

Yet what right do I have to complain about decency and decorum?
No right. And yet I do.

Will I ever be satisfied?

See what happens when one complains?

My perfect brother of the even temper left us: Frank received a command on the *St. Albans*, taking convoy duty to the Cape of Good Hope and traveling on from there to China! While he is gone making preparations . . .

Little Mary of the shallow experiences has her child—and not by easy birth. It is a girl born on April 27, 1807. Her name is Mary Jane, an honour I take with a good deal of humility and self-chastisement for everything ill I have thought (though, with God's blessings, have not spoken aloud).

And then, to make my humiliation complete, Mary does not recover well. She falls into bad fainting fits (having nothing what-soever to do with what she had for dinner), causing us to rant and worry. And pray. Frank has left Mary in our care. Surely four women can be trusted to keep her ever safe and fine.

I hold the child, watching her tiny lips move in a sleeping suckle. Like her weakened mother, she is delicate. And fine. "Dear little Mary Jane. You have many here to love you."

God is good and merciful to us all, in spite of our faults. For little Mary recovers, and I am saved the pinnacle of regret that would have been mine had she and the child incurred any perma-nent suffering and harm.

We are thrilled when Frank comes home for the christening in May and is with us through June, when he sails for the Cape.

An additional blessing is, that when little Mary leaves for a sum-mer visit to her Ramsgate family, I can honestly say I will miss her.

When does one truly grow up? At age thirty-one, I would like to know.

SEVENTEEN

Edward has invited all of us to join him for a visit at his other estate, Chawton House in Hampshire. What a joyous event to see all of them at a location that is so close. For Chawton House is only twenty-nine miles from Southampton, not the one hundred thirty-three miles to Godmersham. In addition, Chawton House is only fifteen miles from Steventon, so James (and company) will join us. What a festive time indeed.

We have never been to Chawton House, and though it is not as grand as Godmersham, it holds our entire family with little effort. It has huge fireplaces, a great hall, and a gallery. The house is heavy with history and the continuity of family.

After our visit, all of Edward's (which of the children only include Fanny and William) will come back to Southampton so we can shew them our home on Castle Square. And to our delight, Henry has come down from London. What a jolly time. We go to the theatre and see John Bannister in *The Way to Keep Him*. It is a fine play, most enjoyable, exhibiting a biting merriment towards wives who stop pleasing their husbands after marriage. We go on a boat trip to Hythe, and then another to the ruins of Netley Abbey. Dear Fanny, at age fourteen, is most impressed and declares, "I am struck dumb with admiration, and I wish I could say anything that would come near to the sublimity of it."

The sublime. Ah yes. For it is all sublime. The family, the laughter, the picnics, and walking with Fanny along Southampton's stores on High Street until late. I enjoy every minute and thank God for one and all.

And yet . . .

Even while I enjoy their company, I wish them gone. Why do I possess this trait? Why can I not be like Henry, who is invigorated by lively company? Why can I enjoy such camaraderie only so long before my spirit rebels and demands quiet attention? I love my family but find rejuvenation in solitude.

Is that wrong?

Wrong or no, it seems I can do nothing to change it. And so, when Henry hires a sociable and takes everyone for a ride in the New Forest, I decline.

"Now, Jane," he says. "Come with us. You can e'en sit on my lap and take the reins."

"If I did such a thing your knees would scream within a mile, and we would surely end in the ditch. No, no, I am fine. Off with you now, before William and Fanny go without you."

I wave as they drive away and enter the house alone. The door closes, capturing the silence and letting it reverberate from ceiling to wall.

I hold my breath, not wanting to disturb the hallowness of the moment. For it does feel holy to me. As holy as any moment in church . . . a moment to be worshipped.

I tiptoe to a chair in the parlour and sit. I lean my head against its back and close my eyes. I expel the breath I have been saving.

And I relax.

❦

"Jane?"

Someone says my name. Someone shakes my shoulder.

I open my eyes to see Cassandra. I am still in the parlour, having fallen asleep in the chair. I sit erect and press at my hair. "You have all returned, then?"

Cassandra removes her bonnet. "Just me. They wished to stop at the Old Bowling Green and I did not. I was worried about you."

I feel badly for causing her to end her day prematurely. "You do not need to worry. I enjoyed the . . ." I do not know how to say it without sounding rude.

"Total silence devoid of human noisiness and movement?"

I stand and busy myself setting some stray books in the shelves. "I adore the company of my brothers and the children." There is a *but* unspoken at the end of my sentence. Blessedly, Cassandra does not fill it in. But she knows. She knows me fair well.

"You need to write, Jane. I was hoping you would use this time alone in such a manner."

"I will. But since moving to Southampton, there is always someone coming or going. We have become quite popular."

She is relentless. "You need to write."

"I will. When the time is right."

"When the conditions are right."

I feel my cheeks redden. "It is lovely here. Such a reprieve from our *other* . . ."

"But it is still not right."

I do not know what she means—exactly what she means. "It is a fine house, in a fine city, with fine company. I have no right to com—"

"Then I will complain for you." She moves to stand before me. "I know what you need, Jane. What you need is—"

I attempt a laugh. "Talent?"

Her face is serious. "Stop that! You possess great talent, but a talent unused is a talent wasted."

"I have written," I say.

"But you must write more. Write anew."

I look about the room where we spend so much of our time. There is nothing to suggest an oppressive quality that would prevent the creative process. So why have I not written? Why is inspiration so elusive? And who am I to be so particular? I am not some bastion of literary genius who must have conditions just so to create a masterpiece. I am but a spinster who dabbles with writing when life affords her the time, inclination, and inspiration.

Cassandra has removed her coat and folds it over her arm. "I will do my best to make it work, Jane. To make life work so you can work."

"I do not deserve special attention or considera—"

"You do. And I will do my best to see you have it."

"But—"

She points at me with a slender digit. "I will do my part, but you must do yours. Agreed?"

"I will try."

❦

It is my turn to visit Godmersham. My dear niece Fanny, who at age fifteen writes letters full of passionate entreaty, has begged me to come. And so, in the summer of 1808, I begin my journey to fulfill her *greatest wish*.

Along the way I stop to see Henry and Eliza. I have oft seen my brother—who frequently travels alone—but have not seen Eliza for far too long. Our initial greeting is replete with hugs and kisses. Once stepped apart, I find her older in countenance (she *is* forty-seven) yet still vibrant in spirit. "It is about time you come to see me!" she says.

And it is.

Their home at Brompton (well east of London) is small and made to feel more so (in a most delightful way) because it is always filled with friends. Oh, the many actors and artists I meet! My brother and his wife are the penultimate host and hostess, and my two months as their guest are filled with dinner parties and numerous outings to see concerts and plays. But beyond the social events, I marvel that there is always time to sit and talk, with never a moment wasted thinking of to-do's or should-do's. At Brompton a guest suffers no cares and my every need is met before its full inception. Eliza knows how to make me feel as if I am the most important person in the world. 'Tis a great talent.

I mean to ask Henry about the publication of *Susan*, which he arranged with Richard Crosby four years ago, but can never find a proper time when such a discussion would not quell some special merriment. Henry *did* deem himself my agent, but I can see he now has little time for such a Herculean task.

Besides, other than offering old stories, long dusty in my trunk, what have I done of late to advance my craft?

Nothing.

And so I leave the subject untested. It is for the best. Life moves on. In most ways I feel incredibly blessed.

Yet even the delights of Henry's must find an end. James, Mary, and their two youngest, James Edward, age ten, and little Caroline, only three, have just collected me. We are off to Godmersham.

We leave at five in the morning. Our first eight miles are hot, but after Blackheath we suffer nothing, and as the day advances it grows quite cool for June. We are crowded, and the children are rowdy. I try to remember it is natural for a child of three to be so fidgety.

At Dartford, which we reach within two hours and three-quarters, we go to the Bull, the same inn at which Cassandra and I breakfasted on a previous journey. It has the same bad butter.

At half past ten we are again off, and, traveling on without any adventure, reach Sittingbourne by three. The innkeeper is watching for us at the door of the George, and I am acknowledged very kindly by Mr. and Mrs. Marshall. I chat with the latter while Mary goes out to buy some gloves. A few minutes, of course, did for Sittingbourne, and so off we drive, drive, drive, and by six o'clock are at Godmersham.

Edward and James immediately walk away together, as natural as life. My two nieces, Fanny and Lizzy, meet us in the Hall with a great deal of pleasant joy. A few minutes later we proceed into the breakfast parlour, and then to our rooms. Mary has the Hall chamber. I am in the Yellow Room and immediately write a letter to Cassandra. It seems odd to have such a great place all to myself, *and* to be at Godmersham without her.

There is a knock upon my door and I open it to find Fanny. "I came as soon as I saw Aunt Mary to her room. May I stay?"

"Of course." We chatter on while I change from my travel attire. She is as dramatic as usual, stating her longing for Cassandra's company. She is grown both in height and size since last year (but not immoderately), looks very well, and seems as to conduct and manner just what she was and what one could wish her to continue to be.

My sister-in-law Elizabeth, who was dressing when we arrived, comes to me for a short moment, attended by some of the other children. She gives me a very affectionate welcome.

I cannot praise Elizabeth's looks, but they are probably affected by a cold. Her little namesake has gained in beauty in the last three years, though not more than Marianne has lost. Charles is not quite so lovely as he was. Louisa is much as I expected, and I am told little Cassandra is suffering a violent breaking-out so severe, she will not come down after dinner.

We go downstairs and I notice how their Steventon cousin, James Edward, finds instant friendship, yet shy little Caroline . . . she is left out. Her cousins are too much for her. A lonely poor-cousin in a large mansion . . .

Elizabeth, though expecting her eleventh child, does well enough, and the older children help with the younger. Yet the way she looks at me . . . as if she disapproves. Because I am not married? Because I am childless? Because I have few responsibilities beyond myself?

Perhaps. And in these liabilities, I find myself accused.

Fanny takes my hand and pulls me towards the front door. "Come walk with me. I have much to tell you."

I set my liabilities aside and assume the role Elizabeth must approve: Aunt Jane.

"I do not see why we must go all the way to Canterbury," Mary tells me.

"It is but seven miles," I say.

Mary huffs and folds her arms. She is full of prejudice today, and I nearly regret taking her with me to visit Edward's adoptive mother, Mrs. Knight. That I would even consider chusing her company on this journey looms as a large question in my mind.

She continues her complaints—about all but herself. "I do not approve of Harriot Bridges marrying that oily George Moore. I do not like him. I just do not."

"I have not met him," I say. To my own discredit I add to her vexation. "I heard they are all coming to dinner tomorrow tonight."

She shudders as though I have stated the Devil himself will grace the Godmersham table. "If Elizabeth will allow it, I will chuse the far end of the table. I will, I tell you."

Her dislike of George Moore—whom none of us has met—only piques my interest of him, for whoever upsets Mary might be a friend of mine.

I ask silent forgiveness for my cruel thoughts.

"And your sister . . ." she continues.

I brace myself, for though I may accept hearing the slights of others, towards Cassandra I am protective. But I do not bite.

"Your sister . . ." she repeats.

Ah me. I know she will not be satisfied till I respond. Towards the hope of eventually changing the subject I open the floodgates with two words: "My sister?"

"Did you know she had tea with a sister of James's first wife?"

"How nice of her."

"Nice?"

I try to think of a more appropriate description. "Cassandra is kind to all relatives, past and present. The woman in question is

Anna's—is your stepdaughter's—aunt."

"That woman is not a relative of any kind. Her sister died. I am the mistress of Steventon now."

"No one implies you are not." Feeling a bit put upon, I take the opportunity to add, "Why did you not bring Anna with you to Godmersham, with the other children?"

"Do your mother and Cassandra wish her to be gone?"

"No, no," I hasten to say. For that is not the issue at all. Yet I am not certain Mary will acknowledge the true concern. "Occasionally the youngest children *are* left behind, but rarely the eld—"

"Anna prefers being with her grandmother and aunt in Southampton."

Although I know Anna enjoys our company—and we, hers—I also know from direct correspondence that the fifteen-year-old keenly feels her stepchild status. And there is no denying she would have enjoyed the company of her cousin Fanny at Godmersham.

If only she had been brought along.

Mary peers out the carriage window. "Oh, when *will* we ever be there?"

Subject suitably changed.

I am certain it is for the best.

Mrs. Knight greets both of us warmly, and my opinion of her genteel, intelligent nature is not changed. Even Mary seems thoroughly charmed, a victory attributed to the generous manner of our hostess.

We have tea and biscuits and chat about family. I take a lesson by the fact Mrs. Knight allows Mary to ramble quite incessantly about the merits of her life, her children (there is no mention of Anna), her fine home, and a new set of dishes that now graces the rectory table. As *my* nerves grow brittle at the monologue, Mrs.

Knight simply nods and smiles and offers an occasional "How nice," which, from her lips and by her countenance, sounds genuinely effusive.

Take a lesson, Jane.

Mary excuses herself to use the facilities. I find her exit a relief. Obviously, any lesson on graciousness has not taken root.

I release a sigh, and Mrs. Knight laughs. Which allows me to laugh. "How do you do it?" I ask.

"All any person wants is an ear, Jane."

"Mary offers too much for my ear."

"She does offer an . . . abundance."

Before I can say more, Mrs. Knight glances at the doorway as if to see if Mary has returned. She leans towards me, her mature face still strikingly beautiful. She presses a small pouch into my hand. "For your use, my dear."

By its weight I know there are coins inside. She has done this before, given me an allowance. And, alas, I am not too proud to take it. "You are too kind," I say.

"Nonsense. I am only kind enough."

Without her generosity, I would have no income to call my own. I take it because her kindness releases a portion of my burden from others. I tuck the pouch into the reticule I have brought with me.

"There. Now that that is taken care of . . . I want you to tell me how you are, Jane."

"I am fine."

She shakes her head. "Triteness does not become you. Again I ask: How *are* you? How are you living in Southampton, holed up with your brother and his wife? Five women . . .'tis the makings of a . . . a complicated life."

"We get along admirably," I say.

"So you like Frank's wife?"

"She is a sweet girl."

"Hmm. And now, with a child."

"It is good we are there with her and little Mary Jane. Frank is long at sea."

"You are a good sister."

I feel my cheeks flush, for I know I am not. At least not all of the—

"You disagree?"

I laugh. "You miss little."

She nods with satisfaction. "The perks of age are few, but the attributes that one *can* collect along the way . . . often come to good use." She gazes at me, waiting. "So? Why are you not a good sister?"

I hesitate only a moment. In truth, I do not mind sharing my failings with such a woman. I only wish to do so before Mary returns. "I complain."

"About . . . ?"

"Too much." I expand for the sake of time. "The house is very nice, there is a garden, the town is lovely, but it does not feel . . . I am not sure it is possible for it to feel . . . I would like it to feel—"

"Like home?"

I let out an expansive sigh. "Yes."

"The feeling of home is often built upon the indistinct."

"I agree wholeheartedly. Although the placement of walls, lushness of carpets, and the pleasure of fine prospects are pleasing accoutrements, the true delineations that make a house a home are ephemeral. 'Tis like explaining the depth and breadth of the wind—one can best explain its effects more than its substance."

Mrs. Knight claps softly. "Bravo! You are steeped in prose. So . . . how goes your writing?"

Oh dear. "It . . . I think about it often."

She gives me a chastening look. "Jane, you know very well that thinking is not doing."

"I do know. And I mean to do it, but the time never seems right and . . ." I shrug. "I should not offer excuses. If I am a writer, I should write."

"But a writer needs more than accoutrements."

I blink, astonished. She understands! "I fear the intangibles that make a home are intertwined with those that provide inspiration."

"If the former existed, the latter would follow forth?"

She makes my mind race. "If I say yes, and yet at some future point it proves not to be so, I have taken away my last excuse."

"So be it."

I press my hands in my lap with determination. "I promise you that once back in Southampton, I will try my very utmost to write. I should not—I will not—let the lack of intangibles keep me from it."

She smiles a sly smile and taps a ringed finger against her cheek. "I have an idea about this. . . ."

"What sort—?"

"Not yet," she says. "But know that I do not forget you, Jane. Nor your mother or sister."

"And Martha Lloyd." I look to the doorway, expecting Mary back by now. "She is Mary's sister but is nothing at all like her; not nearly so . . . abundant."

Mrs. Knight laughs, then looks up. "Ah, Mrs. Austen. Welcome back. Can I pour you some more tea?"

Our visit at Godmersham was ever delightful, but I am ready to return to Southampton. The Bigg sisters are coming to visit, and Mother is going to be in Steventon to bring little Anna home, and Little Mary is still at her family's in Ramsgate, leaving Cassandra and me to entertain alone. What joy! It will be a snug fortnight for four dear friends.

But first I must get there. My initial plan was to ride back with James and Mary, but they have already left, and now I am told that there is no one else to escort me home until Henry visits in two months!

I cannot stay here while this chance to see Alethea and Catherine evaporates. Catherine is soon to be married. This will be our last chance to visit as four singles.

One day in late June we discuss it at breakfast. Elizabeth declares, "I do not see why you are making such a thing of this, Jane. Is our society so tedious that you cannot endure it a moment longer?"

"Oh, Aunt Jane, please stay longer," Fanny says. "We still have a thousand things to do together."

Her plea is flattering and heartfelt but is overshadowed by my need for companionship beyond her sweet adolescence.

I look to the head of the table, to Edward. I have already told them about the Biggs' presence in Southampton and my desire not to miss them, but they see it as a frivolous desire for girl-talk.

Which it is.

But a greater reason *can* be given. One they do not know. One that no sibling knows but Cassandra and James. One I never wanted any of my family to know . . .

Yet if I tell it, I will surely be set free. I believe the gain is worth the loss.

"The scenery will be ever so lovely in September," Edward says. "Besides, at that time Henry can do us a favour by bringing Cassandra here to us, for Elizabeth's confinement."

The next child is due in early October.

"You would not have us be inconvenienced, would you, Jane?" Elizabeth's voice has an undertone of frustration that I would even dare imagine going against their schedule. For what do my wishes matter? I have no important life that must be attended.

And yet . . . I am willing to accept their subtle disparagement if only to spend some special time with the Biggs and Cassandra. I am not one to press, and certainly not one to go against any of my brothers' wishes, but in this . . .

It is hard to explain, this intense desire to have time alone with my sister and our two friends. And I realize as Edward dabs his lips with his napkin, very near the end of our morning repast, that I must press my point. In payment for their kind hospitality, I owe them the truth—or at least a part of it.

"May I speak with both of you?" I ask. "Privately?"

Husband and wife exchange a glance but agree.

Elizabeth gives the servants instructions, warns the children of their manners, and the three of us leave the table. We enter Edward's paneled study, where my brother takes his position behind the massive desk. Elizabeth stands at his shoulder, forming a distinct two against one.

"So what reason can be so important that you take us away from our meal?" Elizabeth asks.

I am embarrassed by the entire situation but have come too far to retreat. I stand with my hands clasped in front and raise my chin, hoping my stance will offer some much-needed courage. "It is very important that I have time with Alethea and Catherine Bigg, because I . . . I was engaged to their brother Harris."

Elizabeth's face shews her aghast. "When was this?"

Edward has a different tack: "You *were* engaged to Harris?"

"I was." I look to Elizabeth to answer her query. "Six years ago."

It is Edward's turn to look aghast. "And you never told us?"

"I did not, because by the next morning I had changed my mind. I broke the engagement."

"But why?" Elizabeth asks. "He is rich, he is handsome, he comes from a good family. Why would *you* turn him down?"

My answer will sound trite, and yet . . . considering my audience . . . "I did not love him." I hasten to say, "You and Edward loved each other when you married. I have always been inspired by your love and want such a marriage for myself. Surely I cannot be faulted in that."

I can tell by the look that passes between them that the point is well taken, and yet . . . the fact I am not from wealth—as the two of them had been—still hangs heavy.

To their credit they do not say it. Do not say any of it. And for that I commend them. Edward knows that his place in the Knight family is a blessing. I am certain he often looks at the financial trials of his siblings and thinks, *There, but for the grace of God, go I.*

In order to solidify my case, I proceed with a half-truth. "Because of my disgrace, I feel the need to repair the damage my actions have caused. I cherish my friends and wish to mend the past so we can continue our dear friendship." I do not mention that the bonds have long been mended, nor that I have been to Manydown since and know that all is forgiven. Yet I *do* know this special time will increase the strength of our sisterhood. And that is always a good and rightful thing.

"Please, Edward," I say. "Please help me make things right."

Edward stands and with a sigh says, "I will arrange it."

It is not surprising that my broken engagement is not spoken of. For it is old news. The four of us—Cassandra, Catherine, Alethea, and I—slip into an easy amity as though the event were but a dream.

It is not possible we are women in our thirties. Women of our age do not giggle and carry on. Yet, alone in our home in Southampton, that is exactly what occurs between us. The years rush away, once again making us hopeful ingenues brimming over with frantic talk of dances and men and gossip and the upcoming nuptial as if we had no cares in the world.

But I admit as Catherine speaks of her autumn wedding, I do not envy her. Herbert Hill is not my first choice as a partner for my friend. For anyone. Without forethought I hear myself asking aloud, "And how old is he?" I know very well the answer.

Catherine's chin rises. "He is not yet sixty."

"Which means he is twenty-four years your elder."

"He is a kind man."

"I would hope so," I say.

"He is a reverend."

"The former does not of necessity go with the latter, although it should," I say.

Cassandra nudges at my knee. "We are very happy for you, Catherine. To find a man who—"

"I will miss her at Manydown," Alethea tells us.

"I will visit," Catherine says. "You know I will. Herbert has assured as much."

"It will not be the same," Alethea says.

Catherine looks about and adds, "Herbert is the uncle to Robert Southey. The poet."

We all nod in appreciation of family ties, but I find myself thinking that I would rather have Catherine marry the nephew—who is sooner our age—than the fatherly uncle.

No one speaks.

I am guilty of lessening the mood. I must make amends.

I stand and retrieve a gift I had planned to give Catherine upon her leaving. My inexcusable dampening of our gathering makes now a better time.

I hand her a cambric handkerchief I have embroidered. "For your wedding day," I say.

"Oh, Jane, it is beautiful."

"You may not think as much when I combine it with this poem." I clear my throat and read from the page I will give her:

"*Cambrick! With grateful blessings would I pay*
The pleasure given me in sweet employ.
Long may'st thou serve my Friend without decay,
And have no tears to wipe, but tears of joy!"

She comes to me with a hug and kiss. "Oh, Jane, that is lovely. I will cherish both forever."

It is what I wish her. For all of us. A lovely forever.

If only I knew exactly what that entailed.

"You wish to move where?" I ask Frank.

He pulls Mary under his arm as she cuddles baby Mary Jane and repeats himself. "We wish to move into our own home on the Isle of Wight, where I am to be stationed. 'Tis not that far, Jane. Just a ferry ride across from Portsmouth."

I know my geography.

"It is not that we do not enjoy your company," Mary says.

"'Twould seem just so," Mother says. She crosses her arms in her peeved mode.

Frank moves away from his family to console her. "Our Yarmouth Division has nice lodgings, and with fish costing almost nothing, plenty of engagements and plenty of each other, we will be very happy."

Mother shrugs.

Cassandra steps forward and kisses Mary on the cheek; then her brother receives the same. "We are very happy for you. You deserve a house of your own."

Frank's sigh reveals his relief. "Thank you, Cass. We knew we could count on your blessings."

"And mine," I say, offering my own kisses.

We all look to Mother, who begrudgingly says, "I suppose I could cure a ham for you."

We laugh. A ham. Of all things. But Frank is ever gracious. "Thank you, Mother. That would be splendid."

The happy family leaves us alone in the parlour. We each look to the other.

Mother speaks first. "Well? Now what?"

"Between the three of us—four, with Martha—we have enough income to stay."

"Not without frugalities," Mother says.

"No," Cassandra concedes. "Not without those."

Vulgar, vulgar economy.

❦ ❦

"Surely you do not pout like Mother," Cassandra says as we ready for bed.

Before I answer, I assess the truth of my response—and adjust. "I do so only in that I do not like upheaval. I am a woman of roots. To be plucked once again . . ."

"We can stay here, Jane," she says, pulling back the covers of her bed.

I nod and climb between my own covers. "I try to see the good of it. After visiting Godmersham and being amongst all those children—dear as they may be—and then coming home to little Mary Jane, and I am sure there will be an increase of children on Frank and Mary's account . . ."

Cassandra nestles into her bed, pulling the coverlet to her chin against the autumn coolness. "It *will* be nice to own silence and the simplicity of adults."

"Adults not with child."

She laughs and turns her face to the wall. " 'Twill be all right, Jane. You will see."

❦ ❦

Our sister-in-law Elizabeth is no longer with child but most certainly has her new child *with* her. Brook John was born just before Cassandra arrived at Godmersham to give her usual laying-in assistance.

An eleventh child. Although I do not deny a single niece or nephew their existence, I do wonder as to the wisdom in it. Not that Edward has not the resources to raise his children in an apt, proper, and prosperous manner, but surely, the wear upon poor Elizabeth . . .

She never complains.

Perhaps she should complain more. Insist on separate bedrooms. Tell my dear brother, "Enough, I say! I have had enough!" Yet for her to employ the gumption to shew such pluck would go against the very reason she and I have never got on. She does not appreciate my pluck, and I do not appreciate her lack of it.

Martha comes in with the post. She has just returned to us from *her* travels, and I find it very fine to have her back.

"Is there another from Cassandra?" I ask. I always ask, for it is my sister's words that please me beyond all others.

"There is," she says, handing it to me.

I break the seal with enthusiasm, eager for news of Godmersham. How is baby Brook John? How goes the weary Elizabeth? I am sure my sister offers more than simple comfort as she—

I stop my mind's meandering and reread the words on the page. The awful words on the page. "No," I say. "No. No. No. No . . ."

Alarmed, Martha comes to me. "What is wrong?"

I clasp a hand over my mouth, unable to say the words aloud. Martha takes the letter and reads for herself. She looks up, aghast. "Elizabeth is dead?"

I run from the room.

More news has come. Details we hate but need to hear. Apparently, Elizabeth seemed quite well after the birth. Just a week later, she had even arisen for dinner, and Edward had felt assured enough to attend to estate business. Yet on the tenth of October, after eating a hearty meal just thirty minutes previous, Elizabeth was dead. The doctor offered no explanation as to why a thirty-five-year-old woman of good health, good breeding, and good attention should pass away in the blinking of an eye.

I try to find rationalization in the fact that death related to childbirth is not a stranger to us. I have witnessed other families suffer this cruel fate. Just a decade ago, during the same week when James's son James Edward was born, two women in tiny Steventon died giving birth. That our Austen family has never lost a child to infancy, nor lost a mother during her confinement, is a miracle attributed only to God. That we would eventually face a break in this string of grace is tragic but nearly expected.

I write to Cassandra, hoping through my words to make atonement for my peevish comments against dear Elizabeth.

Castle Square, October 13, 1808
My dearest Cassandra,

I have received your letter. We have felt, we do feel, for you all—as you will not need to be told—for you, for Fanny, for Henry, for Lady Bridges, and for dearest Edward, whose loss and whose sufferings seem to make those of every other person nothing. God be praised! that you can say what you do of him, that he has a religious mind to bear him up and a disposition that will gradually lead him to comfort.

My dear, dear Fanny! I am so thankful that she has you with her! You will be everything to her, you will give her all the consolation that human aid can give. May the Almighty sustain you all and keep you, my dearest Cassandra, well. But for the present I daresay you are equal to everything. You will know that Edward's poor boys are at Steventon, fetched from school by James. And perhaps it is best for them, as they will have more means of exercise and amusement there than they could have with us, but I own myself disappointed by the arrangement. I should have loved to have them with me at such a time. I shall write to Edward by this post. With what true sympathy our feelings are shared by Martha, you need not be told; she is the friend and sister under every circumstance. We need not enter into a Panegyric on the Departed, but it is sweet to think of her great worth, of her solid principles, her true devotion, her excellence in every relation of life. It is also consolatory to reflect on the shortness of the sufferings which led her from this world to a better.

Farewell for the present, my dearest sister. Tell Edward that we feel for him and pray for him.

I sign the letter and seal it, wishing more could be said but knowing there are no words.

No more words for paper but . . .

I hold the letter to my chest and bow my head. There are many words to be said, but not for any mere mortal's ears.

Dear heavenly Father . . .

I feel most for Fanny.

I know such a declaration might raise more than one eyebrow (considering ten other children, dear Edward, and all the Bridges at Goodnestone who have lost a sister and daughter), yet I cannot change the statement in any well-meaned preference to give it to another.

Edward's loss is terrible and must be felt as such, and it is too soon to think of moderation in grief, either in him or his afflicted daughter. But we may hope that our dear Fanny's sense of duty to that beloved father will rouse her to exertion. For his sake, and as the most acceptable proof of love to the spirit of her departed mother, she will try to be tranquil and resigned in her new role as woman of the household. I hope she finds consolation in Cassandra, and yet I worry she is too much overpowered for anything but solitude.

I vow to be there for her, and yet, what do I truly know of large households and children? Other than offering my respect by wearing bombazine and crepe, I can only offer my presence—either from near or far—along with the occasional hand with some of the children.

The two eldest boys are staying with us now. They behave extremely well in every respect, shewing quite as much feeling as one wishes to see, and on every occasion speaking of their father with the liveliest affection. His letter was read over by each of them yesterday, and with many tears; thirteen-year-old George sobbed aloud, but at a year older, Edward's tears do not flow so easily.

I try to distract them with childish joys and comfort them through their faith. Sunday, I took them both to church and saw fourteen-year-old Edward much affected by the sermon, which, indeed, I could have thought purposely addressed to the afflicted: "All that are in danger, necessity, or tribulation" was the subject of it. Afterwards, the weather did not allow us to get farther than the quay, where George was very happy as long as we could stay, flying about from one side to the other and skipping on board a collier.

In the evening we share the Psalms and lessons, and a sermon at home, to which the boys are very attentive; and yet, in their youth, they have had enough. I am certain God, in His goodness, forgives their inattention and need for normalcy.

We do not want for amusement: bilbocatch, at which George is indefatigable, spillikins, riddles, conundrums, and cards, while watching the flow and ebb of the river, and now and then a stroll, keep us well employed.

Yesterday we had a complete outing. We had not proposed doing more than cross the Itchen River, but it proved so pleasant, and so much to the satisfaction of all, that when we reached the middle of the stream we agreed to be rowed up the river. Both the boys rowed a great part of the way, and their questions and remarks, as well as their enjoyment, were very amusing. George's inquiries were endless, and his eagerness in everything reminds me often of his uncle Henry. My "Itty Dordy" is growing up. . . .

We now sit in the parlour, where George is most industriously making and naming paper ships, at which he purposes to shoot with horse chestnuts. Young Edward is equally intent over Porter's *Lake of Killarney*, twisting himself about in one of our great chairs with book in hand.

Watching them then and now, I feel an odd gratitude that somehow, in some small way, Aunt Jane is able to help.

And yet, as effectively and often as I allow myself to forget our grief . . . my thoughts are at Godmersham. I see the mournful party in my mind's eye under every varying circumstance of the day; and in the evening especially, figure to myself its sad gloom: the efforts to talk, the frequent summons to melancholy orders and cares, and dear Edward, restless in misery, going from one room to the other, and perhaps not seldom upstairs, to see all that remains of his Elizabeth. Dearest Fanny must now look upon herself as his prime source of comfort, his dearest friend; as the being who is gradually to supply to him, to the extent that is possible, what he has lost. This consideration will elevate and cheer her.

Eventually.

For I have learned, as she will learn, that life is ever changing, and the roles we play within it also. Whether we play them well or not is a conundrum even the brightest of minds cannot predict.

The letters fly about the Austen clan, everyone offering their condolences while trying to be strong and merry, when appropriate. I dislike that Elizabeth's death is the impetus for gaining so many letters, but I relish every one.

Upon receiving the post, I close the door against the frightful wind. I read through Cassandra's post where she asks a question that confuses me: *What say you in response to Edward's proposal? I find it most interesting.*

"What proposal?" I ask the parlour.

Mother looks up from her rug making. "Who is getting married?" she asks.

Considering the subject is Edward, I know it is not *that* kind of proposal. "The letters must be out of order. I have Edward's yet to read. I will read it next and find out the mystery."

"Aloud," Mother says. "Read it aloud."

I do just that.

"Forgive my tardiness. I should have made thus an offer far sooner, and in my defense I did think it, but there were extraneous circumstances that did not coincide. . . . I wish to offer you women the use of a house on the Chawton estate. The bailiff at Chawton has recently died and his home is vacant and available. Does this prove intriguing?"

I lower the letter. "Does it?"

Mother has stopped her work. "It does. Of course it does. I have been looking for a home for us. There is one at Wye—"

I shake my head. "But this . . ."

"Does seem more ideal." She removes her glasses to look at me across the room. "I did like Edward's estate there. If the cottage is of the same merit as Chawton House . . ."

"It cannot be nearly as grand, Mother. The estate's bailiff lived there."

She shrugs. "Be that as it may, I did find the surrounding country most amiable."

I realize my heart beats faster. "Chawton is only fifteen miles from Steventon, and its proximity in dear Hampshire . . ."

"I wonder what Cassandra thinks of this."

I pick up her last letter, again reading the words *I find it most interesting.*

As do I.

❧ ❦

Cassandra, Mother, Martha, and I are of like mind: Chawton

Cottage will be ours! We learn that there are six bedchambers—which is just what we wished. Henry wrote to us on Edward's behalf, speaking of garrets for storage places, one of which Mother immediately plans to fit up for a manservant. The difficulty of doing without one had been thought of before. We discover his name shall be Robert.

I do not much care whether his name be Robert, Percival, or Eggplant if it but means we move to Chawton.

I do not know why this place intrigues.

Yet it does.

How can I feel so right about such a place I do not know? One I have never seen?

Yet I do.

I ask God to give me an answer but receive only silence.

And yet it is a peaceful silence that implores me to accept this gift in spite of what is uncertain or unknown.

To go forth, on faith.

And so, we shall move to Chawton.

If I could move immediately, I would. Yet Chawton Cottage demands fix-its and fix-ums before we can reside there, and so we wait in Southampton. 'Twill be months and months, but let them fly by, I say! For I am happy. The anticipation of living in the countryside again sustains me. Like a child holding her breath for Christmas Day, I do the same for Moving Day.

Until then . . . I find myself inexplicably immersed in the joy of celebration. And until Cassandra returns from Godmersham, Martha is my able companion.

"A ball, Jane?" Martha says, pinning her hair into a bun. "I have not been to a ball in—"

"In far too long." I hold my hand in midair as though a gentleman might kiss it as we honour each other before the dance begins. I curtsy—and assume he bows with perfect grace. "But I am not the least bit tired, kind sir," I tell him. "Of course I will dance another with you. And another too, if you but ask."

Martha laughs. "But what if no one asks us to dance?"

I take her by the hand and swirl her under my arm. "Then *we* shall dance together, Miss Lloyd. We shall dance and dance and dance."

We dance and dance and dance.

Our first ball is more amusing than I expect. Martha likes it very much, and I do not gape in energy till the last quarter of an hour. The room is tolerably full, and there are thirty couples in the dance.

We pay an additional shilling for our tea, which we take in an adjoining and very comfortable room.

No one (not even I) expected that I would be asked to dance, but I am asked by a gentleman whom we met on a previous Sunday outing. We have sustained a bowing acquaintance since, and being pleased with his black eyes, I spoke to him at the ball, which brought about this civility; but I do not know his name, and he seems so little at home in the English language that I believe his black eyes may be the best of him.

As for others . . . Captain d'Auvergne's friend appears in regimentals, Caroline Maitland has an officer to flirt with, and Mr. John Harrison is deputed by Captain Smith (being himself absent) to ask me to dance. Everything goes well, especially after we tuck Mrs. Lance's neckhandkerf in behind and fasten it with a pin. The melancholy part is seeing so many dozens of young women standing by without partners, and each of them with two ugly naked shoulders. It is the same room in which we danced fifteen years ago. . . .

I think much about this and, in spite of the shame of being

much older, feel thankful that I am quite as happy now as then.

In the carriage home, I laugh aloud at the memory, causing Martha to ask, "What amuses?"

"Dark eyes," I say. "Fine eyes." I remember a line Mr. Darcy utters in *First Impressions* and I repeat it with some semblance of the rich baritone I imagine him to have. "'I have been meditating on the very great pleasure which a pair of fine eyes can bestow.'"

Martha, who knows my work too well, recognizes it. "'Tis a good line, Jane."

"All Mr. Darcy's lines are good lines," I say. "He would not accept anything less."

We laugh in complete agreement.

EXTRAORDINARY
ENDOWMENTS

EIGHTEEN

I will not miss this closet. This wet, bereft closet.

Nor will I miss the cold winds that blow in from the sea.

People in Southampton say they do not remember such a severe winter as this. For my own opinion, it is bad, but we do not suffer as we did last year, because the wind has been more northeast than northwest. For a day or two last week, Mother was very poorly, with a return of one of her old complaints. But it did not last long and seems to have left nothing bad behind it. She began to talk of a serious illness, her last two having been preceded by the same symptoms; but thank heaven she is now quite as well as one can expect her to be in weather which deprives her of exercise.

I press the cloth into the closet wetness and squeeze it damp into the bucket. Over and over. Our battle of the closet began last November when we had some very blowing weather and so much rain that it forced its way into this store closet. Tho' the evil was comparatively slight, and the mischief nothing, I had some employment the next day in drying parcels.

Now the January wetness offers an encore. We have been in two or three dreadful states within the last week, this time from the melting of the snow. The contest between us and the closet has ended in our defeat, and I am obliged to move everything out of it and leave it to splash itself as it likes. Could my ideas flow as fast as the rain it collects, I might be quite eloquent.

And yet, even as I dip and damp and wring, I do so with a joy far beyond what is due such a moment. *Drip, O house! Apply your worst! Our spirit 'twill not be dampened. For soon, you will be ours no more, and all your vice forsaken!*

'Tis not a laudable verse but the best I can do while wearing soggy shoes.

On April third—Easter Monday—we plan to quit this place and rise anew, to a new life.

An apt and fitting date.

Alleluia!

&—&

I do not know what has got into me, because I am usually not assertive. I am not demanding. I am not . . . a man.

Yet as I awaken this morning, the fifth of April, still in Southampton, yet holding fast to the promise of Chawton, I get out pen and ink and begin a letter.

A letter that will change my life.

I only hope.

And so, with the deepest of breaths to fuel me, and the quickest of prayers to give me wisdom, I write to Mr. Richard Crosby:

Gentlemen:

In the spring of the year 1803 a MS. Novel in 2 vol. entitled Susan was sold to you by a Gentleman of the name of Seymour, & the purchase money 10£ recd at the same time. Six years have since passed, & this work of which I am myself the Authoress, has never to the best of my knowledge, appeared in print, tho' an early publication was stipulated for at the time of sale. I can only account for such an extraordinary circumstance by supposing the Ms. by some carelessness to have been lost; & if that was the case, am willing to supply you with another copy if you are disposed to avail yourselves of it, & will engage for no farther delay when it comes into your hands. It will not be in my power from particular circumstances to command this copy before the Month of August, but then, if you accept my proposal, you may depend on receiving it. Be so good as to send me a Line in answer as soon as possible, as my stay in this place will not exceed a few days. Should no notice be taken of this address, I shall feel myself at liberty to secure the publication of my work, by applying elsewhere. I am Gentlemen & c. & c.

M.A.D.
Direct to Mrs. Ashton Dennis
April 5 1809
Post Office, Southampton

I have held my breath throughout the writing, and expel it loudly before taking another. I smile at the initials, as well as the persona I created for such a letter. If Crosby is a bright man, he should understand the implication.

For I *am* mad. I have waited six years for them to fulfill their promise. That I have not written sooner—nor employed Henry or his lawyer Seymour to do so in my stead—is due to familial circumstances beyond my control. And cowardice. I have been too consumed with surviving like a heroine to truly become one by embracing the heroine's attributes of strength, intelligence, and wisdom in the ways of the world.

That I now pretend to own those laudable attributes is more playacting than sincere, and yet, with the strength sparked by our upcoming move, I will take the chance. *I* will take it, and not assign it to others to do for me.

For ignited within my breast is a new fire. I have set aside my manuscripts too long. It is time they are brought forward and given a fresh start.

Like the one that is being given to me.

I hold the letter in my hand and see the notation of its sender: *Messers Crosby & Co.* "It did not take him long," I say aloud.

'Tis luck there is no one round to hear me.

In my hand lies my future.

With a racing heart I break the seal.

And read the words. And read the words again.

"He will not do it?" I ask the air. "He implies there was no promise? No stipulation? No contract to publish immediately—at all? He lies! And what is this about suing if anyone else publishes it?"

As if a masochist, I go over his final words once more: *If you would care of the retrieval of said manuscript, company agrees to sell it back to Mrs. Ashton Dennis, in its entirety for £10—its original amount.*

I toss the letter on a chair. "It might as well be one hundred pounds as ten. For I do not have it." My usual income—derived a bit here and there from many sources and gifts—is not more than fifty pounds a year. I do not have the ten just sitting about, waiting for this . . . this cretin to grab it back.

I snatch up the letter and head towards the friendly fire. "So much for that," I say. But as I am poised to consign the letter to the flame, I pull it to safety. Most likely Mr. Crosby would appreciate his words being destroyed, all evidence of his deceit and cunning erased.

No indeed. I will not burn these horrid words away. I will keep them close to my heart, fueling my own fire within.

The time has come!

Our exit from Southampton reminds me of another day two and a half years before . . . in leaving Bath I felt release and escape. If running alongside the horses would have hastened our departure, I would have done it.

But this parting is far different, and as our carriage takes us away from Southampton, I peer out the window with fondness. Yes, I am glad to go, but not for any want of Southampton. It has treated me well, and I set it upon a gentle chair in my memories.

As city turns to country, I sit back in the carriage. I look across to Mother, then get an idea. "Will you change with me?"

"What, you say?"

"Change seats with me."

"Whatever for? I can assure you mine here is no more comfortable than yours there."

"Please, Mother?"

With a gruff and grumble she complies. I settle in, feeling oddly triumphant. For 'tis only appropriate that I shew Southampton—and my past—my back.

And welcome Chawton—and my future—face forward.

It is all I hoped for. Dreamed of. All that I need.

Mother and I arrive first. Martha will come after a London visit, and Cassandra will arrive from Godmersham. And though I yearn for the arrival of my sisters, though I am eager to share this happy time with them, I am content to be here, just a little, alone. All the better to drink it in.

Mother has rushed ahead through the house, chattering with a servant who has made things ready. I slip behind to see the house on my own terms, to notice what *I* notice, and linger over what demands me to linger.

The cottage is L-shaped and was once a posting inn. It has been here near forever—at least one hundred years e'en now. It stands red brick, a tall two storeys, with two attic dormers peeking out beneath the tiled roof. From the road, the house looks larger than it is, because the L is not seen. And yet I do not mind the illusion, for inside, it is far large enough.

The house sits on a busy cross of three roads: one leading to Winchester to the southwest, London, just fifty miles northeast, and Portsmouth and Gosport to the south. The church and Edward's Chawton House—which we have visited—are but a ten-minute walk along the Gosport road. And the village of Alton, where Henry has a branch of his bank, is but a mile away towards

London. Edward has informed us that Chawton itself has 64 houses, 65 families, 171 males, and 201 females—205 now. . . . Many of the men work in agriculture, most for Edward, with many others labouring at the looms at Alton. It is said the calicos and fine worsteds make their way to America. I have yet to test their quality but surely will.

Edward's efforts to make the cottage suitable are very amiable. Because of the busyness of the intersection, he bricked a window on the front side and opened another window to the garden. There is plenty of space to dine and relax in the sitting room. He has renewed the plumbing by improvements to the outer pump and privy.

I climb six steps to a landing, then eight steps more to reach the bedchambers. I am immediately drawn to the one on my left, for it is farthest from the main road and overlooks the green garden. It has its own fireplace and, though the room is small, would be enough for Cassandra and me. Although I have been told there are enough rooms for each to have her own, Cassandra has already made it known she is agreeable to leave the extra room as the best bedroom for guests and continue to share with me. We are a pair, the two of us. Our niece Anna even chides that we dress too much alike, and seeing us walk up the lane together—with matching caps—she cannot tell us one from the other. But the truth be that I know Cassandra's starched notions, and she is well aware of my queer meanderings. She is the quiet one, while I am full of fool and folly. We complement each other and perhaps together make a proper whole. The family knows this, and there will be no argument. So . . . although I will allow Cassandra an opinion of this room or another, I know her well enough to be assured that I now stand in *our* room.

I take the deepest breath manageable, drinking the sweet air. The open window brings in wafts of lilac and lavender. The gentle rustle of the beech trees provides the softest accompaniment to the moment. I breathe again. Freely. Easily.

I spread my arms wide and turn full circle.

This is the time. My time. For finally I am completely, positively at home.

❦

Cassandra is here! After a nine-month stay at Godmersham, we are together again. And though I do not begrudge my brother's family her companionship and wise services—especially during their bereavement—I greedily accept her presence as mine, all mine.

I help her unpack, placing items in the dresser drawers I have kept empty for her use. "So?" I ask, unable to restrain myself. "Do you like it? Do you approve?"

She stands erect and arches her back with a groan. "I would like and approve of anything that is not moving right now. Four days in a carriage . . ."

"Cass . . ."

She holds a pelisse against her chest. "It is delightful, Jane. You know that."

"I know that."

We hear the clatter of hoofs upon the road. "It is rather busier than I expected," she says.

"It is no bother. In fact, I quite like the commotion."

She gapes at me, with good reason. "And here I always thought you required complete country solitude."

I sit on the bed, shake my head, and try to explain. "'Tis what I thought too. I often imagined being a hermit might be best for my writing. Merely find me a cave with a flat rock as a table and I would be content."

"A flat rock, but a soft bed."

I shrug. "But here at Chawton, I have the green prospects that fulfill me, as well as the incitement of the world buzzing about. 'Tis like I am the hub of a wheel, set to observe the spokes radiating away from me. Radiating towards me. I am at the best place, Cassandra. Rooted in green solitude, with long branches reaching out to touch the world." I sigh. "I do not know if I say it rightly."

"You say it well enough."

"I now realize I do not write about pastoral fields and flowers. I write about people, and so to see them, yet be able to step away from them . . . it is the ideal."

She tosses away the stockings she has been rolling and faces me. "Writing? You are writing again?"

My cheeks grow warm. "I am."

Cassandra sits beside me, setting a hand upon mine. "Oh, Jane. Nothing could make me happier than to have you feel settled enough to write. I have seen your torment and have agonized over how to make things just right so you could feel at liberty to create. I am so glad Edward listened and—"

She stops talking. I withdraw my hand. "Did *you* ask Edward to give us Chawton?"

"I may have mentioned it. But there were others more influential than I who thought it a grand solution.".

I have only to think a moment. "Mrs. Knight?"

"She is a wise woman and a good mother to all who need her."

I rise to my feet. "I will write to her this very minute!" I say. "I must thank her for—"

Cassandra puts a calming hand on my arm. "You will do no such thing. It proved to be a delicate procedure putting the idea of this place in Edward's conscience while allowing him to think he was the one who came up with it. Mrs. Knight and I have agreed to never speak of our part. 'Tis Edward who must receive your gratitude and praise."

Ah. So that is how it is. "Yet I *may* write Mrs. Knight to tell her how delightful it is here?"

"I am assured you will word it just so."

I give Cassandra a kiss to her forehead. "Thank *you*, sister. This

verse is truly yours: 'Who can find a virtuous woman? for her price
is far above rubies.'"

"Oh, Jane . . ."

I shake a scolding finger at her. "You may not argue with me. I
forbid it."

She wisely holds her tongue, her ruby blush a fine accessory to
my compliment.

❦ ❦

I did not lie to my sister. For I *am* writing. It started the first
evening after we entered this cottage. I retired early to my new
room, feigning exhaustion. For though my body was tired, my mind
was not.

For the first time in the eight long years of exile, I was free,
fortified, and full to overflowing.

I left my clothes unpacked. Chemises, stockings, and dresses did
not deserve to see this room first.

I went to the trunk that was a patient constant in my life, that
had made every journey by my side, ever faithful, ever watchful for
the right moment to demand release.

This was that time.

I opened the trunk and gazed upon the work of my life; pages
and pages of words carefully chosen, drawing images of people who
were as real to me as flesh and blood, who lived lives that had been
put on hold while I muddled through my own struggles and disappointments.

Now all that was over, and they could be set free—as free as I
myself.

But which should be the first to experience emancipation?

It was not a hard choice. The one about two sisters, Elinor and
Marianne—two sisters forced to live with their mother in a country

cottage due to the inequities of the inheritance system. . . .

It is time I address the issue at hand: sense and sensibility.

Which serves a life best?

We shall see.

NINETEEN

If Chawton is my liberation, Cassandra is my liberator. She gives me the time I need to write, and if she would let me, I would lie prostrate at her feet in thanksgiving.

I am not the only one who is willing to let Cassandra handle the household. For Mother has declared herself retired. At seventy, she is quite willing to let the house run as it will and concentrate on her needlework and her beloved garden. She clips and cuts, and directs the willing hands of the villagers, who respectfully accept us as the kin of their patron, Edward Knight. The garden is no idle pastime, no mere cutting of roses and tying up of flowers. She digs her own potatoes and plants them, for the kitchen garden is as much her delight as the flower borders. She has even taken to wearing a green round frock like a day labourer.

And I, from the bedroom window, enjoy the irregular mixture of hedgerow and grass, gravel walk and long grass for mowing, as well as the orchard, which I imagine arose from two or three little enclosures having been thrown together and arranged as best might be, for some ladies' occupation.

With Mother so occupied and happy, Cassandra and Martha have set their stores in all things domestic. Although I have offered to do more, they refuse, and joined to the possession of much good sense, they are both blessed with sweet temper, amiable dispositions, and what is of far greater importance, minds deeply impressed with the truth of Christianity. They live "Thou shalt love thy neighbour as thyself" with their entire being.

And so, with their generous natures firmly in place, I am free to . . . to be Jane. Day to day, day after day, just Jane.

It sounds too simple to be of import, but to me, it is the gift of a life returned.

My life seems effortless and I revel in its simplicity.

I get up first and start each day by playing my newly acquired piano in the drawing room, far away from their ears. To have an instrument again after mine was so sorely sold back in Steventon . . .

Music calms me, and I improve, though I feel no need to use this talent to entertain others. I do not deserve, nor seek, that approbation. 'Tis enough for my ears to hear the notes. And God. Hopefully He is pleased by my offering.

Next, the maid makes a fire in the dining room, setting water on to heat, and I prepare a nine-o'clock breakfast for the rest— merely tea and toast. It is no trouble whatsoever and I almost feel guilty in calling it a duty. I oft feel like a man must feel, with all my daily needs cared for, in some way, somehow, by the sweet women of the house.

Except for my laying the meager breakfast and keeping charge of the tea, sugar, and wine stores, Martha and Cassandra take responsibility for all else: the morning snack and the late-afternoon dinner. And though we employ a cook, these sisters of mine are kept quite busy with tasks to make sure all is right. Martha takes pride in her book of recipes and home remedies and regularly makes new, meticulous entries within its pages.

As I do in my own "book."

I am nearly finished with the edits of *Sense and Sensibility* and actually found little to change. I have read it aloud to the females assembled here, and all appreciate its story, though Mother regrets that Marianne does not end with a passionate love match. Colonel Brandon is too safe for her tastes. And yet, I will not change it. For I like that respect and an amiable affection are the basis for the match. Must everything be passion and fireworks? I think not. And as Marianne's combustive nature revealed, perhaps it is in her best interest to live a life more prone to calm and contentment over fervor and free feeling. As I have learned these eight long years, true black and white rarely exists, and as such, I see no harm in letting Marianne live in a land of gray—as we all must do on occasion.

There can be beauty in gray. Calm in gray.

I know arguments can be made, and I do not mind them. To induce the reader to discussion—whether their opinion post yay or nay—is an author's victory. I do not wish to write a story where all is completely as it should be. At least not without a good bit of trials, travails, and travels along the way.

I finish with my music this morning, and as I play the final chord, I rise and move eagerly to those who call upon my attention.

Not Mother or Cassandra or Martha.

But Elinor and Marianne.

"But he is not for you, Anna. You must not marry him." Even as I say them, I realize my words to my niece will have the consequence of a raindrop on a rushing waterfall. I have often teased that dear Anna can be accused of doing or feeling too little or too much. Finding the middle ground is not her forte.

Anna picks at a wilted rose in the table vase. "He is a clergyman like Father and Grandfather," Anna says. "I would think that would please everyone."

"But he is far over thirty, and you but sixteen."

"I am a woman," she declares, then looks away.

She is a child. A child who seeks escape from her parents' home, from a father who has mellowed to middle age, and a stepmother who much prefers her own issue.

She continues her defense. "Mr. Terry is a fine man, and now that he is related to the Steventon Digweeds through his sister's marriage, there can be no issue of family."

"I am certain he *is* a very fine man," I say. "But what makes you believe he is your man?"

She ignores the question. "Father has given his permission."

"His reluctant permission, or so I have heard."

She removes the offending rose and throws it in the fire. "Father is not capable of great enthusiasm. For anything. But his sermons."

I cannot argue with her. Dear James, the brother who once wrote rousing plays, has used his literary talents to write less-than-rousing epistles. In private I blame Mary. She has overpowered him and drowned the James I once knew. And yet . . . they seem happy. In their own way.

Although never married, I have witnessed enough unions to know that "in their own way" is an obvious preferable alternative to "never at all." Any union between two souls is difficult, at best, and complicated, for certain. But for Anna to chuse a man simply because of his proximity and his ability to remove her from a home in which she finds no solace or nurture?

"I am going to Godmersham, and Mr. Terry is going to visit me there. Does that not say something about his commitment?"

It does, but I will not encourage her in this. "You go," I say. "Time to think is always agreeable."

"I go for pleasure, not to think."

The statement holds meaning—and implication—far beyond her intent.

With a new breath she continues, "I want Cousin Fanny to share in my happiness. Which she will, with her whole heart." With that said, she turns on her heel and leaves me to worry after her.

Which I will do with great intensity and propensity.

"Even after meeting Mr. Terry, Edward and Fanny approved?"

Anna has been to Godmersham and is back again. She flits about the drawing room in the same manner as she did before her travels. "They did, but I have decided against it."

"Against the engagement," I say.

"He is not the one for me." She looks at me, daring me with my own words. "You were against it, Aunt Jane. In this very room you spoke against it."

I run my hands across my face, roughly trying to shock myself into this new reality. "I cannot keep up with you, Anna. You beg to wed Mr. Terry, and now you say it is over?"

"It is," she says, trimming a candlewick with the pinch of her fingers. "I do not expect anyone to understand it."

"Good, because we do not."

"I simply cannot marry him. Surely *you* can understand such a change of mind, Aunt Jane."

The way she looks at me implies she knows about Harris. And yet but for a few choice family members I had assumed it secret.

Secret or not, I am pleased her interest in Mr. Terry is over. She is young. She is pretty and vivacious—albeit a touch flighty. There is plenty of time for her to find another.

"Surely you understand?" she says again.

Although I will never understand this girl, I do approve. "What can I say?" I finally manage.

"Nothing," says Anna with a smile of victory. "Now tell me, what are you writing on? Aunt Cassandra tells me you write every day."

"I do. I currently work on an old story with a new title."

"Which one is it?"

"It was called by *First Impressions*, but now I call it *Pride and Prejudice*."

Her eyes light up. "You have read me a part of that one! It was most capital."

"But now 'tis far different, for I have made many radical alterations and contractions. It has been quite freely lopt and cropt. Do you know it has been sixteen years since I first wrote it? It was truly full of *my* 'first impressions' about life."

"Is Mr. Darfield still in it?"

It took me a moment. "Mr. Darcy?"

"Yes, him. I like him."

"Oh yes," I say. "He is still there, as proud as ever."

"Do he and Lizzy marry? You never read me the ending."

I smile an author's secret smile. "I will not tell you now. You will have to read it once it is published."

"Published? You are getting it published? Really published? Like a real book?"

I have said too much, for nothing is certain. Although I have given my full heart to *Pride and Prejudice*, I wish to hold this manuscript off just a bit and pave its way with another. "Your uncle Henry is working on my behalf for *Sense and Sensibility*."

"Has it been accepted?"

"'Tis not so simple. We have to make the decision whether to sell it outright—which I am wary to do considering my past experience—or find a publisher to print it and give me a portion of the profit, or—"

"The second sounds the better way."

"But the most difficult," I say. "Henry has a friend interested, a distant cousin on the Leigh side, Thomas Egerton, but he has said he is unwilling to take the risk, cousin or no. The last option is the one we have chosen. To publish it through Mr. Egerton but at my own expense. Our own expense. At least for this first one. For I have two other books near ready to publish. But first, I need to get one accomplished. And Mr. Egerton is not alone in his reticence. No one is eager to publish an unknown. Nor a woman."

"So you are putting up the money from your own—"

"I . . . I have no money to risk. But Henry, as my most vocal and enthusiastic supporter, has done it for me. I am in his debt—unless, of course, the book belies the odds and makes a few pence in profit."

Anna takes my hands in her own, her eyes bright. "Oh, it will, Aunt Jane! I know it will. 'Tis a wonderful story. And Uncle Henry is ever so right in backing it."

Henry, with the help of Eliza's money. Although I had not been completely supportive of the match so many years ago, and had wanted Henry to become a clergyman, I have come to realize that Eliza, and London, and his career as a banker, and the vivacity of a life filled with entertainment and society, are perfect for my brother.

And now, perfect for me. For as a clergyman, he would not have had the contacts nor the income to aid me now. Providence is wise even as people only ponder. How ironic, though comforting, to realize that God knows what He is doing.

As—I hope—does my brother.

⟡

"Well?"

Mary stands before us with James proudly at her side. He holds a portrait they have had painted. Of her.

She looks at each of our faces in turn, waiting for effusive compliments. We are not an effusive family—when the compliments would prove false. Father always taught us that honesty . . .

Is not always the best policy?

Mother, being the matriarch and more and more beyond overly caring what others think, takes a step forward, her eyes moving back and forth between Mary and her painted image. She is to comment first.

I admire her courage.

"Well, Mary . . . I cannot say it affords me pleasure. The upper part of the face is like you, and so is the mouth, but the nose . . . the feature that strikes me . . . is so *unlike* you that it spoils the whole and moreover makes you look very cross and sour."

Mary and James stand agape.

I do not know whether to laugh, cry—or flee.

Mary juts out her chin (making the portrait appear more true) and says, "At least I have a portrait. I think it is absolutely deplorable that the Austen men have all had their portraits painted and yet you three women have not. Elizabeth and Eliza have had their portraits taken."

Neither Elizabeth nor Eliza was the wife or daughter of a clergyman.

Mary looks to Martha, her sister. "Surely you, Martha . . ."

"It is a good likeness," manages Martha.

After what Mother has said, this is not necessarily a compliment.

Mary looks at her husband. "James? I believe it is time to leave."

James has not said a word but offers us a quick bow to his head, then follows his wife outside.

"Mother, that was a bit unkind," says Cassandra.

"She asked for our opinion, did she not?"

"She did," I say.

Martha moves to the window and watches her sister ride away. "Mary needs to accept that we Lloyd women are not beautiful. It is this nose," she says, running a finger along the hook of it.

"'Tis an aquiline nose," says Mother. "I too possess such a gift." She huffs out.

The three of us look to each other and laugh. "But alas, I possess no such gift." I trace the line of my nose, which Mother has always disparaged for its lack of curve. I set myself between Martha and Cassandra and whisper, "I think our greatest blessing is that the portrait will hang at Steventon."

❦ ❦

That very afternoon, Cassandra comes into our room, points to the book I have been reading, and says, "Put that down."

"This?" I say, holding up *Ida of Athens* by Miss Owenson. "'Tis no great loss. Nobody ever heard of it before and perhaps never may again. And yet I began my perusal with the hopes that it must be very clever because it was written—as the authoress says—in three months. I am afraid her Irish girl does not make me expect much. If the warmth of her language could affect the body, it might be worth reading in our chilly weath—"

She takes the book from me. "I did not come here for a book review."

Her eyes are intent and she carries her bag of art supplies in her free hand. "So. Why *have* you sought me out this fine afternoon?"

"I wish to take your portrait."

"I have no need to compete with Mary," I say.

"I assure you my talent will not compete."

"For yours is far greater."

She rolls her eyes, then directs me to the other chair, furthest from the window. She assesses the light and adjusts my pose just so.

"I have not assented to this," I say.

She sharpens her pencil with a knife. "I am not offering you assent. I am determined. There should be one portrait taken of Jane Austen, the authoress."

I am happy to play along and lift my chin, attempting regal bearing. "Then do your best. My future fame depends upon it."

❧ ❧

Dinner is called, calling *off* my first ever portrait sitting. I rub the back of my neck. "I did not realize it was hard work."

Cassandra puts away her tools. "Let this be our secret," she asks. "At least until I am satisfied." She studies the small page, a mere four inches by three inches in size.

"May I see?"

She bites her lip. "It is not right. Not yet. Your eyes are too large, your mouth too small."

"I look a bit dour," I say. "Surely, I am not dour."

"As I say, the lips are not right."

"Ah, but the nose is quite perfect. There is no aquilinity about it by any opinion. Mother will be so pleased you did not give me an attribute I do not deserve."

We hear from below, "Girls? Are you coming?"

Cassandra slips my very first portrait under a doily on the dresser. I offer her my arm. "Shall we?"

⊱—⊰

I sit in Henry and Eliza's Sloane Street home in London. I hold the first proof pages of my book—*my book*—*Sense and Sensibility*. As I am paying for the production myself, I have no editor. No proofreader. My submission goes to the printer, they print each page but once, then give them to me for final consideration. I am to say yes, this is acceptable, or no, please change what is not.

I have the power.

I have the last word.

I have the responsibility.

I run my hand across the page: *The Miss Dashwoods had now been rather more than two months in town, and Marianne's impatience to be gone increased every day. She sighed for the air, the liberty, the quiet of the country; and fancied that if any place could give her ease, Barton must do it. . . .*

I feel the words, as if they have true substance.

In a way they do.

Because they are my words.

This is my story.

Based on thoughts from my mind and feelings from my heart.

That others will read.

"Feeling a bit heady, are we?"

Eliza stands at the doorway to the study that they so kindly let me use for this purpose. "So much depends on this. Everything depends on this. All things happen for a reason—but that does not mean all things succeed as we hope."

She nods, and I see a distant look in her eyes. Although Eliza is effervescent, she is hard to fathom, as if she is always set apart by some invisible wall we cannot breech. And yet I know she understands hard experience. Losing a husband to the guillotine, having a son suffer great infirmity, marrying my brother who often is more successful at thinking up, rather than settling down . . .

I look back to the page before me. "I still find this hard to fathom. Can it be real?"

"'Tis only a beginning, Jane. Eventually there will be the two others."

I am brave enough to smile with confidence. "Three."

Her beautiful eyebrows rise. "Oh?"

"I have started a fourth book. As of February."

"What is its name?"

"Mansfield Park."

"No *something and something*?"

"Not this time."

She enters the room in her effortless way, and the study seems more vibrant with her presence. "What is this one about?"

"A poor relation being taken in by rich relatives. A duel of morals and immorality. Temptation and strength." I watch her carefully, wondering what she will think when she reads about the charming Mary Crawford, or Mrs. Bertram, who loves pugs and dramatically lounging just as much as—

"Oooh," she coos. "Will I like it?"

The Jane of last year would say, *I hope so,* but the new Jane I have become says, "Of course."

Eliza laughs. "Our party is tonight. Will you be able to pull yourself away to attend?"

"Of course. Again."

Now that my writing has its own solid place within the moments of my life, I am free to enjoy all the moments more fully.

The rooms are dressed with flowers and look lovely. A glass for the mantelpiece was lent by the man who is making a permanent one for Henry's house. Mr. Egerton and Mr. Walter come at half past five, two very fine gentlemen to begin the festivities. At half past seven the musicians arrive in two hackney coaches, and by eight the lordly company begins to appear. Among the earliest are George and Mary Cooke, and I spend the greatest part of the evening very pleasantly with them. The drawing room being soon hotter than we like, we place ourselves in the connecting passage, which is comparatively cool and gives us the advantage of the music at a pleasant distance, as well as the advantage of the first view of every new-comer.

We are sixty-six in count, which is considerably more than Eliza had expected and quite enough to fill the back drawing room and leave a few to be scattered about in the other, and in the passage. The music is extremely good: "In Peace Love Tunes," "Rosabelle," "The Red Cross Knight," and "Poor Insect." Between the songs are lessons on the harp, or harp and pianoforte together—and the harp player is named Wiepart, whose name seems famous, tho' new to me. There is one female singer, a short Miss Davis all in blue, whose voice is very fine indeed, and all the performers give great satisfaction by doing what they are paid for, and giving themselves no airs. No amateur can be persuaded to do anything. Sometimes wisdom does prevail over a desire for attention.

Wyndham Knatchbull calls me a "pleasing-looking young woman." At five and thirty, *that* must do; I cannot pretend to anything better now, and I am thankful to have such compliments continue a few years longer.

The house is not clear till after twelve. The most interesting news is that Captain Simpson tells us, on the authority of some other captain just arrived from Halifax, that Charles is bringing the

Cleopatra home, and that she is probably by this time in the Channel. But as Captain Simpson is certainly in liquor, we must not quite depend on it. It does give me a sort of expectation and will prevent my writing to Charles until I hear from him. I do long to meet his wife. He met Fanny Palmer far away in Bermuda during his four years there and now has two children we have never seen! To add to the clan, Frank and Little Mary now have a son, his namesake. 'Tis so wonderful they have moved inland, near Alton to be closer to us, for in spite of my complaints, I do feel most complete and at ease among children.

Speaking of children . . . Mother and Martha both write with great satisfaction of Anna's behaviour. She is quite an Anna with many variations, but she cannot have reached her last (for that is always the most flourishing and shewey). She is at about her third or fourth variation, which are generally simple and pretty.

At any rate, the party is in the paper the next day. Imagine. I, Jane, in attendance at such a party. The old Jane would have been wary and quiet until an acquaintance was made, but this new Jane . . .

I keep stating it so: *this new Jane.* And yet I am new. I spent most of my life as someone's daughter, someone's sister, someone's aunt or friend. But now, on the edge of an accomplishment that is wholly mine and mine alone, I have gained a substance that is centered within. It is as though God has finally shewn me my purpose. Like the Israelites, I may have wandered my own desert, wandered aimlessly for years, unsure and confused, but now, I see the Promised Land, and it is good.

I do not know whether my books—and yes, I know in my heart that more than this one will come to fruition—will reach one reader or many. It is something beyond my control. And though I wish great success be heaped upon it, I am willing to let Providence guide its patronage. God has led me this far. He will not abandon me now.

In her last letter Cassandra asks after the book, and I honestly tell her that I am never too busy to think of it. I can no more forget it than a mother can forget her suckling child. I tell her my progress, and Mrs. Knight regrets in the most flattering manner that she must wait till May to read it. But due to the slowness of the printer, I have scarcely a hope of its being out in June. I think she will like my Elinor, but I cannot build on anything else. Henry does not neglect the publishing; he hurries the printer and says he will see him again today.

But until my work is complete, Henry has tickets to the Lyceum to see *The Hypocrite*, and then another day he plans to take us to see the Watercolour Exhibition. I have heard there are many paintings by women—for watercolour is now considered a woman's art.

In the past I have always been agog at the life Henry and Eliza live, often disparaging in its regard. And yet, now, with this new freedom that has infected me, I feel in a celebratory mood and see the advantage of festive minds. As such, I am ready to enjoy the constant celebration that lives at the core of my brother's world.

Life is good. And I am richly blessed.

I am back at Chawton and am thoroughly glad to be here. I find it amusing and more than a little intriguing that since moving to this place, I find little need to leave. In the two years since our arrival, I have not once been to Godmersham. I have but been to London—to Henry's—on business (what a glorious word!) and for a short visit to James's. Although unrealized until now, I believe that my many trips and visits in the past were a means by which I did not need to live in any place that did not cause me happiness. And so . . . I escaped to the homes of others. Yet by admitting this, I also admit a selfish pursuit of said happiness.

For that I am guilty.

Beyond that pursuit (which may be called forgivable, as it is common in all men) is the unforgivable act of complaining. For what good comes from that particular vice—for the complainer, or her unlucky listener?

I am as much guilty of that then as I am guilty of contentment now.

For now, I am content to deal with nouns and verbs, with commas and semicolons, and even with the flawed vitality of my character Mary Crawford against the staid morality of Fanny Price.

I am content to take pleasure in our young peony at the foot of the fir tree that has just bloomed and looks very handsome indeed. I am content to offer a smile of expectation at the shrubbery border that will soon be very gay with pinks and Sweet Williams in addition to the columbines already in bloom. The syringas too are coming out for my benefit, and we are likely to have a great crop of Orleans plums. And our intent is to save the chickens for something grand.

I enjoy sitting with my mother in the front room and revel in her delight as we watch the traffic go by. I laugh (albeit silently) at her habit in rainy weather of sitting with the curtains open. I received a letter from Mrs. Knight that said a traveling gentleman friend of hers (riding by in a post chaise) had seen the Chawton party looking very comfortable at breakfast. If we had but known of his connection to our friend, we would have waved a greeting.

I do not even mind that the stillness of the night is frequently broken by the noise of passing carriages, so thunderous that they often shake the beds.

All these things great, and all these things small, contain the essence of my life. The only betterment will be when I hold my finished book in my hand.

And though I continually fight impatience, in all but this vice . . .

I am truly content.

It rains. We sit in the drawing room and do our needlework. I take an odd joy in such work, as it is the only work men are not allowed to do. It is *our* work, and we each excel in it.

For it is not just the finished work that holds merit, but the working.

As I look about the room at Mother, Martha, and my sister, I marvel at the invisible thread that binds us here. Each busy within her own creative task, we are linked by a commonality of purpose. And though we are pleased—or not—with the results of our labours, unlike those of the male gender, we do not feel the need to compete by assuming a mine-is-better position. We unite through this women-time; we do not divide.

Mother sighs, lowers her crewel work, and rubs her eyes. "'Tis teatime, is it not?"

Martha sets aside her own work and stands. "It can be."

And so we move from one occupation to the next, the delight in each other's company enough to sustain us.

As I gather cups, I think of how different socializing is here in Chawton than elsewhere. Unlike Bath and Southampton, which were often destinations for friends and relatives on holiday, no one comes to Chawton on a lark. In those locales, I always found it hard to concentrate on the light dialogue of such visits and often weighed my words and sentences more than the norm, looking about for a sentiment, an illustration, or a metaphor in every corner of the room. The effort was often wearying, creating a need for *us* to desire our own holiday.

But now . . . there is no such need. Our home is a home, not an inn for lodgers, no matter how amiable and familial.

'Tis not that I utterly disliked their visits. Of course not. But to be here, where the comings and goings of others is more controlled, brings with it a level of serenity that could never be found in those larger cities with their holiday delights.

We are not hermits. We do not sit with doors locked, never to venture out. 'Tis not like that at all. If I have but pride, it is that I am getting to know Chawton in its entirety. I know Triggs, the gamekeeper at the great house, I know Eleanor Papillion, the niece of the rector. (Mrs. Knight once told me I could move to Chawton if I married Eleanor's uncle. I assured her that I would straightaway.) Eleanor and I often visit the poor in each other's company. She is quite as delightful as I.

I also often tolerate the Miss Sibleys, who want to start a Book Society, acting as though it were their own brilliant idea when I have overseen many others. I am conversant with Harriot Webb, who cannot say her *r*'s. I have even tolerated listening to her read— an adventu'e to be su'e.

I know the mighty William Prowting, the justice of the peace, and the Middletons, who let the big house from Edward, at least for a time. (I do hope Edward takes it back, as I *do* long to have *them* come visit and stay so close.)

And I know the lowly. I am on friendly terms with Miss Benn, who has too much extended family and not enough money for any. I call her my "unavoidable" neighbour. She reminds me a great deal of poor Miss Stent back in Steventon. She likes to chatter away, saying absolutely nothing at all. Her taste in clothing is questionable and a bit ratty, and Martha bought her a nice shawl, but on my advice not *too* nice, or Miss Benn would never wear it.

The list goes on, proving that we are not reclusive in our cottage here, but merely . . . selective. The praise to the Almighty goes to the fact that we are the ones who do the selecting. This is a very great blessing, and in execution, probably makes us venture out to meet more of our neighbours than we would meet if the neighbours were thrust upon us.

The tea is ready and Cassandra pours. Once resettled in our favourite chairs, talk turns to the world beyond Chawton. Again, this is a change for us. For in previous abodes we found talk of politics and worldly happenings tedious, and left such discussions to the men. But without men near (or perhaps because we are simply more mature) we have taken an interest in such things.

"I hear the Prince has been made Prince Regent," Martha begins.

"'Tis about time," says Mother. "There is talk the King is once again afflicted with his madness."

"It must be more serious this time," says Cassandra.

"There is to be a birthday parade of Volunteers on Selborne Common next week," I offer.

"Isn't his birthday in August?"

I laugh. "Apparently a Prince can declare the celebration at any time of year."

"As many times as he likes," adds Martha.

"Actually," I say, drawing the word out, a true signal that what I am about to say is a bit scandalous, "I heard that he had a party to celebrate his elevation to Prince Regent at Carleton House in London, and the party cost one hundred twenty thousand pounds."

Mother lets her teacup titter against its saucer. "With our country struggling to pay for twenty years of war? Struggling to feed the poor?"

Martha leans close, her voice lowered. "He did not even invite his wife to the party."

"They battle over custody of Princess Charlotte," says Cassandra. "Poor child."

"Poor child, my elbow," says Mother. "At sixteen she flirts with any man available. One of her parents had better take control of her."

"Their father is busy with his own flirtations," I say. "I personally shall support his wife as long as I can, because she is a woman, and because I hate her husband."

"The new Prince Regent has his supporters—many who are no more virtuous than he," says Mother. "Frank wrote to say the Regent appointed the Duke of Clarence as the Admiral of the Fleet, when the Duke has been making a fool of himself, traipsing about with his mistress, who has born him ten children. In spite of that he also pursues pretty young things while speaking *for* the slave trade in the House of Lords." She shakes her head. "A travesty, that is what it is."

"Our brothers should be admirals," says Cassandra. "They are good men with good character."

"If only women ruled the world," I say.

They are silent and stare after me.

"Surely we could do no worse," I offer.

"There is no guarantee of that," says Cassandra.

"No, there is not," says Mother. "And so that leaves us here to complain."

She says it so seriously that we all pause a moment before breaking into laughter.

Such is our life here at merry Chawton.

I would not change a thing.

It is autumn and I help Mother remove the dead flowers from our garden. It is not work I prefer but work I do willingly to help. Not surprisingly, nor uniquely, I much prefer seeing things grow than die.

I hear the garden door creak open. With a glance I see Cassandra approach. "We are glad for the help, sister."

"Indeed we are," says Mother. She stands and, with a hand to her lower back, arches with a groan.

I pull the leaves of a wilted hosta away from its base. They give up easily, almost as if they know and accept the repercussions of the season.

Cassandra stops beside me, and to look up at her, I must shield my eyes against the sun at her back. "Don't just stand there, help me—"

"Stand up."

"Why?"

"Stand, Jane. You must be standing."

She confuses me, but I comply. I wipe my hands on my apron. "There. I am standing. Now explain to me why I *must* be—"

From behind her back she brings forth a package wrapped in brown paper. "It is for you," she says.

I wipe my hands again, better this time. "'Tis way early for my birthday. Who is it fr—?"

But then I see who sent it. Mr. Egerton.

I look to Cassandra, my mouth agape, asking its own question.

"I do not know," she says, "but I assume . . ."

"Assume what?" asks Mother, walking close.

I answer all our inquiries by removing the string and unwrapping the paper. My heart beats in my throat. I am not certain I can breathe. . . .

In unison we gasp. For there, in my own hands, are three volumes. On the cover are the words that make it real: *Sense and Sensibility*.

I juggle them, one to the other.

"Your book," Cassandra says, finally stating the obvious truth since I, for once, have no words.

Mother wipes the dirt from her hands but does not move to take the volumes from me. No one does. For it is my book. Mine.

She looks over my shoulder. "It says 'By a Lady.' Not your name, Jane? Not your name to take credit?"

'Tis a sore point between us, one that has been discussed and rediscussed. "There is too great a risk in being known. I do not want attention. I merely want the book to be out there, being real, being read."

"But with this . . ." Mother points at the epigraph. "Can I not tell the neighbourhood the truth of it?"

"You cannot. Only immediate family. Not even the nieces and nephews, for surely they are too young to hold the confidence."

"I do not like this," says Mother.

Cassandra's voice is softer. "I do not either, yet I understand." She wraps her arms about me. "I am so proud of you, sister."

I am rather proud of myself too. For now, for once and for all, I am truly an author.

TWENTY

"Jane, Jane! Here is another one!"

Cassandra runs into the dining room and places another parcel on the table. It is from Henry.

I unwrap it and find a letter and clippings from periodicals.

"Ooh," Mother says, leafing through the clippings. "These are about you!"

My stomach knots, then releases. "About the book. Not me," I say.

Mother reads one and shakes her head. "No, it is about you." She clears her throat. "The headline reads: 'Interesting Novel by Lady A—: Who could the mysterious Lady A— be?'"

Martha bumps her shoulder to mine. "Oh, *we* know. . . ."

"And here are two reviews!" Mother says, waving two pages in the air like banners.

Banners were for happy occasions, and having not read the reviews as yet . . .

Cassandra gets us focused correctly. "What does Henry say?"

"Just a moment . . ." I do not wish to read the letter word for word, as Henry oft quotes me numbers in regard to sales, and I wish to keep such knowledge to myself—not because I am unwilling to share whatever level of wealth I acquire, but because I may be embarrassed by the lack of it.

I read the letter to myself. He speaks of the first printing not being sold out—I am not exactly sure how many that would be; at one time he mentioned the number one thousand—but he assures me enough have sold to recompense our expense. His expense. For this I am most grateful and am willing to read no further beyond this good bit of news. Yet I have three other ladies waiting to hear more.

"Henry heard that Lady Bessborough has reported her friends were quite full of the book at Althorp."

Mother claps. "The high-and-mighty readers will certainly aid sales."

"But," I say, reading ahead, "she thinks it ends stupidly."

Silence.

I break the moment by offering, "I know many will think Marianne merely settles on Colonel Brandon, and yet, I see it as a goodly match—considering."

"I do too," Cassandra says. "More," she prods me. "Read more."

I read some lines, then say, "Oh my. Here are some opinions even higher than the last," I tease. "For at the prompting of her uncle, the Duke of York, young Princess Charlotte has read the book and says she feels quite one with the company, and claims to have a very like disposition with Marianne—though she is not nearly so good. The book interested her very much."

Mother puts a hand to her chest. "Royalty, Jane. Royalty are reading it!"

"And liking it," Martha says.

I notice Cassandra has taken the reviews from Mother and has been reading them intently. My throat tightens, but I trust her to tell me true. "What do they say?" I ask.

She holds a finger at a particular place, then reads, "This, from the *Critical Review*: 'The incidents are probable, and highly pleasing, and interesting; the conclusion such as the reader must wish it should be, and the whole is just long enough to interest without fatiguing.' It finds that Marianne and Willoughby are strikingly alike."

I nod. "They are. Too much so to be wise for each other."

"That is what I always thought," says Mother. "The best matches occur when two people share commonalities, yet gain complementaries from their mate."

I smile. "Well said, Mother!"

"There is another review from *British Critic*. It is quite long."

My heart beats faster. I wish I did not care what is said about the book, but I do. "If good, I will read its entirety later, if bad, you may toss it out right now."

Cassandra offers me a knowing smile. "But for a few negativities about the overcharged portrait of Sir John Middleton and a confusion in the beginning about who belonged to what family, it—"

"I like Sir John," says Martha. "He is a most jolly sort."

I am more concerned with the second negativity, for it is one I too had pondered. "'Tis always hard in the beginning to set the story right, to bring in the proper characters at the proper time so as not to cause confusion. I obviously brought in too many too soon."

"I understood it," Mother says. "I understood all of it."

I appreciate her defense, more than she could know.

"What good things do they say?" asks Martha.

Cassandra reads here and there on the page. "'The object of the work is to represent the effects on the conduct of life, of discreet, quiet good sense on the one hand, and on overrefined and excessive susceptibility on the other. The characters are happily delineated and admirably sustained.'"

"Perhaps the reviewer is wiser than I first thought," says Mother. "He does seem to understand the gist of it."

"It delineates a bit of the plot, then says . . ." Cassandra finds her place. "'Not less excellent is the picture of the young lady of over exquisite sensibility, who falls immediately and violently in love with a male coquet, without listening to the judicious expostulations of her sensible sister, and believing it impossible for man to be fickle, false, and treacherous. We will, however, detain our female friends no longer than to assure them, that they may peruse these volumes not only with satisfaction but with real benefits, for they may learn from them, if they please, many sober and salutary maxims for the conduct of life, exemplified in a very pleasing and entertaining narrative.'"

I press a hand to my chest, willing myself to breathe.

"They really like it," Martha says. "Really, really like it."

"*And* they deem it educational," adds Mother. "An added benefit, with added worth."

"I did not mean for it to be educational," I say. "At least not with any conscious intent."

"Your stories portray true life," Cassandra says. "In that there is always education."

"Perhaps it is best I do not *try* to teach. At that I would surely fail."

I look back to the letter, which is nearly complete. And yet, Henry has saved the best for last. "Oh dear," I say aloud.

"What? What?" asks Mother.

As tears threaten, I hand her the letter and point to the ending. Mother reads aloud. "'All this to say, dear sister, that Mr. Egerton is very pleased, and would like to buy the copyright for *Pride and Prejudice*. He offers one hundred ten pounds for the copyright.'"

Mother gapes. "One hundred ten pounds!"

"I was hoping for one-fifty."

Everyone stares, and in but a moment I realize my gaff. "Where did that come from?" I ask sheepishly.

Cassandra smiles. "It comes from being an astute businesswoman. From being a prized author who has been deemed a success."

I put my hands to my mouth, letting the tears loose. The dear women in my life come forth and we all embrace as one.

For in truth, my success is also theirs.

I am excited about a visit to Chawton by both Henry and Eliza. They do not often travel together, so it will be a treat. It will also give me a chance to talk to Henry about the publication of *Pride and Prejudice*. After long consideration I am very hesitant about selling the copyright to Mr. Egerton—for any price. I feel so strongly about this book and its strength (more than any other) that I do not think limiting my return to *any* amount—much less one hundred ten pounds—is wise. For in selling the copyright . . . if it sells beyond that earning, I will get nothing additional. At least not for the fourteen-year length of the copyright. And even then, if it sells well, he may chuse to renew it.

The advantage in living at the crossing of three roads is that I hear the coming of their carriage, the halt of the wheels, and the neighing and huffing of the horses.

I run to the door to be the first to greet them. Henry is already out of the carriage, his hand extended to Eliza as she negotiates the step to the ground.

"Welcome!" I say to them.

He smiles tentatively at me, but his attention immediately returns to Eliza. Once grounded, he takes her arm with great solicitude.

And then I see why.

She is not well. In spite of the warmth of the day, her face is ashen, her features strained—strained beyond the normal stresses of travel.

I step forward to embrace them but find myself barely touching Eliza. I am afraid she will break.

As I lead them inside, I wait for Henry to offer some flippant explanation: *I am afraid my wife is sorely tired of my rambling on about the bank. Can you get her a cup of tea?*

The flippance is checked. Instead he says, "I am afraid Eliza is sorely weary and not herself this—"

Mother appears with a hearty, "Henry! My dear boy! And Eli—" She stops short of a welcoming embrace and says, "Eliza! My dear. You look like death warmed over."

Henry looks quickly at his wife, his face tight with concern, and I realize Mother may have been too apt.

Cassandra and Martha join the welcoming party—which is

quickly turned into a flurry towards getting Eliza comfortably set in the guest bedroom.

We women await Henry's return in the drawing room, our voices hushed as we scatter our concern between us.

"Had they written anything of her condition before?" Cassandra asks.

"Nothing," says Mother.

Martha rises. "I will get my book and see if there is any cure that can help."

As she exits, I whisper, "I do not think any rhubarb roots from China will help what Eliza has."

"Or oil of this or a pinch of that," says Mother. "That book of hers contains more nonremedies than remedies."

I glance at the doorway, fearing her return. But then I hear her voice added to Henry's as two sets of feet descend the stairs. "Thank you for your interest, Martha. But Eliza is very particular about her treatments, for she saw their effect on her mother when she was confined in this way."

The three of us gasp but recover enough to feign normality when they enter the room. Eliza's mother died of a tumor in her breast.

"Well, then," says Henry, playing the jolly brother very well as he joins us. "Please fill me in on all the Chawton gossip, and if there is none too amusing, I am sure I can add a bite or two from London-town."

It is so Henry to avoid distressful subjects.

And it is so *us* to allow him to do so.

We tread lightly; we speak softly.

Although neither Henry nor Eliza asks us to act differently during their visit at Chawton, we adjust our ways to accommodate this changed Eliza, and her husband, who seems intent on pretending there *is* no change.

She spends quiet time in the garden or on the chaise in the drawing room. One morning she even asked me to play for her on the pianoforte, and instinctively, I chose tunes played andante and adagio, leaving the rousing allegros for another time.

Another Eliza.

One afternoon, when Eliza takes a nap, Henry finds me checking the stores in the pantry.

"Jane, just the sister I wish to see, for we have a bit of business to discuss regarding *Pride and Prejudice* and Mr. Egerton. What do you think of his offer of one hundred ten pounds?"

All my grand plans to ask him if it would be possible to finance our own printing have dissolved since first seeing Eliza. I cannot bother him with such a burden—especially when the doctor bills will surely be large. In addition, I cannot bother him to negotiate with Mr. Egerton for more payment at all. What is money when a loved one is dying? "The one hundred ten is quite acceptable," I say.

"It is?"

"Of course." I find I must clear my throat. "I greatly appreciate all you have done for me, Henry. I would not be receiving even ten if it were not for you. And now, with Eliza ill—"

He suddenly stands. "Well, that's that, then. I think I shall go hunt for Mother. She is probably in the garden with her turnips, don't you think?"

"You are probably right. She will be happy for your company."

And so . . . that *is* that. *Pride and Prejudice* will *be*. All in all, my ultimate goal. What do I need with more than one hundred and ten? I am presumptuous to believe it will sell beyond that expectation. That a few hundred souls will read it and enjoy its story will be my true payment.

Eliza and Henry stay quietly as our guests, until suddenly, the calm solicitude of Chawton Cottage is broken by the appearance of Charles with his wife, Fanny, and our nieces, ages three and one—with another baby on the way!

There is no quiet in such a crew, especially considering we have never met his family, nor even seen him in seven long years. The house runs over, and Henry and Eliza discreetly move on to visit Edward's.

Charles brings news of another war. Not with France this time. With America. Again. On June 18, 1812, their President Madison declared war on us! Charles says it is partly over some questionable treatment of their sailors—we are stopping their ships and impressing them into service. He admits our navy *is* sorely depleted of manpower.

And it is partly fought over some issues regarding trade. They wish to trade in some ports that we have blockaded in our battles against Napoleon. And there is also something about our inciting Indians to fight against them. I know nothing about such a savage frontier and can scarce imagine it. I, who take great store in deeply set roots, find it hard to understand the excitement sought—and most likely attained—by those who forge ahead in a brand-new world. They are a more courageous sort than I.

At any rate, Charles and Frank are glad of the war's declaration, because war means the chance for monetary gain in regard to captured spoils. They do not think America can be much of a bother. The country is too new—and too independent in its thinking—to ever have real power.

Mother has a relapse at the bad news (added to her concerns about Eliza) and, after a few days abed, finds solace with her roses, her spectacles, and gossiping with Miss Benn. Lately, we find it best to keep harsh realities from her as much as possible. For her sake, as well as ours.

Yet Mother *is* concerned with the health of one and all—especially in comparison to her own. She is very attentive to news regarding the health of King George, feeling a kinship with him because he came to the throne when she was but twenty-one. She states that they, in essence, grew up together.

The Prince Regent has been in charge for o'er a year, and we have suffered the news that the poor King has been near death many times since. Last year, hearing inklings of the newest death scare, Mother had a black dress of bombazine made, knowing (quite wisely, I will admit) that it would be cheaper to have it made then than after the poor King is actually dead. She assured all of us, "If I outlive him, it will answer my purpose, and if I do not, somebody may mourn for me in the dress. It will be wanted one way or the other before the moths have eaten it up."

After the news of the war, we, in turn, bring Charles up to date. Frank (or should I say Little Mary) has had two more sons: Henry and George, bringing their number to four in five short years. With Charles and Fanny's soon-to-be three ... Cassandra and I—and Martha as an adopted aunt—are always busy seeing to the Austen additions.

This is not to say that I neglect my writing. I do not. I cannot. As soon as they end their visit I work on *Mansfield Park* and await the publication of *Pride and Prejudice* that should come with the new year. Cassandra marvels at my new propensity towards being prolific. I cannot help it. The characters speak to me—e'en when I wish them to be silent!

This phenomenon has made me ask, Why now? Why have I suddenly discovered—or rediscovered—this ability to create? And why did it remain so elusive, so long?

I sadly admit I used to blame the city of Bath for my silence. And though our move there was upsetting, and though in that city I suffered the loss of my father, I hold nothing against it in regard to my creative silence. I now see that my own insecurities and failings made my time there so distasteful. And for my attitude I ask Bath's forgiveness.

I have since read a quotation from Daniel Defoe—that gentleman who brought us *Robinson Crusoe*. He said that Bath was the resort of the sound as well as the sick, and a place that helps the indolent and the gay to commit the worst of all murders—to kill time.

That is my largest crime . . . the years that I wasted. How tragic that time, once spent, can ne'er be renewed.

Nor relived.

Lately, I have found comfort in a verse: *And I will restore to you the years that the locust hath eaten.* . . . Although it will take some time, I vow to dispel my guilt regarding those lost years. For the Almighty will restore them, in His own time, in His own way.

Perhaps He is restoring them even now.

It is my newest prayer.

Which I add to the rest.

It is a small thing to most: buying a sprig of flowers for Martha's hat, a Japanese fan for Cassandra, and some figs for Mother. Yet until this time, I have not been able. But for the charity of others, I have ne'er had income of my own.

'Tis a heady feeling.

The world, as I know it, is movable by my own hand.

It is a small thing to most: buying a sprig of flowers for Martha's
My own darling child is born.

As the new year of 1813 rises around us, *Pride and Prejudice*—by the author of *Sense and Sensibility*—becomes real. *And* . . . it sells for the lofty price of eighteen shillings instead of the fifteen of my first book.

I find it amusing that with his own money at stake, Mr. Egerton has found a way to bring the book to print in but a few short months. . . .

I hold the three volumes in my hand and admire them, turning the pages, checking the spine, making sure it has ten fingers and ten toes.

"'Tis too bad Martha and Cassandra are away," says Mother.

I had not realized she was watching me. "They will see it soon enough. I have had sets sent to the brothers, and to my friend Anne Sharpe."

"Very good, then." She sets three plates for dinner.

"Who joins us?" I ask.

"Miss Benn. The long winter evenings spent alone make her melancholy." She sets the spoons. "Perhaps you can read some of your book aloud. She does love when we read to her."

This is not how I had dreamt the arrival of the book-of-my-heart would occur. But I suppose a corps of drums and trumpets are not readily available in Chawton.

At least not upon this January night.

Dinner complete, we read half of the first volume to Miss Benn. She is unsuspecting of the author and is amused, poor soul. *That,* she cannot help, with Mother and I to lead the way, but she really does seem to admire Elizabeth Bennet. I must confess that I think Elizabeth as delightful a creature as ever appeared in print, and how I shall be able to tolerate those who do not like her, I do not know.

There are a few typical errors, and a "said he" or a "said she" would sometimes make the dialogue more immediately clear; but I do not write for such dull elves as have not a great deal of ingenuity themselves. The second volume is shorter than I could wish, but the difference is not so much in reality as in look, there being a larger proportion of narrative in that part. I have lopt and cropt so

successfully, however, that I imagine it must be rather shorter than
Sense and Sensibility altogether.

I continue to read—about Mr. Collins: "'He was interrupted by
a summons to dinner; and the girls smiled on each other. They were
not the only objects of Mr. Collins's admiration. The hall, the dining room, and all its furniture were examined and praised; and his
commendation of every thing would have touched Mrs. Bennet's
heart, but for the mortifying supposition of his viewing it all as his
own future property.'" I glance up to take a breath and see Miss
Benn's head nodding. I whisper to Mother, "Apparently the duplic-
ity of Mr. Collins is not enough to keep her interest."

"She is an old woman," says Mother. "And uneducated. Do not
take offense, Jane. It reads a fine book, and I take particular pleasure
disliking Mr. Collins."

I take it as high compliment and close the book. Mother exits
to call for Robert to take our neighbour home. I do my duty and
gently nudge Miss Benn to wakefulness.

She opens her eyes with a start. "Is it over?" she asks.

"For tonight."

I help her to stand. "You read well, Jane. And your mother says
you write. Perhaps one day you can read one of your books to me."

Our second evening's reading to Miss Benn did not please me
so well, but I believe something must be attributed to my mother's
way of reading too rapidly. And though she perfectly understood the
characters herself, she could not speak as they ought. Upon the
whole, however, I was quite vain enough and well satisfied enough.

And yet . . . the work is rather too light, and bright, and spar-
kling. It wants shade; it wants to be stretched out here and there
with a long chapter of sense, if it could be had. If not of solemn,
specious nonsense, about something unconnected with the story—

an essay on writing, a critique on Walter Scott, or the history of Bonaparte, or anything that would form a contrast, and bring the reader with increased delight to the playfulness and epigrammatism of the general style.

The greatest blunder in the printing is on page 220, verse three, where two speeches are made into one. Also, there might as well have been no suppers at Longbourn; but I suppose it was the remains of Mrs. Bennet's old Meryton habits.

Listen to me. I ramble on with opinions as if they matter. I doubt Cassandra would agree with me. Being a good Christian, she sees the good far above the bad.

As the months pass on, my authorship remains a secret. I heartily wish it to be a means of saving my family from everything unpleasant. Yet someday they will find out. Secrets do not remain secrets, not even under death.

On the subject of nieces, I am quite enjoying my two grown nieces, Fanny and Anna. If these two would but like my work and tell me so . . . I am exceedingly delighted that Fanny is pleased with the book. My hopes were tolerably strong of her, but nothing like a certainty. Her liking Darcy and Elizabeth is enough (she might hate all the others if she would).

Why do I seek praise?

And yet I do. I heard that the playwright and statesman Richard Sheridan has deemed *Pride and Prejudice* one of the cleverest things he has ever read. And Henry said a literary gentleman of his acquaintance stated it was much too clever to be the work of a woman.

I agree. For everyone knows women can never be clever.

Mr. Egerton has informed me that the first printing has been bought and he begins another. Interest has also increased in *Sense and Sensibility*.

But best of all is that readers seem enraptured with Elizabeth Bennet. And so, my heart is fulfilled.

We are sisters, you know. . . .

Sometimes I wish she were here. With Cassandra and Martha gone, I could use her wise, witty, and welcome ear.

And she mine.

TWENTY-ONE

It is odd *I* have been summoned to London, to Eliza's bedside. Henry has come to Chawton to accompany me. There is an urgency in his actions, and a tightness across his usually animated face.

"It is most serious, Jane. She wants to see you."

That is all that is said.

And so I go. I, who am not particularly well versed in bedside manner. Cassandra is the one called when nursing and consolation is needed. Like Henry, I am not quite comfortable or capable with the ill and their needs.

Yet she asks for me. There is a responsibility in the request that frightens me.

I hold off my questions until we round the last bend to Sloane Street. "What shall I say to her, Henry?" I ask.

"Whatever she wants to hear."

I nod, then shake my head. "And what would that be?"

"That it *has* been all right. That it will be all right."

I assume he is talking about a life not wasted as well as the life hereafter.

"What does she believe?" I ask. "About heaven?"

He shrugs.

Oh dear.

❦ ❧

She is much withered away. It is clear this long and dreadful illness will soon be victorious.

I sit by her bed, still uncertain how I can help. I am relieved her eyes are closed. Do I receive credit for merely being here? I hope—

She opens her eyes and sees me, but the spark is dim, the voice weak. "Jane."

I am glad my name has no more syllables, for by her effort it is clear the one causes more than enough effort.

"I am here, Eliza. If there is anything I can do for you, just—"

"Was it enough?"

I am taken aback. I do not know what she is—

"My life."

Ah.

"Henry loves you. We all love you."

She shakes her head, ever so slightly. "I did . . . little."

My thoughts rush to the Mary Crawford I am now creating in *Mansfield Park*. It is a line Mary would say—if she ever gained wisdom enough to consider all that she is, and is not.

Fiction becomes fact, as my cousin, my sister-in-law Eliza, lies before me. Waiting for an answer.

It is not an easy answer, for Eliza did not do . . . much. My view of her has always been a woman in constant motion, flitting around like a bird looking for the best seed cast upon the ground. Yet she has never been the type willing to dig for it. It had to be there, waiting for her or she would do without, and make the seed seem unworthy of her effort. That a little digging might have proffered her nourishment most delicious and satisfying . . .

With a burst of energy, she reaches for my hand. Her face pulls with worry. I must answer. Now. "You did much, Eliza. Your home was always ablaze with merriment and light. People flocked to your door and vied to be your guest."

As I say the words they sound shallow, as if people came to Eliza's parties for the food and fun, not—

She smiles and closes her eyes. "Yes."

I am surprised by her pleasure, but relieved.

She opens her eyes again, the worry returned. "Henry . . ."

"I will make sure Henry is well taken care of. He will sorely miss you, but—"

She shakes her head. "Children. I wish . . ."

They had had no children. Eliza had not been able, and after the infirmity of little Hastings, even if her body had complied, I am not sure she would have tried. Henry had never spoken of it, but by the way he spent as much time as possible at Godmersham, roughing and laughing with his nieces and nephews, I have always known he would have made an agreeable father.

I have nothing to offer her regret about children, for I embrace my own. I take her hand and squeeze it gently, hoping *it* says enough.

She puts a hand to her chest, pressing against the pain.

Her face contorts.

She moans.

I stand. "I will get Henry."

❦

On April 25, 1813, three days after I arrive in London, Eliza de Feuillide Austen dies. She is buried beside her mother and son. Henry wrote the epitaph:

> *Also in memory of Elizabeth wife of H. T. Austen Esq. formerly widow of the Comt. Feuillide a woman of brilliant generous and cultivated mind just disinterested and charitable she died after long and severe suffering on the 25th April 1813 aged 50 much regretted by the wise and good and deeply lamented by the poor.*

It was oddly worded, but I did not help Henry edit it. A husband has a right to say what he wishes to say, even if only he comprehends the meaning.

❦

As we believed, but moreover newly discovered, Henry's mind is not a mind for affliction. He is too busy, too active, too sanguine. Sincerely as he was attached to poor Eliza, and as excellently as he behaved to her, he was used to being away from her—perhaps more away than together. Because of that, her loss is not felt as that of many a beloved wife might be, especially when all the circumstances of her long and dreadful illness are taken into the account. He knew for a long time that she must die, and it was indeed a release at last.

That he quickly finds female companionship is nearly a relief. Although many who do not know him might be put out by his propensity to let life go on as it may, *most* of the family is relieved.

However ... Henry's penchant for being Henry notwithstanding, I would appreciate he be better at keeping *my* secret. It seems wherever he goes, he cannot resist saying that the author of my books is ... me.

He was in Scotland of late and heard *Pride and Prejudice* warmly praised by Lady Robert Kerr and another woman. In the warmth of his brotherly vanity and love, he immediately told them who wrote it! Then he traveled to see Eliza's family benefactor, Mr. Hastings, and told him. The latter's admiration of Elizabeth Bennet is particularly welcome to me.

When I visit Henry in London, he says that a Miss Burdett wishes to meet me. I see nothing wrong in that until I hear the why of it—because I am a novelist—*the* novelist. I am rather frightened by hearing that she wishes to be introduced to *me*. If she deems me a wild beast, I cannot help it. It is not my own fault.

Yet even as I despair over his inability to remain silent, I do enjoy his company. For in whose presence but Henry's can I visit galleries and search for portraits of people who do not exist? He and I go to the exhibition in Spring Gardens. It is not thought to be a good collection, but I am very well pleased, particularly with a small portrait that looks like Jane—Mrs. Bingley of my story. Mrs. Bingley's likeness is exactly herself in size, shape of face, features, and sweetness. There never was a greater likeness. She is dressed in a white gown with green ornaments, which convinces me of what I had always supposed, that green was a favourite colour with her. I daresay Elizabeth will be in yellow. . . . If only I could find her. But alas, in spite of Henry's and my searching the exhibition high and low, there is no Mrs. Darcy present.

This one exhibition did not halt our quest, for since then we visit Sir J. Reynolds's showing, but I am disappointed, for there is nothing like Mrs. Darcy there either. I can only imagine that Mr. Darcy prizes any picture of her too much to like it exposed to the public eye. I can imagine he would have that sort of feeling, that mixture of love, pride, and delicacy. Setting aside this disappointment, I have great amusement among the pictures, and the driving about in an open carriage is very pleasant.

I even drive alone sometimes. I like my solitary elegance very much and am ready to laugh at my being where I am. I cannot but feel that I have a natural, small right to be parading about London in a barouche.

But enough of such frivolities. Back to chastising Henry for his wagging tongue. Others in the family are far more judicious. I must thank Frank and Little Mary for their discreet consideration of my wishes to remain anonymous. And James and the other Mary too, for they have all been so tight with my secret that not even their children know of it.

Only Henry is unable to be silent. A thing set going in such a way . . . one knows how it spreads. I know it is all done from affection and partiality, but at the same time . . . if only he could do as I wish.

I try to harden myself. After all, revealing my identity is but a trifle and of no care to anyone but me. Society has more important points to think about than this. But I do hate the thought of people believing the stories autobiographical. That an author dips into her own life experience for inspiration or wisdom or fear is a fact I will not deny. And in truth, shades of Jane can probably be found in all my characters. Yet I do not need someone bringing it to my attention or (heaven forbid) asking me about it. If I have used a name common to the family—and I have with Jane, Fanny, Henry, Mary—I make certain the character is far unlike the relative so there can be no comparison brooked.

Towards *Mansfield Park*, I ask Frank if I might use the name of some of his ships, and he agrees, though he warns that such truths might be clues to others looking for the identity of the elusive "Lady A." And so, e'en though I realize I may be laying myself open to complete discovery, the truth is that the secret has spread so far as to be scarcely the shadow of a secret now. Whenever the third book appears, I shall not even attempt to tell lies about it. Rather I shall try to make all the money than all the mystery I can of it.

Second editions of both my books have released. Although I get not a penny more for *Pride and Prejudice*, I do earn for the first book. Instead of saving my superfluous wealth for my family to spend, I plan to treat myself with spending it. Next time in London, I hope to find some poplin at Layton and Shear's that will tempt me to buy it. If I do, it shall be sent to Chawton, as half will be for Cassandra. I depend upon her being so kind as to accept the gift. It will be a great pleasure to me. I will not allow her to say a word. I only wish she could be with me to chuse. I shall send twenty yards, I think. . . .

I am quite the lady of the world now, for I have learnt, to my high amusement, that the stays in dresses are not made to force the bosom up anymore—that is a very unbecoming, unnatural fashion. I am also glad to hear they are not to be so much off the shoulders. When last with Edward and Fanny in London, Edward made a gift of five pounds to each of us, and so we went to Miss Hare's, and since she had some pretty caps, Fanny insisted she make me one, white satin instead of blue. It will be white satin and lace, with a little white flower perking out of the left ear, like Harriot Byron's feather. I have allowed her to go as far as eleven and sixteen on it. My gown is to be trimmed everywhere with white ribbon plaited on (somehow or other). She says it will look well. I am not sanguine. They trim with white very much.

Listen to me. Speaking of dresses and silk caps. And the praise of readers. And a life made busy with concerns hitherto unknown. How can this be happening to me?

I do not know anything of reasons. Only that it is.

Mansfield Park is complete. I do not know why it took me twice as long to write as the others.

And yet I do.

It became a more complicated story than I intended. The characters would not stay as I had planned, but revealed hidden places in their constitution—many that I was not entirely pleased to acknowledge. And how exactly does one write a book about one character when one is more pleasantly drawn to another?

For even more than Fanny, I like Mary Crawford. And Henry Crawford. Just as I like Eliza and Henry. . . . Yet to like someone— even love them—does not mean they are without fault or flaw. Charming people like these draw others like moths are drawn to a flame. Fanny, and finally Edmund, is able to fly away—but not without being singed.

'Tis a painful process, singeing one's own creation. Yet necessary.

'Tis also a painful process to create a character like Fanny who is so full of virtue and morality, yet so . . . unlikable. Mother has called her insipid. And I expect I shall hear worse.

Yet I see such promise in Mary Crawford. She *could* have been a heroine if only she would have learned self-restraint through self-inspection.

I see in her too much *self*.

Which is the problem.

Cassandra wishes me to change the ending—to let Edmund

marry Mary Crawford, and Henry marry Fanny. I realize she will not be the only one. And yet, as much as I respect my sister, as much as I seek and appreciate her advice, in this I will remain strong. As with true life, what is expected does not always come to be. Cassandra and I both know this to be true. Too true.

People do not always make wise choices.

People do not always have control over the choices made *to* them.

People do not always become all they should be.

And yet . . . even within the complicated weavings of life, people *can* find happiness. If they chuse to seek it . . . differently.

It is a question of survival. Adapt or perish. Learn or be defeated. Venture ever forward or cease to be.

Life is not a fairy tale, and happily-ever-after has many measures.

Mr. Egerton does not like *Mansfield Park* as much as my others, says he does not expect it to sell as well, and as such, will not publish it on his own coin. And so I am back to footing the bill for its publication.

I could have said no. I could have put it in a drawer and let it lie.

But e'en as readers might find it disconcerting, I find it to be a good book, one that makes me proud. Perhaps I have hit the mark of true emotion and humanity too close.

I enjoy delving in to emotions which most wish to keep hidden. For often, in seeing such traits in others—through a piece of fiction—we can find revelation within ourselves.

Or not. Novels and heroines—pictures of perfection—make me sick and wicked.

I sit in the attic bedroom of Henry's home in London and compile the letters and verbal comments about my newest creation into a scrapbook. I have never done this before and do not exactly know why I do it now. It seems a bit arrogant—or desperate—to keep track of others' opinions in such a manner. And yet I am fair as I insert the negative comments along with the praise.

I read Frank's words from a letter: *Fanny is a delightful character! You need not fear the publication being discreditable to the talents of its author.* Next to them I paste a note from Lady Robert Kerr: *Your novel was universally admired in Edinburgh, by all the wise ones.*

Whoever they may be.

Next I write down what Anna has told me: *I cannot bear Fanny.*

Anna makes me smile. Anna, who is the Niagara Falls of our lives, would *not* like the self-contained and self-controlled Fanny Price.

Enough of this. I close the book and move downstairs. This freedom to roam is quite delightful. As Henry is gone all day at the bank, I have the apartment to myself. It is my retreat. My writer's haven. I enter the room that opens onto a lovely garden. I love the ability to move in and out, letting my mind meander, as my thoughts coalesce.

For I am working on my newest book—one that is sure to cause a commotion of its own. I call it *Emma*, and once again I have chosen a heroine who is not completely likable and due the respect that Elinor and Elizabeth so aptly earned. Emma's largest flaw is that she believes in herself too much. She stands above the world and directs it to her liking. And when people ignore her and do what they will, she is shocked at their ignorance and audacious behavior. Poor Harriet Smith, poor Mr. Elton, and especially poor Mr. Knightly. They are all sorely tested by Emma, and she by them. To see the error and hard truths in someone you love is difficult. Especially when they see no error in their ways, and in fact see themselves as unapproachable.

In all this lies the story. The story of a young woman saved from herself through difficult lessons learned . . .

I pinch a dead bloom from an aster, letting my concern for

Emma meld into my concern for my niece Anna.

Her infatuation and desire to marry Mr. Terry is long since past. (She now compares him to my character Mr. Collins.) Yet that infatuation has been replaced with her passionate desire to marry Ben Lefroy—the son of my dear, departed Anne. They are, in fact, engaged.

It came upon us without much preparation, which is to be expected of my niece. There is something about her which keeps us in a constant preparation for . . . something. We are anxious the marriage goes well, there being quite as much in his favour as in any matrimonial connection. I believe he is sensible, certainly very religious, well connected, and with some independence. However, there is an unfortunate dissimilarity of taste between them in one large respect, which gives us some apprehensions: he hates company and she is very fond of it. This, along with some queerness of temper on his side and much unsteadiness on hers, is untoward.

James and Mary do not approve. It seems Ben was offered an ample curacy—and declined. Does he think himself too good? If so, he will have to fight for ownership of the feeling with Anna.

My old fear returns: I fear she longs to marry as a means to get away from a home that is uncomfortable. 'Tis an understandable reason but not a good one. Not one good enough. This, after all, is the girl who cut her hair before a ball just to elicit a response. . . .

To Anna's merit (and our surprise), she has written a novel. Just the fact that she has completed *something* deserves our praise. Also to her merit, she asks my advice. I have sent her letters, offering suggestions for her tome, which is entitled *Which Is the Heroine?* I only hope she has an open mind to take it . . . as she asks for criticisms, I would be lax in giving her less than my honest assessments. 'Tis a part of the writing life to hear what one does not want to hear.

To her credit, she writes in an amusing way. There is a great deal of respectable reading, though she *can* express in fewer words what might be expressed in fewer words. There are details about locale and distance, and some dialogue that is too formal. I try to help her in regard to her characters, for I know how they can seem right and yet be wrong. I have advised her not to let her story leave England. She wishes to let the Portmans go to Ireland, yet as she knows nothing of the manners there, she had better not go with them at the risk of giving false representations. It is best she sticks with places she knows.

Cassandra is involved too, giving her opinion. She does not like aimless novels and is rather fearful Anna's will be too much so that there will be too frequent a change from one set of people to another, and that circumstances will be sometimes introduced of apparent consequence, which will lead to nothing. It is not so great an objection to me, if it does. I allow much more latitude than Cassandra and think nature and spirit cover many sins of a wandering story.

Anna describes a sweet place, but her descriptions are often more minute than will be liked. She gives too many particulars of right hand and left. She is collecting her people delightfully, getting them exactly into such a spot as is the joy of my life. Three or four families in a country village is the very thing to work on, and I hope she will write a great deal more and make full use of them while they are so favourably arranged.

She is now coming to the heart and beauty of her book; till the heroine grows up, the fun must be imperfect. Her character, Devereux Forester, being ruined by his vanity is extremely good, but I wish she would not let him plunge into a "vortex of dissipation." I do not object to the thing, but I cannot bear the expression; it is such thorough novel slang, and so old that I daresay Adam met with it in the first novel he opened.

I give her a more detailed accounting of the pros and cons than she probably seeks, but so be it. If Anna is old enough to be married, she is old enough to deal with hard truths.

Perhaps they will aid in her maturity.

Perhaps not.

As news of my authoress identity spreads, I am suddenly the expert in all things literary. And I am suddenly inundated with the need for opinions from a bevy of budding authors in the Austen clan. For it is not just Anna who has decided to dip her creative pen; now it is James Edward, and his sister Caroline, and a few other nieces and nephews who have taken to writing stories—albeit blessedly short. I do not begrudge them their attempts, but it can be wearying to be expected to be a teacher, editor, and aunt—as well as continue to do my own work.

It is also wearying because, where they never have shewn interest in my life before—in any way other than thinking of me as their aunt who made them laugh and listened to their problems—they are now interested in my writing: how I write, where, when . . .

What was a discreet and normal occurrence about Chawton Cottage is now studied by too many curious eyes.

I often like to write on a small mahogany table in the drawing room. There is a creaky door from that room to the offices, and I have resisted all attempts at getting it oiled, as the creak gives me warning that someone is coming. It is then I can quickly put my pages beneath a book and pretend I am doing nothing. Among Mother, Cassandra, and Martha, I hold no such ruse. They go about their work and leave me to mine, but with a bevy of nieces and nephews coming in and out, I have learned to play this hide-and-seek as a means of keeping what is mine, mine.

Yet one day Caroline spots me when I am none too quick, having a particularly delicious sentence flowing between thought and pen. *Seldom, very seldom does complete truth belong to any human disclosure; seldom can it happen that something is not a little disguised, or a little mistaken.* I put the page away, but find her standing before me, her brown eyes seeing too much and wanting to see more.

"What are those pages?" she asks.

"My work."

"They are the size of a book. You fold them like that? Why?"

Too many questions. There is no way out but to order her away, and I cannot do that. Not and stay her favourite aunt.

I pull one of the pages free and unfold it. "I fold it in half so it appears as a book. Then I stitch the pages together." I shrug. "It is a folly. A habit."

"You have a book right from the start," she says.

"I do."

With a nod she says, "I will do the very same with my books."

"You do that."

She skips away, and I return to the line I have barely born . . . something about truth disguised and a little mistaken. . . .

❦

Anna married Ben Lefroy today. My niece married into the family that had been denied to me. Tom Lefroy. My first love.

I suffer few regrets that Tom and I did not marry. He is off in Ireland now. . . . In retrospect and wisdom I see that our love was a young love—frivolous, spontaneous, and flighty. There were no firm roots. And yet there will always be that unknown question: could a union between Tom and Jane have endured and flourished?

It is a moot query. The question at hand is: can a union between Ben and Anna endure and flourish?

They are two stubborn souls. I do not doubt that Anna will force it to work, if only to peeve her parents, who are still against it.

Neither I, Cassandra, nor Mother attended the nuptials, but I heard an account of it from Anna's half sister Caroline, who was a bridesmaid, along with another small Lefroy. The wedding day was dreary and the church in Steventon—my father's old church—held tight to a November cold. There was no stove to give warmth, or flowers to give colour or brightness, no friends, high or low, to offer their good wishes. Mr. Lefroy read the service, and James gave his daughter away.

Caroline informs me that she and little Anne wore white frocks and had a white ribband on their straw bonnets. She does not say what Anna wore.

There was a breakfast after, at the rectory. A festive breakfast in spite of the gray of the day: buttered toast, hot rolls, breads, tongue, ham and eggs. There was chocolate at the end of the table, along with a wedding cake. But the bride and groom left early due to a long day's journey to Hendon. The Lefroys returned to Ashe, and it was done.

I only pray the grayness and solemnity of the ceremony do not portend badly to their future.

Anna is very headstrong and I worry for her life.

Henry is very ill, and I worry for *his* life. I am in London to try to find a new publisher—as Egerton has decided *not* to do a second printing of *Mansfield Park*, e'en though the first has sold out. I will not proffer upon him my *Emma*. She deserves better.

Before taking ill, Henry gave me the name of another publisher, a John Murray. He is the publisher for Lord Byron and writes a letter of interest offering me four hundred fifty pounds—which could have made me dance about the street if he had not added that for that sum he expects to own the copyrights of *Emma, Sense and Sensibility*, and *Mansfield Park*. He is a rogue, of course, albeit a civil one.

Henry refused on my behalf, and now I must print *Emma* on a ten percent commission to go to Mr. Murray. And yet, he will also republish *Mansfield Park*, so that is something.

But then Henry turned sick and did not get better. His fever and pain were so alarming that I sent for Edward and James, and James gathered Cassandra and made haste to our door.

For a week we feared the worst, and prayed and worried, and prayed some more.

But then . . . he was better. If I had not been sorely relieved, I would have chastised him for causing his siblings such alarm!

But as often happens, good comes from bad. While Henry was under the care of the delightful (and deliciously handsome) Charles Thomas Haden, I am told by the good doctor that he is a close acquaintance with the Prince Regent's physician. Because of this connection I hear that the Prince is a large fan of my work and, indeed, has a copy of my books in each of his homes. He has heard I am in London and . . .

So I am thrust into the land of royalty!

The prince sends me his librarian, James Stanier Clarke—who himself is an author, though one of more serious works: *The Progress of Maritime Discovery* for one. I cannot tell him I have read it, as I simply cannot get past the three pages of dedication to the Prince, and then the two hundred thirty pages of introduction before he announces the existence of Chapter One.

But all that is of no consequence as he picks me up and takes me (at the Prince's invitation) to Carleton House. The Prince is currently renovating it with much gold and French taste. I find it a bit overwhelming and am most impressed with its magnificent forty-foot library. I do not meet the Prince—which is just as fine for me—and I do enjoy the company of Reverend Clarke. It is quite agreeable to spend time with a fellow author.

One who is absolutely, completely loyal and enamored with his Prince . . .

Upon leaving I am told by the obsequious Clarke, "I have been instructed to inform you that the Prince Regent has given his permission for you to dedicate your next book, *Emma*, to him."

I am speechless. My condition is misconstrued, and Clarke says, "I know it is a great honour."

I say all the right words—sans giving my promise, and wisely do not detail my true feelings. Those, I keep for Henry.

I pace in front of the fire, with Henry my only witness. "How dare he give *me* permission to dedicate a book to *him*?"

"He can dare many things. He is the Prince Regent."

"But I do not like him. I do not respect him. I do not want his name attached to the book in any way. To dedicate it to him is to give him an honour I do not believe he in any way deserves."

Henry's shrug infuriates me even more.

"Must I do it?"

"Is that how it was presented?"

I think back and am not certain. "He said it was an honour, but beyond that . . ."

"Mmm."

He is no help. "Do you think it would be acceptable if I wrote to Reverend Clarke and ask him to stipulate?"

"Can you not just do it, Jane? Give the dedication and be done with it?"

"I can. But I will not like it."

"Then write your letter and get your options set plain."

So that is what I did.

❦

I hold a letter from Reverend Clarke in my hands. *"It is certainly not incumbent on you to make the dedication. But you certainly might, if you wish. By the by, would you ever be interested in writing a novel with a clergyman—like myself—as the hero?"*

He proceeds to tell me too many details of his life that he thinks I would most certainly wish to include in a book. And if that is not incentive enough, might I be interested in writing a love story based on the House of Saxe-Coburg line of Prince Leopold?

"Am I incumbent to do this too? To write this man's story as my own?"

"Did you agree in some way?" asks Henry.

"In no way."

"Then it is over. Nothing at all to think about."

I hope so. For I know that no matter how much pressure I receive, I cannot write someone else's story. I must write my own, in my own way. For to write otherwise is to be false to oneself.

And that is not an option.

And the story of Prince Leopold? I could no more write a historical romance than an epic poem. I could not sit down to write a serious romance under any other motive than to save my life; and if it were indispensable for me to keep it up and never relax into laughing at myself or other people, I am sure I should be hung before I had finished the first chapter.

And so *that* is that. The dedication I will do with reluctance. But the writing of other people's stories?

I refuse with no reluctance whatsoever.

Emma is released with the following dedication:

To
His Royal Highness
THE PRINCE REGENT
This work is,
By His Royal Highness's Permission
Most Respectfully
Dedicated,
By His Royal Highness's
Dutiful
And Obedient
Humble Servant,
THE AUTHOR

It is not what I wanted. I was set on a short dedication: *Emma Dedicated by Permission to H.R.H. The Prince Regent* but was informed by Murray it was not flowery enough.

I snap the book shut. "Ridiculous," I say.

"You had little choice," Cassandra says.

"Which makes it all the more galling."

"But think of the favour you have bestowed upon him—upon yourself for your obedient, humble service." She smiles.

"The only good to come from this is that Murray sped up the printing process once he heard of the dedication."

"See?" she says. "In such a way the Prince has rendered *you* service."

"We are *not* even," I say, but I have lowered my voice as if there are royal spies even in Chawton.

But somehow I doubt all-things-being-even is a royal concept.

My dear niece Anna has given birth to her first child. It was a difficult pregnancy. In many ways.

For as the pregnancy ripened, Anna's novel withered. I tried to encourage her—for she does have talent—but to no avail.

Today I am in receipt of a letter that states what I have dreaded to hear. I read it aloud to Cassandra. "Anna says,

> *I am sorry, Aunt Jane, but I must set aside the novel, for Ben says it is frivolous—if not even evil—in that it takes me away from him and the child that I have, with much effort, brought into the world. I believe he is right. For it was sure to come to nothing. And yet I thank you for your diligent interest and help.'*

I snap the page against my palm. "She is giving it up! After so much work—on both our parts—she is throwing it all away!"

"You tried, Jane."

"She is rejecting her talent."

"She has a child now. She has a husband. There will be more children."

I sigh with utter frustration. "Are there not enough babies in the Austen clan?"

"Jane . . . you are being unfair. Anna has always wanted to marry and have children. That was her first goal. The writing came about because of your inspiration."

"But what good was it? For her to work and learn, only to give it up?"

"She has made a choice, Jane. One *you* could have made. One that would have changed everything."

She touches an old wound, yet one that is not as tender as it once was. "I never chose *not* to marry or have children. Those choices were thrust upon me. Life was thrust upon me."

Cassandra shakes her head. "That is not true. You could have married Harris and lived in a fine house. You could have had many babies, and kept a household, and been a part of all those noble female vocations."

She is right. For one short night I was engaged, only to discover my own inability to embrace that fate.

I am suddenly overcome with doubt and regret. "Is *mine* a noble vocation, Cassandra? Writing some flit and fluff stories only a few will read?"

To her merit, she does not hesitate. "It is."

"How do you know?"

"I just do."

She comes to me by the fire, takes the offending letter from our niece, and tosses it into the flames.

"Why did you do that?"

"I am ending all second thoughts. Anna has made her choice. It is finished. Long ago, after my Tom died, I made *my* choice to remain unmarried. I have found peace in that. Now you, Jane. It is time for you to make peace with your choice."

I stare at the flames, as Anna's lost dream turns to ash.

Cassandra takes my hand. "What do you love more than anything?"

"You," I say without pause.

She kisses my cheek. "But what makes you arise every morning? What captures your thoughts throughout the day? What makes you feel most alive?"

"My writing."

"It is who you are, Jane. In the same way a wife is committed to a husband, body and soul, you are committed to your stories. They excite you, they ignite you, they complete you. Your books are your children, Jane. With every thought and word and prayer you nourish them and help them grow strong. You give them the romantic endings you yourself have not chosen."

Tears start to flow. "You make it sound so . . . so . . ."

"Right?"

I nod.

"I believe with my entire heart that if you had married Tom or Harris or William or Edward, or any of the other men who could have become your beaus with little effort, you would not have written your books. As you said, life would have been thrust upon you. A good life, but a different life. The world would not have your books if you had married, Jane. I truly believe that to be true."

It is a sobering thought, that a decision *not* to marry could have led to something . . . better.

"God has a plan for each of us, Jane, a unique purpose. I am content in what I have been asked to do. We will pray Anna is content in her choice. But now you need to find your own contentment in being just Jane."

I look back to the flames and see that the letter is no more. Anna's fate has been sealed.

As has mine?

Suddenly, another character steps front and center into my mind. Not a young ingenue in search of a husband. But an older woman, single, hurt by experience, yet seasoned in some good way by all that life has handed her. Her name could be Anne . . . and I would give her a second chance at happiness. I do not know yet how it will end, and perhaps the end is not the essence of the story. Perhaps the journey is the key.

"You are plotting again," says Cassandra. She smiles and points at my eyes. "I can see your mind working."

"I am thinking of another story."

Without another word Cassandra crosses the room to my writing table. She retrieves a blank piece of paper and pen and hands them to me. "Then write," she says.

And so . . . I do that which I am meant to do.

What Happened Next?

Jane finished writing *Persuasion*, which she originally called *The Elliots*, in August 1816. *Emma* was a success, even receiving accolades from Sir Walter Scott: "That young lady has a talent for describing the involvement of feelings and characters of ordinary life which is to me the most wonderful I ever met with." But Jane's health was failing, and though she began another book—*Sanditon*—she could not finish it.

She died—probably of Addison's disease—on July 18, 1817, at age forty-one, in the arms of her "dearest Cassandra." In much pain, she welcomed death. Her last words, said just hours before her death, were, "God grant me patience. Pray for me, oh, pray for me." Cassandra said this of her sister: "She was the sun of my life, the gilder of every pleasure, the soother of every sorrow. I had not a thought concealed from her, and it is as if I had lost a part of myself." Jane was buried in Winchester Cathedral, with an epitaph penned by her brother Henry. No mention was made of her writing:

In Memory of
JANE AUSTEN
youngest daughter of the late
Revd GEORGE AUSTEN,
formerly Rector of Steventon in this County
she departed this life on the 18th July 1817,
aged 41, after a long illness supported with
the patience and the hopes of a Christian.

The benevolence of her heart,
the sweetness of her temper, and

the extraordinary endowments of her mind
obtained the regard of all who knew her and
the warmest love of her intimate connections.

Their grief is in proportion to their affection
they know their loss to be irreparable,
but in their deepest affliction they are consoled
by a firm though humble hope that her charity,
devotion, faith, and purity have rendered
her soul acceptable in the sight of her
REDEEMER

Cassandra never married, lived in Chawton Cottage her entire life, and burned "the greater part" of Jane's letters—presumably the ones that were most revealing—a few years before she died at age seventy-two, of a stroke, while visiting Frank.

Jane's mother, in spite of her hypochondria, lived in Chawton Cottage until the age of eighty-seven, alert to the end. "I sometimes think that God Almighty must have forgotten me; but I daresay He will come for me in His own good time." She and Cassandra are buried in the St. Nicholas churchyard in Chawton.

Frank's wife Mary Gibson died in 1823 after giving birth to her eleventh child. Five years later, Frank married the old family friend Martha Lloyd, who was sixty-three. It was a comfortable arrangement, and she helped take care of his household and children—who did not approve of the marriage. Frank became Sir Francis Austen, and finally an Admiral of the Fleet at age eighty-nine. He lived to be ninety-one. He carefully kept all of Jane's letters, but having given no instructions regarding what to do with them when he died, his daughter destroyed them.

Charles's wife Fanny died after giving birth to her fourth child in 1814 (just two months before Anna Austen married Ben Lefroy). The baby also died. Fanny's sister came to help the household, and under the haze of scandal, Charles married her in 1820 and had another family. His career stalled for decades, but eventually he was made Rear Admiral. He died of cholera in Burma at the age of seventy-three.

Soon after his serious illness in 1815, Henry's bank collapsed and he returned to his original desire to be a clergyman—the profession Eliza had so disdained. He remarried in 1820 but never had any children. He died in 1850 at age seventy-nine.

Upon the death of his adoptive mother, Mrs. Knight, Edward officially took the Knight surname. He never remarried, depended greatly on his daughter Fanny, and lived to be eighty-five.

Jane's niece Fanny married at age twenty-seven to an elder Sir Edward Knatchbull, a widower with six children. She had nine more of her own, meaning she had cared for multiple children since her mother died when Fanny was twelve. One of her sons became Lord Brabourne and published many of Jane's letters, but he later sold and scattered the originals.

Niece Anna Austen Lefroy had six children and lived to be seventy-nine. There is no indication she ever did anything more with her novel *Who Is the Heroine?*

James's health deteriorated soon after Jane died. When he died in 1819 at age fifty-four, his wife, Mary, and children Caroline and James Edward, were forced to leave the Steventon rectory, which Henry and his new wife took over. Just as Mary and James had usurped the rectory when the elder Austens retired to Bath, so Henry now usurped their place.

James Edward Austen-Leigh, James's son, penned a book about his famous aunt, *Memoir of Jane Austen*, in 1869. Not always factual, it has led to many misconceptions about Jane's life, including the fallacy that "Of events her life was singularly barren: few changes and no great crisis ever broke the smooth current of its course." For the book a portrait was painted, based on the unfinished pencil drawing done by Cassandra years before. The portrait is said to have little likeness to Jane. Hence, there is no good picture of Jane for us to ponder.

Tom Lefroy married four years after he left Ashe. He fathered seven children. He sat in Parliament for eleven years, and in 1852 was appointed Lord Chief Justice of Ireland.

Harris Bigg-Wither married in 1804 and had ten children.

Jane's Work

Henry remained Jane's literary champion and helped her buy back the rights to *Susan* from Crosby for ten pounds in 1816. By that time Jane's books had earned her six hundred pounds, with *Emma* still due to be published. A fair living for the penniless Jane. After her death, Henry and Cassandra were instrumental in getting both *Susan*, which became *Northanger Abbey*, and *Persuasion* published in a combined volume. But sales were not brisk, and the last 282 copies remaindered in 1820. No other publisher was interested in reprinting her work for fifteen years. Yet during the 1800s various literary names such as George Eliot, Rudyard Kipling, and Thomas Babington Macaulay praised Jane's work, and during the 1850s people began visiting Jane's grave (to the befuddlement of church workers).

Her popularity grew upon the 1869 publication of her nephew's biography of her life. With his profits, James Edward paid for a brass tablet on the wall near her grave in Winchester Cathedral, which alludes to her work. Yet Jane's popularity did not really take off until the 1900s, when paperbacks of her works became available. In the 1940s, a Jane fan, Miss Dorothy Darnell, founded the Jane Austen Society, which now has chapters in North America, Australia, Brazil, Japan, Canada, and Europe. Most of these groups have annual conferences attended by avid Janeites, many in costume. Miss Darnell was also instrumental in purchasing Chawton

Cottage, where a museum opened in 1949.

Today, Jane's books have sold hundreds of millions of copies, and all of her books have been made into movies, many being nominated for Academy Awards. There are college courses dedicated to studying Jane and her work. There are Jane Austen calendars, posters, cookbooks, gardening books, dating guides, walking guides, quiz books, trivia books, and over seven thousand Web sites. There are books dedicated to her wit and wisdom, compilations of her letters, and novels that take up where her novels left off. Amazon has available over two hundred Austen titles. The woman who sold her first book for ten pounds, who never traveled beyond her own corner of England, who never married, never had children, whose life (according to brother Henry) "was not a life of events," spanned the globe and the centuries by changing the literary world forever.

Dear Reader,

Thirty years after her death, Jane Austen's nephew James Edward wrote a biography of his aunt. There were few people left who'd known her personally. Surely this nephew would offer some profound insight as to the real Jane.

Sadly, James Edward got it wrong. For instance he said, "Of events her life was singularly barren: few changes and no great crisis ever broke the smooth current of its course. Even her fame may be said to have been posthumous: it did not attain to any vigorous life till she had ceased to exist. Her talents did not introduce her to the notice of other writers, or connect her with the literary world, or in any degree pierce through the obscurity of her domestic retirement." Although the last part of his assessment offers some truth, the first line angers me. Barren? Without change and crisis? I try to find excuses for this nephew. I try to remember his memories are that of a young boy and his words may be couched with the prejudices of a nineteenth-century male.

For I found Jane's life to be quite full and eventful. Evident among her days are every dose of emotion. And I find there to be crisis enough for any one life. (I dare James Edward to compete, incident for incident!) Her nephew's disconcerting opinion aside, amid my readings I discovered a Jane Austen whom I would have liked to call friend. She was witty, wise, discerning, creative, and loyal. She was also stubborn, judgmental, insecure, and needy. She was . . . a lot like us.

I find that fact to be one of the most enlightening things that comes out of writing bio-novels about women in history. No matter when they lived, or where they lived, the core of who they were and what they desired from life parallels our own issues and quest to find purpose and meaning. Jane's lifelong search to find a place to belong, a place to feel secure and confident in herself, is our search.

That is one reason why her novels have endured for two hundred years. Jane Austen wrote about people. In her stories, the world does not intrude with catastrophe or universal tragedy. The crises her characters experience develop from their everyday lives, from their families, and from their society—that though small, still wields a mighty influence. There are rules and morals, and right and wrong amid God's constant presence. Conversely, there are people who break the rules, bend the morals, and choose wrongly. And as they do so, and as they suffer the consequences or the victory of their actions, we empathize with them and celebrate with a sense of camaraderie. We are among friends. Jane's stories are our stories, and ours, hers (minus our sad lack of barouches, bonnets, and balls).

How I wish Jane knew the impact her stories have on millions of people around the world. There are Jane Austen societies in the United States, Europe, Japan, Australia, Argentina. . . . Jane, a woman who never ventured beyond England, would be astonished. And humbled. Yet most likely, she would still prefer to spend her days within her beloved Chawton Cottage. Her true home. Her true place to be just Jane.

May you find your true place to be just . . . you. And may you, like Jane, journey forward to find your unique purpose.

Fondly,
Nancy Moser

What Is Fact and What Is Fiction in *Just Jane*?

As a novelist, making things up is my forte. Yet in writing *Just Jane* I strove to discover the facts about Jane Austen's life. In a bio-novel it is my job to "scene-out" true-life events, not to change them. Unfortunately, there are often gaps in the information and I have to do what I am loath to do: guess. There are many biographies about Jane, and many of the letters she sent to her sister, Cassandra, still exist. But after Jane's death, Cassandra purposely destroyed a great many of those letters. Yet the very fact she left us *some* suggests the letters she destroyed were probably the ones where Jane's deepest emotions were expressed. I found a disconcerting silence during many crisis moments in Jane's life. How I longed for a letter where she let it all out! When confronted with these times of silence, I had to fend for her, imagining how Jane might have felt, and yes, perhaps borrowing a bit of how *I* might have felt. For that is probably the largest area of freedom I have taken—in regard to Jane's feelings. Jane belonged to a family where being pragmatic was a given. Great effusions of emotion were not acceptable. Forgive me, Jane, if I got it wrong. I tried to be true to you—and I even used your own words when possible. Below is the truth as I know it . . . and notation where I was forced to fudge. I hope the list adds to your enjoyment of the book and does not disappoint.

Jane never noted the real-life inspiration for her characters, yet many associations *can* be made. The symbolic correlation of certain books being written during certain times was never boldly alluded to, but seems logical. I'm sure there are many more incidents of art imitating life.

✒ The letters to and from publishers regarding Jane's work are actual.

✒ The personalities and relationships of Jane's family are based on facts derived from their actions and Jane's letters. I find the entire family delightful, even amid their flaws and foibles.

✒ Jane's feelings toward household duties, illness, suitors, her sisters-in-law, people at dances, her parents' decision to move to Bath, the rules of society: I used quotations from her letters when appropriate, while employing a novelist's freedom to have her muse about certain subjects while in certain settings. Although the actual moment and method of the musings are my own creation, I truly believe the content of those introspective times suit Jane—and are common to many who deal with such issues.

✒ Jane's love life: No one really knows why she held on to her connection with Tom Lefroy for three years with little encouragement. Jane had plenty of male attention. She was a good conversationalist and a talented dancer. But as she got older, and after witnessing the forced flirtation that epitomized Bath, her savvy realization that finding a mate was often inane, illogical, and unfair made her particular. William Jones, the man she met at Devon, who died before they could meet again, may or may not have been real (his name is my creation). There is evidence of such a romance with an unnamed gentleman, but it is fleeting. (Oh, to read the missing letters!) But the engagement to Harris Bigg-Wither (and the breaking of the engagement) is very real. I believe this event signaled Jane's decision to let the mating game go on without her. Unable to find her own Mr. Darcy, she created him!

✒ Jane and her family often traveled to visit one another. The trips I mention occurred, with the essence of each visit factual. Actually, there were more trips than I had the time and pages to note! Without telephones or e-mail, people had to meet in person. Imagine that.

There is an overlying lack of control in Jane's life. Other people made decisions that affected her in dramatic ways—without her say. This is one reason why she clung to Cassandra and later to Martha. They did not attempt to control her. Her need to find some level of power led to her eventual discovery of contentment within her singleness. She could fight being single and become bitter, or accept it as *her* choice and be happy. This issue of control often found a voice within her books.

True friendship was very important to Jane: Cassandra, Martha, the Bigg sisters. But friendship for friendship's sake (as with Mrs. Chamberlayne in Bath) was tedious. Jane did not need *many*. The *few* sufficed and fed her. And she fed them.

Home and stability were essential ingredients to Jane's well-being *and* to her creative process. For eight years (the Bath years) Jane did not write. There are few tangible details as to why she didn't create, or what she was going through. Facts suggest she *was* miserable. As a writer I know environment and mental state are vitally important. Jane's elucidations during this time are mine but I believe tap in to the essence of what she must have been feeling. Her emotions had to have been strong and unnerving for her to stop doing what she loved to do—for so long. Again, if only we had her letters. . . .

In Chapter 14 Jane's mentor, Anne Lefroy, dies on her birthday. . . . I'd already written the scene where Jane wakes up in the middle of the night when I discovered Anne died on that very day! I looked up the state of the moon and added it to the scene, along with Jane's revelation regarding the timing. A poignant happenstance. An author moment Jane might have appreciated.

Jane is shown taking her manuscripts along wherever she traveled. This is a fact—as is the time when they were left on a coach! Considering all the visiting she did, her unwillingness to have them out of her possession is telling. They *were* her children, even before she realized as much.

In Chapter 17 Jane stays behind when the family goes driving. This is noted in her letters and I believe it is symbolic. By this time she was in her mid-thirties and was starting to go against the grain when she felt the need. She was learning who Jane was—and what Jane needed. She was learning how to be "just Jane."

Were Cassandra or Mrs. Knight instrumental in getting Edward to offer Chawton House to the ladies? No one knows. *I'd* like to know why he didn't offer such assistance earlier. Why were the ladies left to fend for three years before he offered relief? I believe he was a nice man, busy with eleven children, no wife, and a large estate. A man in need of a push. Hence, enter the two women who cared most for Jane and her talent—and who knew of her need for *home*.

I found the Austen pragmatism very interesting. They were not *allowed* to wallow in grief. Although their reactions sometimes seem cold, imagine what Jane's life—including her writing—would have been like if she'd been brought up otherwise.

Jane was a parson's daughter yet rarely mentioned God in her novels. I believe this is because faith was an integral part of her life—of most people's lives. Faith was a constant that held them together. As with emotions, faith was not discussed or analyzed. It just was. God *was*. The scenes in which I mention her faith meld her pragmatic nature with the common need of all people to seek Him in times of extreme crisis and delight.

What did success mean to Jane? Certainly she was thrilled with the independence that came with earning an income, but she didn't seek riches. She just wanted to be treated fairly and to be given *enough*. Most importantly, publication was vindication her work had merit. She loved praise and was bothered by criticism, but did not need fame. In this she and I are the same. "Just let me write" is a philosophy we share.

Jane's voice: I did not attempt to match the unique "voice" of Jane's writing, only to hint at it. No one can write like Jane Austen. Besides, one's speaking voice is different from one's written voice, and since *Just Jane* involves Jane telling us *her* story . . . I hope my attempt is not annoying.

A piece of trivia: The sections of this book were titled from Jane's epitaph: Intimate Connections, Deepest Affliction, Humble Hope, and Extraordinary Endowments. I could mention more items, but this is the gist of it. I wish to thank the following biographers for their insightful books that were invaluable: *Jane Austen* by Claire Tomalin; *Becoming Jane Austen* by Jon Spence; *Jane Austen: My Life* by Park Honan; and *Jane Austen's World* by Maggie Lane. I also want to thank my editor, Helen Motter, who has an amazing eye for fact and fiction and the melding of the two. May the main *fact* of this book be your enjoyment, along with a deeper appreciation of its subject, and her talent.

Discussion Questions for *Just Jane*:

1. In Chapter 6, Jane is faced with a huge disappointment in regard to Tom Lefroy. Yet in her grief, she realizes she has a choice to wallow in her "unhappiness or make a determined choice to leave it behind and move forward. Life is not fair— nor often understandable. But it is ours to live to the best of our ability." When have you wallowed in unhappiness? When have you chosen to set some unhappiness aside and move forward? What were the results?

2. Jane is devastated by her family's move to Bath. Much of her frustration involves not being consulted about the decision. When has a life-changing decision been made in your life without your knowledge or consent? How did it make you feel? How did it turn out?

3. In Chapter 7, after the move to Bath, Jane notices: "The parts people play in Bath are varied, and are actually quite inconsequential. Their desire to be on stage is the driving force here— to be seen, and to see. And to catch, and be caught by the opposite gender." As far as the mating game goes . . . what has really changed between then and now?

4. In Chapter 7, Jane is frustrated with the practice of marrying for reasons other than love. She says, "And what of God? Does He not get involved? Is His will not instrumental towards bringing two people together in a way that is both pleasing to Him *and* suits His plans?" Yet later in the book Jane realizes her singleness was part of God's plan for her life. In society today, remaining single is still a challenging condition. When can it be a calling?

5. Throughout the book, Cassandra and Martha Lloyd encourage

Jane with her writing. Who encourages you to use your talents? Whom do you encourage?

6. Jane finds she cannot create without having certain elements in place. What are those elements? What are the elements you need in order to create? What do you do to insure these elements are present? (What *could* you do?)

7. Jane offers biting commentary about other people. Yet most of the time it is only Cassandra who hears such opinions. We all think bad thoughts about others, so . . . what should we do about them? What is the importance of having a trusted confidante who *could* hear all? Who is your confidante? Who confides in you?

8. In Chapter 13, Jane accepts Harris's proposal—for a short time. What do you think about her choice? Have you ever changed your mind regarding such a life-altering decision? In the end, did you make the right choice? (Did she?)

9. In Chapter 14, Jane says, "I hold on to the meager strength of being . . . just Jane. I will admit that 'just Jane' seems to gain insight from hard times. I wish to ask the Almighty about this, for why do we learn more from struggles than victories? I am certain He has His reasons." Have you found peace in being just *you*? How have hard times helped you in this discovery?

10. Jane recognizes that Cassandra is much better at nurturing others than she is. It's one of her sister's gifts. Looking around the room at your friends . . . what are their gifts? What are yours? How do all of you together make a better whole?

11. In Chapter 20, Eliza is dying and—to Jane's surprise—asks for Jane. Have you ever had someone feel a connection to you that overshadows your connection to them?

12. Jane and her family often had to deal with death. They did so very stoically, in a pragmatic manner. How do you and your family handle death? Is there a *best* way?

13. In Chapter 20, Jane celebrates her big moment—the publication of *Pride and Prejudice*—alone with her mother and a

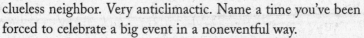

clueless neighbor. Very anticlimactic. Name a time you've been forced to celebrate a big event in a noneventful way.

14. What is your favorite Jane Austen novel? Why? Why do you think it has endured two hundred years?

15. In Chapter 20, Jane is frustrated when her niece Anna gives up her writing. When have you become frustrated with someone giving up their talent too soon? Have you given up *your* talent too soon?

16. Jane's purpose was achieved—though not according to her plans. What do you think is God's plan for *your* life? How has He worked beyond *your* plans? What are you doing toward achieving your unique purpose? How has Jane inspired you?

Looking for More Good Books to Read?

You can find out what is new and exciting with previews, descriptions, and reviews by signing up for Bethany House newsletters at

www.bethanynewsletters.com

We will send you updates for as many authors or categories as you desire so you get only the information you really want.

Sign up today!